"Maybe I don't want anything that badly," Zane said with a shrug.

Rachel folded her arms. "That's a flimsy excuse."

"Like yours is for coming here?"

"What do you mean?"

He tipped his head and walked closer to her. She refused to back away and thus show him how much he affected her.

"I thought that you wanted to keep your distance from any lawman so that the women in your ministry finally learn to trust you."

Oh, that.

"You've come up with a cheap excuse to see me."

Her cheeks hot, Rachel arched her brows. "Aren't you full of yourself? I came here to tell you not to give up."

To prove her point, she dared to take a step toward him. He didn't move. The air stilled around them, and he reached out and touched her chin. His fingers were warm, a striking contrast to the cold air that moved briskly over her face. They stared each other down.

His voice lowered. "Do you want me to stay, Rachel?"

Her heart pounded in her throat. Did she?

Barbara Phinney was born in England and raised in Canada. After she retired from the Canadian Armed Forces, Barbara turned her hand to romance writing. The thrill of adventure and her love of happy endings, coupled with a too-active imagination, have merged to help her create this and other wonderful stories. Barbara spends her days writing, building her dream home with her husband and enjoying their fast-growing children.

Books by Barbara Phinney

Love Inspired Historical

Bound to the Warrior
Protected by the Warrior
Sheltered by the Warrior
The Nanny Solution
Undercover Sheriff

Love Inspired Suspense

Desperate Rescue
Keeping Her Safe
Deadly Homecoming
Fatal Secrets
Silent Protector

Visit the Author Profile page at Harlequin.com for more titles.

BARBARA PHINNEY

Undercover Sheriff

H HARLEQUIN® LOVE INSPIRED® HISTORICAL

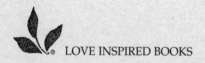

LOVE INSPIRED BOOKS

Recycling programs
for this product may
not exist in your area.

ISBN-13: 978-0-373-42520-4

Undercover Sheriff

www.Harlequin.com

Printed in U.S.A.

Trust in the Lord with all thine heart and lean not unto thine own understanding. In all thy ways acknowledge Him and He shall direct thy paths.
—*Proverbs* 3:5–6

I want to dedicate this book to all of you who think you're not worthy of God's love because of a past sin. There is good news for you. It is by God's grace that we are freed from our sin. Please remember, you are loved and forgiven, so it's time to forgive yourselves.

Chapter One

Colorado, 1882

When Zane Robinson stepped into his brother's rented room, he found a woman rifling through the desk.

He fully expected her to look up, for surely she'd heard him. Zane hadn't exactly tiptoed along the narrow path that led from Mrs. Shrankhof's kitchen to this back addition, determined to locate his missing twin. However, the well-dressed lady in front of him appeared oblivious as she yanked on the desk drawers, pulling out what looked to be a postcard, which she latched on to with the vigor of a miner striking gold.

She then let out a harsh gasp, a look of guilty horror filling her face. For the briefest moment, Zane wondered if she was about to collapse. Thankfully, she did not. Instead, her expression hardening into tenacity, she had the gall to fold the postcard and shove it into an unseen pocket of her closely tailored skirt.

Enough was enough. Zane prepared to charge into the room, settling his Stetson—which he'd removed when he'd come inside—back on his head so both his hands would be free. He felt a twinge as he remembered that the hat was the one his brother had sent him shortly after arriving in Proud Bend.

Alex had written him jokingly that they now had matching hats, and that all they needed were identical clothes and their youth would be repeated. Back then, neither of them had minded wearing the same clothing. Such was the way one dressed identical twins.

That one memory, a shameful one for Zane, lingered.

Never mind it. Alex had long since forgiven him for that foolish ruse.

Back to the issue at hand. That woman was stealing from his brother. Zane cleared his throat. "Who are you?"

With a jump, the woman whirled. Upon seeing Zane, she sagged with obvious relief and smiled broadly. "Alex! You scared me!"

Zane quirked an eyebrow. She thought he was his brother? Of its own accord, his hand lifted to his full beard. Had Alex grown one, as well? His brother usually preferred to be clean-shaven. Yet, this woman saw past the thick facial hair when no one else had so far. Walking through town—albeit with his hat on and his collar turned up against the wind—no one had even noticed that his face was identical to that of their sheriff.

Zane's chest tightened. Alex, his only surviving kin, was missing, gone now a week. Perhaps injured somewhere, or dead. Zane needed to find the deputy who'd wired him to ask if Zane knew where his brother was.

He didn't. Shortly after reading the telegram, Zane had boarded the next train from Canaan, Illinois, to Denver, Colorado, then down the other line to Proud Bend. He desperately needed to see what had been done so far to find Alex. But this woman in front of him needed to answer a few questions first.

She stepped forward, her broad smile still lighting her features. "You're safe! Praise the Lord! Where have you been? I took a card I just—"

Her smile fell like a stone and was replaced by a frown. She cut off her sentence and withdrew that one step she'd taken. "You're not Alex," she accused. Her delicate brows pressed together as she searched his face. "Who *are* you?"

Zane had no time for this. "Considering that you're stealing from my brother, the more obvious question would be 'who are *you*?'"

The woman gaped. "You even sound like Alex! Are you his twin?" She tilted her head, assessing him. "What am I saying? Of course you are. Apart from the beard, you're identical." She touched her chest again as she peered hard. "I don't think I've ever met identical twins before. It's amazing!"

Zane's attention dropped to her hand. Her fingers were rough and callused, nails cut short and utilitarian, a curious contradiction to the rest of this regal woman, whose fine, expensive-looking outfit was perfectly tailored to her tall, slender frame. Her black hair—what he could see of it beneath her bonnet—was arranged in a neat, fashionable knot.

Who was she? Alex hadn't mentioned this woman, or any woman for that matter. "My brother told you he has a twin?" Very curious, indeed. "How did that come up in conversation?"

"It didn't. It's the only logical answer. You just said you're his brother."

Of course. Zane rubbed his brow. He was tired. That was the only reason for the foolish question. The woman was frowning again. Studying him closely.

Wariness tingled through Zane. She was smart. Was she also calculating? It certainly looked that way. He had better watch himself—he'd learned the hard way the dangers of other people's craftiness. He was here to find Alex, not deal with yet another corrupt town.

"I can see that you're perfectly capable of answering questions," he ground out. "So, shall we return to my first one? Who are you?"

She wet her lips in what Zane might call a nervous action. *As she should be*, he thought without the charity he'd been taught as a child. Charity should be saved for those who don't steal.

Or betray their sheriff, as had happened back in Canaan.

Surprisingly, the woman's words were calm despite, he was sure, not wanting to give him a single shred of information. "My name is Rachel Smith."

"Good, Miss Smith. Very good." Zane took a deliberate step closer to her, hoping to appear intimidating. Although she was taller than any woman he'd ever met, Miss Smith didn't compare with his big frame. Yet she stood her ground.

It didn't matter. She'd been caught stealing. He thrust out his hand, palm skyward. "Now give me what you just slipped into your pocket. Before I take it from you."

* * *

Rachel swallowed. Through her skirt, she fingered the postcard. She did not want to relinquish the only clue she had, although she had no idea why her name was scrawled on the postcard or how it had come into the possession of Proud Bend's new sheriff. And she certainly did not wish to hand it over to this stranger.

The postcard could be the last thing Alex had handled before he went missing. If she could learn where he'd obtained it, it could help her retrace the steps he'd taken during the investigation she'd asked him to make into Rosa's disappearance. It could lead her to both Rosa and the woman's young son, Daniel, not to mention Alex, for surely his disappearance had to be related to theirs.

Please, Lord, keep them all safe. Rosa loves You now, I'm sure of it. If someone has kidnapped her to force her to return to that awful trade, change their hearts, Lord. Have all three of them released.

"The contents of your pocket?" the man prompted her, his hand thrust out even farther. Rachel suppressed a shiver.

Don't be intimidated by this man.

He was clearly suspicious of her presence in his brother's room, and if he saw the postcard with her name on it, his suspicions would only increase. She arched her brows and locked her hands primly against her skirt, one palm ensuring the card remained tucked away. "So, since you *are* his twin, what is your name?"

"Alex didn't tell you? You two seem so close." He paused, his brows lifted and his head tilted slightly to the left as if expecting a prompt answer. When she refused to rise to his provocation, he continued, "My name is Zane Robinson."

Rachel ignored his cold tone. His brother was missing, so he was bound to be in a foul mood. Still, she frowned. "Alex said his full name was Alexander *Zane* Robinson."

"That's correct. I am Zane *Alexander* Robinson. Our mother thought it would be whimsical to switch our names."

"Interesting." She nodded, all the while hoping to appear unruffled. She was anything but that. In fact, she felt more ruffled by the second. "Why are you here?" she asked, hoping to move the conversation away from the postcard.

Zane did not move. His hand remained extended, waiting for her to relinquish the postcard still tucked safely in her pocket. Obviously, he did not wish to divert the subject. "Why did you just steal that card?"

When she offered no explanation, he continued, "I want it. If you do not hand it over immediately, I will simply take it from you. By force."

Rachel swallowed. Regardless of her innocent motives, she *had* stolen something from Alex's desk, and this man, his identical twin, had more right to it than she did.

Lord, Your spirit is pricking my conscience. Have it work for Your good.

Reluctantly, Rachel dug out the postcard. All she could hope for was that Zane would find it useful in tracking down Alex. "All I wanted to do was study it when I had the time, because I don't have it now. I would have returned it." She would have, she told herself fiercely, but the look of doubt on Zane's face proved he didn't believe her.

"And the reason for not giving it to his deputy to aid in his investigation? Unless, of course, you are responsible for Alex's disappearance."

"I'm not!" She threw back her shoulders. "I have no reason to wish any harm to Alex! I am, in fact, the one who is working the hardest to find him—and I'm just as capable as the deputy is at following a lead. Perhaps better than him. Otherwise, he would have already found this card himself. He has just admitted to me this very morning that he hasn't yet searched this room because Alex was at the sheriff's office, and before that, at the saloon, and had not been here for several hours before he was last seen. The deputy didn't think searching here would help, whereas I do. That's why I'm here. I'm retracing his last day starting in the morning."

"Really?" Zane's extended hand did not waver, for she had not yet returned the card. "Leads can take a person to places where ladies such as you should never go."

A snicker escaped her lips before she could stop it. "You, sir, have no idea where I have gone. Regardless, this postcard could hold clues to your brother's location. That's the only reason I took it."

Oh, who are you kidding here? You're also afraid you'll be implicated in his disappearance.

Ignoring the sudden internal accusation, Rachel opened the folded card slowly. It was a picture postcard of Castle Rock, the town just a few miles southeast on the same railway line that led up to Denver. The imposing butte jutted up in the picture's background, an ugly formation Rachel knew was normally covered with mining paraphernalia, but in this romantically painted landscape, the artist had removed all that trash. She hastily committed the image to memory before turning it over. Beneath the standard postcard printing was her name, written at an upward angle. She didn't recognize the handwriting, but knew that few people in Proud Bend—assuming the writer lived here and not in Castle Rock—could manage such smooth, readable cursive.

Zane tugged the card from her grip, obviously impatient with her delay. After studying it himself, he glanced up at her. "It has your name on it, Miss Smith."

Rachel swallowed. "Yes. I can read."

"It's in my brother's handwriting."

She lifted her brows, all the while trying her best to stay reserved. She was anything but that. What Zane had just said answered one of her questions but added others. Why had Alex written her name on a postcard from the next town? Where did he get this card? Had he traveled to Castle Rock in the course of his investigation into Rosa's disappearance? If so, why take a postcard and waste it by writing only her name on it?

Worry bit into Rachel. *Lord, You know where they are. Lead us to them.* Rosa wanted to give her life to the Lord, she'd told Rachel hesitantly, and the next day she had promised Rachel she would help her in her ministry to the misguided women who had fallen into a life of prostitution in Proud Bend. That had been over a month ago, for today was the seventh of December. Rosa had gone missing ten days ago. Rachel had gone straight to Alex the day after she'd disappeared.

Two days after that, Alex had vanished, as well. So far, she'd found no clues to his whereabouts—except for this card. It might have nothing to do with Rosa, but if it wasn't important, why keep it? It had been the only thing in a drawer that by now should have been littered with various small items.

"How did you get in here?" Interrupting her thoughts, Zane glanced around the room. "Did my brother give you his key?"

Rachel flushed. "Mrs. Shrankhof unlocked the room for me. Since I'm not privy to Alex's official files on Rosa and Daniel—"

"Rosa? Daniel?" Zane looked baffled as he cut her off. "Who are they?"

"Rosa Carrera is a friend." Rachel clipped her words, not wanting to mention the woman's former profession. "Daniel is her young son, a toddler. They disappeared a few days before Alex did. I reported it."

"Perhaps they moved away?"

Rachel shook her head. "She'd spent the weeks before her disappearance helping me with my ministry, and she was committed to the cause. She wouldn't have just left. Besides, none of their things are missing—nor did she say goodbye to anyone."

"Just what is this ministry of yours?"

She hesitated. She'd hoped to avoid specifying, worried that Zane would lose interest in the disappearance if he discovered that it applied to the unfortunates that society usually considered beneath their notice.

"I minister to the soiled doves of Proud Bend, and attempt to bring them to God."

He eyed her shrewdly. "And Rosa helped you in this ministry? Was she a soiled dove, as well?"

"She used to be," Rachel admitted.

"Maybe she returned to her old habits?"

"No, she has given her life to God." Rachel folded her arms. "Obviously you're not a Christian, to be so willing to discount the work of the Holy Spirit."

Zane raised his brows, looking insulted. "I assure you, Miss Smith, nothing could be further from the truth."

Rachel studied him. Although she couldn't say why, she believed his words. She had no proof, save the indignant look. She had no proof that Alex's disappearance was related to Rosa's, either, but like Zane's answer, she knew it to be true.

His scowl returned. "So you reported her disappearance to Alex?"

"Yes, but as soon as he opened an investigation, he went missing, too." Rachel bit her lip. Had Alex somehow given up on this town and abandoned his duties? Had the work here proved too much for Proud Bend's new sheriff? Too much stress and anxiety?

Automatically, Rachel's thoughts moved to her childhood friend, Bea. Hard times had hit Bea's family and by the time Rachel and Bea were eighteen, Bea had turned to prostitution to help make ends meet. A year later, in a fit of remorse for her choices, Bea had taken her own life. That sad act had cemented Rachel's desire to help the soiled doves of Proud Bend.

That same year, along came Liza, who'd approached Rachel one day on the street, asking for money and followed by a younger, equally squalid-looking woman. It was Rosa, Liza's daughter—a young woman who knew nothing else but to follow her mother in the profession of prostitution.

Rachel shut her eyes, trying to banish the memory. It still hurt to think of Liza and the terrible part Rachel had played in her untimely death.

You should feel guilty.

Two women, two deaths. Another woman missing. You could have tried harder to help Bea. And Liza might still be alive today if you hadn't convinced the other soiled doves to hand over their life savings for you to invest. You would never have been robbed and assaulted that night. And if that hadn't happened, Liza wouldn't have decided to confront the man she believed was the thief. Your arrogance—your belief that you could save those women—played a big part in Liza's death.

Rachel pushed aside the painful memories before they gained a stronger foothold. Right now, she couldn't afford to dwell on them. Finding Rosa and Alex must come before wallowing in guilt.

Had she done enough to help Alex with the investigation? Maybe if she'd spoken to him more, she would have known more about what he'd uncovered—and what had caused his own disappearance. But Rachel had deliberately kept all of her interactions with the sheriff as brief and discreet as possible, seeing him only in the early morning, when most of the women who worked in the cribs behind the saloon were sleeping. Rachel didn't need to be known as someone who was close with the sheriff, considering the distrust and suspicion the soiled doves felt toward law enforcement. Prostitution wasn't illegal, but those women were often arrested for vagrancy and theft, leading them to avoid the law as much as possible.

Rachel sighed. None of this answered why Proud

Bend's sheriff had written her name on a postcard from the neighboring town or even when he'd done so. Rachel stepped closer, indicating the postcard that Zane still held and determined to glean from it every ounce of information she could. "Are you sure it's Alex's handwriting?"

He tossed her a sharp look. "Are you calling me a liar?"

"Of course not." She frowned at his defensive tone. "Are you absolutely certain that's his handwriting?"

"We wrote—write—to each other regularly. When I received a telegram stating he was missing—"

"You received a telegram? When? From whom?"

Zane's mouth thinned before he answered. "This past Sunday. I took that day's train. In fact, I have only just arrived."

"Who sent you that telegram?"

"Alex's deputy," Zane answered. "A man named Wilson. He informed me that Alex was missing and asked if I'd heard from him."

Rachel swallowed. Instead of searching this room, the new deputy had contacted the brother who lived miles away? Why wasn't the deputy doing more to search for answers here in Proud Bend? Instead, he'd sent a telegram and, as far as Rachel could tell, done little else.

Suspicion rose in her, but she crushed it. Not so long ago, the night her father had died, her father's business partner, Clyde Abernathy, had tried to kill her and her mother in an attempt to gain control of the bank he shared with Rachel's father. Now, Rachel felt mistrust at every turn.

No. Suspicion and doubt did not come from God,

she told herself fiercely. Nor should she complain about Deputy Wilson's choice at where he would start his investigation. She hadn't considered this room either until late last night. Rachel wouldn't condemn Deputy Wilson's decisions, not when she was just as negligent, even if her own investigation could not be sanctioned by the law.

With deep concern, Rachel rubbed her arms to suppress a shiver. She couldn't afford to give in to this worry.

She opened her mouth to speak, but Zane cut her off. "I would prefer to be the one who asks the questions," he said. He glanced at the door. "How well do you know my brother?"

His words might have been suggestive, but Rachel heard nothing but concern in Zane's tone. "That's not important," she answered. "How did you know where your brother lived? You said you came straight here from the train."

"Alex had written me about his new home." Zane narrowed his eyes. "Are you intimate enough with Alex that his landlady would let you in anytime you want?"

Now *those* words went beyond suggestive into insulting. Coloring, Rachel tugged on the pocket flaps of her outfit's fine jacket. "Absolutely not!" It was only then that she noticed how Zane had left the door open. Although it was clear and bright this December morning, the cold draft barreling in had dissolved any heat created by the sunshine through the window. "I'm not intimate with Alex in any way, shape or form. Mrs. Shrankhof let me in because she is as concerned over his disappearance as I am and she trusts me."

"How commendable of you." He folded his arms. "Now, the real reason you took the card."

Rachel blinked. "What do you mean?"

"I'm delighted you are so concerned for Alex that you would search his room for any leads as to where he's gone, but I don't believe that's your main reason, Miss Smith."

Her mouth felt dry all of a sudden. "W-why do you say that?"

"You were very focused. You went straight to this desk."

"How do you know?"

Zane pointed briefly to the floor. "There is a skiff of snow outside and you have tracked it only to the desk, not to the wardrobe or the chest of drawers."

Rachel glanced down at the small pools of melting snow that indicated where she'd walked. Zane Robinson was as eagle-eyed as Mrs. Shrankhof. Despite her pounding heart, she shrugged. "It was the logical place to start. I came, and the first thing I saw was the desk."

She threw back her shoulders. "Since I first reported Rosa missing, I have gone to the sheriff's office every day for an update, even after Alex disappeared. When I learned that Deputy Wilson had focused his investigation into Alex around the saloon only, I decided to start my own. I came here and found that postcard. As you have pointed out, that's all I've done."

"And you know for sure Wilson has not searched this room yet?"

"Mrs. Shrankhof confirmed that no one has been in here. It's her job to clean once a week. She'd tidied his room the day he went missing and then locked it up. Believe me, she would notice anyone coming. Unless it was Alex, who has his own key, they would need to ask her to unlock the door. I don't know why Deputy Wilson has not yet searched this room. Perhaps you can ask him that."

Rachel paused. Until this moment, she hadn't considered that Deputy Wilson might have obtained Alex's key and slipped in under the cover of darkness. What if Wilson had taken it after he'd kidnapped Alex?

No. Wilson wouldn't risk incriminating himself in that way. However, what if he'd slipped in here in the middle of the night and planted that postcard, hoping to point the finger at Rachel?

She brushed away the wild conjecture. Such was the result of a stalled investigation and a too-suspicious nature after being exposed to her father's and Abernathy's sly corruption.

"I plan to question Wilson very thoroughly." Zane tipped his head to one side. "So, *Detective* Smith, what's your next move?"

Chapter Two

Rachel blinked away all the suspicions and paranoia and focused on Zane, telling herself again not to be intimidated by this abrasive version of her town's sheriff. "I was going to check out that postcard."

He held it up. "The one that has your name on it? Logically, it seems to point to you, so interviewing you would be the next step, except you claim that you had nothing to do with Alex's disappearance. Therefore, this card is a dead end, so why bother taking it?"

Rachel felt even more heat flood into her face. Before she could answer, he continued, "I've been watching you, Miss Smith. I believe that as soon as you found that postcard, you realized that you might be implicated in my brother's disappearance, which prompted you to try to dispose of it. In fact, I believe that was your sole reason for coming here. To remove any incriminating evidence because you're involved somehow."

"That's not true!" Rachel swallowed, realizing too late that her outburst wasn't such a good idea. "You should be asking the deputy why this room hasn't been searched."

"I intend to, and since we have already established that Mrs. Shrankhof trusts you—"

Rachel tried her best to look knowing. "She's an excellent judge of character."

"I disagree. You're a thief. You stole this card. Since you clearly have Alex's landlady in your back pocket, we will have to consider her a biased witness and disregard any statement she might make in your defense." Zane took a step toward her as his gaze flicked up and down her frame.

Rachel tipped her head up, something she rarely had to do with men, thanks to her height. She studied Zane. She didn't remember seeing the tiny creases between Alex's eyebrows, but Zane had them. He also seemed a whole lot more canny than his easygoing twin. How did he know so much about biased witnesses, statements and such? Was he also in law enforcement?

"You have all but admitted that you have another motive rather than the noble one of finding three people," Zane asked.

Rachel pulled herself together. "You know this because…"

"You call Alex by his first name."

Normally, Rachel wouldn't be so improper as to call the sheriff by his first name, but Alex had insisted on Christian names once he'd learned of her ministry, saying he valued her work. She'd appreciated the friendly personality, but had kept her encounters with him as brief and as few as possible, not wanting the women she helped to believe there was more between the sheriff and her than there really was.

Alex had understood that. He was easy to get along with, candid even, unlike this brother, who currently looked travel worn and testy, as suspicious as that postcard.

Despite knowing why she kept her distance, Alex had been quite companionable, often greeting her in the street. This twin appeared to be the exact opposite. Rachel folded her arms. "What of calling Alex by his Christian name? We had exchanged them."

"Really? He's not in your class."

Rachel bristled but refused to answer. Although her mother had always tried to instill in her the importance of staying within one's class, Rachel knew, even years ago when the Lord had changed her young life, that all were equal at heart. Wasn't that a founding principle that made the United States? She remembered the celebration when Colorado had joined the union. Hadn't the mayor commented on that? It didn't matter. She knew enough not to argue with this man. Not today, anyway.

"As for another motive, it's nearly noon," Zane commented abruptly, "and judging by the freshness of the rouge on your cheeks and the powder under your eyes, I would say that you have only just completed your toilet."

"How does that indicate another motive?"

The corners of Zane's mouth rose slightly. "I can tell that you retired very late last night. What exactly were you doing until all hours? Whatever it was, I wonder if it's making you feel guilty," he speculated.

"Not in the least." She threw back her shoulders

and tugged on the sleeves of her jacket. "The hours I keep are none of your concern."

He was being ridiculous, she told herself. Staying out late did not cause her to feel guilty. Was he goading her?

"And how do you explain these?" He lifted her left hand and indicated her rough knuckles before turning it over to expose the dry, hard calluses. "Are you a washerwoman by night?"

She yanked back her hand, regretting that she'd removed her gloves upon entering this room. "That's none of your business."

"I would say it is. You are full of contradictions, which imply that you're hiding something. Something that I believe is making you feel guilty. I saw it on your face the moment I walked in here."

Rachel felt her mouth thin. "Very observant of you."

"Alex isn't the only lawman in the family."

She narrowed her gaze, knowing that if he was like most lawmen, he would not give up until she admitted that he was correct. They stared each other down as she fought the urge to blink. She fought every fiber in her body that screamed to tell Zane everything, to pour out all the guilt that ate at her.

That would be a very bad idea. Just because he looked like his twin didn't mean he was as understanding as Alex.

His stare continued.

Finally, needing to say something, anything to end the accusatory silence, she blurted out, "Fine, then. I didn't want anyone to think I had something to do with Alex's disappearance. I came here for any clue to help find him, and hopefully Rosa and Daniel, but as soon as I saw this card, I was afraid that if Deputy Wilson discovered it, he would focus on me, to the exclusion of all other suspects. I want him to find Rosa and Daniel because their disappearance must be connected to Alex's. But I'm not responsible for what has happened to any of them!"

Even as she blurted out her words, she knew Zane didn't believe her. As his stare continued, a shiver ran through her.

Not for a minute did Zane believe Rachel's words. He glanced down at the postcard in his hand. A painted picture of Castle Rock? Why would his brother have a postcard from another town? And why waste a good postcard by writing only Rachel Smith's name on it?

In fact, *when* had he written Rachel's name on it? Before or after Rosa's disappearance?

There was also another on that list of hard questions. How was it that he could so easily see the lies on Rachel Smith's face, yet he had not seen how his own staff back in the little town of Canaan had conspired against him?

It was hard to believe Rachel could deceive anyone with a face that open and expressive. It was clear the woman was nervous, an emotion so tangible he could nearly taste it in the air. But did that mean she was involved in his brother's disappearance? Could she be telling the truth about that?

Maybe her nervousness was simply because he'd startled her. And just being an identical twin to a missing man might unnerve another person. Enough to make them look guilty?

Perhaps, but that didn't explain the postcard. Neither he nor Alex had anyone to send postcards to, aside from each other. They had lost their grandparents to old age a few years back, and parents to a flu outbreak last winter. At their parents' shared funeral, Zane and Alex had decided never to lose contact with each other. That was how Zane knew exactly where to go as soon as he'd stepped off the train. In his first letter from Proud Bend, Alex had given him detailed directions to his home and office. Zane would have preferred to go straight to the sheriff's office for an update, but since this room was on the way, he'd stopped here first, just in case his brother had returned.

It was a good thing he'd chosen this detour. Now it looked like he might be taking Miss Rachel Smith in for questioning. He latched on to her elbow. Firmly.

She immediately stiffened. "Let me go! What's the matter with you?"

Zane saw shock flare in Rachel's eyes, but he had no intention of releasing her. Just because a woman was indignant, didn't mean she wouldn't knock him over and bolt the second he released her. This Miss Rachel Smith looked healthy enough to get a good head start on him while he was scrambling to stand. She was taller than most women and if she hiked up that fashionable skirt of hers, she could race out of this room at a fairly good clip.

"We're going to the sheriff's office," Zane ground out. "I want to see if the deputy has heard from my brother."

Rachel dug in her heels. "You don't need to handle me like a wayward child!"

"I think I do." His grip wasn't hard, but firm enough

to ensure her compliance. "I want to question you in a professional manner and that means at the sheriff's office."

"You have no authority here."

He was about to reply when he was cut off by a deep, booming voice. "What's going on here?"

Zane turned. Standing in the open doorway was a large, well-dressed man, middle-aged, with extra weight around the middle. An even older woman, wearing a worn cotton skirt and blouse, with a flour-dusted apron wrapped around her wide girth and a heavy shawl draped over her shoulders, stepped out from behind him. Some of her gray, wispy curls escaped her white maid's cap. Her eyes were wide, taking in every action.

"Who are you?" Zane asked, hearing impatience pepper his tone. He was here to find his brother, that's all, not to confront every townsperson.

The older man drilled him with his own harsh glare. "I believe I should ask that question."

"Don't you recognize our new sheriff?" the older woman answered, peering up at the man. "You wanted me to tell you when he got back. As soon as I saw him pass my kitchen window, I sent my grandson." She drilled Zane with a blatantly nosy stare. "He growed himself a beard, he did."

The man shoved the old woman behind him and puffed up further. "Don't be foolish, Mrs. Shrankhof. I spoke to Sheriff Robinson only eight days ago. He couldn't have grown that thick a beard so quickly."

Zane lit upon the man's confession. According to the telegram, Alex had disappeared a week ago today.

Could this man have been the last person to see him before he went missing?

"But he did, Mayor Wilson!" She pointed at Zane. "Look at him."

Zane felt his jaw tighten. *Mayor* Wilson? The deputy who'd telegraphed him had the same last name. Were they related? Probably. True, it was a common name, but this was a small town. People hiring relatives and cronies into positions of power happened very frequently in these small, isolated towns. This man's young relative didn't sound experienced enough to be voted in as sheriff, but hiring him as deputy was probably as easy as pie.

"Go back to your kitchen," the mayor growled to Mrs. Shrankhof. "I'll handle this."

At the man's order, Alex's landlady reluctantly retreated.

Tugging her arm free, Rachel stepped forward. "This is not Sheriff Robinson, Your Worship," she explained. "This is his brother, Zane."

Zane fully expected Rachel to add that she was also being mistreated by him, but she said nothing more.

Wilson shut the door. After turning, he studied Zane. "The resemblance is remarkable. Discounting the beard, of course."

"They're identical twins." After a moment of thoughtful silence, Rachel took the opportunity to glance back at Wilson. Zane noticed immediately that her expression had changed. Because she had an ally in the mayor? "I believe," she began, her words slow and careful, "that we have a unique opportunity here."

Zane tossed her a cool glare. Rachel's demeanor had switched from defensive to calculating. She now looked far too comfortable, and he automatically bristled. "A unique opportunity for what?"

Rachel glanced out the window before answering, probably to ensure that Mrs. Shrankhof had indeed returned to her kitchen. "Mr. Robinson, our town needs a sheriff because ours has gone missing. Perhaps we can come to some kind of agreement? A temporary one, that is, until you find your brother. If I remember correctly, you said you are also a lawman."

"And you want me to work here so you can make me disappear, as well?"

If he was expecting Rachel to be ruffled at the accusation, he was disappointed. All she did was color slightly. "Alex is missing. You want to find him as much as we do. That's why you're here, isn't it?"

There she went, calling his brother by his first name again, despite her assertions that she wasn't intimately involved with him. Curious, and not something a well-mannered gentlewoman would be expected to do.

"What did you have in mind, Miss Smith?" the mayor asked.

"It's not the most ideal situation, but it's the only one I can think of. Mr. Robinson can adopt his brother's identity."

Zane studied Rachel. What kind of town was this that a well-dressed woman could suggest such subterfuge to the town's mayor with the expectation it would be accepted?

Was it a crooked town, where deception and manipulation were common? It wouldn't be the first. In his town, Canaan, he had seen the wealthy bend the rules regularly. Was he expecting something different in a town where his brother had mysteriously disappeared?

Rachel met his gaze with only a hint of reluctance. "You mentioned that Alex wasn't the only lawman in the family. Are you a sheriff, also? If so, where?"

Zane paused. He didn't want them to know that his latest employment hadn't ended well. If they questioned his competence or honesty, they might not let him participate in the efforts to find his brother, and Alex needed him. Zane's disgrace in Illinois didn't compare to his brother's safety, and, right now, for full access to Alex's files and belongings, he would need to convince this pair he was trustworthy. He would just have to take the chance that they would not ask more than the most rudimentary of questions. "I was the sheriff in Canaan, Illinois."

"Will you take your brother's place?" There was a hint of desperation in Rachel's quick words. "It could lead you to Alex."

Automatically, his lips tightened. "Are you in such a position to offer that to me?"

"No, but I am," the mayor answered, puffing up more.

"Mayor Wilson wants this town to know that his main priority is their safety and well-being," Rachel added.

Ah. That's it. Zane nodded, understanding the situation. "So, it's an election year?"

"Yes." Suddenly, a small smile pulled up the corners of the woman's mouth, one that stated quite bluntly she wasn't the least bit embarrassed by the stratagem. "Our good mayor wants to keep his job. When our old sheriff passed on several months ago, he immediately hired your brother. Like any frontier town, Proud Bend needs a good lawman, and after you find Alex, he can return to his duties, you can return to yours and the rest of the good citizens will remain none the wiser of the switch."

Zane watched Rachel blink at him with affected innocence. Should he take this curious offer? It did tempt him. Taking the sheriff's position would give him access to resources he would not otherwise be able to command. If he didn't take it, what would that do to his chances of finding his brother?

Pare them down to nothing, that's what, for surely one word from the older Wilson to the younger one and Zane would be punished for not coming on board with the mayor's—no, wait, *Rachel*'s—idea of switching identities. He'd probably be run out of town or, at the very least, be denied access to his brother's office, the one that held the information on the investigation into Alex's disappearance.

Oh, how he hated politics. All that sly scheming and manipulation. When he'd refused to bow to Canaan's mayoral pressure to suspend a recent investigation that pointed the finger of guilt at the mayor's son, Zane had been the one accused of the theft. He'd tried to fight back, only to be framed and forced out of office.

Zane pinned Rachel with another sharp look. "I'm not interested in Proud Bend's politics, Miss Smith. Nor should you be. You can't even vote."

She straightened her shoulders. "My suggestion benefits both you and this town."

"So why are *you* so interested? How does this benefit you?"

She blinked, her jaw tightening ever so slightly as she glanced at the mayor. "I have my reasons." She cleared her throat. "You need to find your brother.

What better way than to follow his movements but as his replacement?"

"As his replacement, or acting as him? I don't do undercover work." It smelled too much like what had already happened to him, when those on his staff had bent to the mayor's subtle threats and gone undercover to plant evidence that implicated him.

Rachel studied him. "Or is it that you just don't care for lies?"

Zane stiffened. Miss Rachel Smith was proving to be as good at reading people as he was, with her quirked eyebrow and sharp, blue-eyed gaze. He'd have to be careful.

"Both. I don't care for lies—nor do I care for undercover work," he answered stiffly.

Her demeanor softened. Was that a hint of respect forming in her expression?

"I appreciate your work ethic, Mr. Robinson," Rachel said, quickly recovering her cool manner. "But I can't see you doing anything else. You know you won't be able to waltz into the sheriff's office and demand to see all that Deputy Wilson has done in finding Alex. Or read Alex's file on Rosa and Daniel. The two cases must be related. Two disappearances in a short period of time? You'd need both files."

"My brother could be working on a covert assignment—he might not be missing at all."

"You mean, going undercover without telling his deputy?" She looked skeptical. "Does *he* like undercover work?"

Zane couldn't say for sure. The topic had not risen in any conversation Zane had ever had with Alex. "I expect he would do whatever is necessary to find your friend." Even as Zane said that, he heard the hesitation in his words. Did he not believe them? He hated his own doubt.

Rachel must have heard the uncertainty because she frowned ever so slightly. "Perhaps Alex is dallying where he should not be dallying."

Zane felt his jaw tighten. No. While Alex had often enjoyed life more than he did, his brother would never abandon his job to "dally" with anyone. Rachel's suggestion was ludicrous, he told himself a bit too fiercely.

Wasn't it?

"Do you believe your brother would just walk away from a job?" Rachel asked.

Zane paused and swallowed. The Alex he had grown up with would never have walked away. But after Nicola died a few years back, Alex had taken his wife's early demise hard, even disappearing once for several days and sending their mother into a frantic state. Yes, he'd changed. He'd decided to live more in the moment, he'd told Zane once. Zane knew Alex was running from his grief, but he would say nothing of that aloud, not in front of these people who would judge Alex harshly if he truly had walked away from his life once again.

At his hesitation, Rachel's gaze sharpened and Zane immediately heightened his efforts to appear calm and in control.

"Of course this is a political decision," she said smoothly, wrapping up the conversation as if she was the chair of an important meeting. "But, naturally, one must use common sense here." As she slipped on one of her gloves, she indicated Zane. "One as—how shall I say this?—unceremonious as yourself won't get much out of the people here."

Despite the seriousness of the moment, Zane allowed himself a small smile. If Miss Rachel Smith had tried to be diplomatic with him, it hadn't worked. If she'd attempted to offend him, it had slid from him like water off a duck's back. Regardless, he *had* been "unceremonious" with her. Alex had inherited all the tact, not him. Zane was the more difficult twin.

"If you refuse," Mayor Wilson added with a slight edge, "I cannot allow you to start your own investigation. It would be too disruptive."

To your upcoming campaign? Zane asked himself.

"Why not pick up where your brother has left off, *as your brother*?" Rachel finished, her voice once again as smooth as a silk pillow. "You might just scare someone who can't believe the sheriff is still around and walking. Scared people make mistakes."

True, but scared people acted dangerously, too. Zane drew in a thoughtful breath. He wasn't going to agree to anything simply because it benefited this pair. "So you're suggesting Alex's disappearance is the result of foul play?" Scrubbing his face and beard, Zane knew he had to voice another concern, although he hated it. "What if Alex is dead? Don't you think that his killer would know I'm not my brother?"

Please, Lord, let that not be so.

His words affected Rachel, he could tell. She swallowed and her mouth tightened, obviously hating that they had to consider that possibility. Her answer was soft and hesitant. "Then we shall have to pray that hasn't happened." She blinked, looking remarkably sincere in her grief concerning the idea, but he refused to believe it. "You'll have to shave your beard, too, Mr. Robinson. Alex is clean shaven."

Zane automatically touched it. "Who says that someone else won't realize that I'm not Alex? You saw the truth almost immediately."

"Perhaps I can help you be…less unceremonious," Rachel answered smoothly, not answering his question directly.

"I do not need any help. I know my own brother, and, to be frank, we have switched places before."

That memory cut into him like the ragged edge of a chipped razor. They'd managed to fool everyone except their mother. It hadn't been his finest moment. It was curious that the one time in his life of which he was the most ashamed would be useful right now in doing some good—finding his brother.

"Trust me, Mr. Robinson. I am confident I can help you."

He rolled his eyes. "Quite frankly, Miss Smith, I trust you as far as I can throw you."

Her gaze brightened as it danced over his frame, a moment of impudence that grated against Zane. "We can't allow that, can we? You might hurt your back, for I'm not a small woman." She turned from him. "Mayor Wilson, obviously you must make the final decision."

Zane glanced over at the man who up until now had watched the conversation with little input. Was he looking for weaknesses? "Miss Smith is right," the mayor finally said with his mouth becoming a grim line. "It's risky, but I'm afraid my son is not getting anywhere with his investigation and I want my sheriff back."

Of course. Your political career is on the line here.

Still, Zane scowled, thinking of the three disappearances. In a small town, three persons going missing in a short span of time had to be related. He needed to get into his brother's office and read his files. Fresh eyes might help. "What if I take on the position as myself and not my brother?"

Rachel shook her head. "You'd have to earn everyone's trust, which could take time. Assuming Alex's identity can give you the trust he's already earned. And—" Rachel glanced at the mayor before once more skewering Zane's attention "—you would need to be elected to hold any authority in town if you refuse to take Alex's identity." A slightly knowing smile tugged on the corners of her mouth. "Do you want to schmooze and glad-hand people all while your brother is missing?"

Zane felt his chest tighten.

Her tone softened immediately. "It's not an ideal solution, but you'll have all that's in the sheriff's office at your disposal if you take this offer."

Including Alex's files and notes, Zane thought. They might include information on the lovely Rachel Smith. He frowned, not liking for one minute that he was even considering such an opportunity when his focus should be on finding Alex. Because learning about her wasn't as important, not with the sly political machinations she was weaving.

Zane nodded, wondering all the time if he'd just made a decision he would eventually regret.

Chapter Three

Exactly thirty-four hours after Zane Robinson had agreed to assume his brother's identity, and in the light from the lamp outside her front door, Rachel toyed with the telegram she'd just received. The mayor's young errand boy had brought it over just as she was leaving for her ministry work, as she did most nights. There was no accompanying comment from the mayor, a fact that attested to Mayor Wilson's sharp disapproval.

Rachel swallowed. The mayor had done the sensible thing. He'd checked on Zane Robinson's background. The answering telegram from the mayor of Canaan, Illinois, had only taken a day, and its clipped tone told as much as the harsh words of accusation.

Oh, dear. She had erred once more, this time in her assumption that since Alex was a good sheriff, his twin would also be upstanding. Hadn't he come here to find his brother? He'd been anxious for him. They wrote regularly. Those were good qualities, and Rachel had taken them at face value as testimonials to his character.

In the dim light above the door, Rachel reread the telegram, hoping it wasn't as bad as a moment ago.

Ref. your inquiry of Zane Robinson, he was released from duties, guilty of theft and bribery. Recommend you not hire him.

Her heart sank again. Proud Bend had taken on a thief as sheriff. Would the mayor dismiss him outright? Or wait until Alex was found? All she could hope for now was that regardless of his reputation, Zane would be sufficiently motivated to find his brother before the proverbial ax fell on his limited career here in Proud Bend. Rachel made a mental note to call on the mayor tomorrow.

And hopefully Zane would find Rosa and her son, too.

Keep them all safe, Lord. Please.

"Thank you," she murmured to the errand boy in front of her. With a nod, he hurried away, no doubt anxious to be home.

A breeze rose and chilled Rachel's hot cheeks enough to make her shiver. The weather had turned frigid. Icy air warned of early winter snow, heavier than the skiff that dusted the ground now. Rachel bit her lip, being careful as she stepped down onto the icy gravel that was her home's driveway. In the yard to her left was her late father's coupé, sitting abandoned. It was really a silly conveyance, being so small. Mother had wondered if they should sell the fancy little horse-drawn vehicle.

At the thought of her father, Rachel felt tears spring unbidden into her eyes. She blinked them away. She mourned his death, but she knew that Walter Smith hadn't been the finest citizen of Proud Bend, and had died a victim of his own evil devices.

Father had been accidentally trampled in a stampede just a month ago while trying to blackmail Mitch MacLeod, cousin Victoria's fiancé, into signing over his ranch land's mineral rights. Later that same night, Clyde Abernathy had tried to poison Rachel and her mother, Louise Smith.

While they lay dying in their rooms, Abernathy had hoped to force Victoria into marrying him as part of a plot to cheat Walter Smith's family out of their inheritance. Thankfully, working together, Victoria and Mitch had been able to stop Clyde and save both Rachel and her mother.

Rachel set her basket down on the driveway. From a small pocket, she tugged free her black handkerchief, the only tangible reminder that she was still in mourning. She dabbed her eyes, in part because of the sadness of losing a father and in part because of the sadness of the whole evil affair.

To add to the stress, an hour ago her mother had bemoaned *again* that Rachel would depart for the evening. It was too soon, she'd complained, but Rachel had told her mother flat out that she had souls to win and that mourning shouldn't stop the work. When Louise had reminded her of her health, compromised by Abernathy's attempt at poisoning her, Rachel had assured her mother that she felt fine. Work was the best remedy for her, Rachel believed.

Tonight, though, there would be no escort. Five years ago, when Pastor Wyseman had given her his blessing for this ministry to reach out to the local soiled doves, he'd also insisted she never go out alone at night in the vicinity of the saloon. Tonight, her escort was supposed to have been Jake Turcot, a local ranch hand who worked for Mitch MacLeod. Jake couldn't make it this evening, having caught an early-winter flu.

There was no time to find another escort. It didn't matter. What could possibly go wrong on a cold, quiet evening like this? The men in the saloon knew her and would assume she had brought someone with her as she always did. So one night without one wouldn't even be noticed.

Taking up her basket again, Rachel struck off, her feet crunching the gravel underfoot with even more dogged determination. She had to go. What if Rosa turned up tonight? What if tonight was the night others finally found the courage to leave their profession?

The sounds of harsh piano music rolled down the street toward her as she drew closer to its source. The saloon's entertainer struggled through the song, the sour notes and shaky tempo enough to make even Rachel cringe.

She was only a few yards from the source when something made the hairs at her nape rise. And it wasn't from that one difficult chord.

Stalling her march for a moment, she glanced around the dark and deserted street, but saw no one. With a swallow, Rachel began again, only to stop after a yard and spin back. A dried leaf danced past her, its soft scrape obviously not responsible for the feeling that she was being followed. Perhaps it was just the errant breeze that had caused her hair to rise?

No. She could hear a person's feet crunch the dry

ground between the haberdashery and the barbershop. Errant breeze or not, someone *was* following her.

"Jake? Is that you? Come out at once. Stop this foolishness or I shall report your behavior to Mitch and to Pastor Wyseman."

No answer. Heart thumping in her chest like a giant drum, Rachel hesitated. Should she continue on? Or dash back home and hide?

Fear chilled her core, attempting to nail her feet to the wooden sidewalk. To force her to become a victim once again.

Forget it. She'd come too far with her ministry to run away in fear. She'd seen God's protection time and again, especially with all the terrible things that had happened to her.

Through all of them, God had protected her, and she refused to dismiss His protection now. If the night she'd been poisoned by Abernathy had taught her anything, it was to seize the moment, for time was short. She had to return to her ministry, and no one hiding in the shadows would force her out.

Shoving away her fear, Rachel turned and took a few short, forceful steps, more stationary stomping on the faded wooden planks of the sidewalk with her fur-lined boots than marching forward.

Then, stopping, she spun and waited, her back stiff and her jaw so tight it ached.

A man stepped out of the shadows. And though he froze when he realized his error, she had already seen his face.

Chapter Four

Zane Robinson. Rachel sagged in relief.

He'd shaved his beard since she'd left him in his brother's rented room yesterday morning. The light from the saloon behind her, plus the waning moonlight above his left shoulder, cast their soft glows onto his strong frame and the pale skin where facial hair had been. Although the vertical line between his brows that had defined him yesterday was now erased by his surprise, Rachel knew exactly which twin stood before her.

On the heels of relief came anger. Who did he think he was, scaring her like that? She stalked up to him, giving him a hard poke in the chest. "Is there a reason you're skulking around like a thief in the night?"

Zane pushed away her gloved hand. "Is there a reason why you're trotting around town late at night?"

"I'm not trotting."

"I'm not skulking."

Refusing to be entangled in a war of words, Rachel spun and continued her march down the sidewalk, only to have Zane catch her by the arm. "Are you insane?" He flicked out a nod toward the seedy saloon, the only business open at this time of night. "You're not headed there, are you?" He tapped her basket, now filled with supplies. "What are you planning? A late-night picnic?"

She should explain her intentions here and now. But she still felt the sting from reading that telegram, and she wouldn't waste time on a man she knew to be a criminal.

After yanking back her arm, Rachel tugged the lower hem of her jacket and continued walking.

Zane couldn't believe that Rachel would waltz into a saloon at any hour, let alone this one. The men who had not yet found the shallow comfort that could be purchased would no doubt turn their attentions to her.

Being a sheriff had allowed Zane to see greater people fall. This woman might be unusual, but the ills of liquor and laudanum had caused ruination in many, no matter their social status.

He gritted his teeth. He hadn't come all the way to Proud Bend to babysit a grown woman, except that right now Rachel was his only lead in Alex's disappearance. Zane caught her arm once more, this time hauling her to the bench that sat outside the now-closed haberdashery, plunking her down as if she was a slab of meat hitting a hot fry pan.

He straightened and pulled down on the sleeves of Alex's long, dark coat. Zane had hopped aboard the train to Proud Bend with only a small bag of essentials and his less-warm overcoat, and was glad he now had access to Alex's wardrobe. The weather last week must have been warmer for Alex not to have chosen this coat to wear on the day he'd disappeared.

He rubbed his cold cheeks. *Alex, where are you? Are you warm enough?*

After Rachel and the mayor had left him, Zane had set about shaving his beard and changing into Alex's clothes. Thirty minutes after that, Zane had successfully convinced his brother's deputy he was Alex. Then, thankfully, he'd found his brother's room key tucked in his desk drawer at the sheriff's office and furtively slipped it into his pocket. Now he could lock his brother's room.

When Rachel tried to rise, he pushed her back down. "Don't move," he barked. "If you do, I'll arrest you."

She was suitably outraged. "On what charge?"

"I'll think of something. I'm the sheriff here, thanks to your crafty scheming. Perhaps I'll arrest you for vagrancy?"

"I'm hardly a vagrant."

"Then why would you possibly want to go to the saloon this late at night? And who is Jake?"

She'd called out Jake's name a moment ago. "Jake Turcot was to be my escort tonight, but he's sick."

"So why are you out here by yourself?"

"That's none of your business." She rose, as if refusing to be delayed.

He moved to block her way. Would she back down? He doubted it. She wasn't the type to give in easily, as he knew from the hours he'd spent going through the files connected to her in the sheriff's office. He'd spent the day getting caught up on the various investigations, both opened and closed, including the one into her father's death, and Clyde Abernathy's attack on her and her mother. He'd even read the slim file that had been compiled on Alex's disappearance. Then he'd read about Rosa and her son, the case that had probably precipitated Alex's vanishing act, for he'd been searching for them at the time he went missing.

Curiously, added to the same file was an unsolved crime from five years ago, the murder of Rosa's mother, another prostitute. A note, handwritten by a previous sheriff, told how the mother, Liza, had been beaten to death while working, but she had claimed to know who'd stolen some money the women had given Rachel to invest. Her killer had never been found.

Questions about that had led to yet another investigation. Rachel had been assaulted and robbed not long before Liza's murder. According to the women who worked behind the saloon, Liza had felt responsible for that theft because she had encouraged the other women to hand over their money. She had visited Rachel the day after the assault, vowing that she was going to pay back the money stolen.

Even now, this late in the evening, Zane frowned at the curious events. The robbery connected Liza to Rachel. Liza was connected to Rosa, who was missing. Alex had disappeared searching for Rosa and her son. Did that tie Alex to those old cases? How did Rachel fit into the disappearances?

And just what reason did Rachel have for frequenting saloons late at night?

Zane rubbed his clean-shaven jaw, still unused to it and the chill on his face. The investigations' files read like the plot of a bad Western novel. A murdered woman, another missing, still one, Rachel, tying all of them together.

Walter Smith and Clyde Abernathy, the two men who'd owned Proud Bend's only bank, had both been as crooked as a scenic railway. According to the old adage, the apple did not fall far from the tree. Could he assume Rachel was as crooked as her father?

He needed to find out. "What do you plan to do this late at night?"

She sighed, blowing out her breath in an undignified manner. "I help the women who work at the Two Winks Cribs. The late evening is the best time to meet them because they are often in need then. And there's always the hope that I'll find that Rosa has returned."

"Returned home, or returned to her profession?"

"I *hope* she has returned home, I *fear* she has returned to her profession." Her shoulders slumped. "Rosa is a new Christian. I'm afraid she'll get scared and return to the only thing she knows. But if it means that she'll be back here, unharmed, I will accept it. Right now, I'll take anything!"

"Who's discounting the Holy Spirit this time?"

She stiffened. "That's not fair. I'm only trying to save these women!"

Zane felt his jaw clench. Something drove Rachel to help these women, and he was pretty certain that it wasn't good Christian charity.

"Is that why you were so adamant about me assuming Alex's identity?"

"In a way. Having a good sheriff keeps Proud Bend happy. When they're happy, they keep Mayor Wilson elected. He supports my ministry. The last thing these women need is to be run out of town. There's no way to know what dangers they'd face in a new community, and I'd never be able to reach them for God. So, having you filling your brother's shoes helps my cause."

She made it sound so innocent. But was there more to it? He still believed he'd caught signs of guilt in her behavior. He wanted to know why.

"You care a lot about these women," he observed. "Is there a reason for that?"

"Does a Christian need a reason to care about other people?" she countered.

It was a fair point, but that didn't explain why Rachel's cheeks were so bright red as she spoke.

Humiliation burned Rachel's cheeks. Zane was eyeing her as if he suspected she was guilty of something... and in a way, he was right. Liza, Rosa's mother, had gone to an early grave when she'd attempted to pay back the money that Rachel had convinced the women in the cribs to give her in order to invest. Money that had been stolen from her. She blinked back the memory of that horrible night.

She had been shoved to the ground and had been kicked so brutally the effects had lingered for months. Her escort had tried to fight back, but he had been knocked unconscious, his wounds even more cruel. Both of them had been left for dead. The sheriff back then had not caught the man, and her escort, feeling the strain of the attack, had moved away shortly after recuperating. Even Rachel had almost despaired for some time.

"I just want to help them," Rachel muttered to herself. "I nearly gave up after I was attacked."

The day after she'd been assaulted and left for dead,

Liza had visited her to announce that she was going to pay back the stolen money. She'd even believed she knew who'd assaulted Rachel and planned to seek him out.

From her sickbed, Rachel had protested such a dangerous move, trying to insist that Liza go to the sheriff, but like so many in her profession, Liza mistrusted the law. Too many arrests for vagrancy, theft, disturbing the peace. Too much shunning. So, not wanting to destroy Liza's trust in her, Rachel had not reported the plan to the sheriff.

Rachel had been such a fool—first for being so cocky, thinking she could just invest the money and thus solve all the women's troubles, and then later for not doing more to stop Liza from confronting the thief. If she'd tried harder, perhaps Liza would still be alive.

Of course, there was no way to know for certain if Liza's death had been the result of her going to talk to the thief. She had been working that night. Her killer could have been a customer. The sheriff at the time had said it was a common yet unfortunate end to some soiled doves' lives, but Rachel's heart still clenched at the memory, convinced Liza's death had been at the hands of the man she'd confronted.

Throughout the five years since, the guilt had dogged Rachel, as did the question of why Liza felt she could meet that man who she believed had committed such a heinous crime. Why had she thought she was safe doing so?

Pushing away the disturbing memories and focusing on Zane as he stood over her, Rachel fished a small tract from her pocket. This was why she went out each night, she told herself as she thrust the paper at Zane.

"Here, read this. This is my hope for these women, what I must do."

As he read the pamphlet, leaning it toward the dim moonlight, Rachel slipped into the dark alley between the haberdashery and the saloon. The shadows, long and deep, swallowed her up.

Oftentimes, with her escort, Rachel would first go into the saloon to get a feel of the evening's mood. Occasionally, a surly customer would harass the women and set them on edge. Those nights made it all the more difficult for her to help them.

But, pressed for time tonight and without Jake, Rachel headed straight to the cribs via the alley. This route was dark, stinking of garbage and waste of all sorts. She risked tripping over discarded tins and such, or even the occasional drunk. All she had to deal with tonight, thankfully, was her skirt brushing against the outer walls. Although she would wear last season's styles while doing her ministry work, Rachel tried in vain to avoid snagging her skirt's material on the rough boards that sided the buildings. At least her maid was adept at tugging the threads back in. Mother would be less likely to notice that the fine clothes she'd purchased, albeit last year, were on their way to ruin.

As she entered the yard behind the saloon, Rachel stopped to press herself against the building's rear clapboards.

The yard was empty except for the stray dog that had had puppies this past autumn. It now trotted past with a piece of garbage in its mouth. Rachel glanced around, thankful that no ejected drunk was trying to sneak back into the saloon through its rear door. She took the moment to pray that Zane would give up following her.

"Please, Lord," she whispered. "Hide me."

When, over the lull in the music, she heard firm steps upon the sidewalk pause by the narrow alley, she drew in a breath and held it, eyes shut tight and bottom lip pinned between her teeth.

Then, thankfully, the steps continued on. Zane didn't enter the alley. Rachel dared to let out her breath and look around again. A pair of lanterns on the rear-door posts lit the yard and the cribs, those tiny huts where the women plied their trade. Still clinging to her basket handle, Rachel felt her heart wrench. It always did when she first arrived.

This way of life shouldn't exist. There was no reason why the women here couldn't have decent, safe lives. Rachel had been teaching some of them some basic skills that could lead to jobs as seamstresses or domestic work. If she was going to encourage them to change occupations, she should provide them with some skills to aid their departure.

With a fast glance around the corner, Rachel stepped toward the cribs just as a woman in a filthy pink dress stumbled out of the rear door. Rachel recognized Annie Blake, an older woman who'd been in town as long as she could remember. She was short and scrawny, her face lined like crumpled paper and her teeth stained brown.

Annie fell, and when the woman turned back toward the door, Rachel gasped. Her face was bleeding.

The door stayed open, spilling out additional light as Annie rose unsteadily to her feet. Rachel could see tears glittering in her eyes.

Stirred to action, Rachel rushed over to her. She set her basket down in front of the narrow nearby porch that led to the woman's rented crib before wrapping her arm around Annie's thin shoulders. The woman dropped her head into her hands and began to weep.

Father, have mercy on this woman.

The wind chose that moment to rise, drawing out from the open door the unpleasant smell inside. Rachel held her breath as she led the older woman toward her crib. After setting Annie down on the steps, Rachel opened her basket. In it she had all the things she needed for the night. Bandages, salves of arnica and comfrey and salts to stanch blood, willow bark among her various teas to help with pain because she refused to use laudanum. Thanks to Abernathy's attempt to poison her, she'd learned firsthand the dangerous effects that an opiate could have on a person if overused. It might be the painkiller of choice nowadays, but she knew too many people who seemed to want it overly much, a thought that scared her.

From the small flask of water, Rachel wet a cloth to clean the wound near Annie's eye. She would apply only the salve, given the location of the wound, for the salts could cause blindness. After, she would make tea for the woman and perhaps add some lemon balm to calm her. She reached out to turn Annie's face toward her.

The older woman's expression twisted into hatred as she backed away. "You! Thief! You're the last person I want helping me! Give me back my money!" Then she lunged at Rachel.

Chapter Five

When Zane looked up from the tract Rachel had given him, he was alone. He'd only glanced down for a moment, but in that time, she'd vanished. Feeling sudden frustration, he shoved the tract into his pocket and stalked away. He stopped at the entrance to the alley, but it was shadowed and still. Had Rachel slipped in here? He could hear nothing, no breathing, shifting shadows or anything that might give away a presence.

Where had Rachel gone? She was shrewd enough to try anything to escape him, he was sure, but she was also focused on her mission, which, as his quick perusal of the tract would suggest, was to help the women who plied a disreputable trade. She would hurry to that.

Would she head straight to the saloon? That seemed the most logical place for her to go. Not wanting to second-guess himself, he strode past the alley and hurried inside. The stench of ales and tobacco hit him.

He scoured the main room. Rachel wasn't inside, and a curious wash of relief doused him. At the same time, he studied those patronizing the place. No shocked expressions when he entered, only a few offering mild curiosity. The saloon's customers appeared relatively well behaved, considering the late hour. No one seemed to mind the poorly played chords on the out-of-tune piano, either.

Frustration bit at Zane as he headed to the far end of the bar where he could observe the whole room without being the center of attention. If he had to think something about Alex's disappearance, he'd say that no one here had been involved in it, for surely they would have been surprised to see that he'd returned.

Zane's breath hitched with worry. *Alex, where are you?*

For that matter, where was the lovely Miss Rachel Smith?

A series of guffaws and one female cry of indignation dragged his attention to a nearby corner. Someone shoved a thin woman in a filthy pink dress away from the men playing cards. She was older and looked worn down by life. Zane easily guessed her occupation. Pulling up on the neckline of her dress, she stumbled past him toward the back door and then outside, leaving the door open behind her. No sooner was she outside than she tripped on her drooping skirt and toppled headfirst to the ground.

Zane straightened, but before he could a step toward the back exit, he spied Rachel hurrying over to her from some dark recess of the backyard.

Ah. So she had ducked down the alley between the buildings after all. She hadn't hidden in the shadows until he passed, but must have slipped straight through to this backyard. Zane stiffened his shoulders. Time to see if what she'd told him about her devotion to her mission was true.

It was. She immediately began to administer aid to the older woman. Then, to his shock, the woman screamed out something about thievery and lunged at her. Automatically, Zane pushed away from the corner of the bar to head to her and, and just as quickly, someone caught him.

"Whoa there, Sheriff!"

Zane turned to gape at the bartender, who had leaned across the counter to stop him. The man shook his head. "You need to let Miss Smith handle that."

Zane tugged back his arm. "That woman just attacked her!"

"I know. But Miss Smith isn't going to earn any respect from Annie if you come to her rescue." The bartender straightened and tugged down on his vest. "That's what she needs. Respect from those women. I know you mean well, Sheriff, but trust me on this one. You aren't going to help the situation."

Maybe, maybe not. But letting this woman hurt Rachel wouldn't help, either. Zane pushed himself away from the bar and stalked to the back door, fully intending to save his only lead from a dangerous situation. Annie was screaming something about Rachel being a thief. Who knew what would happen next? Many a soiled dove hid a knife or small revolver in their clothing.

The bartender tore around the counter and caught up with him, his new grip on Zane's arm surprisingly hard for a man who poured drinks for a living. "No! Let Miss Smith figure it out. If you intervene, you'll be making her mission a whole lot harder."

"So you know about her mission?"

"Everyone does. Most don't take it seriously, even this place's owner."

"Is he here tonight?"

The bartender shook his head. "No. He runs several establishments from Denver to Castle Rock."

"If he disapproves, why is she allowed to continue?"

"What harm is she doing?" The man shrugged. "Most of those women aren't going to drop everything they know no matter what some do-gooder tells them. And besides, Miss Smith's father, rest his soul, owned the bank that holds the mortgage here. It's always good to keep your banker happy."

Zane's jaw tightened. More politics to keep straight. When shouts continued, he looked back through the door, to Rachel's hunched back. She struggled to pin the older woman down, most likely to render some aid to the woman, whose face he just now noticed was bleeding. Zane glanced back at the bartender. "Did that woman just accuse Rachel of theft?"

"Yes, but the theft Annie's talking about didn't happen recently."

"How long ago?"

"Years. Five or so."

It had to be the same theft he'd seen noted in one of the files he'd read. The timing was right. Except that the information on it was woefully thin and the trail long cold. Whoever had done the initial investigation had said only that Rachel was carrying a substantial amount of money that belonged to the soiled doves, and it had been stolen after she and her escort had been badly assaulted.

Zane grimaced. Why had Rachel taken the money in the first place? His gut ached at yet another warning of a crooked town.

Or was the ache because he didn't like to consider Rachel a thief?

She is, he argued with himself. *You've seen it with your own eyes.* His gut twisted further. *Just accept that fact.*

But she's a Christian. Look at what she's doing for the Lord.

He peered outside again. By now, Rachel was pushing Annie down, refusing to be bested by the woman. Being stronger, Rachel would win this small battle. Zane closed the door somewhat as he turned to the bartender. "Tell me what you know about the theft."

The man looked him up and down as if weighing his decision to speak. "Like I said, it happened about five years ago and it was more than just a simple theft. Miss Smith took some money that our soiled doves had saved up. Back then, rent on those cribs out there wasn't too much and the women could save a bit. Miss Smith promised to invest it for them, but she was supposedly robbed that same night. After that, one of the women started to work extra so she could pay back the others. Annie here complained the loudest, so she got her share back first."

"Then why is she still crying foul about it?"

The bartender looked grim. "Her memory has gone. She's drunk it away and her mind went along with it."

"Why would that other woman want to pay it back? Did *she* steal it?" Zane frowned. "For that matter, isn't Rachel Smith wealthy? She certainly dresses well enough, and her father owned Proud Bend's bank.

Why didn't she just reimburse them from her own account? Wouldn't that be the Christian thing to do?"

"You'll have to ask Miss Smith all those—" He narrowed his gaze. "Wait, I told you this story when you first came here."

Zane swallowed. "I'd only just got here. You can't expect a man to remember everything from his first day or so."

The bartender shrugged as if accepting Zane's answer. "Shortly after the money was stolen, the woman who'd worked extra was murdered. I feel bad for her daughter."

"Tell me about her."

"Rosa grew up around soiled doves, and once she was old enough she began doing the same thing her mother did. About a month ago, she decided it wasn't the life she wanted. She's got a child and all."

The woman, Rosa, had grown up with prostitutes? Zane's gut twisted. "So she decided she didn't want to remain here and just left?" This was still sounding like a case of a woman moving on.

"Miss Smith doesn't believe Rosa left on her own." The bartender shook his head. "They're a sad lot, aren't they?" He then frowned. "When Rosa went missing, you promised to find her. I guess you haven't been successful."

Oh, yeah. He was acting as Alex. Zane drew in a long breath, remembering how he hated undercover work. When his deputy had found "proof" that Zane had stolen tax money, he suspected that his deputy had planted the evidence through some unsanctioned undercover work. Zane hadn't been able to prove anything, though.

The bartender continued to study him. Zane kept his expression concerned and nothing more, hopefully allowing this man to believe he was Alex. But it still felt like lying. He cleared his throat. "I don't know much about the background. Rosa is missing…"

"Yeah. She and her little boy disappeared almost two weeks ago. Too bad you can't find them. Before she decided this wasn't the life for her, Rosa was good for this business. I'd hate to think she's been murdered."

Zane stiffened. Who had said anything about murder? "Tell me about Rosa's mother." He paused. "Again."

"Liza? She probably worked extra because she'd convinced those women to let Miss Smith invest their savings. Shame they never caught her killer." He shrugged. "I'm not one to spend my money on them. I just work here."

"Who do you think stole the money?" Zane held the man's suddenly shifting gaze. "You must have heard something."

The bartender lifted his eyebrows as he began to move back toward the bar. "That's the big question you lawmen could never answer, isn't it?" he asked, tossing the accusation over his shoulder as he glanced out the back door. "All we have is Miss Smith's word that she can't remember who attacked her. Her escort said the same thing. Sure, they'd been beaten up, but it couldn't have been that bad. They both survived."

What was this guy saying? Zane dug his fingernails into his palms, resisting the urge to grab the bartender and remind him that the attacks had been so brutal they'd been considered attempted murder. There was no statute of limitations on that crime. So, yes, they were *that bad*. And sometimes, memory loss followed. He'd seen it several times in the course of his work.

Only God had pulled some victims through their ordeals. Maybe not remembering was a good thing, considering all they'd gone through. Either way, blaming them for losing the memory of such a vicious attack seemed cruel.

When the bartender reached the long strip of faded and stained pine that served as a counter, he lifted his brows in a smug, knowing fashion. "The money had been stolen. Of course, with her status in town, no one would insist that she pay it back, even as rich as she is."

Zane fought back the annoyance growing in him. He didn't trust this bartender. At first glance, he seemed to support Rachel, but now, he was accusing her. These were tactics of the guilty. Glancing through the open door at Rachel as she continued to dab Alice's eye, Zane countered in a low growl, "But if she is that rich, where was the motive to steal? It doesn't make any sense."

"Thieves take advantage of opportunities. Even the wealthy want more money."

Zane folded his arms, the stiff paper tract Rachel had thrust at him now poking into his chest, right through his coat pocket. "Why would she even consider stealing if she could just walk into the bank and take some of her own money? You've seen how she dresses. Surely someone like that would have a generous amount at her disposal."

The man shrugged again. "It was five years ago, Sheriff, and her pa wasn't dead then. Maybe Miss Smith didn't have any money she could get to without permission. I don't want to speak ill of the dead, but that father of hers wasn't the most generous, and back then, she'd have been underage, so any withdrawal would have to be approved first. Now, though? I heard she owns the bank."

That didn't make any sense. Zane couldn't help wonder where her mother, the bank owner's widow, fit in all of this.

For that matter, who had inherited the partner's share? According to a footnote left in that file, Clyde Abernathy had died of a heart attack in jail the night before he was to face his first day of trial. He'd left no widow or family. The file read that he'd been buried quietly in Proud Bend's cemetery, the expenses to be settled when his will was probated.

Zane grimaced. He would clarify whether or not Rachel owned the bank later. "But, back then, would Miss Smith have orchestrated that brutal an attack just to get money? She lives a comfortable life."

The bartender's small smile turned sly as he shrugged. "Hey, I'm just the man who pours drinks, but if there is one thing I've learned from working here, it's that things can change in the blink of an eye. And sometimes they aren't even what they seem."

That man was not just a simple bartender. For starters, he was too chatty, too willing to offer information. But Zane wasn't about to accuse him of anything just because he freely offered answers instead of keeping the confidences bartenders were so famous for. No, Zane would keep an eye on him.

He returned to the back door and peeked out into the yard. A series of mixed laughs rippled out from another crib, but, besides that, all was quiet.

Annie had apparently retreated into her crib, leaving Rachel to stow the things she'd taken from her basket. In the yellow light from the lamps, her shoulders heaved with what looked like a burdened sigh. It wasn't hard to guess that she felt her night was unsuccessful. If she owned a bank, why was she out ministering to those sorry women? What had driven her to this particular type of mission work? When one of her bandages rolled away from her, Zane resisted the urge to stride out and help her.

No, she wouldn't appreciate that.

The bartender walked up and continued talking as though the din behind them didn't matter. "Ya got a lousy memory, Sheriff. I've told you all this stuff before. You even wrote Miss Smith's name down that first night you were here, after you asked who looked after the women."

The tone was accusatory, the same as when the man was talking about Rachel's status. Zane turned back to him. Either the bartender liked Rachel or not. Time to stop dodging a commitment one way or the other. "How does she look after these women? Does she cook and clean for them? Either she's trustworthy or not."

The bartender shifted his gaze away. "All right. Miss Smith's been trying to help them for years. I've seen her elbows-deep in laundry, scrubbing blood out of those women's clothes, telling them about some new, safe job that opened up in Denver, or which family needed a maid and how important it is to keep yourself clean and disinfected. Most of it falls on deaf ears, but Miss Smith keeps trying."

"So why make it sound like she stole that money herself?"

The tract he held would affirm her faith, and that she hadn't staged a robbery that had gone so horribly wrong. But what if she'd hired someone to rob her without hurting her, only to have him double-cross her and try to kill both her and her escort?

Such a scenario didn't line up with her Christian actions here and now. Cruel deceitfulness toward the soiled doves she worked so hard to help didn't make sense. He took out the tract and weighed it in his palm. He refused to reach any conclusions until he had more information.

"By the way, Sheriff," the bartender called out as he moved away, "you never did pay me for that postcard you took. They aren't cheap, and you wasted it by writing Miss Smith's name on it."

Zane snapped his attention back to the man. Was that the postcard Rachel had found? The bartender said Alex had asked, on his first night here, who took care of the soiled doves. Did that mean it wasn't connected to Alex's disappearance after all? Mentally, he told himself not to discard any evidence just yet. Alex had held on to that postcard all this time—there had to be reason for that. Maybe the card itself was the crucial clue, not the name written on it. "Where did you get it, anyway? It's not a photograph of Proud Bend."

From the far end, a loud, scruffy man called to the bartender, who moved quickly to tend to his request. Only when he'd finished his task did he toss Zane a fast look. He offered nothing more, choosing instead to return to his work.

Frustrated, Zane pushed open the back door a bit more. Rachel had finished stowing her supplies into her basket. Her work looked curiously out of sorts with her fine outfit, yet, she held her head high as she continued to stow her things. However humble the work, she did it with dignity.

Then, abruptly, her head shot up and she stared out at something beyond his line of view. He bent forward to peer in that direction, also hearing the high-pitched, quiet sobs that had caught Rachel's attention.

Zane let out a short gasp. A small, dark-haired boy, barely out of diapers, toddled into the pool of thin light that lit the yard.

Pinned to his dirty coat was a crumpled piece of paper.

Chapter Six

"Daniel!"

Rachel sprang into action, dropping her basket and rushing to the small child. She scooped him into a fierce embrace that crushed that paper pinned to him and forced him to wail out a protest.

Realizing she'd frightened the small child, she set him on the ground and knelt down to his level. "You poor thing! Where is Mama?"

Something swept past them, a blur of dark movement she refused to investigate, keeping all her focus on the child. The toddler cried on and she lifted him and carried him to the step of the nearest crib. At the sounds of his wailings, several women poked their heads from their own small buildings, Annie Blake included.

"Is that Daniel? Where's Rosa? Is she back?" one woman asked.

Rachel shook her head, all the while trying to soothe Daniel. It didn't work. "I didn't see her—but I was focused on Daniel," she admitted. "She can't be far. She wouldn't leave him."

"She's not around."

Rachel turned toward the pronouncement. Zane stood there, his gaze still searching the limits of the lamplight. "How do you know?" she asked him.

"I just checked. I heard someone running off, but lost him or her in the darkness." He grimaced and his voice dropped to a mere whisper. "I wasn't familiar with the area, and with the moon setting, I couldn't see well."

"It couldn't have been Rosa. She wouldn't drop Daniel off and then leave."

Zane's mouth thinned, but he said nothing. Rachel resisted the urge to force her point upon him, instead choosing to cling to Daniel. Thankfully, his wailing had started to abate.

Touching the child's arm gently, Zane snagged the boy's attention. "Daniel? Hello?"

Curious, the child slowed his cries and watched him. Zane smiled gently. "Can you tell me who brought you here?"

Thankful that Zane knew how to speak to a small child, Rachel held her breath.

The boy didn't answer, but he did stop crying. Encouraged by this, Rachel asked him, "Was it Mama who brought you here?"

Zane shook his head. "Don't ask him a leading question. He'll want to answer you the way he thinks you want to hear." He tugged lightly on the boy's jacket and smiled softly. "Who came with you, son?"

Abruptly shy, Daniel buried his head into Rachel's jacket. She held him tight and sagged. "He's too young for this. I'm not sure he even understands what we're asking."

Gently prying the boy some inches from Rachel, Zane unpinned the note. "Where's your mama, Daniel?"

The boy began to cry again. Rachel felt his face. "His forehead feels warm and he doesn't look well. And yet his hands are cold. I think he's caught a chill." She looked at Zane. "It's a shame you didn't find who dropped him off. They could know what's wrong with him."

"I'd say whoever dropped him off didn't want to deal with a sick child. As soon as I heard you call his name, I raced off in the direction he'd come. I could hear someone, but I couldn't find them." Zane's voice slipped into a whisper. "Whoever dropped him off knew their way around—certainly better than me."

Keeping the boy close, Rachel stood and sighed. "Well, we can't leave him out here in the cold. We need to get him home."

"Do you know where he lives?"

She flicked her head toward the cribs. "Rosa can barely afford to rent a crib, so this is home."

"It hasn't been offered to another soiled dove?"

"I expect she's paid for a full month's rent." She hugged Daniel tighter. "I'm taking him to my house."

"Do you think it's wise?"

Appalled that he was questioning her judgment, Rachel asked, "Why not?"

"If you stay with him here, he might be more comfortable and be able to tell us where he was and who brought him."

"Believe me, he won't be more comfortable here, and frankly I doubt he can tell us anything. He can barely string a sentence together."

"But is it safe to have him in your home? He might be contagious. Or become a real handful."

"I know this child." She clung to him. "He's better off at my house. I'm certainly not going to keep him here in the crib. My cousin, Victoria, has had her fiancé's children overnight several times, and there are five of them. If we can survive those mischief makers, we can handle one sick little toddler."

Zane shot her a dubious look. Experience told him that taking the child out of the place he was used to would hinder any chances of the boy telling them anything.

Still, admittedly, the chances that the child would have any useful information to share were slim. Zane scanned the darkness, his ears pricked to hear anything suspicious, but the noises from the saloon and the cribs masked the rest of the night sounds. A mongrel dog slunk by, tail between her legs.

This was not a good end to his first full day of filling his brother's shoes. He looked down at the stiff but crumpled paper in his hands. It was too dark to read it, so he tucked it into his breast pocket beside Rachel's tract. Besides, the night was getting colder and he didn't want to stand in the doorway so close to the bartender and patrons, none of whom he fully trusted. The child's health was more important.

Taking up Rachel's basket for her, he said, "Fine. Your house it is. Lead the way."

He had a pretty good idea where she lived. Earlier today, he'd done a bit of exploring on Alex's horse. The beast had known instantly he wasn't his brother, but, after a few sniffs of Alex's coat, had accepted the replacement wearing it.

He'd noted all the major homes and businesses in Proud Bend. There were only a handful of fancy houses in town, all close to the river. One was closed up, and, after reading all the files he could, Zane assumed it was Clyde Abernathy's, for the man's estate had yet to be fully settled.

The fanciest house, with its fine, glimmering stone facade, he now discovered was the Smith residence. Wordlessly they walked up the long driveway. Gravel crunching underfoot, Zane could not deny the swell of suspicion. Here was the town's richest family, a banking family, and, from Rachel's slight drawl, he would say their heritage was old money from New England. From reading his brother's reports about Walter Smith, he knew that corruption was rife in this family, and with each step Zane took toward the house, his resentment and ire grew.

Lord, take away my prejudice.

He set his jaw, keeping his breath short and waiting for his black mood to pass. Rachel had done nothing to implicate herself in her father's corrupt schemes. In the matter of Walter Smith's death, she had been, along with her mother, as much a victim as he'd been in Canaan.

Zane hated the memory of the treachery. Did Rachel know what Zane had been accused of? Unlikely. Not even Alex knew yet. He'd been fired and had received Deputy Wilson's telegram the same day. It had happened so quickly that Zane had felt it better to tell his brother to his face than put the bitter incident down on paper, a reminder for years to come how wealth bought its own privilege to do as it pleased.

"It's a fine home," he muttered tightly as they approached the front door. To the right was a small horse-drawn coupé, horseless at this time of night, but in the lamp lit above the door, Zane could tell the carriage had cost a pretty penny.

"Yes, my father wanted the best of everything," Rachel said.

"And you?"

"I have to admit, there was a time when I was very pleased that I lived in such luxury." She pursed her lips and shook her head. "Not anymore. I have seen too much evil and trouble to simply be happy to sit in the front parlor sipping hot tea and looking out at the world going by."

She shifted the drowsy child in her arms and opened the front door. Several lamps burned in the deep, wallpapered entrance, casting a warm glow on the curved staircase farther in. Warm air, scented with a mix of supper and a perfume to mask the smell of burning coal and wood, greeted his first inhalation as he crossed the threshold. A young man dozed in a chair nearby, and as Rachel quietly shut the door, he jumped to his feet, startled.

"Jasper," Rachel said to him, "Please stay here until Sheriff Robinson leaves. Then you may put out the lamps and go to bed."

"Yes, Miss Rachel."

Zane followed Rachel up the wide, ornately carpeted stairs. On the third tread, Rachel paused to adjust the child and lift her skirt.

"Here," Zane said, setting down her basket, and

peeling the sleeping child from her arms. "I don't have a fancy skirt to trip over."

He held the boy close and frowned at how thin and light he was. Gone was the baby fat that should have carried a healthy child into its toddler years. Long gone.

Holding him snugly with his left arm, Zane removed his right glove and touched the boy's forehead. The boy had a fever, all right, and could easily be very sick. They needed to do something soon.

"I know," Rachel answered his unspoken concern softly. "I have some medicines upstairs. Let's take him to the room we've made up for Victoria's new family. But be quiet. I don't want to wake anyone."

"Considerate," Zane murmured.

"Thank you, but I'm thinking that it's easier to handle Mother when we're both rested." She trod quietly down the hall toward a far door and, with a slight cringe, opened it. It creaked lightly. Hurrying in, she found a candle and lit it from the one burning in the hall. Then she lit a small hurricane lamp. Within a few minutes, the room was filled with a yellowish light.

After Rachel took Daniel from him, Zane glanced around, cataloguing the contents of this small bedroom, one crowded with two beds, a desk and a large chest of drawers. As he removed his Stetson, his gaze lit upon a potbellied stove that stood in front of a walled-up fireplace. The room was too cold to ignore all and simply read the note. "I'll start a fire."

While he busied himself with that task, Zane tossed a glance over his shoulder. Rachel had already found a thick clean nightshirt and cap from the chest of drawers. After setting a pot of water on the stove top to fill a hot-water bottle he found sitting at the end of one bed, Zane finished stoking the fire. Though he knew it was necessary, he disliked the thought of preparing the child for bed in this chill. But, picking up the child's clothing that Rachel had already removed, he shook his head. No wonder Daniel was sick. The clothes were dirty and damp. Damp? This town had the driest air he'd ever felt. Where had the boy been? Somewhere near Proud River?

The clothes also smelled different from other children's clothing, but the scent was nothing he could identify. The fire now blazing, Zane stood and bundled them up. He turned the tiny jacket inside out to protect any traces of whatever might be on them that caused that odor.

"Leave them," Rachel said. "I'll have them washed. There are some of Mitch's children's clothes here I can dress Daniel in tomorrow morning."

"No, I'm taking them. I want to look at them in the light of day. They may give me a clue as to where he has been."

Rachel's brows lifted. "I hadn't thought of that."

Zane wanted to remind her that was why he was the lawman, but he kept quiet. Rachel had been through enough tonight. Her battle with that Annie woman and disappointment at not finding Rosa were only tempered by finding Daniel, but why only the child had returned was still not answered. Zane took the bundle of clothes and set them on the small stool near the door.

He fingered the note. Just as he was preparing to read it, Daniel, chilled from the change of clothes and cool room, stirred and sat up, his face scrunching up in preparation for a wail.

"Shh," Rachel told him softly to ward off the scream. "It's all right. It's going to get warm in here. Didn't Mama ever light a fire?"

She drew him into her arms and held him close. Zane handed her one of the spare counterpanes draped neatly over the end of the other bed. She tucked it all around Daniel and it settled him immediately. "See? You're warm and safe here and we'll give you something to make you feel better; okay? Look around, Daniel, what do you see?"

Zane looked around, as well, finding a soft, stuffed toy—a rabbit or a dog, he wasn't sure. He gave it to Rachel.

"Look at this. Who is this?" she crooned quietly.

"Puppy?"

"Yes, it's a dog."

Daniel looked up at Rachel. "Puppy! Me see puppy."

She smiled over his head to Zane. "There's a mother dog that hangs around the saloon. She had puppies this fall and I think Daniel has seen them." She tucked him into the bed, along with the toy. "I'm afraid it's probably the only pleasant thing in this boy's life. Rosa can barely afford to feed him. I often bring food for her, and I have been trying to teach her to cook simple things like biscuits, but it's hard. She's given up that awful life, but still lives in a crib. She has only a bit of savings, and spends a lot of time looking for work."

Zane swallowed. The child's life wasn't off to a good start. Rachel turned to him. "I have some medicine that will bring down his fever. I'll get it."

She slipped out of the room. Seeing how Daniel had closed his eyes, thankfully, Zane turned to fill up the hot-water bottle. The water would be only warm, but that was probably best for Daniel's young skin.

Rachel clearly cared very much for the boy, which was a credit to her. Corking the bottle securely, he turned back toward the bed. There was a piece of paper on the floor near the door. Obviously it had fallen from Rachel's pocket as she left. Zane quickly slipped the bottle in between the sheets and against the boy's icy toes. Already Daniel was drifting off to sleep, although his rest would be fitful if his fever didn't come down.

After tucking the bedclothes in again, Zane scooped up the paper from in front of the door and returned to the bed. Sitting down in the rocking chair between the beds, Zane unfolded the sheet and bent it toward the lamplight. It was a telegram. The name of his hometown flew off the page toward him, as did the sender's name and every awful word in between.

Dread filled him as he read the stinging accusation.

A noise, soft and swooshing, drew his attention away from the telegram.

Rachel had pushed the door farther open and then shut it tight to keep in the slowly building warmth. She carried in her hands several bottles and a small silver spoon.

When she saw him with the telegram, the hand holding the spoon slapped the pocket of her skirt, and a look of horror flushed her face.

"You checked up on me," Zane stated flatly, his tone neither accusing nor congratulating. "It's good to see that at least Canaan's mayor is prompt in answering."

Chapter Seven

Rachel swallowed. Shifting Daniel must have dislodged the telegram. Carefully, she set her medicines down on the high chest of drawers. Her heart racing, she tried her best to keep her voice smooth. "It's impolite to read other people's telegrams."

"Then what are you doing with it? It was addressed to Mayor Wilson. Did you steal it, too?"

Rachel colored even as she walked over to him and held out her hand. "No, and you know perfectly well that I am not a thief. I took that postcard to keep the deputy from wasting time on me. Besides, the postcard could reveal valuable clues as to where they are."

"Unlikely. I learned tonight that the postcard was part of a pile sitting on the bar at the saloon when Alex first went there. He asked if anyone looked out for ladies like Rosa and Annie. When the bartender gave your name, Alex took the card and wrote your name on it. It happened long before Rosa went missing."

Rachel remained standing in front of him, her hand outstretched for the telegram. "That telegram was in my possession. You must know it's unlikely that I would be able to steal it from the mayor, so it's logical to assume that he gave it to me."

Zane continued to finger it. Rachel could see his jaw tightening. "So he was checking up on me?"

"It was a wise precaution."

They stared each other down for a long minute, the tension in the air crackling like the small logs in the wood stove. Finally, Zane handed over the telegram. She folded it back up and tucked it deeper into her pocket.

"Isn't this the part where you tell me I have to leave?" Zane asked.

"Leave?" She was genuinely surprised. "Why?"

"Because I'm a crook?"

Rachel fingered the paper deep in the folds of her skirt. She'd faced her share of scorn for her ministry, with some going so far as to suggest that she had only attempted to help the women so they'd trust her with their money—after which she'd arranged to have the money stolen from her five years ago. Zane had spoken to the bartender, and Rachel knew perfectly well, thanks to Rosa's warning once, that he'd been spreading rumors about her.

She wasn't a thief, but the suspicion persisted despite all the good work she'd done. Hard work all these years was still not enough to dispel one single rumor.

Her gaze wandered up to Zane's tight expression. Was it possible that there was another side to the story that the mayor of Canaan had told? How could she insist on her innocence and not allow Zane a chance to speak in his own defense? Rachel lifted her chin. "I'm willing to listen to your side of the story, if you like."

Zane's brows shot up, causing Rachel to fight back

a small smile. Was he impressed with her? "So, what do you have to say for yourself?"

He hesitated. "You might be willing to listen, but what about the mayor? No doubt he will want to fire me."

"We both know the situation is complicated."

"You made it that way by insisting I impersonate my brother."

"If you tell me the truth, I'll talk to the mayor on your behalf."

Zane's expression hardened. "What if I admit I'm a thief?"

She swallowed, indecision waffling through her. She honestly didn't know what to say. Thief or not, he was their best chance to find Rosa and Alex.

Zane stood, his expression staying firm as he walked back to the small stove. He donned his Stetson and gloves, strode over to the bundle that was Daniel's clothes and scooped it up. After opening the door, he turned. "Good night, Miss Smith. *Rachel.* I will return before noon to see how the boy is."

Rachel stood. "What about that note pinned to Daniel? What does it say?"

Zane battled the irritation rising in him. "It says it's evidence."

Outside, after bidding the footman a curt goodnight as he strode out the front door, Zane tugged his collar up to battle back the cold wind. Should he have told Rachel his side of the story? He had not a single shred of evidence to prove his innocence except his word that he hadn't taken the money he'd been accused of stealing. But the "evidence" against him was piled up like that solid rock structure called Castle Rock.

He couldn't prove his innocence, so he would say nothing, even to the mayor who would no doubt confront him in the morning. It was better that way. Rachel and the mayor would keep him at a distance and thus remind him that he couldn't trust them, either. He already had his suspicions about Rachel and the missing money, and who knew how crooked the sheriff's office was with the mayor's son as deputy?

Zane quickened his pace away from the Smith mansion. Was the missing money connected to Alex's disappearance? Had Alex found out something incriminating about the Wilsons? Or the sheriff's office? Or was it related to that missing woman, Rosa?

Slipping his hand up to his coat's breast pocket, Zane reassured himself that the note attached to Daniel was still there. He would read it as soon as he could, but out in the cold, dark night wasn't the time, not while he was still stinging from the discovery of that telegram.

Which left his thoughts to wander back to Rachel. For a woman with biting wit and suspicions of theft twirling around her, she certainly knew how to garner sympathy. She'd taken a ragamuffin child into her home, one filthy and sick with who knew what disease, and seemed prepared for him to stay as long as necessary. Remembering how she'd pulled Daniel in close to her at the suggestion that he be returned to his home, Zane could see she had a compassionate heart as easily as he could see that she had done this without forethought or devious planning on her part.

But he'd caught her stealing.

Although, he hated to admit, her reasons for doing so were logical. She didn't want to be the sole target of the investigation, nor did she believe Deputy Wilson was a capable investigator.

Zane had his doubts, too. He'd met the man. He was barely twenty and too inexperienced to do a proper investigation. Zane had managed quite easily to convince him that he was Alex, the boy not even noticing the whiteness of Zane's jaw after so many months wearing a beard.

Gripping Daniel's clothes closer to him, Zane stomped across the barren street toward his brother's rooming house. Within a few minutes, in Alex's room, he'd set down the bundle and was stirring the barely glowing embers in the stove to coax out some warmth. Alex's lantern needed fuel, but he'd risk running out of it in order to study the note Daniel had delivered.

It was a postcard of Castle Rock, that ugly chimney-like rock that jutted above the town with the same name. The picture was a softly colored print in which the artist had made the town seem serene and idyllic. Zane had not been there, but with all the mines around, he doubted that a mountain like Castle Rock would look so romantic.

Fingering the card, he frowned. Why that town and not a postcard of Proud Bend? Did that mean the kidnapper had kept them in Castle Rock? Surely the boy hadn't been dragged for miles in the cold?

Zane flipped the card over, smoothing it again and, with his fingernail, pressing out the puncture marks made by the pin. On an afterthought, he rose and pulled the pin from the coat pocket. It was a brass-and-steel safety pin, weathered and old. It offered no clues, being too common. Every household would have some.

Returning to the card, Zane peered down at it. Thankfully, the words on the back held more promise. His heart pounded in his throat as he read the words.

Mizz Smith,
you want Rosa and sheriff back, you leave $2,000
at wite horse bluf. box at top. saturday nite at 10.
you only. then I let them go.

He sat back, rubbing his jaw. Rachel again, this time mentioned in a ransom note. Whoever had dropped Daniel off had known that Rachel would be at the cribs, but that didn't seem to be a secret.

Zane lifted his head and stared unseeingly out the window. What drove Rachel to this work? How could the town—how could *Alex*—allow her to walk into such a dangerous situation each and every night?

He yawned. Tomorrow evening was the time of the drop-off and in the light of day, he'd see the case more clearly—and Miss Rachel Smith, as well.

In the morning, he'd remember that he wasn't going to be here long enough to form friendships. He was only here to find his brother. He couldn't prove his innocence back in Canaan, but maybe he could do some good here, like finding Alex.

Maybe? There was no maybe. He *would* find Alex and that was all there was to it.

Suddenly, that burden felt like two bricks on his shoulders, and fatigue stole his concentration. He added only one small log to the fire and it caught immediately, tossing out enough light for Zane to prepare for bed.

His sleep was surprisingly restful for being so short. It was early dawn, but this late in the year that meant around seven o'clock. Not one to sleep in, Zane threw off the blankets and, after stirring the fire to life again, he quickly prepared for the day. Mrs. Shrankhof would have breakfast ready for all the lodgers shortly. If Zane hurried, he'd have time to do a bit of work before she rang the bell to call them to the kitchen table.

At the desk, he carefully spread out Daniel's clothes, taking advantage of the new sunlight that streamed in the window. He sniffed them. They smelled of old grease, cheap perfume and something he couldn't identify. Plus, they were stained beyond repair. Zane felt regret bite into him for suggesting that the child return to his home. It was clearly unsuitable for any toddler.

The jacket appeared to carry the most clues. The front of it was soiled with the dust and dirt that one expected a small child to have after wearing the clothes for far too long. But the back was more interesting. An unusually shiny dust was smeared across the upper portion of it, where the shoulder blades might sit.

Zane retrieved his razor and a sheet of writing paper. After slipping the paper under the jacket, he carefully shaved the dust from the material. When a small pile of it accumulated, he examined it at an angle, squinting in the morning sunshine that hit his face. The dust looked pale, almost a pinkish beige. It twinkled like those shiny rocks every child coveted. He folded the paper into a makeshift envelope, like those used for single doses of a pain powder.

Zane tucked away the envelope into the back of

the desk's top drawer. He wasn't sure what it might tell him, but it proved that Daniel had recently leaned against something dry and dusty enough to transfer to his jacket. Yet, the clothes were damp. A curious mix. Once Zane discovered the reasons, he'd know where to start looking for the child's mother—and hopefully find his brother with her.

He checked the pants next, finding the same material on the seat and a small metal cube in one pocket. Turning it over in his palm, he noticed it bore the letter *A* on one side. A dull metal, stained with black and scratched on the adjacent surfaces, it looked like a child's building block. He doubted Daniel would ever be educated formally, but there were plenty of quality toys out there designed to teach children. Had someone cared enough to give Daniel an educational toy? Was it Rachel?

After tucking the block in the drawer, Zane carefully bundled up the clothes again and set them to one side. He then retrieved the card that had been pinned to Daniel's dirty jacket. At the desk, he smoothed it out.

Interesting. Yes, he was sure this was identical to the card that had Rachel's name scrawled on it, but that card was in his desk at the sheriff's office.

The breakfast bell rang, reminding Zane that none of his questions could be answered right now.

He flipped over the note. The words were poorly written, but that wasn't a surprise or even a clue, either. Most in town would have only the most rudimentary education. If it was someone who could read and write more proficiently, they could have altered their style on purpose.

One thing was certain. Rachel would not be going

to White Horse Bluff tonight, and no money would leave this town.

He would go and confront the kidnapper. *He* would find Alex and then move on with his life, such as it was.

Chapter Eight

"That's the most ridiculous idea I have ever heard," Rachel announced a few hours later. It was nearly ten, the grandfather clock in the main hall having just struck the three-quarter hour. She'd arisen early, a rare thing considering how late she usually stayed out, but with both Daniel and Zane on her mind, she couldn't stay abed.

After seeing Daniel fed and changed into a set of clean clothes, Rachel had left him to rest in the nursery in the care of her maid. The boy was still lethargic and had promptly dropped back off to sleep after what was probably too big a breakfast for his size and habits.

"You can't simply make demands of a kidnapper. They have Alex and Rosa!" She stood in the morning room, several feet from Zane, holding the ransom note and gaping at him. "The logical thing is to pay the money. Don't you want your brother returned safely?"

"I didn't come here to argue, Rachel. This was a courtesy call," he gritted out, deliberately using her Christian name. "You will do as I say."

Rankled, Rachel reread the note. "Don't you think

they are going to notice that it's you and not me delivering the money?"

"There won't be any money delivered tonight. As I just told you, I'm going to leave a note demanding that they prove that Alex and Rosa are still alive."

"How are they going to do that?" She swallowed, resisting the urge to bite her lip. *Please, Lord, keep them alive.* "Do you believe they aren't?"

"I don't know one way or the other. On the one hand, the kidnapper—or kidnappers, as I suspect there must be more than one—would know they need us to believe that Alex and Rosa are alive if they want the money. On the other hand, they have already returned Daniel."

"All that tells you is that they needed me to receive the note, and they didn't want to deal with a small, sick child."

Zane took a step closer to her, his voice dropping to a gentle burr. "We have to face facts, Rachel. If Rosa is dead, the kidnappers wouldn't want the burden of caring for her child. And if Rosa is dead, we can probably say that Alex is, also, since my brother would never stand by and let a woman be harmed without trying to interfere. If that's the case, it would be logical to give Daniel up by having him deliver the ransom note, hoping we will think that Rosa and Alex are also alive. Whoever it is knows you will take the risk and pay."

Rachel blinked rapidly, feeling the swell of tears sting her eyes and cause her throat to close. "How can you think like that? Alex is your brother! Your twin!"

"I'm not going to do him any good if I give in to fear, Rachel. I'll deliver a note that states you want proof that both are alive, and that you need time to get the money."

"I only need an hour."

Zane's lips tightened and Rachel could hear his sharp intake of breath. She cocked her head. Why would that bother him?

Although the paperwork had yet to be finalized, Mother now owned the bank, fully and outright thanks to a clause that stated that should Clyde die without issue, his share would revert to her father or his heir. Mother was allowed to inherit her husband's business. She didn't have much of a business head on her shoulders, but the manager was competent and trustworthy, so since Father had passed, the manager had taken over the day-to-day running of the bank, reporting weekly and explaining everything patiently to Mother. Of course, Rachel would be able to access the money left specifically for her by her father, so why should Zane appear disapproving? Her inheritance was a tidy sum—and surprising considering her Father had cut her allowance off when she'd refused to marry Clyde.

"I can get my hands on two thousand dollars quickly enough." She had just over twice that in her private account.

"You're not to take out a single cent. You don't need to ruin a perfectly good business by draining its revenue in one withdrawal."

Rachel frowned. She opened her mouth to correct him, but Zane held up his hand. "I'm the sheriff, not you. I know how to deal with criminals."

She arched her brows. "And I, after ministering to those women for years, having been assaulted and left for dead, don't know anything about criminals?"

Folding his arms, Zane's expression turned cold. She'd struck a nerve, although how she wasn't sure. "That's an investigation that I plan to reopen," he muttered. "Where is the women's money, Rachel?"

She stepped back. "How would I know? I was robbed and beaten."

"I gave this some thought on my way over. The man who was supposed to have been protecting you that night has disappeared."

"No, he left town. He moved on."

"Why?"

"Our pastor said he wasn't the same after the attack. The emotional toll on him was too great, so he moved south. He found work in Texas, I hear."

"Convenient."

She gasped. "What exactly are you accusing me of?"

"The money was never found, and I have learned that your father wasn't the most generous man in town."

"That was no secret."

"And he had at one time expected you to marry Clyde Abernathy."

"Yes, but I refused. Who told you that?" Although Alex had known, he had assured Rachel it would remain in confidence. He wouldn't have told anyone. Perhaps one of the servants had spoken out of turn. Regardless, Zane couldn't have learned that tidbit from one of them so soon.

She then nodded to herself. *Mrs. Shrankhof.* The woman was like a bloodhound with a good bit of gossip. Rachel's shoulders sagged. She'd had a small inheritance from her grandparents, but the bulk of her spending money had always come from Father. When he'd withheld it as punishment for refusing Clyde's proposal, he'd hoped that his daughter was as shallow as his wife and would give in. All this to keep the bank fully in the family.

But Rachel had continued to refuse to marry Clyde and, over the subsequent years, she'd drained her savings to provide for her ministry.

"Your father withheld your allowance, didn't he?"

"So you believe that I staged the assault to pad my own meager savings."

"Did you? You would have been around twenty. Old enough to marry and certainly old enough to plot out a theft."

She folded her arms. "Tell me, then. What do I spend the majority of the money on?"

"Clothing?"

Rachel shook her head. "Mother's allowance has always been sufficient for that. She's always insisted I look my best, and since I don't care about clothes, she buys them for me." She sighed. "If you must know, I spend my own money on my ministry. So why would I rob those women, only to give it back to them?"

"I saw your basket, Rachel. It held supplies needed to provide for them."

"Exactly."

"Would those women spend their money in such wise ways?"

So he thought she might have stolen from them to use the money to help them? That was a good point and Rachel couldn't argue with it. Still, the accusation hung in the air between them. Even if she'd chosen to use the money virtuously, stealing it and lying to the women would still be wicked and cruel. Why on earth would he even consider that she'd robbed those women?

Because that was where his own thoughts went? She recalled the telegram Mayor Wilson had sent over. Perhaps Zane's thoughts went straight to thievery because he was a thief himself.

The thought cut into her surprisingly deeply. She needed to talk to the mayor as soon as possible, if only to find out what he planned to do. Bristling, she straightened. "Well, since you have me figured out, I guess there is no reason for me to try to explain my actions."

At her words, he stilled. His only movement that Rachel could see was a slight bob of his Adam's apple. Then he worked his jaw.

She shrugged. "I can't prove anything, anyway. The attack happened five years ago. The only other witness left town. No one's searching for that money anymore, not even the women after half of them got their money back."

"Half?"

"Liza had earned enough in one night to return Annie's life savings, along with one other woman's."

Zane's brows shot up. "Are you telling me a soiled dove found it in her heart to pay back what was stolen?"

"Just fifty percent."

"And you didn't find that suspicious?"

Rachel swallowed. She had. "Liza believed she knew who'd assaulted me and planned to seek him out to convince him to return the money."

"You didn't try to stop her?"

"Of course I did. I told her to go to the sheriff, but Liza didn't trust him and I didn't want her to start mistrusting me by going behind her back. Instead, I tried to convince her to reconsider her plan. The next night, Liza was dead, murdered, I believe, by the man she'd said she was meeting. Whoever killed her was also the one who'd assaulted me. I'm sure of it.

"I told the sheriff only after she'd died, but he didn't think my attacker was her murderer. He just said that Liza was a beautiful woman, but she wasn't the smartest. He also reminded me that her profession is a dangerous one. Liza knew a lot of men, so trying to narrow down who had attacked me, or her, based on who she knew would be fruitless." Rachel swallowed and looked away.

"And that's why you go to them every night? Because you know you're to blame for this?"

She whirled back to face him. "No! I am not to blame for Liza's murder! Nor did I steal their money! But since I can't prove it to you, I'm not even going to try."

Zane furrowed his brows, a handsome gesture she found more unique to him than shared with his twin, although her dealings with Alex had been limited to a few polite chats after church and reporting Rosa and Daniel's disappearance.

She shut her eyes. *Rosa, come home if you can. Bring Alex.*

Opening her eyes again, she studied Zane. Last night, when she'd asked for his side of the story behind his mayor's accusations, he'd walked out of the nursery without defending himself. She'd taken it to mean he was guilty. But then, hadn't she done the exact same thing here?

Doubt trickled in. Stung by his accusations, she had refused to say anything more in her own defense. Had Zane done the same thing for the same reasons?

He leaned down to her slightly. "We're getting off topic, Rachel. You are still not going out to White Horse Bluff tonight. And you are not to withdraw money from your bank, either."

She wanted to correct him that it was her mother's bank, not hers, but another thought hit her. If he was a thief, wouldn't this be the perfect opportunity to insist she withdraw money and take it himself? He could claim he'd completed the drop-off without her and keep the money, saying the kidnappers had taken it.

Instead, he was insisting the money stay safely in the bank. Relief surged through her, but it was short-lived. Even if his decision seemed honorable, it didn't mean he wasn't guilty of theft back in Canaan. Just because she couldn't defend her innocence didn't mean he followed the same reason for refusing to explain himself. There was still the matter of why he considered her the main suspect in her own assault. It must have been because he would do the same thing.

"Did you hear me, Rachel?"

She focused back on him. "Yes. You don't want me to withdraw any money."

Zane took a step closer. His expression softened as it had when he'd warned her that Rosa and Alex might not be alive. "Rachel," he began, her name barely above a whisper, and she hated that she liked the sound of it on his lips. "It's for the best. When you suggested I fill in for Alex, it was on the assumption that he was still alive and someone might give themselves away should 'Alex' return to work. Now, we also need to consider the fact that Alex and Rosa might be dead."

"How can you say that?" Tears again blurred her vision.

"Because Daniel has been returned. A mother would fight to keep her child with her, rather than having him returned to town with nowhere for him to stay and no one to see to his care. But if Rosa is no longer alive to look after her son, then he'd become the kidnapper's responsibility. A toddler isn't easy to look after, especially one who's ill. But the kidnapper can safely use the boy as a means of sending in a ransom note because Daniel can't identify his captor."

The small meal she'd had for breakfast sat heavily in the pit of her stomach. "Don't say that. Please, don't. I can't bear the thought of losing a third woman."

"A third? Who was the other besides Liza and Rosa?"

"A childhood friend of mine, Bea." Rachel swallowed, feeling the struggle to hold in her emotion even now, after all these years. "I don't often talk about her." It had been cruel the way things had turned out for Bea.

But maybe she should tell Zane the bare facts. "As soon as I learned Bea had begun to sell herself after her family had fallen on hard times, I offered her some of the money my grandparents had left me. She refused. It was her pride that ruined everything." Rachel blinked. She'd fought her own pride when she'd realized she should have checked up on Zane before encouraging the mayor to hire him.

"So she was too proud to take your charity?"

Rachel set her jaw. "Yes, but I didn't try hard enough. The money could have been a loan, one of those open-ended types. I know I could have convinced her, but I didn't push it. She hated what she'd become. She took her life. I've had to live with that."

She rubbed her temples. "I should have promised her to make up a simple contract. I could have taken her home that night I saw her selling herself. But instead I went home by myself to a warm, comfortable bed, feeling sorry about everything. I even remember my maid bringing me hot milk to drink in bed. I woke refreshed, until I learned what had happened in the night. Because of Bea's death, I decided to help all those women. I do what I can to lighten their burden. I cook, bandage, and I have even cleaned their cribs to try to keep the women from catching diseases." She curled her fingers and hid her hands. "The soap the doctor suggested is harsh."

Suddenly she glared at him. "As you can see, I didn't need that money you suggested that I'd stolen from those women. I used an inheritance from my grandparents for my ministry. My father couldn't take it away from me because my mother was in charge of overseeing it."

"Was it enough to last you all this time?"

Rachel bit her lip. "Well, no. It ran out shortly after my father began to withhold his allowance. After that, I was doing the ministry with precious little. But Mother would give me some on occasion. Yes, she can be far too shallow when it comes to keeping up appearances, but, oddly, she would give me money every now and then so I could continue. Her only stipulation was that I didn't tell anyone. Until now, I never have, so please don't mention it."

"I find it hard to believe that your mother would approve of you going out like that and even help fund it."

"Believe it or not, my mother is a Christian, and our pastor had already set in place a system to ensure my safety." Rachel frowned. "My mother is a rather complex woman. She's hard to figure out, so don't even try. As for the money, I wasn't going to look a gift horse in the mouth. I took whatever she offered and it has kept me going."

"I look forward to meeting her."

Rachel suppressed a smile at Zane's acerbic tone. "You say that now, but hold that thought," she answered spritely. "If you must know, I think Mother wanted to be known as disapproving of this lifestyle. And she does a good job of presenting it. Rosa commented once that she thought my mother was mean."

"Is your mother a social leader in this town?"

Rachel laughed, but it was short. "She is *the* social leader in this town, yet, deep down, she has a caring heart."

Zane's shoulders dropped slightly. "I'm sorry I had to bring up the reality that Alex and Rosa might be dead, but we need to face that possibility."

Rachel looked down at her hands. Without warning, Zane took them in his, holding her fingers lightly. She could feel his warm touch even through the thick calluses that covered her fingers and palms. It was a comforting action, and shame at having such awful hands caught in her throat.

How could she have let them get so bad? Zane had already noticed them, even commented on them.

She quickly withdrew her hands.

Chapter Nine

Zane allowed her hands to slip from his fingers. At least he had the reason for why they were so rough. He'd seen her last night, dealing with Annie's injuries. He could easily imagine, as the bartender had suggested, that she did all the cleaning. Lye soap was hard on the skin, as were the cold nights out here. The air was too thin and dry and it would be hard to bandage women up wearing fine calfskin gloves.

She stepped away from him, her cheeks becoming a bit too pink. What was going on in that aristocratic head of hers?

It didn't matter. What mattered was that she was going to do as he said and stay home. She'd be able to help the case from there. Perhaps if Daniel was feeling better, he might be able to communicate what had happened to him since he had been kidnapped, in his own simple way that maybe Rachel could interpret, as long as she didn't lead him in her questions.

A wry smile twitched at the corners of his mouth at the thought of an obedient Rachel Smith. Yes, the best chance for success was if he went out alone to White

Horse Bluff to see who showed up. He'd have to be careful, though. If there was more than one kidnapper, capturing the one who came expecting money might result in Alex and Rosa being killed. There could be a plan to shoot them if the one who was to meet Rachel didn't return.

"So, where is White Horse Bluff?" he finally asked.

Smoothing down the neat, lightweight jacket she wore, the one that matched her skirt perfectly, Rachel straightened. Whatever shame or conflict she'd felt was now gone. "Come into my father's office. He has a map there. But I'm sure the sheriff's office has one, as well."

"I expect so, but I am not supposed to be so much of a newcomer that I have to study maps. The deputy might get suspicious. Remember, Alex has been here for months."

With a nod, Rachel led him into her father's office. It sat to the left of the front door, and its window looked out at the front yard, a large square of crisp, dried grass, frosted by a thin layer of snow. A fine picket fence cut through the southwest view of the town. Zane had also seen the view from the morning room a moment ago. It looked out at the flagstone patio and yard that rolled southeastward toward the river. It was a pleasant morning view. But this view, so appropriate to a banker's private office, looked out onto the busy main street.

Rachel left the door open and walked to the desk. "You'll need a horse."

"I've met Alex's gelding already. He knew I wasn't him but he's fine. Wearing Alex's clothes helped."

"They're smart animals. But I think you should take one of our mounts."

"Why?"

"It's possible that the kidnappers would recognize the horse. My mother and I use several fine piebald mares that are well-known in town. They're quiet and calm, but sturdy enough to reach the top of White Horse Bluff."

"Have you been up there?"

"Not for years. The church in Castle Rock once hosted a picnic and invited our church up there. It was very exciting. I remember the boys daring each other to get close to the edge." She pulled a rolled map from a brass urn behind the desk.

Automatically, Zane helped her smooth it out. "That's a fine urn," he commented with a glance back at it. "It looks like it could hold a lot of maps."

"Father liked to collect maps of all the places where the bank held mortgages. He even had an original map drawn by General Pike himself when he explored the source of the Arkansas River. When he died, Mother donated all but one large map to the Recording Office. The new Recording Officer, Mr. Livingstone, was glad for them as theirs were getting tattered. If you need to know anything about the county, it's best to go there. But today, we need a map that's a little closer to home."

She pointed to the middle of the paper. Proud Bend was clearly shown. Zane could see the map was well detailed with prominent businesses and even contour lines. It would be an appropriate map to keep.

Within minutes, Rachel had located and pointed out White Horse Bluff. They leaned close to identify the surrounding landmarks, but the printing was small. Zane could smell the faint scent of cologne on her, something flowery, but what it was he didn't know. He was a lawman, not a horticulturist.

Still, he found himself drawing in a deep breath, and, he realized with a frown, enjoying it. He immediately pulled back and waited as Rachel took a magnifying glass from the top desk drawer. The glass sat on its own stand and offered a powerful view of the map's small details.

"It's south of Proud Bend and west of Castle Rock." She glanced up from the glass. "When I was up there, we traveled in a cart. It took a long time, but it wouldn't if you were on a horse."

They were still too close and Zane shifted back. Yes, the office door was wide open, but considering a household like this would boast a large staff, it would do no good to cultivate any rumors about Rachel and Alex. It wasn't fair to either and nor was it proper. He was leaving as soon as this terrible business was over and refused to drop his brother into the rumor mill. "What exactly is White Horse Bluff? A cliff?"

"Yes. Look at the contour lines. It's a hill with one steep side. They say the bluff looks like a horse's head when viewed from below." She shrugged. "I don't remember seeing it."

Zane pointed at one ranch that had been circled. "What's this?"

"It's Mitch MacLeod's ranch. He's going to marry my cousin, Victoria, in the spring. Father had wanted the mineral rights under the ranch, but Mitch refused. It was where my father lost his life."

Of course. He'd read all about the various attempts

to ruin Mitch MacLeod with the hope of forcing him into bankruptcy so as to claim the property away from him. "I remember reading about the accident. As well, you mentioned you have clothes that belong to his children up there in your nursery."

"He's a widower with children. Victoria often has them here for an evening of games, mostly on Saturdays." A playful smile hovered on her lips. "Personally, I think she prefers to ensure they have a decent bath before church the next morning."

"She lives here, too?"

"Yes. She's out with Mother this morning doing some wedding planning." Rachel lifted her chin and her smile turned sly. "I'm going to be her maid of honor. Jake is going to escort me down the aisle. He's Mitch's best man."

Their gazes locked and Zane could feel something hard form in his chest. Why had she told him that? A reminder that Jake had stood her up the previous night, albeit only because he was sick, lingered on Zane's lips. But he held his jaw tight.

He focused back on the map. He could hear Rachel chuckling softly and found himself irked that she seemed to be teasing him. When he turned his head, he gave her a stern look. "This is not the time for games, Rachel. The note said at the top of White Horse Bluff there will be a box. I see there's a trail that reaches it from the west. Is it flat up there?"

Rachel's smile slid away. "At the top, yes, but beyond that is an open-pit mine. The bluff has a good view of Castle Rock, but it won't be as pretty as it's shown on those postcards. It's full of scaffolding and mining junk. I don't know why all that stuff is still there, because it's not even used anymore. But the slope coming up to it from the west is much gentler." She studied Zane. "I'm sorry for teasing you. I am taking this seriously, but at the mention that I am to be a maid of honor, you seemed a little scared."

"I'm not afraid of anyone."

"Not even a maid looking for a fine young man to accompany her to a wedding?"

"You'll have Mitch's best man to escort you." He felt irritation grow again. "What's his name again?"

Rachel looked surprised. "Jake Turcot. How much do you know about weddings?"

"Enough. I was Alex's best man."

The surprise increased. "Alex is married?"

"He was. His wife died a few years back." Despite the passage of time, and even the fact that Zane hadn't had the opportunity to get to know Nicola well, her death continued to sting him. But it had hurt Alex far more. Perhaps that was what hurt Zane.

He didn't want to talk about it. Didn't even want to think about it. Alex had been running from his grief for a long time. Zane had hoped that Proud Bend would help to settle him down, but in case it hadn't, he didn't want anyone, especially Rachel, to know that Alex might have disappeared of his own accord because of that grief.

It didn't seem likely now. Not with the ransom note. It mentioned Alex. Or was the kidnapper lying to get more money? Zane stole a fast glance toward Rachel. Who would be aware that she would be willing to pay for both Rosa and Alex?

He didn't know enough people in town to find the answer to that question. Roughly, he began to roll up the map again. "I'll need to borrow this. I'll keep it in my room. I don't want the deputy to suspect I needed a map."

"I doubt that Deputy Wilson would suspect anything based on a map."

"I don't want to take the chance. The day he disappeared, Alex said he was going south. That's what the deputy put in his report, so perhaps he saw Alex consulting another map."

Rachel bit her lip. "When will you leave?"

"Tonight, about an hour after dark. The note wants me there at ten."

"They want *me* there at ten. With the money," she reminded him.

"Forget it. You have a ministry to run and a child to care for." He eyed her sideways. "Do you think that this whole plan is to get you away from those soiled doves?"

She frowned. "To what end?"

"What trouble do the women here face the most?"

Rachel scoffed and Zane knew it was a naive question. "Not getting paid. Proud Bend doesn't have an establishment that controls the women and demands payment up front." She looked grim. "It used to, but the old lady who ran it died. Afterward, Mayor Wilson was asked to rid the town of the women, but I managed to get his support to help them. Now they are a loose group with no protection."

"They have you."

She sniffed. "But I don't run a brothel, if that is what you're suggesting."

"No, you're trying to help those women out of a difficult life choice."

"That would be a noble goal, but I have a better one. I want them to learn about the Lord and allow Him to guide them away from that life. I want those women to trust that God can protect them. He has protected me many times over the years. I've learned to trust Him."

Zane swallowed. She trusted God that much? Given all the suffering she had seen—and experienced—firsthand, he wouldn't have pegged her as a woman so devout, one crediting God for her safety. Was her faith the reason she was willing to trust him, in spite of the disgrace he'd faced in Canaan?

And that was another question—how had the mayor reacted to the telegram? He'd probably already left a message for Zane to report to the town hall.

Rachel reached for the map Zane had rolled. "Let me tie it up for you."

Immediately, their hands touched, and Rachel pulled hers away just as quickly, taking the map with her. Zane recalled his tactless remark back in Alex's room, how he could tell she'd worked outside and in less than favorable conditions just by seeing her rough hands. He'd been insensitive to draw attention to them.

Alex wouldn't have and, once again, he felt the loss of his brother keenly. Zane watched as Rachel took a silk ribbon from the top desk drawer. With deft movements, she tied the rolled map securely.

"Thank you," he said in a tight voice as she handed it back to him. Her expression looked calm, but he noticed a definite strength of purpose around her jaw. Why on earth had he felt the need to point out her imperfections back in Alex's room?

Because you aren't perfect, either. You ran off like

a pup with his tail between his legs instead of staying to prove your innocence.

Ramming the map between his upper arm and his rib cage, Zane gritted out, "I'll return it tomorrow. In the meantime, look after that boy and stay in the house." He strode to the door.

"What about the horse?" Rachel called out.

He stalled, his free hand on the office door. "I'll be back to your stables this evening after dark for it." He dared to turn back for a glimpse of her, hating the stricken look on her face. Was she worried for him, or upset that he wouldn't allow her to assist? "Please see that it's ready."

Then, without a nod, Zane departed, not even waiting for the young footman to hurry over to the front door ahead of him. He threw it open with far too much force.

Outside, he inhaled the crisp, dry air. It was definitely colder today, and as he looked up at the sky, he could see weather moving in over the mountains. *Lord, keep it fair until we find Alex.*

He swallowed. *Can I really find him and Rosa tonight?* he asked himself. *Please, God, guide me to them.*

There was no answering wash of peace his minister had often spoken of when God was listening. *Why should there be? You haven't let Him into your life for a long time. He can't fix your kind of troubles, not with so many against you.*

Zane quickened his steps. With this ever-increasing pace, he would be running by the time he reached Alex's rented room.

* * *

Still in her father's office, Rachel ran her fingers over her palms. Yes, such rough skin. No wonder Zane had noticed them. They told an awful tale of an unsuccessful ministry and hard work that had little to show for it. She curled her fingers and pressed them to her chest.

The crunch of feet on gravel drew her attention from her shame. She walked to the window in time to see her mother and Victoria returning just as Zane strode away. Victoria was planning a simple country wedding, and the thought of it brought a wan smile to Rachel's face.

At the memory of her slight tease directed at Zane, she chuckled. He'd looked horrified. But as the women approached Zane, Rachel recalled how he'd said that Alex had been married and was now a widower.

How many young ladies in town knew that? The sheriff had been a popular target for husband hunters since his arrival. Would it make a difference to them to know he was still mourning his late wife?

Rachel watched Zane tip his hat and nod to the ladies. Even through the closed window, she could hear his deep voice greet Mother first, then Victoria. Thinking he was Alex, Mother asked him how he was and where he'd gone, for she'd heard he was missing.

"Sheriff's business, ma'am. No need to worry about it," Zane answered, his deeply timbered voice reaching Rachel even through the closed window.

Mother arched her brows, but a small smile hovered on her lips. "Let's hope you were successful in whatever you undertook, Sheriff. And that your reason for coming to my house wasn't anything as serious." Reproof and curiosity dripped from her words.

Rachel sighed. Mother was difficult to understand sometimes. She wanted her life to be as genteel as it had been back in Boston when she was a debutante. But at the same time, she was as mischievous as Victoria's future stepchildren.

Zane turned to face the front facade of the house, and Rachel found her gaze slamming into his. He didn't seem to appreciate Mother's sense of humor. "Coming here was nothing but a small matter, ma'am," Zane answered. "I assure you that there is no cause for alarm."

His gaze drifted from Rachel's to the brickwork. In fact, he stood there a moment and studied her home, his expression pinching into a tight frown. Victoria, having said nothing yet, followed his gaze before returning hers to his face, her expression becoming puzzled, indicating she didn't understand his fascination with the mansion.

Noticing it, Zane tipped his Stetson again, said his goodbye and pivoted. His boots crunched on the pea gravel as he walked away. Rachel caught her mother's sharp look before turning from the window to meet her family at the door.

"What was the sheriff doing here?" Mother asked as she brushed past the young footman.

"He came to borrow Father's map." It was all she should say to Mother on the matter.

After handing her purchases to the footman, Victoria pulled off her gloves. "Why? Did he find that woman, yet? Is that why he was missing? Was he looking for her?"

Mother gave her niece a knowing look. "Where men are concerned, Victoria, dear, it could be any reason. I think coming for a map was just an excuse. Surely the sheriff's office has maps, or he could have gone to the Recording Office."

"It's Saturday, Aunt Louise. I think they close early today." To Rachel, Victoria asked, "Isn't the map you kept the best one? Perhaps he wanted one with more detail than he could find at the sheriff's office."

"Most likely." Louise eyed her daughter. "Although I was just hoping he might have come with another purpose in mind. There are few respectable men from which you can choose a husband, Rachel."

"Aunt Louise!" Victoria laughed as she shed her coat. "You're as subtle as a bolt of lightning."

Louise shrugged. "Sometimes a mother has to be. I think we'll have lunch early. All that walking has worked up an appetite in me." She departed toward the kitchen.

Rachel walked up to Victoria. Since her father had died, she'd grown closer to her cousin, who'd also lost her father years ago. "Thank you for deflecting her," Rachel said. "Mother bounces between throwing up her hands and giving up, and insisting I mend my embarrassing ways and settle down."

"I'll try to keep her busy with my wedding plans." Victoria paused. "Did the sheriff find that woman, yet?"

"Not yet. In fact, he has a ransom note and wanted the map to find exactly where the drop-off is."

Victoria gasped. "He's paying the ransom? Or are you? I know that missing woman is important to you."

"I wanted to, but he refused to allow it. So, no, he's

not paying a thing. He says we have to first find out if they are alive."

Victoria took her cousin's hands. "They? Who else is missing?"

Rachel swallowed, realizing too late her folly.

Victoria frowned. "Don't tell me it's her son, because early this morning, I went into the nursery after hearing a child's cry. You have our maid caring for a toddler. He looks sick. That's her son, isn't it?"

"Yes, but don't tell Mother. I'll break the news to her at lunch."

"Of course not, but we both know that if he cries out, she'll realize he's in this house. Your home is big, but not that big. So who else is missing?"

Rachel led Victoria into her father's office and shut the door firmly. She had no reason to be concerned that Mother might waltz in here, for the woman avoided the room completely now that she'd sorted out her husband's estate. Still, Rachel bolted the door just to be careful.

Victoria studied her face. "Mitch told me that the sheriff was also missing, and even Aunt Louise knew that when she asked where he'd been. I had assumed the two missing-persons cases were related, but who else is there?" She waited for Rachel to speak, but when her cousin hesitated, she rushed out, "What's going on, Rachel? You're never up this early, and why would the sheriff borrow a map when he has access to others? And how long have you had that sick child up in the nursery?"

Rachel and Victoria sat on the leather chesterfield. The whole story poured from her, how she'd gone to search for clues in Alex's room and had been confronted by Zane. Plus the plan she and the mayor had formed to have Zane impersonate his brother.

"He's a twin?" Victoria asked, blinking. "They really are identical. Except that Zane's face seems paler."

"He's recently shaved his beard. I don't think anyone has guessed yet. But, Victoria, he won't let me pay the ransom, even if it could save his brother's life."

"Maybe he feels that it would only encourage more kidnapping?"

"Not if it's kept quiet or we capture whoever is doing it. He's adamant, though, and yet, he's a crook himself."

Victoria started. "He is? How so?"

Rachel realized she'd neglected to mention the telegram. "He's been accused of stealing in his town. Our mayor telegraphed his mayor, who warned us not to hire him. Oh, Victoria, I've rushed into a situation too quickly again! What makes me think I can solve everything with one hasty decision at a time?"

"Calm down and stop blaming yourself. I know you. You don't rush into things. You make wise, timely decisions." Her cousin patted her hand. "It will all work out. Zane wants to find his brother, don't you think? No matter what he did in that other town, he has every reason to do good work here. You trust Zane and can convince the mayor not to kick him out of town. Just go and talk to him."

Rachel looked down at their fingers, comparing hers to Victoria's. Victoria took such good care of her hands. She pulled hers away. "I don't know if I really do trust Zane. I asked him to defend himself against what his mayor said, but he refuses. He's told me to stay put tonight and do nothing."

"Wait a minute. Somewhere in your story just now, you mentioned not wanting to defend yourself against the charge of theft because you couldn't, so perhaps he's thinking the same way?"

"I thought of that."

"And if Zane was a crook, why didn't he take your money? It seems to me like an easy opportunity."

"I thought of that, too." Rachel shut her eyes and shook her head. "I don't know what to think. He's ashamed of something that happened in Canaan. I wish I could just trust him and be done with it. But, Victoria, two lives are at stake here! Can I risk trusting a stranger?"

Victoria merely gaped at her cousin.

Rachel stood. "I can't! This has to end tonight. Proud Bend doesn't need a crooked sheriff. It needs its old sheriff back. How do I know that Zane isn't going to just drag this out so he can try to steal from us, like he did in Canaan?"

Victoria stood and took Rachel's hands again. "You're overthinking things. Zane will want to find his brother first and foremost."

"I don't know anymore. I saw him out there talking to you, sizing up this house. What if he's thinking of robbing us?"

"Stop that! He was looking at the brickwork, that's all. I've done the same thing. This is a beautiful, unique home."

Rachel pulled away her hands. "No. I need to end this. I need to withdraw the money from the bank."

"You were just saying how you shouldn't rush into things!"

"And you were just saying that I don't." Rachel

strode to the door. "Tell Mother not to delay lunch for me. I'll return as quickly as I can."

"Rachel—"

But Rachel didn't stay to hear her cousin's protest, choosing instead to charge out the front door. Yes, she was jumping into things right now, which was not how she normally behaved. Sometimes, however, quick decisions were necessary. And now was one of those times. She feared that Zane was right that Alex and Rosa were no longer alive. If that was the case, she wanted to know right away, without letting the kidnapper or Zane drag this out any longer. The sooner she ended this kidnapping, the sooner Zane Robinson would be gone.

If he was a crook, this town would be better off without him.

If he wasn't a crook…

Rachel paused, thinking of how close they had stood back in the office when they'd pored over the map. She'd been able to smell the soap he'd used during the morning's ablutions. Oh, yes, she absolutely didn't need a distraction from her work and Zane Robinson was definitely that.

Chapter Ten

The night air had stilled, making for a trip that could almost be described as pleasant.

If it wasn't for the circumstances, Zane amended grimly.

He'd spent much of the afternoon memorizing the route, the landforms and landmarks, and when he'd slipped into the Smith stables just over an hour ago, he'd found the young groom had saddled a beautiful piebald for him.

If it had been her selection, then Rachel had done well at choosing a horse. The mare was calm and sturdy, a perfect animal for a ride on an unfamiliar trail. Zane had found a long duster coat among his brother's clothes, one lined with warm flannel. He hoped that the material covered him sufficiently to mask his identity. He'd left his hat behind. Even in the light of the quarter moon, the Stetson, a gift from his brother, would tell anyone watching that a man was arriving. He'd just have to pull up the collar of the duster and hope the night air wasn't too cold.

Thankfully, the road was easy to follow, and within

an hour of setting out from Proud Bend, he found his way to the base of the hill that held White Horse Bluff. Strategically, it was a good place for a meeting, having a panoramic view to ensure no one could advance unseen. But he was early. Zane hunched down in the saddle, hoping he might look smaller.

At the base of the hill, Zane reined in the horse and dismounted. Tying it off at a small tree, he left the animal enough leather to sniff the ground. He crept up the side of the trail, keeping behind the scrubby bushes that lined the way to ensure his advance wasn't easily spotted.

He'd written a note demanding proof that Alex and Rosa were still alive, and insisting that more time was needed to get the money. He'd tried out his most lively cursive script, because he'd neglected to ask Rachel to write it out. Now he felt his inside jacket pocket. The letter was still there.

He left the trail when he saw the flat top of the hill and the steep side called White Horse Bluff. The soil and stone were pale in the waning moon, and at one point, when Zane stopped to listen to the noises of the late evening, he could make out the profile of a horse's head in the bluff face.

A few more steps and he stopped again. Only the quiet of the night met his ears, although his heart pounded in his temples and the tiny hairs on his arms and neck were erect and alert.

Someone else was there. He'd honed the skill of wariness early on in his career, and it was paying off now. Too bad he hadn't utilized that skill for watching his back. He might have prevented being framed for theft.

He unbuttoned the coat to allow better access to his revolver, should he require it. The breeze up top here chilled and sharpened him. He took a few more stealthy steps closer to the top of the hill, keeping as hidden as possible. Again, he stopped to hear even the slightest noise, but nothing reached him.

I know you're here. I can feel you. Where are you?

No one answered his silent question, but Zane's senses were alive with warning that someone was out there. The flat top of the bluff was deserted except for a wooden crate sitting on a natural raised ledge. Scanning the area, Zane inched over to the box, keeping himself low. He slipped the note he'd written inside.

Doubt now trickled in about leaving the note instead of the ransom Rachel had been willing to pay. Alex was his brother. Rosa, a young mother. It would be best for all if they were safe. What if he'd been wrong in his theory earlier—what if they were still alive, and the refusal to pay caused them harm?

Zane clenched his teeth and kept his body rigid. There was no point in second-guessing himself now. He wanted nothing to sway him from the decision he'd made, and if he gave in to doubt now, he'd talk himself into returning to Proud Bend and asking for the funds.

Forget it. He needed a guarantee before he paid one red cent, even for his brother. It was the right thing to do, though a part of him hated it.

With a grimace, Zane slipped behind some sagebrush. They tended to be short, but crouching down, he knew this type covered him well while the lack of snow hid his large footprints. Slowly he peeked around to find a vantage point that delivered a view of the town and, to his right, the distinct form of Castle

Rock. It also provided an excellent view of the wooden box in front of him.

He checked his watch. Nine thirty-five. Frost streamed from his mouth and fogged the crystal, hiding the hands. He slipped it back into its pocket.

A few hundred feet away and below, his horse whinnied, the sound clear in the cold air. Zane searched the darkness once more for movement. Nothing. He hadn't tied the horse too securely in case it needed to move to defend itself against a large cat or wolf, but the whinny didn't sound stressed, so he returned his attention back to the box.

Shuffling, a scrape, jerked his attention away. Someone was coming. He waited. A grunt on the other side of the brush told him someone found the last few feet of the climb to be tough. Finally, long minutes later, there was a rustle of material as someone stood up on the top of the bluff not ten feet from him.

A woman.

She hurried over to the box and lifted the lid and the carpetbag she carried at the same time. She turned at one point to glance around her.

Rachel?

Furious, Zane rushed forward and clamped his hand over her mouth while the other arm pinned her close. She fought like a wild animal, but he was stronger. He hauled on the carpetbag to free it from her grip. It fell with a thud to the dirt. He tried to kick it behind the nearest sagebrush, but the bag was heavy and merely rolled once to land just beyond his feet. With a grunt of disgust, he ended up ignoring it before hauling her back to where he'd been hidden. She continued to fight until he pinned her down and whispered harshly in her ear.

"It's me, Zane! Stop fighting! I only wanted you to be quiet."

Rachel stilled, and Zane pulled her farther back behind the shrubs and farther from the box. Without ceremony, he plunked her on the ground and crouched down, separated from her by only inches. Her back was to the box and, immediately, she twisted around.

"Stay put! Don't move a muscle. I'll be right back."

Craning her neck, she followed Zane with her attention. He went to her bag and scooped it up. She let out a gasp when he returned with it and shoved it under the sagebrush next to her.

"What are you doing? You need to replace that note with the money!"

"Didn't anything I said to you stick in your head?" he hissed.

"Of course it did."

"So why did you come?"

Rachel folded her arms. "I disagree with your methods. I want to pay the ransom."

Zane threw up his hands in obvious frustration. "That is the worst idea I have ever heard. Do you want to know why?"

"Not really." She glanced away. She was kneeling primly on the dusty rocks behind a large sagebrush shrub, for her skirt hardly allowed anything else. "But I expect you'll tell me regardless."

Zane leaned close to her. "What happened the last time you walked through Proud Bend with a large sum of money?"

Her lips tightened, and she didn't answer.

"Do you know who wrote that ransom note?"

She turned her head away. "No."

"Neither do I. And that makes them all the more dangerous. We don't know who will meet us here. We don't know what they're capable of."

"They returned Daniel, so they must have some compassion."

"I doubt it. He wasn't useful to them, so they disposed of him in a way that would be most likely to influence you. Daniel was a tool to them, a means by which to deliver a ransom note."

"He wasn't hurt."

"He was hungry and sick and cold and dirty, Rachel!" Zane immediately lowered his voice, knowing how sounds traveled so easily in the cold air. "Paying that ransom encourages them to repeat the lucrative plan again."

"So you'd rather let Alex and Rosa die?"

"If they're still alive at this point, then it's in the kidnappers' best interest to keep them that way. Look, I'm not going to argue with you up here. If those kidnappers want their ransom, then they have no reason to harm Alex or Rosa. They'll figure out some way to prove they are still alive and then demand their money again. But give it to them tonight, and it's quite likely they will kill their hostages and disappear. If we do this my way, there's a better chance of getting Alex and Rosa back alive."

Her heart chilled. Zane looked down at her and his voice dropped to a whisper. "You don't trust me, do you?"

Rachel wet her lips. Up here, miles from home,

waiting for a kidnapper or two or three, she didn't want to reveal that she didn't trust Zane for fear that he'd abandon her in disgust. She was tough, she liked to think, but she didn't want to be left here alone. Not after being reminded of that terrible assault five years ago.

"It's all right if you don't trust me," he said, still whispering. He leaned closer. "But it's not all right to be wandering the countryside with a large sum of money. I can't do my job if I have to be watching out for you all the time."

"I had an escort five years ago. He nearly died."

"I won't die. I know how to take care of myself."

His voice might have been soft, but it was rich with confidence. Rachel swallowed. She'd always expected God to look after her when she worked for Him.

Was she doing that now? Or by paying the ransom, was she merely displaying her fear? Had God given her Zane tonight to ensure her safety so he could tell her His will and escort her back to town? She shut her eyes to the unwelcomed indecision waffling through her.

"Rachel, listen to me—"

He cut off his own words and jerked up his head. Rachel, hearing the scrape herself, spun. Zane pinned her down with one strong arm, no doubt wanting her to keep their location a secret.

As much as she hated the decision Zane had made, she saw the logic in it. She shut her eyes a moment and prayed. *Lord, let this be over right now.*

Despite it all, Rachel swallowed and fought against her short, nervous breaths. Her heart pounded in her throat. She felt Zane shift closer, continuing to prove that even when it came to something as simple as holding still, he didn't trust her.

He shouldn't. If anything happened to Rosa and Alex, she would be to blame and she could trace that blame for tonight all the way back seven years to Bea's death. She should have insisted Bea take a loan to help her family.

So much regret. She should have realized she wasn't a banker with the knowledge and experience in investments, foolishly insisting she could make money for those women. She should have forced Liza to go to the sheriff if she'd known who'd robbed and beaten Rachel and her escort almost to death.

The cold air stung Rachel's eyes. She should have insisted Rosa move out of the crib she called home the minute she had told Rachel she wanted to know more about Jesus. It couldn't be a coincidence that Rosa had disappeared so quickly after leaving her awful trade.

Rachel swallowed and blinked. Beside her, Zane shot her a fast look, the expression full of concern. But was that also suspicion in his eyes?

What if something happened to them tonight? How could they save Rosa and Alex then? Rachel felt her hand start to reach for him, to both reassure him and calm her racing heart. Tears welled further in her eyes, and she resisted both the urge to sniff and take hold of Zane, forcing her hands into her lap as she knelt behind the sagebrush, hating that she couldn't see what was going on beyond their hiding place.

Zane patted the air between them and pointed to her. He wanted her to stay still. He then took two of his fingers and pointed them at his eyes and then at the box. Was he going to move so as to see whoever had arrived? Was that what his actions meant? Or was she to look at the box?

Lord, keep him safe.

The urgency of that need struck Rachel. She didn't want anything to happen to Zane, and nipping at the heels of that realization was that her concern didn't come from worry for Rosa and Alex's safety. It was for Zane alone.

No. She would not allow her suddenly silly heart to rule her. Zane didn't trust her. He thought of her as a crook, and when this was all over and done with, they would go their separate ways. He'd have no reason to stay—and she wouldn't want him to. Rachel could hardly help those soiled doves of her town if she was seen sharing affections with a lawman.

As Zane shifted silently to peer around the brush, she did the same. A figure approached the box. Rachel couldn't make out the person, only that they didn't seem as tall as she was. But since she towered over most men, it hardly narrowed down the kidnapper's identity. Even the coat revealed nothing, as those long dusters were designed to keep a person warm from top to bottom.

A small hand reached out and opened the box. The sharp sound of exasperation cut the still air.

Slamming the lid, the person straightened and the collar of the full-length duster fell back. With a gasp, Rachel recognized the slight frame and the wide, fancy skirt that poked out of the duster as the woman's hands dropped. A skirt saved for working nights. Her hair fell forward, loose and long, its color as black as Rachel had always known it to be.

Rosa Carrera!

Chapter Eleven

R osa? Why was she there? Rachel automatically opened her mouth, but Zane's hand descended on it, just as his other gripped her shoulder to still her movements.

As quickly as Rosa appeared, she grabbed the note and disappeared again. Only after a few seconds did Zane remove his hand from Rachel's mouth. She turned to him, ready to tell him she was going after her friend, but Zane's finger pressed against her lips. He shook his head violently. Although the night was deep and dark, she could see his fierce expression warning her to say and do nothing.

What did Zane expect would happen? Something awful?

Zane slipped around the sagebrush and crept away. Rachel's heart pounded like horses' hooves at full gallop, but she knew that in her narrow skirt, she could never catch either of them. Even Rosa's skirt allowed freer movement. The woman could easily outrun Rachel.

Instead, Rachel sank against the bristly bush, still

shocked at what she'd just witnessed. Rosa? How was it possible? She'd been kidnapped, hadn't she? Alex had not been able to find any trace of her or her son, nor any indication she'd left of her own accord. The ransom note mentioned her. So how could she be the one who'd come to collect the ransom?

Rachel leaned forward, barely hearing over her thrumming heart the sounds of Zane scrambling down the side of the hill after Rosa. She bit her lip. What would he do if he caught her? It didn't take a genius to realize that Zane didn't care to be made a fool of.

Praying for wisdom, Rachel stood. Uncharacteristic indecision floated through her and for several minutes she stood, listening to the chase sounds as they carried through the cool night.

Then they died off. Rachel swallowed. When scraping noises drew her attention again to the edge, she hurried over in time to see Zane climb back up. She held out her hand to help him the last few feet.

He refused it, pulling himself up with the ease of a man fit for any duty. She turned to watch him dust off, realizing then that he'd shucked his coat before starting his pursuit. She retrieved it for him. "You didn't catch her?"

"No." His tone was sharp. "Like whoever dropped Daniel off, she disappeared too quickly. *Perhaps because they were the same person?*"

Rachel recoiled. "Are you thinking Rosa abandoned her own son?" She shook her head. "I don't believe that."

"Was that Rosa who just retrieved the paper?"

"Yes, but—"

"Then I absolutely believe she abandoned her own son."

"Zane, I don't believe this, not at all. There was no evidence."

"We just saw the evidence. I know what we saw last night, too. Whoever dropped off Daniel scurried away pretty quickly. Rosa did just that, and how many people would know where to drop Daniel off? How many people could keep him quiet right up until that moment? And who else would know about the ransom note? Who else would want to see Daniel safe in all of this?"

"A short time ago you said Daniel was merely a tool."

"That's exactly what he was, with Rosa as the kidnapper, using her own son as a courier. Of course she'd want him safe for that."

Rachel pressed her hands to her mouth and cheeks. This was insane, impossible. "But the note! It mentioned both Rosa and Alex!"

"And was poorly written, too. You've been ministering to those women, giving them tracts. I saw one of them. They are designed for people with a minimal reading ability. Were you teaching Rosa to read and write, too?"

"Of course. I'd like her to be able to read the Bible someday."

Zane leaned forward. "So it's possible she wrote that note. Does she have that much skill?"

"I—I don't know. I only glanced at the note. I had just begun to teach her basic writing." Rachel rubbed her arms. Rosa had been showing the promise of being a fast learner. Yes, there was a definite possibility she could have managed a simple note, but there were many people who could write at that poor level.

She didn't want to point that out to Zane. He probably knew it, anyway.

Zane retrieved her carpetbag. "We're leaving. Even though Rosa is involved, she might not be alone in this. I don't want to be around if that partner decides to show up, especially after not getting the money they demanded."

"So you don't think she's responsible?"

"Oh, she's responsible, Rachel. And when I find her, she'll go before the judge for it. But she must have help. Alex is as big as I am, and as well trained. Even if a thin woman such as Rosa could overpower him using the element of surprise, she wouldn't be able to drag him to a hideout by herself." He grabbed her upper arm.

Knowing what he planned, Rachel hiked up her skirt and allowed him to propel her along the trail that led down the easy slope at the back of the bluff.

"I can't believe this!" she said as the trail smoothed out and Zane released her arm. "It's like a nightmare where everything goes wrong."

"How did you get here?"

"On Mother's mare."

"Where is it?"

Rachel indicated down to where the trail met the road into Proud Bend. "There."

He continued on for a moment, then stopped and looked down at her. She waited for him to comment, but he ground his heel into the dirt and walked down the bare, open trail toward her piebald. Rachel had given him her own horse and she'd patted him once to reassure him as she'd passed him on her trip up to the bluff. Again, Zane tossed a curious look over his shoulder at her.

Rachel stood and watched him. "What is it, Zane?"

"Nothing."

She hurried up to him and caught his sleeve. "No, something is bothering you. What is it?"

He stopped. Holding her breath, Rachel waited for him to do something, say something. Finally, he pivoted. "Fine. You want to know what's bothering me? I'll tell you. The bartender at the saloon suggested to me that you arranged to be robbed five years ago. He suggested you didn't get any allowance from your father and this way, you could have the money you wanted and not worry about paying it back." He held up his hand as she began to protest. "It makes me wonder if you aren't trying the same thing again. This time with Rosa to help you. Anyone with any basic education could have written that note."

"And Alex? Did I manage to kidnap him, too?"

"Like I said, it doesn't take much strength to surprise a person. And there are two of you to carry him."

She pointed to the carpetbag Zane carried. "I used my own money!"

"*Your* bank's money."

"No! My own money." She shook her head, still shocked by his accusations. "You think I would steal from the bank—simply walk in and demand cash from the till—to spend the money on a ransom?" she questioned. "That's got to be the silliest notion ever." Then she narrowed her eyes. "You're saying I am in league with Rosa?"

Arms folded, Zane didn't answer. Truly miffed and

with arched brows, Rachel also folded her arms. Her breath streamed out in a long, frosty sigh. "So that's it, is it? You speak to one man and appear to know my whole life? You didn't think to confirm this with me? You think I stole the money five years ago. You also seem to think I own the bank, and can just waltz in there to take some of the money." Before he could answer, she continued, "Of course, if you'd asked me, I would have told you the truth. I did neither of those things."

"And five years ago? Did you arrange your own assault?"

"No!"

"Did your father withhold money from you?"

Her shoulders stiffened. "Yes. He often did. My father wanted me to marry Clyde Abernathy, hoping to control all the shares in the bank. All the while, Clyde was trying to connive his way into full ownership, too. In the end, they both lost, and my mother became the sole owner of the bank."

Rachel threw up her hands and let out a short laugh. "Another of life's great ironies, because she has the least head in Proud Bend for business and has had to leave the care and control of the bank to its manager."

Despite the time of night, Rachel continued to laugh. She was freezing cold and bone tired and stunned by all that had happened, but the look of shock on Zane's features was nothing short of hilarious.

"Yes, my mother is the owner of the bank—not me. And while my mission work often makes her uncomfortable, she still supports me." Rachel paused. "Perhaps it was because of what happened to my friend, Bea. It made Mother realize life isn't always fair."

Even now, recalling Bea made Rachel's words catch in her throat. "Mother was horrified when she learned that Bea had taken her life, but surprisingly compassionate after that. She even defended me when Father said he wanted me to marry Clyde. I can't help but wonder if Mother has made the connection between soiled doves and brides of convenience, of which my mother was one, believe it or not."

"She was a bride of convenience?"

"Yes." Rachel straightened her shoulders. "Anyway, as for arranging my own assault, I did not do any such thing. I nearly died that night, and the money was never recovered. I could arrange for you to peruse my accounts to prove to you that I did not deposit any of it. Nor did I stash it away or spend it. After my father cut off my allowance, I used up what was left of my fund from my grandparents. When that money was gone, I depended on donations from my mother. I hope to use the funds I will inherit once my father's estate is settled."

Rachel shut her mouth. She had no intention of allowing him access to her financials, but the words had simply gushed from her like a burst dam.

"And now? Tonight?" Zane prompted.

"I want this nightmare to end so I withdrew personal money from an account Mother set up for me after Father died. She knew it would take time to settle the will. She has her own family money that she rarely touches. I want Rosa and Alex to be freed! There would be no need of a ruse to steal my own money if it was mine to begin with—and if you ask the bank manager, he'll tell you I touched no one's accounts but my own. I was as shocked as you were when Rosa showed up. I can't explain how that has come about, either."

She suddenly grabbed the carpetbag from him. "I don't know anything more than that! I always felt, and still feel, that Rosa would never endanger her son. She truly cares for Daniel. She would never have abandoned him. There has to be another explanation."

"Such as?"

"I don't know. Yet. But I will find out." She marched past him, down to her horse and strapped the bag to the saddle with shaking hands. She then turned to him, her expression as frosty as the night. "I require assistance mounting. If you please."

Surprisingly—and wordlessly—Zane walked over to offer the help. Rachel held her breath.

Before he stooped to assist her, he placed his hand on hers as she gripped the pommel. It was a far too intimate act and she tried to pull hers away, but his grip was firm. "Listen to me, Rachel. You will do nothing more with this matter, do you hear? I know you want to get to the bottom of this and you don't feel I am capable of that, but you can't involve yourself."

"I'm already involved. The note wanted me to deliver the ransom."

"Well, it ends tonight. You have to trust me to find Alex."

"You didn't even know where this hill was."

"The geography might be unfamiliar to me, but human nature isn't. There are other leads I can follow. I will find Alex, arrest all the people involved and not spend one red cent of your money."

How odd. She'd been completely willing to leave the money, but Zane had refused. In fact, the grit behind his words cut through the cold air and chilled her further. It was as if he hated the sight of it. In that moment, she knew his motive truly was what he claimed—he would find his brother, or die trying.

But that telegram to Mayor Wilson told of a different man. As she'd spoken of a different Rosa. Rachel swallowed, realizing they'd been mistaken about Zane. Was she also wrong about Rosa? She wasn't sure. The woman had said she wanted to know more about Jesus. Had that been a manipulation on the woman's part? Had Rachel, in her desire to see fruition in her ministry, read more into the request than Rosa intended?

"Will you do as I ask?"

After a pause, Rachel nodded. "For now."

Accepting her concession with a grimace, Zane released her hand and stooped to help her mount. Once sidesaddle atop her horse, she glanced around. She could see more of Castle Rock, both the squat butte and the little town below it. Even this late, there were a few lanterns burning and the odd window lit, offering a small sense of comfort to her. Still, she would be happy to get home. Often, her work kept her out very late, but it had always energized her, even on those difficult days that felt as futile as tonight. So much so, she'd often needed a cup of chamomile tea to calm her down before retiring.

God had been leading her then, surely, but tonight felt like a frustrating, confusing waste of time and energy, and they faced a cold trek home of an hour or more. God seemed now as distant as her home, maybe even more so.

She looked down at the carpetbag attached firmly to her saddle. It was a considerable sum of money.

Would any man who might be working with Rosa suspect that Rachel had come with it? Would he try to waylay her on her way home? It was possible. And even if he didn't, the deep of the night was a dangerous time for a lady to be out and about, let alone carrying money. Zane had been right to scold her for bringing it.

She'd been a fool to carry the money five years ago.

As much as Zane would want to escort her to her home and as much as the money might be safe there, it would be safer locked up securely in the bank. Of course, that would not be possible until first thing Monday morning, for it would be unfair to awaken the bank manager tonight. He'd been kind enough to open the bank for her a few hours ago, and tomorrow was Sunday.

The second-best place would be the safe at the sheriff's office. She'd seen it when she'd first reported Rosa missing. Alex had told her that he used it to store prisoners' effects, important paperwork and extra ammunition.

But could she trust Zane to do the same?

Before fatigue nudged doubt into her decision, Rachel untied the carpetbag. She handed it to him. "This should be put in your office safe."

"Don't you trust your staff?"

"I don't want to risk their lives if there is a chance a man out there knows I have withdrawn such a large sum of money. He may try to rob us. Would you please put it in your safe?"

Zane had not yet reached for it. "Do you still trust Rosa?"

Did she? An hour ago, she would have been adamant in her answer. But now she wasn't sure. "I don't know, and tonight is not the time to make that kind of decision." She paused. "It's best done after a good night's rest when we see things more clearly. I—I don't want any emotion to get in the way of trying to save Alex."

Zane waited for more, but Rachel wasn't sure she could add that she trusted *him*. When she kept silent, Zane reached for the carpetbag. "If you come to the office Monday morning, I'll escort you and your money to the bank."

"Thank you. We should also meet with the mayor."

"And say what?"

"Answer his questions."

"I don't have any answers he'd like."

Rachel straightened. "Well, then, perhaps he needs to hear my opinion."

Zane's mouth quirked, but he said nothing, instead looking away.

"And Zane?" Rachel recaptured his attention. "I know you're only thinking like a lawman, but you need to think with your heart about this."

"About what?"

"About why I can't believe Rosa could kidnap Alex or endanger Daniel. It makes no sense." She held up her hand. "I know. I know. I see she is involved, somehow, but I can't help thinking that we should put at least a little trust in *my* instincts here, since I'm the one who knows her."

Zane took the bag. Their fingers touched. Through the thin calfskin leather of her glove, she could feel his hand. She fought the sudden urge to grip him, to find comfort in the strength of his fingers and warmth in the broad palm. The need for both lingered even after he had taken her bag.

Did she trust him more than Rosa? She couldn't even answer that. One thing was certain, though. He was the last person she needed in her life. He was only here to find his brother and he suspected everyone of devious intentions—intentions that she feared he shared.

She was married to her ministry. Looking for comfort from him would be dangerous. And futile. The man would put his back to Proud Bend the second Alex returned.

Her heart surprisingly tight in her chest, Rachel turned her mount around and started along the trail toward Proud Bend, more than a little anxious to see the night end.

Chapter Twelve

Zane quickly returned to his horse and attached the bag of money. With a fast glance around them to ensure they were alone, he spurred the mare to follow her stablemate.

Rachel was an odd woman, indeed. She recognized her mother's shortcomings and yet clearly cared much for her. And indeed, her words about her father seemed tempered with some kind of affection, even when she was speaking of his attempts to force her into a marriage she didn't want.

As for Rosa, Rachel didn't want to believe the woman had duped her. Zane could hardly blame her for that. No one liked to have their trust betrayed. He knew that firsthand.

He'd also considered that Rachel was part and parcel of this kidnapping, but that made less sense than Rosa being a part of it. He was also starting to believe she had brought her own money, not the bank's, for her story would be easy to confirm.

Another item on his list. Check to see who exactly owned Proud Bend's only bank. And if it wasn't Rachel? As he reached her and allowed her mare to walk in front of him, he was beginning to see that such a thing was quite probable.

She was also right about another thing. He was foolish to take only the word of a bartender. Since when was he so stupid?

Since you were betrayed and hurt. The words pierced him and he shoved them out of his mind where they could no longer linger like a winter cold.

Even if she wasn't lying about the bank, that didn't mean she hadn't staged her own assault, he argued back to himself. He doubted she'd intended to be hurt that badly, but the robbery could have been planned differently than the disastrous way it had turned out.

Would he be able to find out the truth about that? Did it matter?

Yes, it did.

Ahead, Rachel slowed her horse and turned it sideways, waiting for him to come alongside.

"All my adult life, my goal has been to help those women, although I sometimes despaired. Rosa helped make that vision come into sharp focus when she asked about Jesus. She's been the only one and I began to believe my ministry was turning around. It felt so right. That's why I said we should trust my instincts. But I just find myself going around in circles. Maybe my ministry has been a waste of time all these years."

He was so lost in his own thoughts that it took him a moment to follow her words. She was resuming their last conversation as if no break in time had occurred.

"You can't give up your ministry because of one setback," he said slowly, although he was not sure why he said it. He certainly hadn't done much to fight his own failure and disgrace in Canaan, choosing to give up, instead.

She peered through the darkness, and Zane could feel that gaze of hers more than he could see it. "I don't want to give up. What I'm saying is that what we see isn't always the truth. That's where faith comes in. There are many around us who will only accept one kind of proof, but I say all you need is faith."

Zane eased his horse into a steady walk beside Rachel's. Reminding himself he needed to protect both of them, he scanned the area. But the horses weren't sensing anything amiss, and he couldn't see anyone on this lonely road between the towns.

"Then faith is all you need." Not knowing what else to say, he allowed his piebald to stick close to Rachel. She'd said her mother was complex, but she was equally so.

Again, his thoughts returned to her plea of innocence. Returned as if drawn to it.

As you are drawn to her.

Why? Was it for her playful charm that displayed itself when it was totally unwarranted? Her big mansion and fancy clothes that she seemed to be so unimpressed with? Her dogged determination when it was needed?

Yes. And more.

He shoved the attraction from his mind. He was just passing through her life, pretending to be his brother for a short time. If he started a relationship, however sweet and proper, Alex wouldn't appreciate having to deal with the consequences should people witness it.

Rachel certainly didn't want a personal relationship with him, either. She was friendly with Alex, but had said that she kept him at a distance, claiming it wasn't good for her ministry. Zane tightened his jaw. He'd just be giving her more headaches.

Let it go. You can't fix your own troubles, so you don't need to be making more for others.

Some Christian he was, that he couldn't stay in Canaan to prove his innocence and protect those who were now subject to that corruption, whether they knew it or not. All because he'd been framed and kicked out of a job that he'd loved so much. The sting of rejection still hurt and would do so for a long time to come.

If it hadn't have been for Deputy Wilson's telegram coming the day he'd been forced to resign, a week ago tomorrow, then he'd have probably wandered the West all winter looking for work. He might have shown up in Proud Bend, but Alex was just starting his career here as sheriff and didn't need to be stuck with his wayward brother, one whose career as sheriff had ended in disgrace.

Yet if he'd still had a job, he wouldn't have been able to get away to come here. Rachel talked about ironies. Here was another big one.

The main road between Proud Bend and Castle Rock finally widened and Rachel urged her horse out of a careful walk to a decent trot. The valley floor was clear, the road well worn and safer for both man and beast. Following her tall form, Zane found himself wondering why these events were playing out the way they were. Could he have been brought here to save Rachel from the wrong path in life?

When they were children, Alex had saved Zane's life. Against their parent's rules, they'd been playing down by the river one spring day when it was still swollen with the previous winter's runoff. Zane, the more daring one back then, had been climbing a tree by the bank when he'd fallen in. Alex's swift thinking had saved Zane from being swept away and drowned.

Later, Alex joked that he'd been born solely to pull Zane from various dire straits. Time, along with experience, had tempered Zane's adventurous spirit— that and the betrayal of those he'd trusted. The mayor in Canaan, along with the deputy, had accused him of stealing the tax money Zane had collected, as was part of his job. The evidence had "appeared" in his safe. Zane believed he could not fight that battle and had resigned.

Curious how Alex, after losing his wife, had become the daring one, willing to risk more than Zane would now. Was Alex's new recklessness the reason he'd been kidnapped so easily?

Proud Bend appeared in the distance, the saloon's garish lamps cutting through the frosty night just as Zane realized he'd eased his own mount's speed. The horses' breaths streamed out in front of their long faces and Zane pushed the animal to come alongside Rachel's.

"When we reach town, we'll stop at the sheriff's office first," he told her. "I want to put your bag into the safe before I escort you home."

She nodded stiffly, and they said nothing more until they reined in the horses at the front of the office. Zane pulled out his watch. It was just after midnight. Tucking it away again, he said, "I hope that you don't plan to do ministry work at the saloon tonight."

Rachel accepted his assistance in dismounting.

"No. I don't want to go tonight." On the firm, frozen ground again, she sighed.

"Is it because of Rosa?" he asked gently.

She tugged her hand from his. She opened her mouth to speak and shut it again before finally blurting out, "I want to say it's because I'm bone tired and frozen and aching from the ride. But that's only part of it. Seeing Rosa tonight surprised both of us."

He answered with a grim nod. "Come inside. It should be more comfortable in there."

As they stepped into the office, the wood stove's cheery warmth greeted them. Zane could hear Rachel inhale deeply the homey scent of a crackling fire. "Deputy Wilson is most likely out making some rounds, but it's good to see he's kept the fire going."

He lit the lamp on his desk, looking up as Rachel removed her gloves and coat. She shrugged as he lifted his brows in curiosity. "I don't want to get overheated, although I'm freezing right now."

Zane took her coat and hung it up. A curious sensation lingered in his stomach. Relief? Disappointment? He couldn't tell and refused to allow himself the luxury of examining it.

"You have no one in the cells?" she asked as he set her carpetbag in front of the safe.

Zane looked toward the door concealing a short hall to the pair of cells. There was a slate attached to the wall to record whoever was incarcerated, but it was blank. "Not yet. I expect a few will come in soon to sleep off whatever poison they've taken."

"You don't drink?"

"No." His expression darkened. "It's not appropriate—nor do I wish to imbibe. And you?"

She laughed. "Hardly. I often trumpet the virtue of abstaining, but it just as often falls on deaf ears."

"Even Rosa's?"

Rachel sagged. "With her, I don't know anymore."

"Which is why you feel you need a night off?"

Rachel smoothed her skirt and adjusted her cap. It seemed ridiculous for her to dress up for a ransom drop like she had, but he expected she'd chosen her outfit with the night in mind. It was warm and dark, basic in style. Even the cap had small, tasteful ear flaps that blended into the fur trim, offering extra warmth if needed. But her skirt was slim in cut, creating her need for assistance mounting. She had known he would be there and would help her.

"It's all right to take a night off, Rachel," Zane advised as he opened the safe and tried to stow away the carpetbag. It didn't fit so he opened the bag to flatten it further. "It's also all right to reevaluate your ministry, especially when your most promising woman has deceived you."

"I shouldn't judge her." Her words sounded crisp. "I strive to be compassionate and understanding. But at one time, I also thought that I could simply hand over all the soiled doves' money to the bank and make them enough of a tidy profit to convince them to abandon their work with joy. It was a naive thought. In retrospect, even if my plan had succeeded, I think it would have made things even worse."

"How so?"

"It would have encouraged them to work more with the hope I could earn them more money." She paused and he glanced over his shoulder to see her dejected look. "Perhaps that's why Rosa is doing what she's doing. She only wants to provide for Daniel."

"Don't focus on the betrayal, Rachel. It will eat you alive."

She sharpened her attention back on him. "What else can I do?"

The bag now fitting into the safe, Zane closed it. He straightened and folded his arms. He found himself questioning the wisdom of putting money in the safe, which Wilson had access to, but nothing could be done this late at night. He'd just have to pray that Wilson would not need to get into it. Not every person they threw in jail had valuables to be stored away.

"You need to focus on the immediate situation," he told her firmly. "You have Daniel, who needs care. Who's looking after him right now?"

"My maid." Rachel suddenly looked a little lost, an expression he didn't think he'd ever see on her face. "I expect I'll have to hire a nanny. He's a busy toddler."

"If you intend to raise him, then eventually you will have to formalize your care of him. And report that Rosa has abandoned him."

"I hadn't thought of that." A stricken look dashed across her features. "When should I do that?"

"I'll need to check Colorado's laws, but you probably have a few days, I'm guessing." He cocked his head. "What does your mother think? Or does she know?"

"She discovered him tonight." Rachel offered him a self-deprecating smile, another expression he hadn't expected from her. "I honestly believed she wouldn't notice. But Daniel decided to throw a tantrum just after supper when my maid wanted to bathe him. He's still a bit sick, although he's better. Regardless, his screams certainly brought Mother into the nursery. She knew Victoria hadn't asked to have Mitch's children this weekend, so the nursery was supposed to be empty."

"How did she react?"

"She was horrified, especially when she saw his runny nose. I told her the whole story. All she asked is that he be kept upstairs until he's healthy." Rachel smothered a giggle. "The look on her face was priceless. But, in keeping with my mother's ability to surprise even me, she ordered more milk be purchased because Daniel 'should be bigger than he is' as she put it. There are some days I feel my mother is deliberately trying to confuse me."

"And what will you tell her tomorrow? Or didn't you tell her you were going out tonight to pay the ransom with the hopes of ending the whole affair?"

Rachel shrugged. "I told her, and no, she wasn't happy that I was going out to pay it. Well, that's putting it mildly. She was nearly as horrified as when she discovered Daniel. But I did tell her you'd be there, and that actually satisfied her, although she was surprised that you were not Alex. I expect she'll tell me that she knew Rosa was involved or some other foolishness. Remember, she wants to keep me guessing."

"And Daniel? What will you say if he asks for his mother?"

He should be more worried for Alex, because Daniel was already safe at the Smith home. But even though some people might brush the toddler off as beneath his concern, Zane couldn't think that.

Here was a chance to change a child's life for

the better, just as Alex had changed Zane's life all those years ago by pulling him to safety from that fast-flowing river. One decision, made even hastily, could affect a whole life.

"What should I do, Zane?"

His brows shot up. Was she really asking him for advice? When she saw his reaction, she stiffened and turned toward the coat rack. "I'm sorry. I shouldn't have bothered you with that question."

"No. You're feeling betrayed and uncertain of the right path to take. I am the right person to ask. I was betrayed, too."

She looked over at him, a question on her face. "By whom?"

"By the mayor who sent that telegram, and by my deputy. I can't prove it, but I believe the mayor's son stole the tax money I had collected, then his father bribed my deputy to plant some of it on me so that I would be ousted before I could catch the real culprit. However, I can't prove it."

"How would he do that?"

"I haven't got it all figured out yet, but the deputy had the safe's combination, and there were some other things that happened to make me suspect the mayor's son had come to the sheriff's office the day the money went missing. I knew I was closing in on the truth when 'evidence' was suddenly found that incriminated me. You see, the mayor's son has some bad habits that cost him money and I know the deputy has wanted my job for a long time. The mayor would do anything to save his family from scandal."

Rachel gasped softly. "You were framed? Why

didn't you say this before? Mayor Wilson needs to be told. Were you charged?"

"No. My mayor said if I resigned, he'd overlook everything and get the deputy to do the same. Either way it went, I'd be run out of town. That same day, Deputy Wilson sent a telegram asking me if I'd seen Alex, because he'd found a letter I'd written in Alex's desk here." Zane patted the top surface of the desk in front of him. "I no longer cared about my job. Alex was missing and that meant more to me. I booked a seat on the first train and came straight here."

The frustrations of the night, exacerbated by his fear for Alex, weighed down on his shoulders like a heavy sack. It might seem as though they were closer to saving Alex, what with Rosa appearing, but in reality, they weren't. They could only speculate that Rosa had hidden Alex somewhere close to White Horse Bluff. The whole area around Castle Rock, though— as he had learned from studying Rachel's map—was pockmarked with legal and illegal mines, some still used, some abandoned. Alex could be in any one of them. Or Rosa could be holding him in town. A prostitute wandering the streets at night wouldn't be a surprise to any person out that late. And Castle Rock, being bigger than Proud Bend, probably had plenty of places to hide a man, especially if he was gagged and bound.

What Zane needed was a strong lead. He'd thought he could follow whoever took the note, but leaving Rachel up on that bluff just wasn't an option. When Rosa had melted into the night, leaving no trace as to which direction she'd gone, he didn't dare search farther.

Or was he too lily-livered and just using Rachel as

an excuse? Had the fight gone out of him? Caring for Alex was one thing, but doing something about it was another. Yet, instead of tearing the countryside apart looking for Alex, here he was, sitting in the sheriff's office, chatting with Rachel.

Zane sagged. Yeah, he'd lost his fight.

That truth squeezed his heart as he stood. "It's time to get you home before the men in the saloon call it a night. Trust me, you don't need me protecting you."

Chapter Thirteen

Rachel felt her heart squeeze at the bitter note in Zane's voice. Did he really think he was no good as a protector?

Did she even believe what he'd said about being framed? It was plausible. More than plausible. Sheriffs sometimes collected taxes, and, if she'd learned anything about men and money in the last few months, it was that when you put the two together, it could make for ever-increasing greed. Father and Clyde had conspired together against people like Mitch, and also against each other, even to the extent of Clyde attempting a double murder.

If such greed could happen so easily here, it could happen anywhere, even in that distant town of Canaan.

Rachel stepped close to Zane. "I'm sorry for what has happened to you." She wanted to add that he still had fight in him, but she wasn't sure he had that. The night was waning, and so was their strength. Perhaps sleep was needed to rejuvenate the fight.

Or maybe there really wasn't any left. She laid a

hand on his as it sat on the desk beside his leg. "Don't let your town's betrayal eat you alive, either."

He didn't move his hand away. "It's too late for that."

She grimaced. What more could she say? She touted herself as a missionary to the soiled doves of Proud Bend, claiming compassion and understanding, but suddenly she found herself without a decent word of comfort. What good was she?

It was just as well. She shouldn't be dillydallying around here, anyway. She'd only ever wanted to earn those women's trust, and if they learned she'd spent the evening with the sheriff, especially alone in his office, who could say what would happen to that trust?

Had she ever had it? She'd thought she had with Rosa, but even that didn't appear so. Carefully and slowly, she withdrew her hand and turned away, grabbing her coat and quickly shrugging it on. "Yes, I think I will call it a night. But perhaps I will walk the mare home. I've had quite enough riding for the evening."

Outside a minute later, Zane tied one mare to the other, and, with Rachel walking beside him, he led the pair of piebalds toward the Smith stables. They said nothing the whole way, and Rachel knew their thoughts were too heavy to be spoken. As they reached the front door, she stopped, looked up into his somber expression and bade him good-night.

Zane watched Rachel disappear into the house. A moment later, the young footman slipped outside to extinguish the lantern above the door. The poor man had to wait up each night that Rachel worked.

Leading the horses into the stable, Zane glanced

around, found no stable boy or groom awake, so he quickly removed the tack and gave the animals a hasty brush-down. Thankfully, their stalls were warm and dry, and the reassuring scents of hay, horseflesh and leather, along with the mindless task of combing, calmed his edgy thoughts. Ensuring the mares had water, he suppressed a heavy yawn and left to return to the sheriff's office. No doubt his deputy would soon be filling up the cells with men who needed to sleep the night off.

Like Rachel, he was chilled to the bone and grateful for the hot stove in his office. Zane took a moment to drop into his chair and ease it back to revel in the warmth. He should have stayed out all night and searched for Rosa and Alex, but he would not risk Rachel's safety. Alex would agree, especially considering the bag of money.

Zane opened his eyes and let them stray to the tightly locked safe. Had she really taken her own money to pay the ransom? Was she that naive to think the nightmare would end so simply? Or was she so desperate she'd disregarded all logic? He didn't know her well enough to say, and his first impression of her was hardly stellar.

Surely someone in this town could vouch for her? Or even explain why she did what she did. That bit of information would go a long way to figuring out the woman. All he could tell right now was that she wore a mask of calmness and confidence. But it was only a mask, and he wanted to know exactly why.

Concern. Guilt and fear. Those words popped into his head. But why would Rachel feel those things? Because of her friend, Bea?

Such questions would have to wait, he decided, hearing his deputy approach with a boisterous drunk.

Once the man was incarcerated, Deputy Wilson turned to Zane. "Sheriff, you don't need to stay."

"I know," Zane answered, thankful that the man still didn't know he was not Alex. "Where is the file on Rosa Carrera?"

Wilson found it on his desk. Zane had already read through it once but wanted to take it back to his brother's room. There had to be something he'd missed. Alex was a good investigator. Surely he'd have guessed that Rosa had staged her own disappearance, possibly with the assistance of Rachel and with the intention of kidnapping Alex.

He weighed the file Wilson handed him. "It's bigger than I remember. Did you add something to it?"

"I did. I put in the notes I'd made when you disappeared, though I imagine you can scrap them now. You never did tell me where you went, you know." Wilson's tone turned petulant. "I ought to be told."

"Sorry about that."

Wilson waited, brows lifted. For a moment, Zane wondered why the man's own father had not yet taken him into his confidence. Was the older Wilson more trustworthy than Zane expected?

"I forgot to tell you," his deputy added, "I sent a telegram to your brother while you were gone, asking him if you'd shown up there. I guess I'll have to telegraph him back to let him know you've returned."

"I'll take care of that. We write frequently."

Wilson shrugged and finished logging in the drunk. Thankfully, he had no valuables to lock up. Zane opened Rosa's file. "I need the file on Miss Smith's assault, too."

Looking up, Wilson asked, "When Rosa first disappeared, you dug that file out. Do you still think there's a connection?"

"Yes." Zane felt his gut clench. So Alex had also believed they were related. "I want that file on Liza Carrera's murder, too." He'd already looked at all these once, but in the meantime, the deputy had refiled them.

"There's not much in it," Wilson warned testily. "She's been dead a long time, and Rosa's gone and she ain't coming back, either. It happens sometimes. We may as well close Rosa's file, just like Liza's."

"Are you saying Rosa has been murdered like her mother?"

Wilson gaped at him. "Is that why you think they're connected?"

"I don't know. But right now, I need to read over everything again." He stood wearily. "I'll have them back Monday morning. Good night."

The next morning, the weather cloudy with tiny grains of snow drifting down, Zane made his way into Proud Bend's only church. It would be, thankfully, a quiet day, with no businesses open and those in the cells sleeping until they were sent packing with a fine and a reprimand. Deputy Wilson could handle those tasks, having bedded down in the back of the office. Zane was glad for the easy schedule. It allowed him time for worship. And one small task at the same time.

Before he found a seat, he noticed the owner of the

general store making his way to a pew on the other side. He'd exchanged greetings with the man on Friday.

Taking the unexpected opportunity, Zane doffed his hat and approached him. "Good day, sir, may I ask you about your merchandise?"

The man allowed his wife to enter the pew as he faced Zane. "Certainly, Sheriff. Are you looking for something in particular? I'm open at eight tomorrow morning."

"I don't want to purchase anything, but want to know if you have any postcards of Castle Rock."

The man shook his head, as if confused. "Why would I have postcards of another town? I carry a small selection of humorous ones, and ones of the bandstand. I'm afraid the townsfolk around here don't have much use for them. If you want one of Castle Rock, you'll have to see the printer down there. I hear his shop is very close to the rock itself. I used his services to print out the postcards of the bandstand. The others I purchased from a printer in Denver."

"What is his business's name?"

"I'd have to check my records, but if you want more information, try the Recording Office. It's supposed to be located in the county seat, but it's here in Proud Bend until a proper office can be built for it. I do know that one of the men working there is from Castle Rock, and they might have maps to help you locate the printer. Also, there's a young woman there, Miss Walsh, who is excellent at reading a map."

Zane made a mental note to see them both in the morning. "Thank you." After nodding to the man's wife, Zane found a seat on the opposite side at the back of the small church and waited for the service to begin. And to see when Rachel arrived. She claimed she was faithful in her ministry, working for the glory of the Lord. Would she be there today?

Shortly after that very thought, Rachel and her mother arrived. Smiling at her fellow congregants, she made her way to the front. Zane looked away, unwilling to catch her eye.

When the service ended, Zane lingered in his pew, watching Rachel as she exited. She hadn't acknowledged him during the greeting time, mostly because he'd sat in the back, but now, as she slipped into the aisle, she stole a furtive look at him.

He scowled as unwanted heat rose into his neck. He needed to know if he could trust Rachel. Alex's safety could hinge on it. As the stragglers finally left, Zane made his way to the door. Pastor Wyseman was busy shaking the hand of the last parishioner and finally looked up at Zane.

"Sheriff, it's good to see you back. When Rachel asked me to pray for your safety, I—" He reached out his hand, but stopped and then started again, slower this time as he studied Zane. "I… I asked our Bible study groups to also pray."

Zane glanced around before shaking the minister's hand. The man's expression was troubled, leaving Zane with an uncomfortable lump in his throat. It was one thing to remain undercover, posing as his twin for the regular folk of Proud Bend, but another to keep up the pretense for this man of God.

Zane hadn't even liked keeping his true identity from Deputy Wilson, but until he could prove without a doubt why the young man had handled the investigation into Alex's disappearance so ineptly, and why his own father had chosen not to trust the young man, he wasn't about to reveal who he was. Not when back in Canaan his own deputy was ensconced as temporary sheriff, awaiting a shoo-in election with the mayor's endorsement to confirm his appointment.

Pastor Wyseman was still frowning. "How are you, Sheriff? You look tired this morning. Pale, almost."

"It was a late night. We had several 'guests' arrive."

Wyseman looked resigned. "I expect you did. Even from the parsonage, I could hear the saloon. They often wake me on Friday and Saturday nights. There wasn't any trouble, I hope?"

"Nothing we couldn't handle." Zane paused, still waiting for the man to say something, anything about his true identity. Rachel had guessed he wasn't Alex, and she hardly knew his brother, or so she claimed. Although, Zane had had a full beard then.

Automatically, Zane's hand lifted to his cheek, thankful he'd been up early enough, despite being late retiring, to give himself a close shave. Wyseman's frown deepened.

"Is there something wrong, sir?" he asked the pastor.

The man's eyes narrowed. "I was about to ask you the same thing, but I'm not sure who I am addressing. You're not Sheriff Robinson, are you?"

"Why do you say that?"

"Alex Robinson is thinner, albeit only slightly, and you have deeper frown lines. Your cheeks are paler, which tells me you've recently shaved off a beard, one Sheriff Robinson did not have. His cheeks are ruddy. He likes the outdoors."

Zane lifted his brows. Impressive. Not too many

people would have noticed minor details like that. "You're quite observant. Have you considered a career in law enforcement, Pastor?"

Wyseman smiled. "I have one. The law of God. So, who *are* you?"

"I'm Zane Robinson, your sheriff's twin brother."

"Older or younger?"

"I beg your pardon?"

"Are you the older or the younger twin? You can't both have been born at the same time."

"I'm the younger."

Wyseman looked surprised. Then again, people always did. Alex had been the easygoing one, pleasant in tone and temperament. Even after his wife passed away, Alex had managed to push aside his grief and keep the more genteel personality. Zane had become more serious, better suited to be the older son. No one but their parents knew it was Zane who'd misspent his youth by rebelling against authority, a trait often connected with younger sons.

What did it matter? It had been only minutes that separated their births and could hardly define a personality. Zane pinned the minister with a hard look. "I need to talk to you, Pastor."

"Indeed." Wyseman studied Zane, who waited with decreasing patience for the inspection to end. "When did this switch happen?"

"Thursday morning, after I arrived by train. Alex was already missing. I was, shall we say, met by Miss Rachel Smith, as well as the mayor."

"Not at the train depot, I imagine. That would be too obvious. Did your brother's disappearance bring you here?"

"Deputy Wilson telegraphed me to ask if I had seen Alex after he went missing," Zane said. "I left as soon as I received his telegram. Deputy Wilson does not know who I really am, though."

"Why not?"

"I went straight to my brother's room, where I met Rachel and the mayor."

"A curious place to meet."

"It's a long story that involves Mrs. Shrankhof."

Wyseman laughed. "There isn't too much in Proud Bend that doesn't involve her in some way. She runs the largest boardinghouse."

"Rachel and the mayor suggested I assume my brother's identity so that I can continue the investigation into Rosa's and Alex's disappearances."

"Yes. I can see Mayor Wilson suggesting that," Wyseman answered drily. "Next year is an election year and he wouldn't want anyone to know the sheriff he endorsed has vanished. The mayor prides himself at being in full control of this town."

"While one soiled dove is murdered and her daughter, five years later, disappears? And what about the circumstances that led to Bea's suicide?"

"You've been doing your homework, Mr. Robinson. Or should I call you Sheriff? I expect I'm allowed to call you that since you're undercover." The smile returned, but was grimmer. "Don't worry, my lips are sealed. I'm good at keeping secrets."

"*Sheriff* is fine." Zane paused, then continued. "I want to ask you something about Rachel Smith."

Wyseman glanced down at his feet, the small smile growing on his lined features. Zane caught a glimpse of his furtive look up at him. "Rachel has a strong personality."

"Yes," Zane answered. "I have run afoul of that. But that's not what I want to know."

"I expected you to have already realized it. She used to be much more comfortable to be around. Even quite charming."

"So you agree that now she seems tense? Wary and even guilty?"

"Yes. Since Rosa disappeared, she's been very concerned."

Zane folded his arms. "How can you allow her to continue her ministry?"

Smiling even more broadly, Wyseman waved to a couple passing the front of the church in a small carriage. The smile dropped away as soon as they passed. "Have you told Rachel what to do yet?"

"Yes, actually."

"How did that work out?"

Despite everything, Zane chuckled. "Not well."

With a slight smile, Wyseman nodded. "You can see my dilemma. I may be this town's pastor, but I can't force anyone, least of all her, to do anything. Nor should I. I should be leading by example, and guiding them to make the wisest decisions, with Christ as *my* example. In Rachel's case, we struck a compromise. Don't get me wrong. I don't have anything against the work. Mission work can and should happen in one's own town. But I was concerned for her safety."

"So what was the compromise?"

"She never goes into the saloon or to the cribs behind it without a male escort. We arranged for the men of our congregation to rotate through that duty."

"That's a big commitment."

"We're a mission-minded church, Sheriff."

"It's also not being followed. It wasn't last Friday night, at least. She went to the cribs unescorted."

Wyseman frowned. "I'd heard that Jake Turcot was ill, but I would have thought that she'd postpone her visit."

"She didn't. She was hoping that Rosa Carrera would return that night."

"That disappearance weighs heavily on her. I think she blames herself." With a shake of his head, Wyseman added, "I'll have to remind her again of our agreement."

Zane took a moment to glance around the small, silent church. Its scent of wood and candles offered a bit of comfort, but the dim stillness that might incite quiet prayers left him as empty as the pews. Three unsolved cases, one of them his brother's disappearance—and Rachel at the center of it. "Why does she minister to them?"

"As you may know, she had a childhood friend who slipped into that trade and then took her own life. Her parents never fully recovered from what they'd allowed their daughter to do. It's a terrible burden they can't unload. They think God isn't big enough for their mistakes. I still try to convince them otherwise."

So Rachel's story about Bea was true. Had he really thought it wouldn't be? Zane felt his jaw tighten. "What happened? How did she get into that life in the first place?"

"Her parents fell on hard times. Her father hurt himself in a mine accident shortly before she and Rachel turned sixteen. I remember it because their birthdays are close together and always around Easter. That year, Bea's birthday fell on Easter Sunday, but she didn't celebrate it because her father was at home recuperating."

"So the family forced her into that trade to help pay the bills?"

"Bea was a beautiful woman, tall with long, red hair. Quite stunning and apt to catch a bachelor's eye. It wasn't hard to see how she could earn a lot of money. But that decision didn't happen right away. Her family struggled along for a while, getting deeper into debt as her father's medical bills rose. In fact, none of us learned what they'd allowed Bea to do until it was too late."

"Didn't anyone help?" He glanced around, looking for an alms box. "Don't you have a benevolent fund here?"

"Her father was too proud to accept any donations our church offered."

"Too proud to take charity, but not too proud to sacrifice his daughter?"

Shrugging, the pastor walked deeper into the church and began to snuff out the candles. His long black robe swished as he moved past Zane. "I won't profess to know what went on in his mind."

Zane followed, coming to stand in the center of the aisle to watch him. "Rachel didn't force her friend to accept charity? You've just told me she has a strong personality."

"As bold and persuasive as she is, she wasn't here at the time. Her father had sent her east to an academy for young ladies. By the time she'd returned, Bea was well into that trade and said she couldn't force her family back into poverty again. She claimed that she had accepted her new position in life, and while Rachel still tried to change her mind, I don't believe she realized how fragile Bea had become. Wyseman sighed as he walked back down toward the door. "Rachel still blames herself."

Another confirmation. "Rachel is a curious woman."

"She is that. But she's a faithful parishioner and we are all God's children." After they walked outside again, Wyseman turned and closed the church door.

"So Rachel's mission has your blessing even though it's dangerous?"

Wyseman stiffened. "God will protect her."

Zane felt his jaw tighten. "God doesn't bless foolish behavior."

The pastor said, "Apart from this last Friday, she's always had an escort."

"She had an escort the night she was assaulted. God didn't protect her then."

"True." The pastor looked contrite. "But our ways are not God's ways."

"Nor are your ways necessarily Rachel's ways."

"What do you mean?"

"The sheriff back then never did find who assaulted her. He never recovered the money, either, but Rachel continued with her ministry."

"After she recuperated, yes." Wyseman gave Zane a harsh look. "What are you suggesting, Sheriff?"

There was no use beating around the bush. "My brother is missing, and I need to know if I can trust Rachel. She is the person closest to Rosa Carrera, who I believe is somehow involved in my brother's disappearance."

"Of course you can trust her." Understanding dawned on Wyseman. "You think she staged that assault to use the money for her ministry? Her ministry is to those women. Why take money from them?"

"Because we both know how most of those women will spend their savings."

"They didn't spend it, Sheriff." His words were cool. "That's why they called it savings."

Zane glanced around the ground. "Perhaps Rachel felt it would be better spent elsewhere. She didn't have an allowance from her father because she'd refused to marry Clyde Abernathy."

"I don't know who has told you she stole the money, Sheriff, but it couldn't be further from the truth. Yes, she didn't get an allowance, but there were donations. Like I said, we are a mission-minded church." The older man laid a heavy hand on Zane's shoulder. "Son, 'trust in the Lord with all thine heart and lean not unto thine own understanding. In all thy ways acknowledge Him and He shall direct thy paths.'"

Zane swallowed. Proverbs three, verses five and six. They were his mother's favorite verses, often quoted to his father when Zane, as the wayward youth he'd been, had acted out. Still, he held himself stiff.

Wyseman lowered his hand. "Sometimes, we get hurt by people we trust and it's hard to trust anyone again. But you can always trust God." He led Zane down the steps of the church. Off to the right was a good, solid home with a middle-aged woman standing by the gate. Mrs. Wyseman, Zane assumed.

He bade the pastor good day, and watched as the man donned his narrow-brimmed hat and walked toward the parsonage. The harsh wind that suddenly rose chilled his hot cheeks.

Trust God? Not when there were men like Canaan's mayor and his son walking the earth. Or that deputy. They didn't care about the Lord, and, frankly, with men like that, there wasn't much God could do. If Zane was to trust God, would that mean returning to Canaan to clear his name? That would be impossible. He had no proof he'd been framed. The mayor and deputy had been too careful in covering their tracks. Besides, Zane wasn't sure there was enough fight left in him, and what little was left he wanted to be focused on finding Alex.

His jaw ached as he ground his heel into the dirt and strode away from the church. If nothing else was gleaned today, it looked like he could trust Rachel.

Heart leaping in his chest at the thought, Zane pushed his steps farther. *Don't bother looking forward to it. You're not going to be here that long. Besides, begrudging trust isn't the way to start a relationship that's doomed to end too soon.*

Chapter Fourteen

Rachel swallowed and blinked back tears, telling herself they were from the biting wind and not because of the stiff, stubborn set of Zane's shoulders as he strode away from the church. She smoothed her dark green coat and readjusted its matching bonnet, all the while hoping no one could see her apprehension.

She wouldn't have even noticed him talking to Pastor Wyseman if it hadn't been for Jake Turcot's mother stopping her at the street corner nearest the church to give Rachel an update on Jake's illness. Normally, he lived at Mitch's ranch, but since his illness, he'd been recuperating at his parents' house. He was on the mend, but tired, as the flu often drained a person. Feeling a bit guilty for not asking about him earlier, Rachel squeezed the older woman's arm and thanked her with a forced smile.

As Mrs. Turcot had said her goodbye, Rachel had turned and noticed Zane. She was too far away to eavesdrop accidentally on the conversation, but it was clear from the expressions and the tight shoulders that Zane was hearing something he didn't like. Why would he even tarry after church in the first place, unless it was to speak to Pastor Wyseman in private?

She knew exactly what, or whom, was being discussed.

His harsh words up at White Horse Bluff still stung her. He'd actually wondered if she was working with Rosa to steal from the bank he'd assumed she owned, and then keep the ransom money.

That hurt. She'd tried to convince him, and had even thought she had had some success in that. Obviously, her protest needed to be confirmed by her pastor.

Here she had been trying her best to instill trust in those like Rosa and Liza, and she couldn't even convince Zane to believe in her. That painful realization sank onto her shoulders.

Pastor Wyseman hadn't looked happy during their conversation. Rachel spun away. She shouldn't speculate. It was nearly as bad as eavesdropping. If Zane still couldn't trust her after talking to her pastor, then she would have to move on with her own investigation.

Yes, she'd do exactly that. It was better that way. She wasn't going to be disappointed by Zane, for surely she was a terrible judge of character. Look at Rosa. She'd trusted her.

Not sure what steps to take now, Rachel sent a short prayer upward. She had to find Alex. She had to confront Rosa, too, but Alex was the more pressing need. He couldn't be dead. She refused to believe it.

Fatigue weighed down on Rachel. Last night had been long and cold and disheartening and she would have loved to linger in bed this morning, but church often revitalized her. Besides, there was little Daniel to care for. He was feeling much better this morning, up and playing with the few toys they kept for Mitch's children. Rachel had tried to ask him some simple questions, although she knew he could barely answer. She'd just been hopeful that maybe he could say something that would give her a clue. But all he'd done, when she'd asked where his mama was, was talk about the puppies. One in particular. She would take him to see them, perhaps this afternoon if she could find where the mother dog was keeping them.

"Oh, Rachel?"

She turned to find Mrs. Turcot returning to her. "You must come for lunch. I have made a lovely chicken stew. Jake still isn't eating as I would like him to, so now we have far too much of it. I've invited Mitch and Victoria, too, plus the children."

Rachel forced a smile. "That should take care of all the stew."

Mrs. Turcot laughed. "I made quite a lot of it. I always do." She leaned forward to squeeze Rachel's arm. "Please say you'll come. You do so much for our community, and I hear that you have taken in that small boy. Bring him. Mitch's boys can entertain him. It will do them all good."

Rachel relaxed. She'd known Mrs. Turcot all her life. The woman had only been blessed with one child, Jake, and Rachel knew for a fact that she loved all children. She'd run the Sunday-school program at the church for years, including teaching Rachel. In the small Sunday-school annex off to the side of the church was probably where Mrs. Turcot had learned about Daniel, for Rachel had brought him to church, only to have him taken from her by another helper so that Rachel might enjoy the service.

Rachel nodded. "I'll be there. I've sent Daniel home with my maid, but I'll walk back and get him. It won't take too long."

Mrs. Turcot's smile broadened. "I'll keep the stew and rolls warm until everyone comes."

Zane set down the file he'd been reading. His room was quiet. In fact, the whole main house was deadly silent. Sunday was Mrs. Shrankhof's day off, and she often spent it with her son and grandchildren, he'd learned. The only food available to her lodgers was either leftovers or bread and cheese. No doubt most of the other lodgers took advantage of the day of rest to sleep in. Not hungry, Zane decided to forgo lunch, then find a quick bite at suppertime.

He'd wanted to review the files on Liza, Rosa and Alex one more time. And Rachel, also—the thin one about the assault. Now, setting down her file, Zane rubbed his face and peered out the window above the desk. Despite the hazy sun that had tried its best to break through the clouds, it had begun to snow lightly.

He returned to the file. A man named Robert Bale had been Rachel's escort five years ago when she had been assaulted. Days after, according to Rachel, Liza had said she knew who had done it and had wanted to confront the man. But there was no record of who Liza had suspected.

Even Zane, when he'd first read this file, had not thought much of it. Rachel had reported that she'd taken the money from Liza that night, after Liza had gathered it from all the soiled doves. It had been a Friday night and the saloon had been full.

Zane flipped back a page. Robert Bale had moved to Texas. The report had marked his address when he was still in Proud Bend as in care of Mr. and Mrs. Turcot. The same Turcots whose son was to have been Rachel's escort last Friday night?

Perhaps. There didn't appear to be other Turcots in town.

Their address was near the church. It wasn't uncommon to take in a boarder to help make ends meet. Perhaps they knew exactly where Bale had moved to, for surely they would need his new address to forward any mail. Perhaps they knew something about what had happened to him that night. Surely, Bale would have recuperated at their house. He could have said something. Zane noted as he scanned the thin file that the Turcots had not been interviewed.

It was a long time ago, but they still might remember something. He needed to speak with them. He checked his watch. They should be done eating lunch by now.

Zane found the house easily enough and, surprisingly, Rachel answered the door. "I wasn't expecting to see you," he said with raised brows. "Another ministry?"

She smiled with her own brows arched, obviously not wanting to be bothered by him. "No. Mrs. Turcot is ministering to me by means of lunch." She stepped aside from the door. "Please come in. I'm assuming you want to speak to her or Mr. Turcot?"

"Both." He stepped inside and removed his hat. Immediately, he inhaled with the warm scent of chicken and vegetables, noting also the yeasty smell of fresh bread. His stomach growled out in protest that he'd decided to forego a meal.

Rachel took his Stetson and his coat. "We're ready to sit down to eat."

"I'm sorry to disturb you. I'd expected your lunch would be over and done with by now. I could come back later, if that would be better for the Turcots."

"Nonsense," she answered briskly. "You look hungry. You should stay. I've been helping Mrs. Turcot in the kitchen and know for a fact that there is plenty to go around."

Zane looked down at her small, frilly apron, noting her hands set neatly in front of it. She noticed where his eyes had fallen, and immediately Rachel tucked her hands beneath the material. Several children's screams of laughter filled the warm air. "There's already a full house here," he commented.

"Victoria and Mitch and his brood are here. I brought Daniel so he'd have someone to play with. He's feeling better and the other children are quite excited to have a new playmate."

Out from the kitchen came a short, heavyset woman, wiping her hands on her own apron. "Sheriff, what a pleasant surprise. It's not bad news, I hope."

"Nothing of the sort, ma'am," Zane answered. "I need to ask you some questions about an old case I'm working on."

"On a Sunday? Surely not!"

"I was merely reading the files and knew you'd be home. I wanted to catch both you and your husband at the same time, and didn't want to wait until later in the week. I'm sorry to disturb you on your day of rest."

The older woman's laughter pealed throughout the short hallway. "A woman's work is never done. I do honor our Lord's day, of course, but people still need to be fed." She looked him up and down. "And so do you. Come in and eat with us."

"Ma'am, it was not my intention to come looking for a meal. I thought you would have finished eating by now."

"Normally, we would, but with a full household, everything takes longer." She beamed. "The children are happy to play while they wait. Besides, I have plenty and we should have had you over for a meal before now. I know Mrs. Shrankhof goes to Castle Rock on Sunday afternoons to visit her son and his family. You wouldn't be fed at her house today."

"She always leaves plenty of leftovers for us."

A man who had to be Mr. Turcot appeared from the parlor, a pair of young boys gripping his calves and causing him to drag his feet. He grinned, obviously loving the attention. "You have come to save me, I hope, Sheriff, from these wild beasts."

Zane smiled back, deciding then to stay for the meal after all. Lunch was a chaotic affair, reminding Zane of his own childhood on Sunday afternoons. The meals on those days were always something warmed up from Saturday night, but with all four of them around the table, the time was meant for fellowship and fun, with Alex and him trying to capture and hold their parents' attention. His mother had not been able to have any more children after delivering her twins, so their family had been small.

He remembered how often he would be caught flinging a crumb at his brother or slipping an unwanted vegetable to the dog. His parents had the patience of Job, like the Turcots here, who clearly loved their house being filled with people.

A pang of homesickness hit Zane, but he ignored it. There was no going back. His childhood had come and gone, and though it was generally a happier time, it was only for a season. His life was far different now. He was a disgrace, the pitiful end to a wild childhood. His parents were gone. Save Alex, there was no one left to help him recall his youth.

Once he found Alex—and he would find him—Zane would leave. He didn't want to hang around a town that so clearly admired his twin, where Alex was striving to do his best. The much-admired Sheriff Robinson didn't need to have his black sheep of a brother marring his ideal life here.

Zane stole a glance at Rachel. Her life was as mapped out before her as Alex's was. Though Rachel's choices were atypical, they filled her life with a strong purpose, while his was a wayward mess of questions and accusations. What Rachel thought of him shouldn't matter. And what did it matter to him that she had purpose?

Because he could not fit into her life?

No, it's not that. It was more that her purpose lay before her like a lush valley full of the promise of spring. Yes, it was a challenge, but the reward would more than make up for it.

Clear was her vision of her ministry, while his had nothing but desert waste. With more vigor than he thought he should have, he dug into his chicken stew and put the whole train of thought out of his mind.

A young man introduced as Jake came down to

eat, but did so only sparingly, much to his mother's consternation. He returned to his room shortly after. Mr. Turcot finally broached the subject of Zane's visit.

Zane's demeanor turned formal. "I need to ask you some questions in private."

Victoria rose suddenly. "Mitchell, why don't we take the children into the kitchen to clean up?"

Mitch rose and, with the help of the children, they quickly cleared off the dining room table and departed. One of Mitch MacLeod's older children scooped up Daniel.

Soon Zane was alone with the Turcots and Rachel. "What are you able to tell me about the attack on Rachel and Robert Bale? He used to live here, did he not?"

"Yes, but I'm not sure how we can help you," Mr. Turcot began slowly. "We weren't there that night."

"But you did board Robert Bale, correct?"

"Yes."

"Did he convalesce here after the assault?"

"I took care of him," Mrs. Turcot answered, her expression serious. "He was badly injured. It took him months to stand without getting dizzy."

"So he didn't work during that time?"

She shook her head swiftly. "Oh, no, he couldn't. For the longest while, he could barely sit up in bed. Why do you ask? How can his recovery help your investigation?"

"I wondered if he could have spoken to someone about that night. If he took so long to recover, he must have spent quite a bit of time here in the house. It doesn't sound as if he was able to leave to go to work. How did he pay his rent?"

Mrs. Turcot's eyes widened. "He didn't pay anything. But we could hardly turn him out, could we? So we took care of him. Although, as soon as he was well, he left."

"My wife did most of the caring," Mr. Turcot amended. "But I did help her move him."

"Did he ever speak of that night?"

Mrs. Turcot wet her lips and glanced at her husband. "Not for a long time." She blinked and swallowed. Rachel leaned over and rubbed her arm.

Zane spoke. "Are you saying that he spoke to you *eventually* about that night? Why didn't you tell the sheriff? The case file indicates that the sheriff never spoke to either of you about the attack."

"Robert didn't really tell me anything directly." Mrs. Turcot looked down at her hands. "But what I heard, I did tell the sheriff, although nothing came of it."

"What do you mean nothing directly? What did Robert say?"

"He talked in his sleep. And one night, we heard a terrible crash, and found him on the floor."

Mr. Turcot spoke up. "I helped him back to bed. He was clearly not himself when he spoke. We told the sheriff, but he dismissed it, so I said we should, too."

"I stayed with him for a little while that night," Mrs. Turcot explained. "He was in pain, and he kept calling out."

"What did he say?"

"Some words I will not repeat," Mrs. Turcot warned with a tone full of decision and her shoulders stiff. "They aren't fit to be said in polite company. But he was angry at someone."

Zane leaned forward. "Did you ever question him, ask him later what he was saying?"

"Oh, no!" she said, her words strong. "He was very upset that night. I was afraid he'd... I mean, he was just starting to mend."

Having stayed mostly quiet during the questioning, Rachel asked, "Did the sheriff come by to question him?"

"Only one time shortly after the assault. Robert wasn't well enough to leave his bed."

"Did you hear any of the questions?"

Mrs. Turcot looked insulted. "I'm not an eavesdropper, Rachel. You know that."

"No, you're not, but you might have heard something in passing that might help us now." Rachel's words were gentle. "Mrs. Turcot, the sheriff has passed away, and Robert is long gone to Texas. If there is something that might help close the case, you should tell Sheriff Robinson."

Mrs. Turcot glanced at her husband, who nodded. "I know you heard a few things, dear," he said. "Perhaps you should get it off your chest."

"But what good will it do? It's an old case and you'll never find out who did it." She patted Rachel's arm. "We prayed so hard for your recovery, too, and when God blessed us with it, and with Robert's return to health, we were just plain thankful. Digging back into it again feels like I'm being ungrateful to God for all He's done."

"You're not, Mrs. Turcot," Zane said firmly. "Everything in its own time. If you help with this case, we may be able to find—um, Rosa."

Zane felt Rachel's sharp look on him. Had she been afraid he was going to mention Alex?

His heart pounding, Zane realized that he very nearly had. The Turcots were open and honest people, and generous to a fault. He didn't want to hide the truth from them, but he needed them to focus on the questions he posed, not create more in their heads.

"Do you think that soiled dove's disappearance is related to the assault on you and Robert?" Mrs. Turcot asked Rachel.

"The attack on Rachel came directly before Rosa's mother was murdered, so one might assume those two cases are related," Zane answered firmly. "And while Rosa and her mother had hazardous jobs, I think it's too much of a coincidence that the one woman is murdered and the other, her daughter, disappears. I can't ignore the possibility of a connection."

Zane held his breath. What he'd just told Mrs. Turcot made it seem as though he felt Rosa was an innocent victim in her disappearance. And to his shock, he realized he was actually considering the possibility. How could he think that? He'd seen her with his own eyes.

Faith. Rachel had said you sometimes needed it when nothing made sense. But faith wasn't his strong point, even though he firmly believed in God. He didn't even have enough faith in God to believe that He could help Zane clear his name in Canaan.

How had he become such a coward?

"That makes the attack on me related to Rosa's disappearance and Liza's death," Rachel summarized.

"Liza Carrera has been dead for years," Mr. Turcot warned.

Rachel turned to him. "It's the only thing we have to go on right now."

Mr. Turcot nodded to his wife. "Tell him what you told me, dear."

Mrs. Turcot dug from her pocket a small handkerchief. She dabbed her eyes. "Robert kept calling out Liza's name, over and over. He also said, 'Liza, stop him! Stop him!'"

Chapter Fifteen

Rachel sat back, feeling her jaw fall open in shock. "Robert said that Liza was there?"

Zane turned to her. "Do you remember her being there?"

She shook her head, still reeling from Mrs. Turcot's revelation. With a self-conscious clearing of her throat, she shut her mouth. "But my recollections are foggy at best, and I have never been able to fully recall what happened that night. No, I don't remember Liza being there."

Zane turned back to Mrs. Turcot. "Is that what you told the sheriff?"

"Yes!" Rachel had never heard Mrs. Turcot so adamant.

"What did he say?"

"Only that I must have been mistaken and that Robert had called out a different name. Or else that Robert knew Liza anyway, so calling out her name might not mean anything."

Zane shifted his gaze to Rachel. "Is that true? How well did he know her?"

Rachel blinked. "Well enough, but it's not what you think. Robert was one of my regular escorts. He'd been with me more than any of the others. He believed in my ministry. Both his father and uncle were missionaries overseas and Robert often spoke to Liza while I tended the others. Liza reminded him of some of the women his father and grandfather spoke of."

Zane looked skeptical. "Robert would actually minister to the women? How?"

Rachel blew out a sigh and set her shaking and suddenly moist hands down on the lace tablecloth. It had yet to be removed, and the far end, where the children had eaten, was need of a good scrubbing. She rubbed her fingertips over her calluses, wondering if Mrs. Turcot had anything to help soften them.

Suddenly hating them, she tucked her hands back under the table and straightened her shoulders. "Robert often just sat and talked to Liza, and any of the others who were willing to listen, and told them about his father and uncle's work overseas. He would tell them about people from all over the world who gave their lives to the Lord. He would tell about their desperate living conditions. Africa, in particular."

"But when he said her name that night, was he recalling her being there at the assault or was he delirious?" Zane asked.

"Both," Mrs. Turcot whispered. "But the sheriff didn't think he was believable, not in the same way I thought he was."

"So you believed him?"

"I asked him about it later, but he claimed he didn't remember. Except once, when his fever returned, he called out her name again. I think he didn't want to remember, but his brain kept pushing the memory on him anyway." She leaned forward and gripped Rachel's arm. "I know I only have some muttered words, and they really don't sound credible, but I believed him. I just couldn't convince the sheriff, so I had to drop it. I didn't say anything to you because I didn't want to upset you."

"When did he start to call out her name?" Zane consulted his small notebook before looking back at Mrs. Turcot. "Do you remember how soon it was after the attack?"

"Fairly soon, within a few days, I think."

Zane looked down at his notes as Rachel finished his thoughts. "But within *two* days, Liza was dead." He frowned. "Did you tell Robert that Liza had died?"

Mrs. Turcot shook her head. "He was in no shape to hear any bad news, Sheriff. I would never have said anything to upset him."

"Did she come to visit here like she did Rachel?"

"That sort of woman keeps her distance from respectable folk."

"That's not Christian, my dear," her husband told her sharply.

Rachel grimaced. She'd heard that some towns forbade their soiled doves from going wherever crowds gathered. They were shunned, refused service at stores except on certain days. Thankfully, Proud Bend wasn't so harsh, but the prejudice lingered.

Mrs. Turcot stiffened. "I'm sorry. You're right. Of course, I wouldn't have turned the woman away if she'd come around to visit, but she didn't."

"Surely you knew he would learn of her murder eventually?"

"Of course." She dabbed her eyes again. "When Robert was told, after he healed, he was upset with me for not telling him sooner. I think learning of her death added to him wanting to leave. I probably added to it, too. I hate myself for it, now, but what could I have done differently?"

"Nothing, Mrs. Turcot," Rachel told her firmly.

Zane looked up at her across the table. In the kitchen, the sounds of noisy cleanup told them the children were enjoying the time alone with Victoria and Mitch. "The money that was stolen that night was never found," he said, locking his gaze to Rachel's.

She pursed her lips and sat taller. Oh, Zane was a good investigator, asking questions calmly and listening carefully, all the while instilling confidence in his audience. She could appreciate that, but that was where her admiration ended. He still thought she'd stolen the money. How was she ever going to persuade him otherwise?

"That's what I've been told," Mrs. Turcot said. "You've read the file on Liza. What was on her person when she was found?"

"Nothing. Just her clothes." Zane looked at Rachel. "I've read the file and it says nothing about Robert's words. Do you know if your old sheriff questioned any of the other soiled doves?"

"The file didn't say?" Rachel sighed. "That sheriff wasn't the most trustworthy. Some of the soiled doves said he demanded money to look the other way. But, as far as I know, he didn't question them. And if he had, I think I would have heard the complaints from the women."

"What about Liza's regular customers?" Zane asked Rachel. "Do you know if he spoke to them?"

"He told me that Liza knew a lot of men, so it would be pointless to track down each of them," Rachel answered. "It's hard to believe he'd say that when a woman had been murdered."

Zane closed his notebook. As he tucked it away, he tilted his head and asked Rachel, "So you didn't know anything about what Robert said?" His words held a small accusatory edge.

Mrs. Turcot spoke. "Apart from my husband and the sheriff, no one else knew."

Rachel offered him a short shrug. "I was recuperating, also, though I wasn't as bad as Robert. I tried once to talk to him about it, but he got belligerent. I really hadn't thought that Mrs. Turcot could shed some light on our attack, so I never asked. Anyway, by the time I was up for visiting, the trail had gone cold and the soiled doves were keeping to themselves. Robert was very upset about it, too, and shortly after he got better, he left."

Zane stood. "Thank you, Mr. Turcot, Mrs. Turcot, for both lunch and the answers."

Everyone rose. "I'm sorry we couldn't be more helpful," Mr. Turcot said.

"You've done well for the amount of time that has passed. If you think of anything more, please let me know. I would like to hear it."

Mrs. Turcot turned to Rachel. "Dear, why don't you see the sheriff to the door? I want to check on both the kitchen and Jake."

Rachel slid her chair slowly toward the table, looking everywhere but at Zane. When he indicated with his hand that she should go first, she swept from the room. At the front door, she threw it open. A gust of icy wind barreled in. Zane leaned closer to her to retrieve his Stetson from where Rachel had set it on the rack.

She stepped in front of the door. He donned his hat, saying, "You're letting out all the heat, Rachel."

Lips pursed, Rachel directed Zane out the door and shut it behind her. She pinned him with a sharp look. "You still don't trust me, do you? You talked to Pastor Wyseman, you've interviewed the closest you have to eye witnesses, you've heard my plea for you to believe me, but you still don't. Why?"

"I'm trained to question everything that's said. You take unnecessary risks and I can't help but wonder why."

"Those women need me. They need help!"

"It's been my experience that people aren't nice, Rachel. They don't care back. They're out for themselves, and if that means stepping over people who can't defend themselves, so be it."

Rachel glared at him. "What are you talking about? Who have I stepped over?"

He sighed. "You haven't stepped over anyone. But clearly, those women will do it to you if you don't watch it. I can't believe that you're so naive that you wouldn't know this, or that Pastor Wyseman is also so naive as to think that you can save those women and God will take care of you along the way. I know you're an intelligent woman, so it's hard to believe you could be so blind. It makes me wonder what your true motivation is."

"My true motivation?" An understanding dawned

on her. "You're not talking about my ministry, are you? You're warning me for some reason."

"No, I'm not, and if you think those women wouldn't betray you in a heartbeat, you're sadly mistaken. Look what Rosa has already done, and we have just learned that her mother was there the night you were attacked."

"That may not be true, Zane. Robert was badly injured. We can't say for sure why he was calling out Liza's name."

"I doubt that he was recalling a time he was chatting with the woman. More likely, he was still reliving the attack, which proves what I just warned you about."

Rachel rubbed her arms to warm herself. It was too cold to be standing outside without a jacket, but this conversation was too important to splinter in a quest for outerwear. "Yes, let's discuss your warning. Do you think that because you were betrayed, you see subterfuge at every turn?"

"There *is* subterfuge at every turn. The circumstances around the investigation into Liza's murder prove it. As sheriff, it's my job to protect you from whoever has already killed one woman and tried to take two more lives."

"If protecting people is so important, then why didn't you stay and fight in Canaan? That's what you're really upset about. You told me you were framed for theft, but where are you now? Here!"

He stiffened. "My career doesn't compare to my brother's life, Rachel."

"That's true, but when this is all over, do you plan to return to Canaan to fight the corruption that ruined your life and put its citizens at risk? Or is Canaan on its own?"

His lips thinned. Rachel thought she would feel a surge of victory, knowing she'd hit the nail on the head, but there was none. His reaction made it clear to her that Zane wasn't going back to Canaan. He was going to let the corruption live on. Suddenly, Rachel winced with a pang of sympathy.

She couldn't believe he would really do it—abandon the town he had sworn to protect. In the short space of time, a mere few days, she'd seen Zane at work, and hadn't seen any evidence that he would stand for *any* corruption. He seemed as honorable as his brother. A person who would fight for those who could not fight for themselves.

So why walk away from his job, his career, his *honor?* Something cold sank deep into her stomach and she swallowed. The wind picked up and stung her eyes and chilled her hot cheeks as she realized she knew the answer.

He still hurt too much.

Abruptly, the front door swung open, and Mrs. Turcot peered out. "Is there something wrong? Rachel, dear, you shouldn't stand out here without a jacket. You'll catch your death."

"I'm fine, Mrs. Turcot. I won't be long."

"She's just coming in, ma'am." Zane said, his voice so low Rachel could barely hear it. "I won't keep her."

When, with a skeptical look, Mrs. Turcot shut the door, Zane leaned in closer. "Nor will I be here long. *Because there's only enough in me to fight for Alex.* After this, I'm moving on."

He turned on his heel and left her.

Chapter Sixteen

The fine chicken stew—and it was the best she'd had in a long time—sat like lead in Rachel's stomach as she approached Alex's rented room. She needed to talk to Zane, and this late Sunday afternoon, before Mrs. Shrankhof returned and while the other boarders dozed, was probably the best time.

She found Zane piling the firewood by the back door to the kitchen. His jacket had been tossed aside and he'd already shoved up his long sleeves. Rachel stopped a moment to watch him wipe his brow. He'd been at this task for a while.

"Mrs. Shrankhof will be impressed," she said as she approached, keeping her expression calm even while her heart pounded for absolutely no good reason. "You're leaving a precedence that Alex may not want to live up to."

Zane kept working. "As long as he's around to berate me for it," he answered tersely.

"And you? Does that mean you'll stay to hear it?"

"I told you. I don't plan to."

Disappointment plunged deeper into her chest than

she had expected. Surely she wanted him to leave? He'd been a thorn in her side since he'd caught her taking that picture postcard, always ordering her around, always acting like she was the most unwise person in town and, quite frankly, always believing the worst of her.

He's hurt. He's lost. Have compassion. She took a step forward. "You're a good lawman. It's possible you might find work here."

"Doing what?" Zane strode back to the messy pile in the center of the backyard and refilled his arms. Mrs. Shrankhof's hens scattered with disgruntled squawks. "Working for Alex? No, thank you."

"Why not? Or do you not like taking orders from your brother?"

"It's got nothing to do with that. I was a sheriff and that ended poorly. What makes you think I would be happier as a deputy? Besides, I don't want to be hired because I have some influence with the sheriff. I left that kind of corruption behind." He dumped his armful of firewood down on the running length that was already waist high.

"We're not corrupt here."

Although he shot her a skeptical look, he said nothing, rather, he continued piling the wood he'd retrieved.

"All I'm asking is that you not give up fighting for what's right. It sounded back there at the Turcots like you've just given up on life."

"I haven't." Having finished with that armload, he retrieved more firewood. "I'm putting all I have into finding Alex. Unless you don't think that's important?"

Her voice went soft. "That's not fair. Finding Alex is the most important thing right now. It will bring him back and it will lead us to the truth about Rosa."

"Why do you think she waited so long to deliver a ransom note? Alex had been missing over a week by the time we found Daniel. Why didn't Rosa deliver the note the next day?"

Rachel lifted her shoulders briefly. "That's a very good question. Perhaps because Daniel got sick? And before that time, she hadn't figured out a way to deliver her demand?" Her words held a note of reluctant yielding.

"Perhaps she waited until she thought you were desperate enough to pay handsomely?"

"I don't believe she's that cunning, and there was no evidence she ever returned, no hint that she might have kidnapped Alex."

"What hint would there be?"

"Rosa kept some food hidden in a tin beside her bed. Just some biscuits and such for Daniel mostly. You'd think that keeping both Daniel and Alex, and getting hungry herself, she'd have slipped back to get it. But each time I've peeked in her window, hoping to see her back, I've noticed that the tin hasn't moved."

"Maybe she emptied it."

"Normal people would just take the whole tin." Rachel paused. "Has anyone else in town complained that food has disappeared? Have any eggs gone missing? Or hens from henhouses?"

Zane glanced over at Mrs. Shrankhof's chickens. This time of year, they laid fewer eggs, but his brother's landlady had not mentioned anything unusual, and he had a feeling the woman would know exactly how many eggs to expect. She probably counted the chickens each night. He hadn't heard any complaints from other townsfolk, either.

"She could be getting food from Castle Rock."

"I've peeked in the window several times. Nothing in her crib looked disturbed," Rachel said. "It seems an odd way to kidnap someone. I don't believe she had planned to do so with Alex."

"Which means she could be working with someone and they changed the plan."

"Which was what?" Rachel sighed and stepped into the weak sunlight in hopes of warming herself. "And how did she avoid drawing attention to herself? In that time, she had to keep Daniel quiet and unnoticed."

Zane met her gaze. "I'm afraid that a small urchin like Daniel could blend in just about anywhere. There are plenty of them around and some are employed because they go unnoticed and uncared-for. Think of those who pick pockets, for instance."

Rachel shut her eyes. "I can't even think about how that could be Daniel in a few years. Poor mite."

Zane studied her. "Pastor Wyseman said you've changed."

The odd switch in subject caught her off guard. She bristled. "Changed what?"

He walked over to the long length and threw down the armful of wood. "Don't be defensive. I'm talking about your demeanor. He said you had a strong personality, but it's changed since Rosa disappeared."

"He's mistaken. I'm just as opinionated as ever."

Zane's brows shot up in a knowing manner. "He's very perceptive. He knew right away I wasn't Alex."

"Really?" Rachel hadn't thought that Pastor Wyseman knew Alex that well.

Zane lifted one corner of his mouth. "Imagine that. Pastor Wyseman is as smart as you."

Rachel's lips thinned, but she chose not to speak. Still, her stomach tightened. Yes, she had changed, and it wasn't for the better. And seeing Rosa last night honestly hurt her. Why would the woman leave without saying goodbye? Had she changed her mind about helping Rachel with her ministry and couldn't tell her to her face?

What if she had moved her trade to another town, like Castle Rock, and had kidnapped Alex down there when he had finally found her?

Rachel stiffened. She shouldn't allow herself to get bogged down like a carriage wheel in a rut. The other women needed her as much as ever to help them.

Zane slipped closer to her. "I'm just saying you need to be careful, Rachel."

She smiled, trying her best to push the worry behind her. "Where's the fun in being careful?"

He didn't share her attempt at humor. "Is it fun to risk your ministry work by being alone with a lawman?"

Smile dropping, she hastily glanced around, but the tiny backyard was fenced in on two sides. The front was shielded by the kitchen annex, and Alex's room filled in the remaining side. No one from the street could see in, and no one in the kitchen was peering out the solitary window, either. She turned back to Zane. Her reputation was safe for the moment. "I came to ask you not to give up."

"And who are you to give advice?"

The walls around them weren't the only walls she was up against. "I'm someone who works in a ministry that would have any normal person flee like a little girl seeing a spider. You don't get anywhere in your life if you give up when things get tough."

"Then how do *you* keep going?" He peered intently at her. "What gets you up in the morning, Rachel?"

She refused to admit her stamina was fading. "Nothing. I wait until the afternoon, usually."

Zane didn't seem impressed with her humor. "You don't get far in life being insolent, either."

"Look, Zane, if you want something, you have to work for it, plain and simple. I want those women to learn to trust God and let go of a profession that will surely drain away their spirit and might even kill them. I've seen it happen twice. That's what gets me out of bed each day. I know that I need to work at my ministry if I want it to succeed. I know I have days where it seems like nothing good happens, but God gives me strength, and on those days when He seems to be looking the other way, I get strength from knowing that in the past, God carried me through, and He will do so again when it gets bad."

Her words surprised even her. But she beamed inwardly. Yes, she'd managed to encapsulate exactly how she felt.

"Maybe I don't want anything that badly," he said with a shrug as he returned to the messy pile of wood, "outside of finding Alex, that is."

"And your honor?"

"I guess I don't want it badly enough, either."

"I don't believe that."

He walked over to her and touched her chin. His

fingers were warm, a striking contrast to the cold air that moved briskly over her face. "It won't do me any good," he whispered softly. "God can't control those who framed me."

"God is in control of everything."

"Then I guess He doesn't want to bless me." Hurt dashed over his face. "Maybe I'm still paying for that reckless youth."

What could she say? She'd seen women who lived reckless lives remain unblessed. Here in Proud Bend, the soiled doves scraped by. Barely, bitterly.

But they didn't all have misspent youths. Bea was a shining example of how horrible a woman's circumstances could become through no fault of her own.

"We're made new creations in God," she answered quietly. Was she becoming that? How could losing her drive make her a new creation?

He dropped his hand. "Yes, we're made white as snow. I was there for that Sunday-school message. But that doesn't mean the consequences of our actions don't catch up with us. They caught up with you that night of the assault because you felt, incorrectly, I might add, that you could solve those women's troubles with money."

"I know. I just feel…"

"Guilty? Don't. Others choose their own paths for their lives. You didn't force them to do anything."

"That's the problem. I should have forced Bea to take a loan. Forcing her might have saved her life."

"Be careful it's not pride speaking."

Was Zane talking about himself or her? She stepped back, watching him load up his arms with more wood. "And Liza? If I had insisted that she avoid the person she felt had assaulted me, she might still be alive. I didn't do enough."

"She died only two days after you were attacked. You were still recuperating."

"I should have been stronger."

Zane dumped the split wood down, his expression fierce. "That guilt will eat at you, Rachel. I've told you that before. Why can't you believe me?"

"Why can't you believe me when I say that I didn't orchestrate the assault on me?" She paused before her voice turned soft. "It's hard to trust, especially when you've been hurt. But if you won't trust me, try trusting God."

Zane glanced away. "It's just my own suspicious nature that's saying that you might have had a hand in your own assault. There aren't too many people like you in this world."

"For which I'm sure you're grateful."

Despite everything, he chuckled at her sarcasm. After a heavy pause, as his smile fell away, he added, "Trust doesn't come easy to me. I left my job in disgrace all because I had trusted those people I worked with, the ones who betrayed me."

"Why didn't you stay and fight?"

He shrugged. "Maybe I'm not a gambler. Maybe I couldn't. It didn't matter. That same day, Deputy Wilson's telegram arrived and I took it as a sign that it was time to move on. It was all that corruption that made me unable to accept that someone can actually care."

"You would have come here anyway, as soon as you learned Alex was missing." She cocked her head. "Do you feel guilty he is missing, possibly…in danger?"

"Or do you mean *dead*? You may as well say it."

Zane's mouth took on a grim edge. "Yes. Alex has always protected me. Or at least tried." He paused. "Once, when we were about fourteen, I got into some mischief that I am thoroughly ashamed of, and Alex took the blame for it. He said he was the one who did it."

"That was very noble. He must really love you."

Zane rolled his eyes. "As noble as it might be, it wasn't smart. When our parents learned what had happened, we were both disciplined."

"Why?"

"Our mother wasn't so easily fooled. Yes, we'd even changed clothing to complete the ruse, but she could always tell us apart and knew as soon as we walked in the door that Alex had lied when he'd taken the blame. In fact, she'd heard about the misdeed an hour before we arrived home. Then I tried to tell her that I had bullied Alex into accepting responsibility, but she saw through that lie, as well."

"Oh, dear."

"The point is that Alex has always looked out for me. That wasn't the only scrape he's pulled me from. I owe him. Without him, I would have gone down the wrong path in my life and who knows where I would have ended up."

"So why are you insisting that I'm wrong to feel guilty when you're letting it rule your life?"

"Because those you feel guilty about don't care. Alex cares for me."

She folded her arms. "A flimsy excuse."

"Like yours is for coming here?"

"What do you mean?"

He tipped his head and walked closer to her. She

refused to back away and thus show him how much he intimidated her. She could see beads of sweat on his brow, unexpected considering the chilly and dry air. He really had been working hard here. "I thought that you wanted to keep your distance from any lawman so that those soiled doves could finally learn to trust you."

Oh, that.

"You've come up with a cheap excuse to see me. Last night at White Horse Bluff was another cheap excuse."

Her cheeks hot, Rachel arched her brows. "Aren't you full of yourself? I went out to the bluff to pay the ransom in the hope that I could end this nightmare. I came here today to tell you not to give up."

To prove her point, she dared to take a step toward him. He didn't move. The air stilled around them, and even the hens in the far corner, those scratching at the dry end to the season's kitchen garden, eased off on their soft clucking. She and Zane stared each other down.

"Do you want me to stay in town after we get Alex back, Rachel?"

Her heart pounded in her throat. Did she? Her ministry would prove to be all the harder then. He wasn't like Alex, who understood and kept his distance. Zane seemed to be everywhere she was, stirring up defensive emotions with every encounter.

No, Zane could not be a part of her life.

And with his ideas about corruption, especially among the wealthy, he made it doubly difficult. Did Zane see that same thing in her? Tears filled her eyes.

"Well, Rachel?" Zane asked, his voice still low as

he interrupted her thoughts. "You just keep staring at me. Can I assume you want me to stay?"

She snapped out of her reverie and pulled in a sharp breath. She wasn't going to waste her own strength fighting Zane. Like him, she only had enough to find Alex and return to her ministry.

"I merely wanted you to know," she answered tightly, "that if something is worth having, you should fight for it. And a person's honor is always worth fighting for."

"Not my honor," Zane gritted out, hearing the bite in his words.

"You're arrogant."

Zane stepped back, smarting from her words for some odd reason. "Once Alex is back, I'm gone."

Then, maybe to soothe the sting, he took another step toward her. He didn't want to end the conversation with harsh words between them. On the Lord's day, of all days, he just wanted a rest from the distrust and tension. An insane thought popped into his head. It would be nice to court her for one evening. To be normal for one day, and able to reflect on that memory as he wandered the West for the remainder of his life. "Perhaps before I leave, you would allow me the honor of an evening with you? Maybe it would give me the honor you think I need."

"Do you think honor comes from courting?"

"No. It comes from doing something on principle alone." He shrugged and stepped back. "But you're right. It isn't deferrable. I beg your pardon, Rachel. It was rude of me to proposition you."

Rachel's cheeks flooded with color and he noticed

again how she pulled herself together. Those hands, still chapped and rough, smoothed down her skirt before lying neatly folded in front. Her shoulders back, her posture stiff, she looked like she was posing for a fine portrait, motionless for the few minutes needed to secure a good exposure.

"Perhaps I'm like you in that there is not enough fight in me except to find Alex and continue my ministry. My concern is how they spend their evenings—and, indeed, the rest of their time—not how I spend mine."

Zane frowned. "What do you mean? How do they spend their time outside of their evenings?"

"Secluded away as if they carry the plague," Rachel said, her distaste at the idea clear. "The sheriff before Alex kept those women outside of the town, allowing them to shop for necessities only during specific hours. He often had them arrested for vagrancy and petty theft regardless of whether or not they were guilty. The sheriff before him was the exact opposite. He wanted his share of the profits, so you can see why they are mistrustful of authority."

"And Alex? How does he see them?"

"With civility."

"Then we need to continue to show them their new sheriff can be trusted." He paused. "I have an idea."

Her eyes narrowed slightly.

"I have to escort you to the bank in the morning. And since I have read over the files yet again and interviewed Mrs. Turcot, the only other lead I have to follow is the ransom note. The postcard it was written on is the same type as the one Alex used to write your name. Alex got that one at the saloon. Would you like to come with me as I interview the bartender? I plan to do that after we visit the bank."

"How will that instill trust with anyone?"

"I'll be searching for Rosa. She's still a missing person, and if I show that I'm looking for her and concerned for her safety, it may go a long way to helping repair the soiled doves' trust in the law."

"How will they know what you've said to the bartender?"

Zane folded his arms. "What I say and do will get around."

Pleased she was actually considering his request, Zane returned to the pile of firewood. He needed to keep his hands busy. A few minutes ago, he'd touched Rachel's chin and had been sorely tempted to take the liberty of brushing his fingers against her cheek. Or even stealing a kiss.

It wouldn't do either of them any good. She was devoted to her ministry and convinced any relationship with a lawman was detrimental to it. She'd shown no signs of interest in his suggestion of courting.

Rachel nodded slowly. "Fine, I'll go with you. Perhaps an extra set of ears and eyes may help. I'll be at your office at ten tomorrow morning."

He nodded, busying himself with the wood. There was a long pause before he heard her leave.

The yard became too quiet and empty afterward.

Chapter Seventeen

With daylight beaming into the sheriff's office, Zane pulled out his pocket watch. It was exactly 8:30 a.m. He had one-and-a-half hours before Rachel would arrive to collect her money and allow him to escort her to the bank. Plenty of time to complete one important errand.

A few minutes later, he opened the door to the Recording Office. Three people looked up from their work as he entered. The young clerk in front who was busy helping an older couple was obviously the man from Castle Rock, for the other clerk in the far back was a young, attractive woman, Miss Walsh, most likely. Still farther back, in his own glassed-in office, was the Recording Officer, Noah Livingstone.

The woman came forward. "May I help you?"

"I need some information on the printer down in Castle Rock."

"What exactly do you need?"

As Zane answered her, the Recording Officer walked up beside her. Miss Walsh shot Mr. Livingstone a fast look with shining eyes. Zane felt his brows furrow. Was there a romance between them? Although Livingstone was nothing other than professional as he told Zane the name of the business, allowing Miss Walsh to retrieve one of the rolled maps, it was obvious the young woman admired him.

Just as Zane was concluding that the affection wasn't reciprocated, he caught the one single, furtive look Livingstone offered Miss Walsh as she unrolled a map.

A pair of juvenile screams drew everyone's attention to the window. Zane could see a pair of young boys race past. He'd seen them when he was walking over, no doubt playing before needing to go to school. Whoever their family was, they had their hands full.

When he turned back to the maps, he caught Livingstone's scowl and Miss Walsh's reddening face.

"I'm sorry," she muttered to Zane.

"It's all right," he replied. "It's hardly your fault. They're just boys. I wonder—"

Barely in time, he cut off his words, realizing that Alex might know the children. Miss Walsh frowned at him. He clamped shut his mouth.

"What do you wonder?" she asked.

Zane cleared his throat. "It's nothing."

"You're probably wondering why they aren't heading over to school. They'll wait until the last minute when Miss Thompson rings the bell." Miss Walsh smiled ruefully. "They are a handful for my mother, especially since I work, and she's been unwell. My father has been in Denver on business all week, which doesn't help."

She tossed a fast look up at the clock. "They'll be heading to school shortly."

When she resumed her directions, Zane drew in a relieved breath. He had to be more careful. It was bad enough that some astute people could tell he wasn't Alex, but to ask a question that his twin could already know the answer to was foolish and dangerous. The more people who knew he wasn't Alex, the bigger the risk that they'd complain, which would force the mayor to action. This morning, he had received the long-awaited order to report to the mayor. That meeting would happen later today. No doubt Mayor Wilson would believe the other mayor and send him packing.

That would make two towns washing their hands of him in one week. That would have to be one for the record book. Armed with the information he needed, and glad to be outside, Zane donned his Stetson and pulled it low to block out the early sunshine. He didn't have time this morning to travel down to Castle Rock to find the printer, but the first chance he had, he would. The train, the one that had brought him here mere days ago, would be arriving soon. It would carry on to the next stop on the line, Castle Rock. Zane noted the time.

His deputy had reported that Alex had been heading down to Castle Rock when he'd disappeared. What for? Rachel had wanted to follow the lead the postcard offered and Zane actually believed she could. Did that mean he fully believed in her innocence? And that her leads might come to fruition?

He clamped down on his jaw as he returned to the sheriff's office, refusing to answer it. It could lead him to wanting to stick around after Alex was found.

* * *

At exactly ten, Rachel opened the sheriff's office door and stepped inside. She'd expected Zane to be there and wasn't disappointed.

In fact, as she'd spied him through the window, her heart had taken an uncharacteristic leap.

Once inside, she noted that he was dressed respectably, in a dark but handsome suit, the badge of office clipped on his breast pocket. She'd seen Alex wear the same suit and realized that Zane was wisely wearing his brother's clothes. It appeared that perhaps Zane was a little broader in the shoulders, for the suit fit more snugly.

He glanced up when she shut the door. Was that a genuine smile on his face or merely a screen to hide something else? Whatever it was, it didn't quite reach his wary eyes. She smoothed her basic dark green outfit, oddly thankful that she'd taken pains with her appearance.

And last night she had used rose-scented cream borrowed from her mother to help heal her hands. For the briefest moment, Rachel shut her eyes. What on earth was it about this man that made her so insecure?

Forcing away doubt, she smiled, far more broadly than his wary expression merited. "Good morning."

Zane nodded as he stood. "Good morning. Are you ready to go sleuthing?"

"The bank first, please. I don't care to be toting money around while investigating a felony."

"A wise decision." He walked to the safe and removed the carpetbag. "You don't mind if I carry it?"

"Of course not."

He locked up the office and after a few minutes of

silent walking, they reached the bank. The beefy security guard, reputed to have been a Pinkerton detective at one time, opened the door for them and greeted Rachel politely. Her father had hired him years ago, and he was as much an institution as the elderly teller, Mr. Claymore.

Claymore carefully counted the money Zane set on his counter, and took Rachel's bankbook to update it. Rachel knew him to be professional in every way, but she could tell the man was relieved to have the money returned. Saturday evening, when she'd withdrawn it, the manager had stopped by Claymore's home and roused the man from his comfortable parlor chair to assist him.

If truth be told, she, too, was glad the money was back where it was safest. As Claymore took the bills to the safe, Zane gently extricated Rachel's bankbook from her hands.

She allowed him. They were the only clientele in the bank at the time, so all was quiet.

"Satisfied?" Rachel asked with arched brows.

"Quite. I was waiting to see how the money would be handled." He handed back the small book.

"And you can see it was from my own funds."

"I should have held off on that assumption until I had it verified." After they'd stepped outside, he added, "And I was rude to simply take your private bankbook from your possession without asking permission first. Please accept my apologies."

Rachel laid a hand over her heart. "As I live and breathe, I didn't think I'd hear that from you."

He donned his Stetson, leaning closer to her. "Just

as I didn't think I would see the interior of your bank-book."

"I would have shown it to you willingly if you'd in-sisted." She smiled wanly. "Don't look so surprised. I actually understand your mistrust in me."

She couldn't believe she'd said that. Yes, she did understand him. She also understood that he had only enough fight in him to find Alex.

An ache rolled through her, and she resisted the urge to reach out to grip his arm, to give him some of her own determination. To share in the anguish he must feel.

Zane stepped away. "Don't, Rachel."

"Don't what?"

"Don't sympathize with me. I don't want it and I don't deserve it."

"Why not?"

He scowled. "Because I'm not as strong as Alex. Nor can I do anything to redeem myself."

"You think you need to pay for past sins but also think the cost is too high."

The look he shot Rachel cut her to the core. Wary, watchful, haunted almost, it was like nothing she'd seen on him before. "Don't tell me God has already forgiven me. I know that, but there are some things He can't fix, because they are the consequences of my sins."

"Zane—"

"And don't go thinking I'm worthy of saving like your soiled doves, either."

She could feel her heart pound. Her emotions con-cerning this man had bumped up and down like one of those bucking bulls she'd seen when the town had hosted a rodeo. Did she think she could barrel into his life and make it all better? Was that the only reason she found herself thinking so much of Zane?

She'd wanted to make things better for the soiled doves, but she hadn't been able to. And when she'd pushed to have Alex find Rosa, he'd disappeared, as well. Tears stung her eyes. No. Zane was right to push her away. "I'm sorry."

"Don't be."

She couldn't help it. She was sorry that he felt he was unredeemable, and she felt sorry for herself that she couldn't help him. They were a fine pair.

Still, a part of her wanted to help, *needed* to help. But there could be nothing more between her and Zane, not as long as her ministry defined her life, as it always would.

That made her heart ache.

By now, as they crossed town, they'd reached the bandstand. A skiff of snow lay hidden in its shadow, refusing to be melted away by any weak winter sunshine. Zane stopped her at the closest corner, one where wayward sagebrush had been allowed to grow. It was the backside of the bandstand, and since Proud Bend didn't even have a band yet, no one had bothered to trim back the bush. She felt its branches brush her skirt and jacket as a breeze rose. When a few grains of snow stung her cheeks, Rachel said, "Zane, let me help you."

"It won't work."

Frustration flared in her. Why on earth was she so interested in helping this difficult man? "You won't let me try. You just want to run away to lick your wounds." She grabbed his arms, ignoring the etiquette of not touching a man. Forget that. Zane needed to know he was important, too.

"So what if I want to hide away? Am I not allowed to do that?"

"No! It's not right. You say you don't have the strength to do anything but find Alex. Well, fine, then, I'll accept that. I feel that way, too, sometimes. But think of Alex. He writes you often, you said. Would you say his opinions are worthless?"

"No."

"He thinks you're worth fighting for, right? He wouldn't want you to run away from your life."

"My life right now is finding him. That's the only thing that matters."

Her voice dropped. "You matter, too." She swallowed. "To me, too."

Was it inappropriate to say that? Rachel was hardly one to follow convention and good deportment, but sudden shyness washed over her.

Too late. You've said it. But it only means that you like to fix things. It means nothing more. It certainly doesn't mean you want him to stay.

Zane stood, his arms folded across his chest and his expression as stiff as his posture. He looked as tough a lawman as there could ever be. "You care only because I am your best chance to find Rosa and get to the bottom of this investigation. You feel guilty for all that has happened—to Bea, to Liza, to Daniel, to Alex, even. I could tell you to stop feeling guilty about them, just as you want to tell me to stop feeling guilty for my misspent youth and for the situation in Canaan. But let's not fool ourselves. Neither of us is going to listen to the other."

How could she answer that truth?

Abruptly, Zane unfolded his arms and took her hands to draw them close to his chest. She wore her best kid-leather gloves, but they were thin and she felt his warmth seep through to her fingers. "We're a fine pair, aren't we? Thrown together to find my brother and hopefully solve an assault, a kidnapping and a murder."

"How are they all connected? Besides through me."

"I don't know. I'm going on instinct here." He leaned closer. "But listen to me, Rachel. You have a good heart under that boldness. Don't waste it on me."

"And under your abrasiveness, you don't really want to run away. I believe you can fight for your innocence. You just think you shouldn't because it's some ridiculous payment for the sins in your past. Maybe you're afraid you won't win."

"I won't."

"It's not about winning or losing. It's about justice being served. We don't always win. Oh, believe me, I know that! But we keep up the good fight and trust in the Lord. He will guide us."

Zane's expression clouded. "Pastor Wyseman said something similar."

She felt a smile twitch her lips. "Then it must be true."

He searched her face, his gaze finally settling on her lips. Rachel's heart leaped. She really shouldn't be standing so close to him, not in broad daylight beside the bandstand for all to see, not if she didn't want her heart to wander so far from the safety of her ministry, where disappointment was tempered by new hope each day.

But she couldn't stop herself. She leaned closer.

Chapter Eighteen

A horse's loud neigh rent the cold air. Zane caught himself just in time. Was he really thinking he could just lean down and steal a kiss?

Hardly stealing. Not if he was judging Rachel's expression rightly. She wanted him to kiss her.

He pulled away from her, and Rachel stumbled slightly back into the bushes behind her. This had to stop. She was married to her ministry, and even though she voiced a valid argument that he was important, too, he was the last person she should involve herself with. He would be moving on soon, no longer welcomed after Alex returned.

He may or may not be strong enough to prove his innocence, but he knew one thing. If he showed his face back in Canaan again, he could easily find himself charged with theft. Rachel didn't need that kind of man in her life. She had a strong personality, to quote Pastor Wyseman. She needed a strong man, too.

Oh, yeah, she deserved way more than him.

"We'd better get to the saloon before the men start

to come in and that bartender can't answer our questions." His words sounded gruff even to his ears.

Rachel brushed down her skirt. He caught a glimpse of her nervous expression before it was whisked off her features. "I hope you know what questions to ask."

"I do. Don't worry." He took her arm and they stepped onto the street. The ground was frozen and made for easier walking. That was one good thing about winter here. It wasn't as messy as back in Illinois, where a winter's storm could bring both snow and rain.

The saloon, although open, was empty of patrons. The bartender was sweeping under a table and looked up with surprise as they entered. "Miss Smith, Sheriff Robinson, I didn't expect either of you this time of day."

"Yes, Eddie, it's quite early," Rachel agreed.

He propped the broom against the wall and walked behind the counter. "I only just opened. May I offer you some coffee?"

Rachel and Zane glanced at each other. From what Alex had told him in his first letter, Eddie knew how to run the saloon, but he made terrible coffee. Alex had compared it to the tar served in train depots. From the look of alarm masked quickly by politeness on Rachel's face, she agreed with that assessment. "No, thank you," Zane answered.

With an expectant look, Eddie asked, "How can I help you, then?"

Rachel walked up to the counter, her posture stiff. Zane pulled from his breast pocket the two postcards. He laid them on the smooth wood of the counter, pictures face up. Zane was reluctant at this moment to reveal their messages. "These two postcards are the same."

Eddie nodded. "I can see that."

"I know that this one—" he pointed to the one he knew had Alex's handwriting on it, even though the bartender could not see that "—came from here." He hesitated a moment.

"Because Sheriff Robinson here took it and wrote my name on it," Rachel hurriedly added.

"And he hasn't yet paid for it," Eddie reminded him with a sharp look to Zane.

Zane pulled out a coin and, after examining it, slid it across the counter to the man. Eddie took it and slipped it into his pocket. He should have paid for it when Eddie had first reminded him, but he'd had other things on his mind.

Why hadn't Eddie put the coin in the cash box that had a small ledger slotted into its lid? The owner might not agree with that kind of bookkeeping.

"Are you the only place in town that sells them?" Zane asked.

"The general store has postcards," Eddie hedged.

"Not this type." Something felt off. Zane didn't want to, but he might need to say more than he should about the ransom note. "This one—" he indicated the card with the ransom demands on its back "—is a ransom note, addressed to Rachel."

"Really?" The bartender reached for the postcard, but Zane was quicker. He didn't want the man to see the message that revealed Alex was being held hostage, also.

He inwardly grimaced as he tucked away both cards, still not liking that he was playing Alex. It was turning out to be a hindrance because no one seemed to be concerned that "Alex" had returned after a disappearance of nearly a week. Did they expect such an undedicated lawman?

"How many of these postcards did you get in?"

"You saw the pile, Sheriff, when you wrote down Miss Smith's name. That's why I couldn't understand why you came in here last Friday night and wanted me to repeat it all again." He nodded to Rachel, his mouth turning up slyly. "Don't you trust her, Sheriff?"

Rachel's brows were high when she looked questioningly at Zane. He refused to take the bait. Eddie was playing them off each other, much like Zane used to do with his parents when he'd found himself in trouble. He'd often hoped that if he could turn his parents' attention away from him, the punishment would be forgotten.

It had never worked, but in his immaturity, Zane had kept on trying. Eddie was going to be taught right now that it wasn't going to work with him, either.

He drilled the bartender with a hard glare. "How many postcards did you acquire, Eddie?"

Eddie shrugged. "I don't know. A big stack."

"How many were sold? And to whom?"

"I don't remember."

Zane felt his patience thin. "Why sell postcards of Castle Rock?"

"Why not? There isn't anything as pretty as that mountain around here."

That was a lie. First up, Castle Rock wasn't *that* pretty, and Proud Bend, with its crystal-clear river meandering around the town limits, set against a backdrop of Proud Mountain, was a far more pleasant image. The streets were wide and the buildings neat and tidy. The bandstand had a fresh coat of paint on it. Everything around here was prettier than Castle Rock.

"You don't have any town spirit, Eddie? Isn't Proud Bend more attractive than Castle Rock?"

Eddie looked away, busying himself with wiping down the counter. "Is that why you're here, Sheriff? To check on my town spirit?"

Rachel leaned forward, setting her gloved hand on a cleaned spot. Her expression looked plaintive and innocent. "We just want to find Rosa. Help us find her, please. We think that ransom note came from here, so it's possible the kidnapper frequents this place. Do you remember who may have bought any of those cards?"

"Most of them get stolen." He tossed an accusatory glare at Zane. With a tightening jaw, Zane resisted the urge to arrest Eddie. Perhaps a few hours cooling his heels in a cell might improve his disposition.

"Even telling us who you think may have stolen some might help," Rachel added. "I know you care what happens to these women."

Eddie folded his arms. "I care that they do their jobs. You're trying to get them out of that occupation. If that happens, I could lose my position."

"You're the only bartender in the only saloon in town," Zane growled.

Rachel smiled sadly at Eddie. "Neither of us is going to be out of a job. There will always be men who want to spend their money foolishly and there will always be women willing to help those men spend it. Will you help me find Rosa? Allow me to save at least one of them?"

Slowly, his mouth pulled to one side, Eddie waffled a moment. "You're too good to them, Miss Smith."

Rachel looked away. "Thank you." When she focused back on Eddie, she said, "Do you remember anyone who bought the cards, or who you think might have stolen them?"

Eddie turned and wrung out the cleaning rag into a dry sink. "I don't remember. I'm sorry."

"Where did the cards come from, anyway?"

He hung up the rag. "I get lots of peddlers in here, Miss Smith. I'm supposed to haggle with them and pour drinks, too. We don't have the money for security like your bank or a manager who can decide what products to buy."

Her bank. Zane remembered how Eddie believed Rachel owned the bank. He was wrong. "Then who has been unusually interested in Rosa? More than the obvious interest?"

"She has some men who like her, but nothing out of the ordinary. For people treating her special, there's only Miss Smith. Rosa's pa comes around once in a while, but he's good for nothing except asking for money. And there's you, Sheriff. Ever since that first day when you asked who looks after the women."

A pair of cowboys shuffled in right then, diverting Eddie's attention a bit too quickly. Zane knew the conversation was over, especially considering how the patrons' attention lingered on Rachel and him. He ended the questioning quickly and led her outside.

Out of earshot, Zane muttered, "He's lying."

Rachel fell into step beside him, feeling as disappointed as Zane's expression hinted. "That much is obvious. But why?"

"It's been my experience that either love or money motivates people."

"Love?"

"People do stupid things when they're in love."

She blinked, her expression curious. "Speaking from experience?"

"No."

Well, that was short. "I don't think that love is the issue here. So that leaves money." She looked at Zane. "Was it love or money behind the plot to frame you?"

"Money. The mayor's son stole the taxes and the mayor arranged to frame me. He convinced my deputy to plant the evidence."

"By paying him?"

"In a way. By promising him he would be the new sheriff."

"And that means more money for your deputy."

"And a position of authority he can use to pressure others, like your former sheriff who asked the soiled doves for bribes. With those two working together, the sheriff and mayor can help keep each other in power. Again, money—because the mayor will be well paid."

Of course Zane wouldn't trust this town, with Mayor Wilson wanting to be reelected and his son as deputy. "So, here it's about the money. Rosa getting some by ransoming Alex?"

"No. I was thinking about Eddie and his pack of lies."

"Pack?"

"More than one. The first being about you owning the bank."

"Well, he could have been mistaken." Why was she trying to absolve Eddie from any deliberate lying?

"Bartenders aren't usually mistaken. They do hear a lot of tall tales, but they hear a lot of truths, too."

"From whom? I doubt my mother has spent her hours in the saloon bemoaning to others about how I own the bank."

"But one of the employees could have."

Rachel fell silent. One of her household staff, or did Zane mean the bank employees? She bit her lip and slowed her step.

"What is it?" Zane asked.

"Mr. Claymore from the bank prefers a hot cup of tea and an evening fire to going out. But I've seen the security guard in the saloon on some evenings. Still, you think the bartender is deliberately lying. What was the other thing?"

"The postcards. I'm sure of it. Did you notice that he pocketed the coin I gave him instead of putting it in the till?"

"I did notice that."

"It's possible that he's bought those postcards knowing they were stolen and is selling them on the side."

"Can't be much of a market for postcards that would force a person to steal them."

"You wouldn't think."

Rachel turned to Zane to change the subject. "You asked the bartender about my honesty?"

"I didn't. Eddie is trying to turn us against each other. Didn't you do that when you were a child?"

"I'm an only child. Did *you* do that?"

"More often than I care to remember. Sometimes I would include my brother, but mostly, I tried to turn my parents against each other so they would argue and forget that I was supposed to be in trouble. It's a sign of immaturity and I was a good example of that."

"You must have been a delightful child to raise."

Zane nodded ruefully. "Alex was always the likable one."

"I look forward to hearing even more about that." Rachel murmured. "Why don't we check out Rosa's crib again? I know that Alex searched it. I have, too, but perhaps we missed something. Your fresh eyes might help."

They hurried around back through the alley Rachel had used last Friday night. The area hadn't changed since the night Zane had watched Rachel administer aid to Alice. A fresh dusting of snow from last night, not yet touched by the sun, seemed to brighten the yard. "Rosa's crib is the second one from the end. We should be quiet. The women don't appreciate being awakened."

Zane consulted his watch. "It's nearly noon."

"And if we awaken them, we're less likely to get any answers should we need to question them again." Rachel hurried over to the crib. At the far end of the short stoop sat a battered flowerpot with the withered remains of a plant. As Zane stepped up to the door, Rachel slipped her hand free of her glove and dug into the dry, dusty soil. "I know that Rosa kept the key in here, but I can't find it right now."

"Don't bother," Zane said, gripping the older-style door handle.

She glanced over her shoulder. "Why?"

"Because the key is in the lock." He turned the lock and the door opened an inch.

Immediately, the hairs on the back of her neck rose. Something wasn't right. Rosa never left her crib unlocked, and Rachel was sure she had been the last person to enter, having searched it after Alex had told her he'd done so. Rachel had returned the key to the flowerpot.

Zane quietly pushed open the door. Her heart leaping in her throat, Rachel watched him also push back his jacket, her eyes widening as they lit upon his revolver. He looked at her. "Stay out here while I see who's inside."

What if Rosa had returned in the night and had forgotten to remove the key? She could have been upset, or so tired she only wanted to fall into bed. Rachel couldn't keep her curiosity at bay even a minute. She hurried in behind Zane.

Though the day was bright, these cribs had few windows and the inside sat in relative darkness. Zane stood at the end of the bed, his hand on his revolver as he scanned the entire room. Rachel quickly lit a lamp. When she turned back to Zane and the bed, she gasped. The room looked like it had been turned upside down.

Except the bed. Even though the bedclothes were heaped in the center, one thing was obvious when the bedding shifted. Someone was in it.

Without any warning, Zane crossed the room to slam her to the boards beneath their feet, all the while covering her with his frame. On her trip to the floor, she caught a glimpse of his revolver as he pulled it from his holster.

Two deafening shots rang out. She heard a man cry out.

Zane!

Chapter Nineteen

No, not Zane!

How badly had he been hurt? He felt like a dead-weight atop her. Rachel tried to squirm loose, but couldn't free herself. All she could do was lie there as whoever was in the bed hit the boards near her head with stocking feet.

Another shot rent the air, and she tucked her head farther into her shoulders and shut her eyes tight. The door banged wide open as their assailant bolted from the room.

Everything went silent. The pungent odor of gunpowder lingered. Above her, Zane didn't move. "Zane?"

"I'm okay." He shifted his weight and groaned. When Rachel moved to free herself, she also let out a groan and looked down at her elbow, the source of her pain. No blood. Good. But her whole weight had landed on that arm and it was going to be black-and-blue tomorrow.

She finally eased herself free of Zane and sat up. He stayed prone beside her. "Zane!"

"I'm okay."

"You're not moving. Are you hurt?"

"Yeah, a little. He caught my side." He raised himself, cradling his left arm as he hugged it to his chest. Rachel gasped and sank down beside him, realizing it wasn't his arm but his ribs he was protecting.

"You've been shot!"

"It's not bad. Here, help me out of my coat," he said. "He shouldn't have been able to take me by surprise."

Zane's coat off, Rachel answered, "You pulled out your revolver so quickly!"

"I was a sheriff, remember? I do know how to defend myself. Or at least, I used to." He blew out a sigh. "It's my own fault. I didn't draw fast enough."

"It looked pretty fast to me."

"I should have been ready before I entered. I only had my hand on it." He tried to stand, grimacing as he did so.

Rachel helped him. "Here, sit on this chair." She brought it close to him. "Or, better still, lie down."

He looked at her with scorn. "I'm not fatally shot, woman. It's just a graze along my ribs. I could even wrap it up myself, if necessary. But before we bandage me up, did our friend here leave anything behind?"

"No. I saw him take his boots, because my face was only inches from them. Whoever it was is agile."

"What happened here?"

Both Rachel and Zane looked up to see Eddie in the doorway gripping the jamb. Behind him appeared several of the women, the closest one being Annie.

"Just a squatter," Zane muttered. "We surprised him."

"What are you doing here?" the bartender asked.

"We wanted to see if Rosa had returned in the night," Rachel answered testily.

"We would tell ya, I'm thinkin'," Annie snapped back, her tone bitter from being rudely awakened. "We'd hear her."

"Did you hear that guy come in here?"

Annie looked to the other woman whose crib was closer. That woman, Mags, shook her head. Annie followed with the same motion.

"Then how would you hear Rosa returning?" Zane pointed out, his tone cold. Annie looked away.

"Was anyone hurt?" Eddie asked.

"Just Z—the sheriff," Rachel blurted out. "Annie, did you see anyone hanging around here last night? A man?"

Annie pulled her coat closer to her thin frame. "No, it was a quiet night."

Eddie looked back at the other women, but they shook their heads. When the bartender returned his attention to Rachel and Zane, his expression was tight. "Rosa shouldn't have left her door unlocked."

"She didn't," Rachel snapped.

Eddie said nothing. A man from the bar called out and forced him to twist about. He pushed himself between the women to return to his work. With wary looks, they left, too. None seemed interested in the fact that their sheriff had been shot.

Rachel felt her shoulders sag. "I didn't really expect anyone to have seen anything." She turned and gasped at the sudden move.

"Sorry," Zane said, lifting his elbow to check his wound. A blotch of dark red had formed on his light shirt. "I shouldn't have pushed you down so hard."

Rachel set to work hastily. "Turn around, Zane."

"What for?"

"Just turn around."

He obeyed, with a grimace and Rachel lifted her skirt to tear a strip from the hem of her petticoat. She then took Zane's handkerchief and folded it into a small bandage. After lifting his shirt and pressing the handkerchief against his wound, she bound it with the strip of white cotton hem.

"Thank you."

"Just keep this snug until we can clean it up properly."

"I'm sorry. I should have done better."

"Forget it! You saved my life! I walked right up to that man in the bed, and he would have shot me if you hadn't shoved me down."

"I tried to twist around to shoot him, but it went wide." Zane searched the ceiling and upper walls.

"Let's not worry about him." She set her hand on the key. "I'll lock up this place and take the key with me. Rosa will come looking for it if—*when* she returns."

"Rachel?"

She turned back to him. "Yes?"

He offered her a bleak smile. "She'll be back. We'll find both of them."

"With the leads we have? Each day that goes by makes it that much harder to find anything substantial." She sagged.

His gaze became thoughtful. "We have more than we realize, but it's putting all the pieces together that makes it hard. It's like a puzzle without the picture."

Reluctantly, Rachel scanned the room. "All I saw

was stocking feet as he jumped out of bed and picked up his boots."

Zane pulled a face. "Whoever it was is used to getting caught unawares. Throw back the bedclothes, Rachel. He might have left something behind."

She tossed them back. A small clunking sound rang out. Walking around the bed, she searched the floor until she found the culprit. "Here. This was in the bed."

She handed a small block to Zane. It was metal and had a letter on it. "It's exactly like the one I found in Daniel's pocket. It must be a toy."

Rachel looked at it. "It's got a backward *P* on it."

"Backward?"

"What was the letter on the other block?" she asked.

"It was an *A*." Zane rolled the block around in his hand. "But I wouldn't have noticed anything unusual because the letter *A* is the same forward and backward."

Rachel scanned the room for anything else. "It's a stamp. I'm pretty sure that block isn't meant as a toy. It's too small." She looked at Zane. "Ink and paint are too expensive to be wasted on children. Even Victoria gives only slate and chalk to Mitch's children."

Zane checked his wound before looking around. "Was Rosa this messy?"

"No. She was very neat, but she didn't have much of anything. That's why I knew she hadn't left town. She only owned a few dresses and such, and they were still hanging in her wardrobe."

"Then we seem to have a squatter."

"Well, that's not unusual." Rachel walked to the back of the room where a small pitcher and basin stood. "But never mind him—let's get your wound tended to."

"I hardly need a doctor."

"Nor do I want to take you to him. What if Alex has a scar or had an injury that the doctor tended?" She peered into the jug, but the water held a film of dust. It had been sitting since Rosa went missing.

Pulling a face, Rachel announced, "We should tend your wound up at my house. I have all my supplies there, not to mention clean water and soap."

She sounded so no-nonsense, but a moment later, she found her hands no longer cooperating in the simple task of helping Zane into his coat. It went from bad to worse when she tried to lock Rosa's door. "Look at me. I'm shaking like a leaf!"

Zane covered her hand with his, drawing her attention away from the door and up into his eyes. "It's all right, Rachel. It's just a graze. I'll be fine and, most importantly, you weren't hurt."

He took the key from her, and Rachel marveled at how calm he was as he locked the door. He looked down at her, smiling. "It's all right. Really. I'm just glad you're safe."

Was he? She'd been nothing but an irritant to him for days, and yet he'd thrown himself atop her to protect her.

Her heart stalled. She dared to peer into his dark eyes and found him smiling softly back at her. Her knees turned to jelly and she reached for Zane as if he was the only thing that could stop her from falling. "Hold me, Zane," she whispered. "I think I need it right now."

He took her in his arms, and she clung to him, gingerly, so as not to hurt him further. For a long, comforting moment, she shut her eyes, pushing away all the danger they'd just experienced. As she pressed her left cheek against his coat's lapel, she felt him stiffen and suck in a sharp breath. She opened her eyes and her gaze fell on the bloodied and scorched hole in the side of his coat.

Rachel quickly stepped out of his embrace. He'd been shot, and she shouldn't be foolish, begging to be held as though her fears were more important than tending his wound. She was far stronger than that.

She tugged down on her jacket, smoothing the front of it. "Let's go to my house. I can even mend your coat if you like."

He nodded. Rachel pocketed the key and hurried down the steps. Thankfully, they were alone, but not wanting to tarry, she propelled him away toward the main street. The sooner they were safe at her home, the better she'd feel.

Zane allowed Rachel to cross her threshold first. Before they'd embraced, she'd been as pale as a fresh layer of snow. And her gaze on him? He'd seen it on Alex's wife the day they'd married.

It was a look of trust, mingled with a touch of nerves. Even now, rethinking it as he walked into her front hall, he felt warmth rush through him. It wasn't because of the woodstoves.

Zane swallowed. Having Rachel's trust was attractive. It was dangerous, too. She shouldn't trust him. He refused to fight for his own honor. And today, he hadn't even had the good sense to draw his revolver first.

Rachel led him into the parlor where, a few minutes later, she laid out her supplies on a small table set between two fussy high-backed chairs. She took his Stetson and coat and handed them to the young footman who'd followed them in, his eyes wide. Rachel gently directed Zane into the nearest chair.

"Oh my! What's going on here?"

Both he and Rachel looked up to find Mrs. Smith gliding into the room, a young maid trailing behind. Both were dressed in warm clothes, and Louise was pulling off her gloves as she approached.

Automatically, Zane began to rise, but Rachel's hand descended onto his shoulder. "Stay where you are."

"What happened?" Louise cried out, having spotted the blood.

"He's been shot, Mother."

"Shot! We should call the doctor, then."

"It's just a flesh wound, ma'am," Zane told her. "Hardly worth his bother."

Louise peered over Rachel's shoulder as she began to lift his shirt. Zane watched the older Smith woman, curious about her. Her steely calmness told him that she was tougher than she looked. More practical, too.

She turned to her maid. "Stoke the fire in here and bring in some boiled water." To Rachel and Zane she added, "It's chilly in here and, yes, I agree with you, Sheriff. It's not as bad as it could have been. I'd like to ask what happened, but, in retrospect, I'm not certain I want to know."

"It was behind the saloon, Mother."

"What on earth were you doing there this early in the day?"

"We went to see if Rosa had returned."

"Has she?"

"No." Rachel returned to her task, her mouth a thin line. She turned to her mother again. "You've been out?"

"We took a basket of baked goods to the Walshes. Mrs. Walsh is in my Bible-study class and has fallen ill. Poor Clare. She's now stuck looking after those wild brothers of hers on her own."

She removed her hat and jacket and handed them to the footman. "I don't know what that family is going to do with those boys if she gets any sicker. Clare will have to stop working, but that could easily put them in the poorhouse."

Rachel's head shot up, but all her mother did was hand her a clean cloth even before she reached for it. Zane lifted his brows. As brusque as Louise appeared, she was rational and efficient in her movements. He knew right then where Rachel had acquired her no-nonsense attitude. Her mother had it, although the older woman's was tempered by decorum.

"There, Sheriff," Louise announced after she'd supervised her daughter's ministrations. "You'll be just fine. I wouldn't go riding or tackling the evils of this town head-on for the next few days, though. Give that wound a bit of time to heal, in case it becomes septic."

"Mother's right," Rachel said softly. "If it gets red or swollen or hot, you may have to see the doctor. But for the next day, don't remove the bandage."

Louise swept from the room, calling with a heavy sigh over her shoulder as she went, "You'll be off doing what you want in no time at all. Although I expect it will be something equally dangerous as today's adventure."

Chapter Twenty

Rachel couldn't stop her mother's words from cutting into her like a thousand tiny knives. Zane would mend soon enough for he was robust and healthy, which meant he would indeed get right back to doing what he had come to do. He'd find his brother. And then he'd leave.

His wound had been deeper than she'd first thought, though. It would take time to heal. Mother was right about being careful it didn't get septic. Surely her warning would be heeded?

Gathering up her supplies and stowing them back in her basket, Rachel tossed a look over her shoulder at Zane. "I can mend your coat."

"Never mind. I will ask Mrs. Shrankhof to do it. I need to be getting back to work."

Rachel whirled. "Mother and I agree that you shouldn't work for a few days." She cleared her throat. "We rarely agree on things, so you should listen."

Zane shrugged into his coat. "I'll be careful. I need to speak with the mayor. I've been ordered to report."

"What if Mrs. Shrankhof asks what happened to you?"

"I'm the sheriff and I'm sure she expects some days to be like this. I imagine she's already heard the whole story by now anyway." He stared at her, his gaze sweeping up and down her frame.

The moment lingered for far too long. She stood in front of Zane like a dumbstruck teenage girl. Panic swelled, a thoroughly unwanted emotion she couldn't check. She wanted to blurt out to Zane a series of foolish orders.

Do not go back to work.

Do not find Alex. Don't learn the truth about Rosa.

Don't get even more hurt.

Again, Rachel swallowed, but the lump that had formed in her throat returned, hard and hot as ever. As long as Zane recuperated, as long as Alex was just missing, and as long as Rosa was just a big question in the investigation, Zane would still be here.

And all the while, Alex would still be in danger.

Oh, what an awful person she was.

Rachel tightened her jaw, set her shoulders back slightly and refused to relent to the selfishness inside of her. She had no right to lecture him that honor meant something. Where was her honor? She wanted time to stand still. What about her work? She was there each night trying to dispel a guilt that would never leave. She'd already started to doubt her work and her faith in Rosa. There was nothing honorable there, either.

"Is there something wrong?" Zane asked.

She forced out a firm smile. "Nothing. I was just concerned for your wound, that's all."

Zane walked to the door, where Rachel saw him reach gingerly for his Stetson, resting on the small table. "I promise to treat my injury with the utmost tenderness."

She didn't believe him. "No riding."

"I promise. But, Rachel, someone shot at us. I need to investigate it now. I can't let it wait until I heal."

"You have a deputy."

His expression darkened slightly as he bade her farewell with his thanks before disappearing out the parlor door. Rachel stood in the center of the room like a silly woman, and she fought the urge to cry. What a horrible person she was. No wonder Zane had made a hasty exit.

A tear slipped from her eye and rolled down her cheek. She brushed it away angrily and finished tidying up. It was time she grew up and accepted the fact that her life was already set before her and it didn't include any man, least of all Zane.

The next morning, Tuesday, Zane looked up as Rachel entered the sheriff's office. In one hand was her basket of medical supplies and with the other, she slowly led in Daniel. Immediately, Zane rose and smiled down at the little boy. The child looked so much better than even a few days ago. His cheeks had lost their hollowness, and his hair, as black as Zane would expect when the child's mother had Spanish roots, was washed and combed. He wore an outfit that was slightly too big for him but looked comfortably warm and clean. Daniel smiled up at him, a testament to his natural friendliness.

Zane allowed his gaze to settle on Rachel's smiling

face. She looked far calmer than she had yesterday. When he'd left, he'd felt disconcerted by her expression. Getting shot at must have shocked her more than he'd initially realized.

"We've come to check on our patient," Rachel said brightly.

He rolled his eyes. "I'm fine. Whatever that salve was that you put on has done its job. I expected the wound to sting and redden, but it's healing nicely."

"How do you know that? Didn't I tell you not to remove the bandage?"

"I bathed. I needed to do so, or Mrs. Shrankhof might refuse to feed me."

She smiled. "That would never happen."

"Couldn't take the chance. By the way, I saw Mayor Wilson. Without saying too much, I convinced him to keep me on. Being shot at has helped my case, I think. It's clear that the town needs someone on the job until Alex can return."

"Effective persuasion technique, although dangerous." Rachel set down her basket and lifted Daniel to sit on a nearby chair. She tugged off his woolen hat and mittens, and set them on the desk beside him. "Stay here, Daniel. Look, I have a toy for you." She pulled a small wooden truck from her basket and handed it to him. He immediately dropped to the floor to play with it.

With a shake of her head, she sighed. "Another man who doesn't listen."

With a chuckle, Zane peeled off his jacket, trying to keep his face neutral. He tugged his shirttail free to pull up the material just enough to expose the bandage. Rachel unwound it. At the sight of the gash, she grimaced.

"It's not that bad," he told her. "It's not even red and tender. No need to worry like you did yesterday."

She shut her eyes a moment, as if to gather her wits together. "You're right. It's healing nicely." After she cleared her throat, she added, "I just don't want you to work for a while."

Didn't she want Alex found and Rosa in custody so she could answer why she was involved with the kidnapping? He studied her. "Have you ever seen a gunshot wound before?"

"No. Lots of bruises with a few cuts, and once a minor knife wound. I guess it's just the thought that if you had shifted even a few inches to your left, that bullet could have ended up in your heart."

"It didn't." He watched her as she set out her supplies. She was obviously determined to bandage the wound again. "Do you remember anything more from Rosa's crib?" he asked.

Rachel shook her head. "Nothing, I'm afraid. I didn't have time. Mother bombarded me with a litany of questions after you left. It was exhausting."

"She was polite when I was there."

"Her breeding would allow nothing less in your company. But not so the moment you closed the door. She came storming down the stairs like the cavalry. My mother would have made an excellent solicitor, by the way. No one would dare lie to her." Her smile turned rueful. "I simply didn't see your shooter's face. All I saw was his feet."

Zane wasn't surprised. It had all happened so fast, and he'd been ill prepared to properly defend them.

While he'd had his hand on his gun as he'd entered the dim crib, he should have forced Rachel to stay outside until he knew it was safe to enter. He should have had his gun drawn fully from the holster, too.

As soon as Rachel had lit the lamp, he'd noticed the boots and guessed a man was in the bed. If he hadn't acted as quickly as he did, things could have turned out far differently.

But he still hadn't acted fast enough.

"All I saw was his feet and a glimpse of an arm as he bent down to pick up his boots," Rachel was saying as she continued her mercy task.

Zane tipped his head to look up at her. "What kind of boots were they?"

She stopped. "What do you mean?"

"You're a woman with refined tastes. Were the boots stylish? Common? Polished? Scuffed?"

"Refined tastes?" Her brows shot up. "I'm a woman who accepts fashion advice from her mother because it keeps her from interfering with my ministry. A small trade-off, I might add."

"But that taste is refined. You're used to dressing fashionably."

Rachel shrugged. "I suppose it is refined. But it's not that I insist on wearing only the best, just what Mother wants me to. She does have nice taste."

"And I'm sure she also dressed your father, so you must have learned something from her about men's styles. What color were the boots?"

"Black, and quite dusty. A pale dust that was almost shimmery. I saw the way the lamplight made the dust look a bit pink."

Rachel stood back, a look of wonder on her face.

"Now that I think about it, I would say that it almost looks like the color of the outside of our house when the lamp above the door is lit. I know, I've seen it enough times late at night."

Zane tensed. Ignoring the bandage dangling from his ribs, and the twinge of pain, he leaned over and removed a bundle from the bottom drawer of his desk. "I brought Daniel's clothes in with me this morning, hoping that we might be able to identify the dust I found on them. Maybe even compare it."

"To what?"

"To the clothes on the person we finally arrest for kidnapping Alex."

Rachel stiffened. "You mean Rosa?"

"If we find matching dust on her clothes, that won't prove anything. She's Daniel's mother. It's a good chance that whatever dirt he's touched, she'd have on her, as well. And vice versa. No, I still think she has a partner."

"You mentioned it at White Horse Bluff. What makes you so sure of that?"

"It wouldn't be easy for a small woman to haul Alex around if he was unconscious. We're not small men. She'd need another pair of hands because it would be too easy for Alex to try to escape while she was sleeping, or while she was away. Should we ever find her accomplice, I'm hoping we can compare the dust." He undid the bundle. Along with the clothes, he'd also tucked inside the bundle the small envelope of powder he'd scraped off Daniel's jacket. "If her accomplice has the same dust, it will prove he has been there with Daniel."

"First, let me finish wrapping you up." She quickly

completed her task. Zane watched her face. A troubled expression marred her beautiful features. Again, she'd been careful with her toilet, with fussily pinned curls and powder perfecting her complexion.

Her mouth remained pursed, though not so tight as to threaten lines like those small ones between her brows. With her clenched jaw, Zane knew she was upset.

Of course she would be. Disappearances, kidnappings, shoot-outs. An abandoned child. He could understand why her mother had announced that she didn't want the details. Far too stressful.

When Rachel was finished, she took the tiny envelope from Zane's hand and carefully opened it on his desk's blotter to study it. "It's hard to say for sure, but it looks like rhyolite."

"Rhyolite?"

"It's a type of stone quarried here. There are several large deposits around Castle Rock. That's why all the fine stone buildings around here, my house included, have their front facades made of it. They're constructing some government offices in Castle Rock, and the whole building is going to be made of rhyolite. That's why the Recording Office is temporarily in Proud Bend. We're not the county seat here, but we have it until the office is built."

"I met the Recording Officer."

She chuckled. "I'm sure you like him. He has no sense of humor, either."

Zane tossed her a sharp look. She tried to hide her smile as she folded the envelope and returned it. "I remember there was a lot of dust on that shooter's boots," she said.

She turned away before gasping and spinning back. "His hands! I saw them as he leaned down to grab his boots! They were tanned and wrinkled." Rachel gasped again in realization. "They had spots on them like my mother's. Don't tell her I said that. She'd be mortified."

"I won't." Zane tucked the envelope again back in with the clothes. "So the man wasn't young. You did well, Rachel. That's good."

She beamed and began to tidy up her things. "Try not to do too much for another day or two. And don't tell me that you've had a gunshot wound before. I'd rather not hear that."

"I couldn't even if I wanted to. I've been shot at, but not hit until now."

Rachel finished her task quickly, her mouth tight and the slight creases returning between her brows. When she'd finished repacking her supplies, he laid a hand down over hers. Her gaze slid up to his. Those beautiful eyes, a blue as clear as the sky on a fine summer's day, widened.

They were wary, wanting to trust, but not so open as yesterday. She bit her lip.

"Thank you," he said, holding her gaze.

"You thanked me yesterday."

"I'm thanking you again today."

Her cheeks pinkened. When they'd met, she'd been as bold as the magpie that frequented Mrs. Shrankhof's yard and whose ridiculous nest teetered high in the tree behind the chicken coop. If he'd known he could knock Rachel off center simply by showing gratitude to her, he'd have tried it before now. Apparently, Rachel Smith wasn't used to flattery. The men in Proud Bend must be idiots.

She cleared her throat. "I'm the one who should be thanking *you*. You saved my life yesterday." She shook her head. "I wonder who he was."

Zane had his theories, but he needed to confirm a few things first. He didn't want Rachel insisting on accompanying him like some battlefield nurse. She had Daniel, and getting shot at had truly rattled her. "Forget him," he muttered. "He's long gone. I've asked the blacksmith to change the lock on Rosa's crib, too, in case there is another key."

"Nothing seemed touched. Alex searched her room as soon as I reported her missing, and I had looked in it, as well."

"Didn't you trust him?"

"I believed I could add to the investigation. You know, a fresh pair of eyes." She sighed. "It was a fool-ish thought. I don't own a gun, let alone know how to fire one, although Father bought Mother a small pistol once. I can only thank the Lord that no one danger-ous was hiding in that crib the day that I went. No, the only thing I could do was identify a few personal items and that tin of biscuits."

"Did you notice if it was all still there yesterday?"

She lit up. "It was, but the tin had been opened. I remember seeing it under the bed. The last time I saw it, it was closed and on the bedside table." Her eyes shone. "Do you think that means anything?"

"Only that our squatter searched around for food before he fell asleep. He must not have been that drunk, then."

"Or he knew what was there. It's not one of those

fancy tins. It was plain and could easily be over-looked." Rachel shook her head. "I wish I was more helpful."

"Think of the dust. You're more helpful than you realize. You're also one of the bright spots in my trade, Rachel Smith."

She laughed shakily. "And not a bad nurse? I think we will keep your wound covered with salve for one more day."

Zane nodded. Odd that they had managed to survive the shooting at the crib with only his slight injury. Even now, thinking of how differently things could have turned out sent a shiver through him.

Thank You, Lord.

He'd started an investigation immediately. Zane didn't think the bartender would offer anything to him, so this morning he'd sent the deputy to ask people around the saloon if they'd seen anyone lurking around Rosa's crib the night before.

It left him alone here with Rachel.

His heart leaped at the thought.

No, it was not appropriate. Just like yesterday. Back there in the crib, after the shots and after the shooter had left, when the mood had shifted, Rachel had asked to be held, a request he'd never expected from her. And he'd obliged. Willingly. Even now, the memory of holding her in his arms rushed through him like a hot summer breeze. He'd liked the feel of her. She was tall and slender, with light, lithe curves. Rachel had a fragile feel to her, like she needed to be protected.

He'd seen her up close, too, her blue eyes and long, luxurious dark hair. Yes, she kept it well under control, but he knew it would have to be long and wavy

to do all the artistic things she had going on under
that small, neat little hat. After he'd thrust her to the
floorboards and after she'd helped him up, he'd noticed that some of those rich black waves had escaped
and tumbled down her slender neck.

Her skin was clear, pale and creamy, tempting him
to brush his hands along her cheeks before he cupped
her jaw and dared to take the kiss he'd wanted since
yesterday morning beside the bandstand.

Zane stood and reached for Rachel. She looked up
at him, not pulling away. They stood for a moment,
staring at each other, Zane searching Rachel's face,
yet not knowing what he was looking for.

Suddenly, he didn't care about anything but holding her. His eyes drifted shut as he lowered his mouth
to hers.

"Puppy!"

Rachel jumped and quickly stepped out of Zane's
embrace. Her attention immediately fell on Daniel.
He had crawled back up onto the chair she'd plunked
him into when they'd first entered the office, and was
now twisted around in it and pointing out the window.

Glancing outside, she saw a number of people, with
one hurrying by, his head down and mostly hidden by
his battered bowler hat. Beyond him, far in the distance, was a dog, but it wasn't the one from behind the
saloon who'd birthed puppies. Still, to a small child,
all dogs probably looked the same. She looked down at
Daniel, who peered up with expectation on his expression. He banged the toy truck on the back of the chair.

"What does he want?"

"The puppies, I guess," Rachel answered with a

shrug. "I should take him to visit them. I think the mother has them hidden at the end of the cribs or behind the haberdashery. There are a number of bushes and small sheds there."

"Will the mother let you near them?"

"Yes. I've even petted her before. I'll bring her a few bones from our kitchen."

"There must be one puppy in particular he likes," Zane commented. "He keeps asking for just 'puppy.'"

"Either that or he doesn't know the difference. He's only two and a few months. The pastor's wife once said that boys sometimes take longer to learn to speak than girls."

"Women have a lifetime of things to say. May as well get started early on it."

She smiled at him. "Don't insult your nurse, Sheriff. I have access to stinging medications."

Zane laughed and the bold heartiness of it caught in Rachel's breath. She hadn't heard it before now, and it was rich and full. A woman could listen to it for hours.

She cleared her throat. "Well," she said. "I think we will walk over and see if we can find the puppies."

"Don't go back to the cribs, Rachel."

"Now or tonight?"

"Neither." His expression darkened. "Not until we've found Alex and the investigation is closed."

Rachel ran a nervous tongue over her dry lips. If she did as he asked, what would that say about her ministry? That she was willing to discard it for a man who had nearly kissed her? What did that say about her?

"If you won't do it for me," he added, "think of Daniel."

Rachel shut her eyes. She had planned to go. Jake was supposed to be her escort tonight, but that had been arranged weeks ago. He was in no state to escort her.

Daniel needed caring for, too, and until she could arrange for a nanny, her maid had been assigned the bulk of that task. But the girl split her time between Rachel and Victoria already. Besides, Rachel thought as she looked down at the boy watching expectantly out the window, she had started to enjoy having Daniel around.

So, was going out the wisest thing to do? Before tonight, Rachel had answered to no one, and oddly, she now felt as though she answered to one small child. Daniel had had enough dangerous living, for his mother's lifestyle wasn't the kind that offered safety and she was all he had. Rachel never even asked who or where the boy's father was. The least she could do was give Daniel a safe life until Rosa returned.

But what if Rosa had kidnapped Alex and simply returned to take Daniel back, without a care for Alex? Could Rachel refuse to surrender him?

She was getting ahead of herself. Surely, Rosa was a victim, too. She had endured so much, with her mother's unsolved murder and her own father mostly absent from her life. Rachel wasn't sure she could deny the woman her only family, regardless of her faults.

"Rachel?" Zane prompted her.

She pulled herself from her private questions. Zane was watching her closely, hopefully, and Rachel felt a powerful desire to do what he asked. But was she going to stay away from the cribs for Daniel, or for Zane? Daniel needed her. How did Zane fit into this?

Her heart thudded in her chest. What about her life's work? Was it no longer important? She swallowed, hating herself for her questions.

Finally, Rachel nodded. "All right. Just for a few days." Her words gripped her, but as she glanced out the window at the cold day that warned of more snow, something else clutched at her insides, something that chilled her more than the fear of discarding her life's mission.

What was it?

Chapter Twenty-One

"Puppy! Poppy!"

"I should take him there now, before he gets too tired and cranky." Rachel found Daniel's small mittens on the floor under the desk. He must have grabbed them and tossed them down. Now, where was his hat?

"Here." Zane handed it to her as if reading her mind. She lifted her gaze to his face to thank him and got lost for a moment in his warm, dark eyes.

Glancing away, she quickly bundled up Daniel, then tugged on her own gloves.

"I'll walk you over."

"There's no need. Perhaps—"

"It's early. No one will be up, Rachel. No one will suspect that you are friends with the sheriff. We've already been seen together and have explained that we're still looking for Rosa."

Biting her bottom lip, Rachel acquiesced with a slight nod. "I suppose. I didn't go there last night, though."

"What did you tell your escort?"

"Jake was supposed to be it. Tonight, also, but obviously, that's not going to happen." She offered him an aimless shrug. "I didn't want to go out. Not after what happened at the crib."

She turned away, feeling her eyes prick with tears. She hadn't taken a Monday evening off in five years, except shortly after Abernathy had tried to kill her. Last night, after toying with the idea of checking up on Zane, she'd chosen to spend her time with Daniel. Whatever had caused his fever had left him, and he'd played with Rachel until he began to whine and she realized he was tired.

She'd loved the evening. She'd read to him, held him, brushed his curls until he'd fallen asleep, and even after that, she'd sat in the lamplight and watched him. At twenty-five, she wasn't too old for children, but with no suitors waiting for her, her time to settle down and have a family was ticking away slowly. Yet, with each moment last night, she'd felt the desire for children swell and grow.

A gentle finger lifted her chin and she glanced up to find Zane raising her head to face him. He searched her expression. "Does it bother you?"

"Not going out? No. But knowing that fact bothers me."

"Why?"

She swallowed. "I've been at this ministry for five years, and in that time more things have gone wrong than right. The only encouragement I received was from Rosa, and now she's involved in Alex's kidnapping. Now I can't feel the same energy and purpose pushing me forward every night. I'm actually agreeing to stay away entirely for a few days. What have I done wrong?"

"Sometimes you can do everything right and still not win."

She shut her eyes and sighed. It felt good to have him close and caring. His hand slid to cup her chin, his thumb to brush her cheek. Rachel wanted to lean into it, to gain strength from him.

He needed strength, too. He needed to know he could go back and fight to redeem his honor. Except with her feeling her own strength sapping away, she wasn't the one who could help him realize that.

Her heart ached as she stepped away from him.

"If we're going to find that dog, we need to go now."

A slight frown marred his expression as he nodded briefly. A short while later, with Zane carrying Daniel, they found the mother dog. The puppies, more friendly than expected, welcomed them with short, wagging tails and sweet yips. The mother, used to people, especially Rachel, lounged nearby.

"See, Daniel," Rachel said. "Puppies."

He looked up at her, then looked around in bewilderment. "Poppy?"

"No, puppies. More than one." She pointed to all the little dogs. "Puppies."

Daniel made a face. For some reason, he clung to Rachel, all the while watching the dogs with confusion. When she encouraged him to step forward, he grabbed her skirt and held back. "I don't understand," she said to Zane. "He's been asking to see them for days."

"Now that he has his wish, he doesn't want it anymore," Zane commented. "Maybe he was just telling you about the dogs."

"That must be it. But why keep telling me if he didn't want to see them?" She shook her head. "Children. I guess I'm not meant to be a mother."

"Why do you say that? I think you'd make a good mother."

"You think so?" She felt herself beaming at his words.

"No one really knows until they become one." He paused. "Where is Daniel's father?"

"I don't know anything about him and I've never asked. I think Rosa is ashamed of the fact she had a child out of wedlock."

"Does she see her own father much?"

"Not often. I've been told that he comes by sometimes, asking for money, but we haven't crossed paths in years." Rachel felt a spark of something ignite inside of her and her gaze dashed over to Daniel. The child chose that moment to drop to the thin layer of snow and howl for some reason Rachel couldn't fathom. "He's getting tired," she said. "I should take him home."

"I'll walk you there. Rachel?"

She scooped up Daniel. "Yes?"

"Don't think it's too late for yourself."

Her heart jolted. "For children? I don't even have a beau." She tried to lighten the mood. "Are you volunteering?"

His expression darkened. "You wouldn't want me." He took the toddler from her and began to walk out toward the street.

Following him, Rachel watched his stiff back as the grouchy Daniel wriggled in his arms. Zane would make a wonderful father. A real papa. A pappy.

Poppy? Was that what Daniel was trying to say?
She slowed her pace. Her heart chilled.

The next morning, a Wednesday, Rachel weighed
heavily on Zane's mind as he alit from the train. To his
left, the Castle Rock butte jutted up above the depot.
He'd chosen the train over riding down here, thinking
of his side. No need to constantly jar it.

To his right was a large building, one that housed
the local printer, the newspaper and a small store
whose wares were of more interest to tradesmen than
ladies.

It was Rachel's words on stone masonry that had
brought him here. The fine dust on Daniel's clothing
was most likely rhyolite, mined within view of Castle
Rock and the printer of the postcards, which he now
had tucked in his coat's breast pocket. That couldn't
be just a coincidence.

He stopped in front of the printer's shop. It was
logical to start here, the origin of those postcards that
were so intrinsically tied to the case. How they had
ended up in Proud Bend was still unknown, but if
they were printed here, Zane reasoned as he looked
up at the sign above the door, the printer would have
a record of whomever had bought them. Perhaps the
answer to that question would also explain why Alex
had kept one of the cards.

Zane pushed open the door and stepped inside. The
smell of metal and ink filled his nostrils. A rhythmic
smack and grind told him one of the presses in the
back was working. He walked up to the counter as a
man wearing a well-stained leather apron approached.

His sleeves were gartered and protected and atop his head was a snug cap. "Can I help you?" he asked.

After introducing himself as the sheriff of Proud Bend, Zane pulled out the postcards and pressed them onto the wooden counter, keeping the pictures face up. "Do you recognize these?"

The man gave them only a cursory glance. "Yes. If you turn around, you'll see it's the view from this very shop."

Taking back the cards, Zane walked to the window. He compared the view to the cards. They were almost identical.

He turned back. "But these cards are obviously stylized."

"Who wants to see all that scaffolding junk the mine has up there?" the printer asked. "It's a vicious circle."

"What do you mean?"

"For years, we needed the mine to keep the town alive. The mine needed that awful scaffolding, which makes for an ugly sight that obscures the view that visitors and new arrivals alike would see when they first arrive. The mine as it looks now would never attract tourists."

"Tourists? Out here?"

"The weather is good for the health, some say." The printer shrugged. "So, I had an artist remove all that junk and give me a nice picture I could sell and show tourists what this town *should* look like."

"So you print these postcards and sell them from here?"

"Yes, I print them here, but I sell them to local businesses."

"Any customers in Proud Bend?"

The printer shook his head. "No. Wait a minute. Let me see those postcards again."

Zane returned to the counter. The printer dug out a magnifying glass and studied them. "I had a break-in a month ago and these postcards were among the items stolen."

"They're an odd thing to steal."

"More a crime of opportunity, I'd say. I had some sitting on the counter above the cash box. These two were part of that stack."

"Are you sure?"

"Yes. I had smeared the artist's signature, and felt they weren't good enough to sell. That's why that stack was separate."

"What else was stolen?"

"Some ink and a few printing tools. But I believe the reason I had the break-in was because I'm usually paid that day by the newspaper and keep the money in my safe to pay my early workers the next morning. I used to keep the cash in the cash box. Maybe the thief didn't know that I have a safe now, because the cash box was busted open."

"So, money wasn't stolen?"

"Actually, I wasn't paid that day because the bank closed early, and the newspaper's paymaster didn't get to it in time. Seems the bank employees here wanted to attend the funeral of the bank owner in Proud Bend."

That fact would be easy to check. Rachel would know the date of her father's funeral, and Zane had read in a file that Clyde Abernathy had had no funeral, having died in a prison in Denver awaiting trial.

"Why do you wait for the newspaper's paymaster?"

"The newspaper is my main client. From that money, I can usually pay all my employees."

Zane nodded. "So that night, someone broke in, expecting to find cash?"

"They tried to get into the safe, but couldn't. Nor could they take the safe away with them. I recently had it attached to the floor."

"Who noticed the break-in?"

"The night watchman reported it during his ten-o'clock rounds. Now, before you ask, the sheriff checked on my employees, but everyone had an alibi. It wasn't a bank employee, either, because they all traveled back together from Proud Bend, and got back quite late. Besides, they would know there was no money that day."

"So who else knew the money was usually there?"

"I've employed a few men now and again for extra help, just some miners whose mines have dried up. I get them to do the lifting because they're used to hard work. But they come and go as their fortunes see fit. Although—" the printer looked reflective "—there is one who always seems to be looking for work more than others, so I hire him more often."

"Would he know when everyone gets paid?"

"Oh, yes. Everyone is paid the same day, just at different times, depending on when his shift starts. He would know when the paymaster from the news-paper shows up. Come to think of it, the last time I hired him, I hadn't bought the safe yet and only had the cash box."

Zane lifted one of the postcards. "Are you sure these are two of the stack stolen?"

"Absolutely. I'd put them on the counter above the

safe. I think whoever it was just grabbed whatever he could find, once he realized he wasn't going to get any money. I lost a whole tray of metal printing blocks, too. I expect they'll be melted down and sold as scrap."

Zane's attention pricked. "Metal blocks? Like the ones with letters on them?"

"Yes." The printer dug through something behind his counter and produced a large block, twice the size of the one Zane had found in Daniel's pocket. "Like this but smaller. They had a different typeface than this. This one is serif, which means it has little wings on the ends of each line that makes up a letter. It's the most popular style. I wasn't using the blocks that were stolen anymore, so I had put them in a tray beside the postcards. I suspect that was why they were taken. They were the easiest thing to grab."

"What could they end up doing with the blocks? Is there another printing press here in Castle Rock?"

"No. The closest is Denver. Those blocks are in an old-fashioned typeface, so I can't imagine anyone wanting to use them. The thief will have to melt them down and sell them as scrap metal. That's what I had planned to do."

Zane had asked the blacksmith next door to the sheriff's office to change the lock on Rosa's crib door. He'd been willing, boasting that he could do just about anything. Making a mental note to speak with the man tomorrow about someone looking to melt down any blocks, Zane thanked the printer for his time and left.

The postcards had been stolen and the bartender was selling them under the table for a bit of extra cash. That didn't reflect well on the bartender, but it didn't necessarily make him a suspect, because the postcard used as the ransom note could have been stolen from the saloon. Or even bought.

What about the blocks? How would one go from the thief's hands to a child's pocket? Or to the bedding in a soiled dove's crib? The whole tray was missing, the printer said. Zane noticed a tray of letter blocks sitting back near the press. It would be too heavy for a woman to cart away, assuming Rosa had been the thief.

Zane adjusted the brim of his Stetson. The sun, being low in the sky as expected in December, already shone almost perpendicular to the south-facing wall. Which meant that the east wall glinted with oblique rays. Glinted almost pink.

Rhyolite. Zane stooped and looked at the clumps of soil and dead grass that peppered the corner where the building met the ground. This soil was pale, but the stonework wasn't dusty at all. He brushed his knee against it and then inspected it. No transfer of stone dust. But a mine would see much more.

"Is there a problem?"

Looking up, Zane found the printer standing near the open door. "Is this stone rhyolite?" he asked the man.

"Yes. It's common, but not cheap. We here in Castle Rock only use it for the best buildings."

Zane glanced up the height and breadth of the building. "Even this one?"

The printer lifted his shoulders once. "This used to be a rhyolite mill, a place to carve the best stone for the best facades. It's logical to use your own building as advertising, but the mill has been closed for years."

"Your shop is clean inside. You've removed all traces of stone dust."

"Of course. I can't do a decent job printing otherwise."

Which meant that Daniel couldn't have been in there.

Just follow the facts, Zane told himself. He glanced around, stepping back enough to catch the top edge of White Horse Bluff. It wasn't that far as a bird might fly. "Where can I find the rhyolite mine?"

"There are a number of them."

"Which is the closest?" Zane was working on a hunch right now. Rachel had thought the hands that had grabbed the boots in Rosa's crib were old. And an old miner wouldn't want to travel too far to find work when he had been laid off.

"Well, Castle Rock has one, but was never the best source. The mine behind White Horse Bluff had the best rhyolite, though it's been closed for a few years."

That was interesting. "Is there a road to it?"

The printer nodded. "The trail to the bluff meets the road between Castle Rock and Proud Bend, about a mile north of here. There is a second trail sprouting from it not far in. It dips down so it's not as easy to spot at White Horse Bluff's trailhead, but if you look hard enough, you'll see it. It wraps around the hillside, because the mine entrance is behind the hill. You can't miss it, because you can still see the cart tracks. It's less than half an hour's walk around the hillside."

Encouraged, Zane thanked the man once again. Taken separately, each of these leads didn't feel like anything important. A break-in a month ago, a stolen printing block that mysteriously ends up in Daniel's possession, another in a soiled dove's crib, and a suspected casual miner who might have worked near where the ransom was to be dropped off.

Taken together, these leads were far more powerful. Rachel would like this.

Zane had no intention of telling her. She had a curious ability to attract trouble.

"One more question," Zane said. "Can you give me a description of that one miner who you hired so many times?"

"I can do better than that." The printer retreated into his shop and returned a few minutes later with a photograph. "This is my staff on our one-year anniversary." Slipping on a pair of spectacles, he peered down at the photo before pointing to an older man in the back row. "This is him."

It was all starting to make sense. "May I borrow this?"

"Certainly. Turn it over. The man's name is listed on the back with all the others."

Five minutes later and armed with a decent description, Zane was on his way to White Horse Bluff. There was plenty of light left, despite the short winter day, but Zane didn't want to waste the time. Thankfully, the printer was able to arrange for him to borrow a horse. Pressing his elbow against his revolver, Zane also reminded himself to remove it from the holster as soon as he dismounted.

Rachel had been right when she'd warned that riding would bother his wound. But forcing himself to relax eased the pain.

Sunshine brought a new look to White Horse Bluff. As he approached it, Zane studied the distinct outline— that of a horse's head. He recalled how, against his explicit instructions, Rachel had had the gall to come up in the deep of night to pay the ransom.

In a way, he couldn't blame her. He was anxious for this nightmare to end, too. Even now, the temptation to pay the ransom and hopefully see the return of his brother hovered just under the surface, always there reminding him of that option.

But give in to Rosa and her accomplice? Wouldn't that be like giving in to those who'd framed him?

You already have. You left with your tail between your legs.

Swallowing back bitter bile, Zane urged his horse faster as he put the bluff over his left shoulder. The trail up to the top was ahead, and he soon spied the side shoot of the other trail that the printer had described. He carefully tucked his jacket behind his revolver.

Time to end this nightmare.

But he wasn't about to ride in with gun a blazing. He was one man, with no clear picture of what he was about to face. He needed to scout out the area first. At a spot close to the trailhead, Zane quickly dismounted and hid the borrowed mount behind some larger sagebrush. With an encouraging pat, Zane left the gelding and began a quiet advance on the mine.

A short, soft nicker ahead stopped Zane. With the wind blowing from his back, he knew another horse ahead had already smelled him.

And had recognized him.

He moved cautiously around several low bushes that, while bare of their leaves, were tangled enough to obscure him from whoever was ahead.

Then he saw her, frozen in her steps, having already interpreted her piebald's quiet hello.

Rachel stood at its flank, a small ladies' pistol pointed right at Zane's heart.

Chapter Twenty-Two

Rachel sagged as soon as he stepped forward. Immediately, Zane snatched her mother's pearl-handled pistol out of her grip, completely disarming her before she even had a chance to finish her sigh.

In the next instant, Zane had her pinned to his chest. Her horse sidestepped the whole event, skittish at Zane's unexpected move. Rachel cried out.

"Hush, woman," he hissed, "or I'll gag you! I don't want to be shot twice in one week."

"I wouldn't have! Zane, you scared me, that's all."

"Oh, yes, no one has ever fired off a pistol after being scared."

His sarcasm was the least of her worries. She tilted up her head. "Let me go. You're hurting me."

He released her. "What are you doing here?"

She turned and began to unfasten a bag from her saddle. "I'm going to confront Rosa."

He shoved his hands onto his hips, pushing aside the twinge of pain at his ribs. "How do you know she's here?"

"I put the leads together and this is the only logical place she could be."

"How did you figure that out?"

"Yesterday, after we saw the puppies, it occurred to me that Daniel hasn't been talking about dogs, but telling me where his mother was. That's why he kept saying the singular 'puppy.'"

Zane frowned. "I don't understand."

"He wasn't saying 'puppy.' He was saying 'Poppy.'"

Not making any connection to the mine, Zane gaped at Rachel. As she continued her task of removing the bag she'd brought with her, she explained, "*Poppy* is a nickname for *grandfather*. I couldn't figure it out until after I put Daniel down for a nap. A man had walked by the sheriff's office, heading to the blacksmith's shop. I remember having the feeling that I was missing something."

"You recognized him?"

"Not at first, but I think it was Rosa's father. I haven't seen him in years, though. I think he's Rosa's accomplice. It's the only thing that makes sense. I believe Daniel saw him and that was why he called out 'Poppy.' I think his grandfather was our squatter, and yesterday he strolled by because he was following Daniel."

"So why look for him here?"

"Rosa's father is a miner, hence the rhyolite on Daniel's clothes and on the squatter's boots. My father's map noted the major mines in the area. Father had always wanted to acquire mineral rights, so his map would show places known to contain large deposits. But it's an old map, so I expected this mine to be exhausted, which would make it perfect as a hideout."

She watched as Zane slowly nodded. Then he

pointed to the horse. "You're just going to leave your horse here for all to see?"

"I had planned to hide her. I've ordered a carriage to meet us where White Horse Bluff's trail meets the road, so that if I do get Alex, I can get him home." She studied Zane. "How did you know where to come?"

"I found the postcard's printer. It was the bartender acting suspiciously that made me wonder if I should be following up on that lead. Daniel had a printer's block, and the printer confirmed that his shop had been broken into a while back and a stack of post-cards, plus a set of printer's blocks, were stolen. He mentioned that he's occasionally hired a few miners to help him. All separately, those leads mean nothing, but put them together and I could see a whole picture forming. The building used to be a rhyolite mill. It no longer had enough rhyolite dust to have transferred to Daniel's clothes, but a mine might, even one that has been abandoned. When the printer told me the near-est mine was behind White Horse Bluff, I knew that they'd chosen a drop-off for the money close to their hideout. It was starting to make sense, then."

Zane pulled out the photograph the printer had given him. He showed it to Rachel. "Can you find Rosa's father in this?"

After scanning it, Rachel pointed to the older man at the end of the back row. "That's him. I'm sure of it." She continued to unhook the bag.

"That better not be the ransom money."

"It's not. It's medical supplies and food."

At his quizzical look, she explained. "Alex could be injured and most likely hungry and thirsty. You'll need me to help you with him."

"But you were planning to do this on your own."

"Not quite. They want money, I want Alex. I've withdrawn the money again from the bank and left it with someone I trust in Proud Bend. If I don't come back alive and well, they return the money to the bank. I'll remind Rosa and her father that I have custody of Daniel. If I'm injured in any way, or killed, what will happen to him? I've contacted my solicitor and he's begun to draft up papers that will state my mother gets custody of Daniel if I die. I'm counting on Rosa wanting her son back."

"What if she doesn't?"

"She will. I know how she is around Daniel. She'll want him back, which means she'll have to let Alex go."

"And the money?"

"Her father may not see it quite the same way. The money is for him. But only if I get Alex back to Proud Bend first."

"That's blackmail."

"No, it's simply a switch with insurance. Rosa knows I will care for Daniel. That's why the ransom note was addressed to me and why Daniel was delivered to the cribs when I would be there. She won't risk him."

"Who is to say she won't decide to hold *you* for ransom? Your mother would pay handsomely for you."

"Yes, she would, but Rosa believes my mother will rid herself of Daniel if I'm not there to defend him. Remember that Rosa doesn't think my mother approves of my ministry."

"She doesn't."

"Not openly, no. But I know my mother will take

care of Daniel. Rosa doesn't know that, though. In fact, very few people know how much Mother has helped me out in this ministry and no one knows how my mother has decided to care for Daniel even now." She touched Zane, her stare strong and determined. "I can save Alex. Trust me."

Could he? Zane's heart leaped into his throat at her last two words. There was no perfect plan here. Each suggestion that ran through his head had some element of risk. But Rachel was here, ready to help, ready to use all her experience with Rosa to save Alex. She was ready to fight. She was learning to push past the doubt and fears.

It was time for him to fight, too.

He nodded and held up her small pistol as she hefted her bag. "You said you'd never even held a gun before."

"This morning, Mother showed me what she'd been taught. I actually fired it and hit a tree down by the river."

"I hope you were aiming for it." He handed the pistol back to her. She quickly hid it in a small concealed pocket where her jacket flared out. It made for easy access, he noted.

"I can't believe your mother allowed you to come here."

"She knew she had no choice. Once she knew she couldn't convince me to stay, she decided that I needed to be armed." Rachel blinked at him, and Zane suddenly recalled the expression *butter wouldn't melt in her mouth*. Yes, Rachel was that cool and calm.

"Ready?" she asked primly.

He nodded. "Just a couple of things."

"Such as?"

"Don't you think you should have that pistol more accessible?"

"No." She adjusted her bag. "Rosa should see me as she always does. Unarmed."

Zane coughed out a laugh of disbelief. "If you think I'm going to let you just stroll down there by yourself, you don't know me as well as you think you do."

"That was my plan before you caught me. I now expect you to be very close, but hidden." She set down the bag. After she opened it, she pulled out a small whale-oil lantern with a rounded globe. Lighting it took a moment. She then fastened the bag again and lifted both the bag and the lantern. "The oil doesn't make for good light, but it was all I could find at a moment's notice. It's probably a good idea to have less light, anyway, if you are to stay hidden. You'll be just out of the lamp's reach, but right behind me. Now, what was the other thing?"

"Are you going to tell Rosa you forgive her?"

Rachel stilled. "I want to forgive her for this." She sighed. "But it's hard."

"Did Rosa ever forgive you for your part in her mother's death?"

Rachel paled. "She always said that I wasn't responsible, even though I always thought that I was."

"So you're saying that what you did was unforgivable? That you are unforgivable? That's rather arrogant, deciding that for everyone."

"No!" Her eyes flared. "How can you say that? I'm not arrogant at all!"

"Then what makes you think you can devalue God's

grace? And the forgiveness of others? What makes your sin unforgivable but not the sins of others?"

Her eyes watered and she blinked. The bright but waning sun glinted off the thin layer of snow the scrubland around them had received, adding to the pallor of her expression.

Zane knew then that they both needed to hear his words. He'd learned last week about sin and forgiveness and trust in God. "You say your sin is the worst, but I say that it's no worse than anyone else's. Rachel, what makes it disgraceful is that you can't forgive yourself. There's a difference between knowing you've sinned and feeling so awful about yourself that you can't forgive yourself. You need to acknowledge your sin while also accepting God's grace so you can try to be a better person. You need to forgive yourself and move forward. Forgiving someone frees you more than the person you're forgiving. Forgiving yourself even more so."

Rachel lifted her chin.

"You need to trust that God can and will forgive the one who is truly repentant," he added softly. "Can you trust Him?"

"Yes," she whispered. "You're right. If God can forgive me, I shouldn't try to tell Him I'm not worth it. Yes, I need to forgive myself."

Zane cradled her face in his hands and kissed her soundly. He lifted his head far too soon. He wanted to hold her, keep her safe while she fully sorted out all he'd told her. He wanted her to know she was forgivable. Lovable.

He swallowed. His own advice hit him hard in a powerful, piercing way.

* * *

Searching his face, Rachel knew she had to say this. "And you, Zane? Can you forgive yourself for what has happened to Alex? Regardless of what we might find in that mine? I think you feel badly that he's been kidnapped while you, the defiant one, have escaped danger. You think it should be you in that mine because of the sins of your youth. It's stolen your fight."

"But you built it back up."

"What do you mean?"

He paused, then stood stiffly. "I'm going back to Canaan when this is all done. I'm going to clear my name." He looked grim. "We'll talk about this later."

Later? She didn't want to hear any more of it. His words sank like a cold stone inside of her. He was leaving, and if all went well and Alex was safe, he would be leaving sooner than later.

How selfish of her to be upset about that. They'd have Alex safe. They'd have answers to who was helping Rosa and why she was doing this, and all would return to normal in Proud Bend.

Not quite normal. Rachel's breath caught in her throat. Though the town would have its sheriff back and Rachel would return to her ministry, it wouldn't feel normal at all. It would feel lonely.

She straightened. She needed to be strong for when that day would come.

It hurt.

Zane moved her horse behind a large sagebrush and rock, hiding the beast. Then, returning, he led the way. They found the mine opening. As they stepped in the maw, the wind, which had begun to gust, died away, offering a pocket of warmth that Rachel needed.

She peered in, holding her lantern high. Since rhyolite was often mined from open pits, this short opening had probably been carved out to search for other minerals.

Stooping, Zane stepped gingerly in ahead of her, and against the mine wall. Rachel held her breath, knowing he was trying to find a way to both protect her and stay hidden.

Tears formed, blurring her vision. She wanted this day to end, but she also wanted Zane to promise her that he wouldn't leave right away. It was a selfish thought, but the more she tried to push it away, the stronger it seemed to latch on to her.

Finally, she couldn't stand it any longer. She grabbed his arm and whispered, "Zane, before we go any farther, can I ask you something?"

He stopped and faced her. But the answer didn't come from him. A noise cut the still, cold air. They both spun to face deeper down the shaft from where the sound originated.

Zane looked from the depths back to her face, his expression perplexed. She knew he wanted to hear her question and yet wanted to find his brother as fast as they could.

But her heart's desire meant nothing against Alex's safety. "Never mind. Time to go," she whispered with false briskness. Keeping the lantern in front to guide her steps on the uneven rock floor, Rachel moved downward, deeper into the mine. The air warmed as she descended, and grew stale. Her route was careful, and she wished she had a free hand to lift her skirt. Still, this way, her progress was slow and quiet. She could feel Zane's silent presence close to her.

She tried not to breathe deeply, afraid the air was contaminated. The floor turned slick despite the dry air. Rachel tossed an anxious look behind her.

Still stooping, Zane stepped into her circle of light. "I'll lead the way, but stay as far back as possible," he whispered. "Remember, if there is anyone down here, their eyes will have already adjusted to the lack of light, giving them an advantage over us."

Rachel nodded. As they moved painfully slowly, she noticed a warm, yellowy glow ahead, exaggerating each cut and crag of the damp walls. No sounds, just the gentle wobble of light that told Rachel a basic lantern was lit somewhere beyond the next bend. Zane stayed out of sight.

She could smell moisture and now could hear the faint trickle of water coming from some small spring ahead. Even though this whole area was dry, the mine was not. It explained Daniel's damp clothes the night he'd returned with the ransom note.

Stepping around a small bend, Rachel peered into the small cavern ahead. Two battered wooden chairs stood back-to-back, and tied in the one facing Rachel was Alex, gagged, his head down, his shoulders slumped. She gasped.

At the noise, the occupant of the other chair came fully alert. Rachel tossed an incredulous look to Zane to make sure he also saw the whole shocking scene.

Chapter Twenty-Three

Rosa? Zane stepped out of the darkness, his jaw dropping as he spied her gagged and tied in the chair back-to-back with Alex's. How could this be?

Her eyes were wild and fearful in the dim light of the small miner's lantern set some feet away. Rachel hurried over to her to yank free the filthy cotton strip that bound her mouth. After holstering his gun, Zane moved straight to Alex, gently lifting his brother's head to peer anxiously into the face identical to his own. He quickly removed the gag.

Alex coughed softly, though his eyes remained closed. He obviously wasn't well, but he was alive. Zane sagged and sent a short prayer of thanks upward.

Rachel hurried over to examine Alex.

"He's drugged," Rosa cried out over her shoulder. "I'm sorry! I couldn't stop it. I couldn't fight back when he took Daniel, either. I was so scared he was going to hurt him!"

"Who was going to hurt him?" Zane asked.

"Never mind all that right now," Rachel snapped. "Help me untie Alex. We need to get him to a doctor."

Rachel carefully peeled away the thick twine that bound Alex's wrists. Zane winced. The wounds underneath must sting like fire-ant bites, for the cord had cut deeply into his skin. The length had also been tied to Alex's belt and, in disgust, Zane tore it away.

Still Alex didn't move. In fact, his head lolled farther forward. Rachel took it in her hands and brushed away the bits of fabric caught in the burr that was his growing beard. "He needs fresh air. Perhaps the cold will revive him?"

Zane slung his brother over his shoulder and heaved up to standing. His side burned with the strain on his wound. Rachel turned to Rosa. She hesitated for a moment.

"Untie her, Rachel," Zane urged her. She looked over her shoulder at him, her expression torn. With a nod, he encouraged her further. "She couldn't have tied herself up and I doubt Alex did it. Have some faith. You're strong enough to do this."

A small wobbly smile formed on her lips and pride shone in her eyes. She untied the woman quickly. With her basket handle looped over her left arm and that hand gripping the lantern, Rachel used her right arm to help the woman toward the entrance of the cavern. Rosa stumbled and Zane noticed that she was limping slightly.

"Are you hurt?" Zane asked her.

She pulled a face. "A bit. Pa kicked me in the thigh once, then tied my ankles so tight I still can't feel my feet."

"What's his name?" Zane demanded.

"Samuel Carrera."

"Come on, Rosa," Rachel said. "I'll help you. Walking will bring the blood back to your feet."

"I'm so sorry, Rachel," Rosa cried softly, stopping to cling to her. "About a month ago, after I prayed by myself for the first time, I knew I could no longer keep the secret I've carried for the last five years. I've always known it was Pa who assaulted and robbed you and, over the years, I couldn't help but be impressed at how you never gave up."

"You've known?"

Rosa nodded mutely, her eyes shining. Then as Zane turned away, she added, "Ma had sworn me to secrecy that night. She was scared. She'd witnessed what Pa did to you and Robert. She even tried to stop him, but my pa threatened her. Ma told me what happened 'cause she was going to find Pa to tell him to return the money and she wanted me to know in case something happened. But she said it was too dangerous to tell anyone else, so she begged me to keep quiet."

So Mrs. Turcot had been right, Zane thought grimly. Robert had seen Liza. "You knew she went to confront your father?"

Looking at Zane, Rosa nodded. "After he killed her, Pa disappeared for a while. About a year ago, he came back, threatening to hurt Daniel if I told anyone what I knew."

Zane shook his head. "He had all that money he'd stolen. Why didn't he just leave and never come back?"

"He couldn't go anywhere. He's wanted for murder down south, and I think he's getting too old to be moving around, trying to avoid the law. And he could never hold on to money for long—always drinking or gambling it away. He bullied me into giving him money every month."

That was it, Zane thought. He was in control of his daughter here, and living off her wages. No wonder she had nothing but the bare essentials in her crib. She couldn't afford anything more.

"But after I prayed like you'd taught me," Rosa went on, "and Pa came back one more time to remind me to keep quiet, I told him I couldn't live with it anymore. That's when he took Daniel."

Zane didn't want to waste time, not with Alex still unconscious. "Let's go," he growled.

They moved forward around the corner, the pace slow so that Zane could choose his footing well. As the shaft straightened out, Rachel asked, "How did your father know I had the money?"

"He'd come by once in a while, demanding money from my mother, but that one time, she let it slip that she'd just given it all to you. Oh, please forgive her, Rachel. She didn't think he would attack you!"

"She should never have approached him afterward to ask for the money back."

"Ma thought he'd never hurt her. She loved him."

"Where's your father now?" Zane demanded, hoping the man wasn't close by.

"I don't know!" Rosa looked at Rachel, her expression stricken. "He may have gone to find Daniel."

"So he cares for Daniel, but no one else in his family?" Rachel's tone held a sharp edge.

"He doesn't even care for him. He wants to kidnap him back so he can use him against me to keep me from turning him in. The only reason he released him last Saturday was because he was getting sick.

Pa didn't want to catch whatever Daniel had. That, and Daniel was an ideal way to get that ransom note to you."

"He used Daniel as leverage," Zane muttered as he readjusted his brother's deadweight. He shot Rachel a fast look to remind her that she had planned to do the same thing.

Catching the look, Rosa gripped Rachel. "Is Daniel all right? What were you going to do to him?"

"He's fine," Rachel answered crisply. "Doing very well, in fact. I'm sorry, Rosa. I thought you were working with your father willingly, and I wanted to use Daniel to force you to let me leave with Alex." She cleared her throat. "I'm as bad as your father."

"No, you're not. You were trying to save lives. Pa wants to cheat and steal and hurt. Oh, Rachel, I wish I knew where he was!"

"We saw him outside of the sheriff's office," Zane muttered through the pain in his side and the weight of his brother. "Even Daniel recognized him."

Rosa nodded. "He was going into Proud Bend to see the blacksmith. He said he had some metal to melt down and sell."

"The printer's blocks he'd stolen," Zane muttered, heaving up his brother to find a more comfortable position. "He broke into the printer's office to steal their money because he knew when the payroll was usually there. But when he couldn't get into the safe, he stole whatever he could get his hands on."

"How do you know that?" Rosa asked.

"I found a small printer's block in Daniel's pocket and in your bed. Your father squatted there the night before."

By now, his eyes adjusted to the dimness, Zane was able to turn around and see the women's faces clearly. Rachel's expression was pure concern, and yet, when she met his gaze with hers, she softened.

His heart lurched. If only…

"Pa gave a block to Daniel," Rosa continued. "He also forced me to tell him where I kept the key to my crib, so he had a place to sleep off a night of drinking. He would drug us when he wanted to go out for the evening. He'd smother our faces with a rag soaked in something sweet smelling."

Chloroform. This wasn't the first time the drug had been used in the execution of a crime. His jaw tight, he pushed upward, the incline mild but slippery and treacherous with the moisture from the spring somewhere in there. Rachel helped Rosa. Zane felt the incline tighten his legs as he carried his brother. When Rosa slipped, Zane knew he needed to leave Rachel behind to continue helping while he and Alex keep going. Alex needed air and attention, neither of which could be given where they were. He encouraged Rosa to keep going.

"Ma saw you get assaulted. She never forgave herself for letting it happen." Rosa kept talking. "She worked hard the next night to try to earn enough to pay everyone back."

Rachel shook her head. "She couldn't possibly earn enough in one night."

"No, but she managed to earn enough to pay back Alice. She was complaining the loudest. Ma realized she couldn't earn enough money to pay everyone back—not if she wanted to have enough to feed herself and pay the rent on her crib. She needed to speak to Pa."

"I know," Rachel said. "She came to see me the day after I was assaulted. I was still recuperating, but she seemed certain she knew my attacker."

"Pa knows he could still be tried for the crime, Rachel," Rosa moaned. Zane could hear them close behind. The long shadows caused by the lantern in Rachel's hand made every crevice in the mine floor look deep and treacherous, and he chose his steps carefully. He could barely do that and listen at the same time.

"Yes, there's no statute of limitations on that type of assault," Rachel answered. "Not to mention what he did to your mother."

Zane paused, taking the moment to catch his breath. "Rosa, did you give Rachel money, too?"

Rosa shook her head. "Only a little. I didn't have much. But I don't care about the money. I've been thinking about all you've said about confessing your sins and being forgiven, so when I decided to pray, I knew that I had to tell Sheriff Robinson the truth. Then Pa came by, throwing his weight around and twirling that pistol he owed. It was to remind me to keep my mouth shut. He must have heard that Rachel had been talking to me and that I was starting to listen."

"When did he kidnap you?" Zane asked.

Rosa nodded. "It was early in the morning just as the sun was rising. I was already up with Daniel when he dropped by. He took Daniel first, while I was dressing and Daniel was out on the stoop. He drugged him and put him in a cart under a cloth. When I tried to stop him, he did the same to me." She sobbed. "He kept me tied up until I well and truly knew he would kill Daniel if I didn't do as he said."

Zane started to move again.

Rosa followed, all the while her words spilling from her. "Then Sheriff Robinson showed up looking for me and Pa knocked him out."

They all stopped. "How did Alex know where to find you?" Rachel asked.

"I don't know, but Pa knew he needed to change his plans. That's when he decided to send Daniel back to you, Rachel, asking for ransom money for us both. He was getting sick being in this mine. Pa knew you would pay for our release. He boasted that with the money, he'd have enough to escape to Mexico, where no one would find him."

Zane listened carefully to Rosa's confession. Far up ahead, daylight lit the tunnel, a small circle of brilliance offering fresh air. Thankfully, the extra light helped with his careful steps.

They continued to climb. "Does your father realize there are two Sheriff Robinsons?" Rachel asked.

"Yes, he saw him when he delivered Daniel and the ransom note. When he came back, he was furious, saying he'd seen another Sheriff Robinson. He laid a beating into the sheriff, demanding to know what had happened. The next night, he sent me to get the money, saying that if I didn't come back, he'd kill the sheriff. I couldn't let that happen! Oh, Rachel, I know how guilty you feel! It's terrible, isn't it?"

"I've learned a lot about guilt, Rosa," Rachel muttered. She helped Rosa come up beside Zane. Only a few more feet and they'd be free of this mine. The air already smelled fresh and cold, and would hopefully revive his brother. "We have a photograph of your father. We'll stop him easily enough."

"Not as easily as I am going to stop all of you."

Zane's head snapped up. Stepping into the mine entrance not more than two feet away was a man, his frame silhouetted against the bright light of the maw. Zane couldn't see his face, but he knew one thing.

The man had a rifle pointed right at him.

Chapter Twenty-Four

Rosa stepped out of Rachel's supportive embrace. "Pa, even you can't kill all of us."

"Oh, yes, I can, girl, so shut up," Carrera snapped.

Zane eased his unconscious brother to the stone beneath their feet. He'd be able to defend himself more effectively with his hands free. And if necessary, he would fall on him to protect Alex from getting shot. One thing was certain, though. He wouldn't be able to free his revolver before Carrera had a chance to fire.

Then it happened. Rachel shoved Rosa to the right, causing her father to hesitate momentarily, not knowing which way to point his rifle. In those few seconds, Rachel swung the lantern to clock him along the side of his head. Thankfully, the oil remained in the reservoir, but the unprotected globe broke and the flame flared outward for a second, blinding Carrera.

Fearful of getting burned, Carrera raised his arm to protect his face. Rachel let go of the lantern as it flew by his head, and in the same swift motion, dropped her basket and wrenched the rifle from his grip.

Zane leaped forward. With one sharp uppercut,

he subdued the man. Carrera slumped to the stone, unconscious. While he was out, Zane quickly hand-cuffed him.

Rachel set the lantern aright. "That cart I ordered should be down at the road by now. I'll get my horse so we can take Alex to it."

She was gone only a few minutes before return-ing with her piebald. Zane slung Alex over the side-saddle, wincing when he realized the ladies' pommel was probably digging into Alex's stomach. Carrera was beginning to stir, but Rachel and Rosa had used the cord that had remained around Rosa's waist to tie her father to the horse, forcing him to walk or risk get-ting dragged. He stumbled as he stood.

Rachel's groom was waiting beside the carriage and hurried up as soon as he spotted them. Together, he and Zane eased Alex down across the carriage's seat. With the rope from his waist, they secured Car-rera's ankles to his manacled wrists through the back of his belt and twisted him in the carriage, as well. He lay uncomfortably on the tiny floor space, his front arched due to the short rope. Wisely, the groom pulled a handkerchief from his pocket and blindfolded the older man. "Just for extra insurance," he said. "He won't try anything if he can't see."

Zane nodded. "Get my brother to the doctor and this man to my deputy for arrest on murder, assault and kidnapping. Tell my deputy that I want him in a cell by the time I get back. Then take Rosa to Rachel's house to see her son. In that order."

Rosa beamed. She scrambled up beside the driver and the carriage rumbled away. Zane turned to Rachel and bent down to help her mount. "Follow them. I'll get my horse and catch up."

When Zane had returned to the trailhead with his borrowed horse, he found Rachel still waiting there. "I couldn't leave you." Her smile was wobbly as she shrugged.

His heart leaped, but he suddenly realized that their lives weren't going to end happily ever after. In fact, he recalled with another sudden lurch of his heart that, with Alex safe now, there was no reason to stick around. He no longer had a job, and, as much as the idea of spending time with Rachel appealed to him, he had nothing to offer her. He was simply a discharged sheriff with an unsavory past and no future.

He swallowed. Rachel might not be able to leave him, though. That meant he had to leave her.

The trip into Proud Bend was silent. Rachel sensed Zane's reticence as his horse trotted beside hers. What was he thinking? She hated how fear curbed her desire to question him.

Yet she clung to the foolish idea that as long as they rode on, not saying a word, as long as Proud Bend remained in the distance, barely lit in the dying daylight, the future remained open. Anything could happen.

But that anything might not be good.

When they reached town, Zane said curtly, "I'll meet you at your house. I'm going to check on Alex and then make sure Carrera is locked up."

"Let me come with you to check on Alex."

"No. He's my brother, and you need to see to Rosa and Daniel." He galloped off.

Dejected, Rachel returned home. Louise met her

on the stairs, her face tight with disapproval. "That woman, Rosa, has taken her son. I don't dare think where they are headed, but it can't be any place suitable for the boy. He needs a good home, and I have already ordered cook to buy more milk for him."

Rachel didn't feel like dealing with her mother, not while her mind remained on Zane. "You barely noticed him here, Mother. So why the concern?"

"It's not that at all. The child should not be punished for his parents' sins. When Clyde tried to kill us, it was a direct result of your father's misdeeds. I won't allow that to happen again, certainly not to a small child—"

A sharp knock on the door sounded. Still on the stair treads, both women froze. The footman hurried to open the door.

It was Rosa, carrying Daniel. When he spied Rachel's mother as she hurried down the stairs, he smiled broadly, his arms outstretched. "Gamma! Gamma!"

Eyes wide, Rachel turned to her mother. "Gamma? Gramma?"

Louise haughtily lifted her chin. "Well, he had to call me something. I've been up visiting whenever you were out. It's not like you're going to give me any grandchildren."

Rosa didn't let her son go. Instead, she shifted him and the small bag she was also holding. "I'm only here to say goodbye."

"Goodbye?" Rachel echoed. She could hear her mother suck in a sharp breath.

"I'm leaving, and I have to hurry if I'm going to catch the train. I have a cousin in Pueblo. I'm going to stay with her for a winter. In the spring, I'm going back to my mother's hometown."

"What will you do?"

"My mother's family owns a general store. I know I'll be welcome to stay and raise Daniel there. Maybe learn about the business."

"What about your father? You'll have to give a statement to the sheriff."

"I dictated it to your mother before you came, even how he sold the stolen postcards to the bartender, who suspected where they came from and bought them anyway." She looked incredibly sad. "I can't stay here, Rachel. Daniel deserves better."

Tears swam in Rachel's eyes. "Will you remember all I've taught you?"

"About God? Oh, yes! I hate how much I must have disappointed Him, but on the way here, I realized that I've just been running from God. I was always too scared to stop living this terrible life, and feeling guilty and not worthy, and it would start all over again. But while I was tied up and wondering if I was going to die, I started to pray. God gave me peace, and I know I'll be okay as long as I trust Him." She dropped her bag, gave Rachel a one-armed hug and then picked up her bag again. Within a minute, she was hurrying down the driveway. At the street, she turned toward the train depot. Daniel was watching the house, and when Rachel saw her mother lift one hand to wave goodbye, he did the same.

Rachel stood beside her, the cold seeping into her along with the painful knowledge that she hadn't trusted God, either. For a long time, even after her mother had retreated into the warm house, Rachel watched Rosa disappear from sight.

Hooves on gravel snagged her attention and she saw Zane, on horseback, trotting up to the front door. Her heart surged and she knew right then what she needed to say.

Zane dismounted. "Alex is fine. He came around and I told him all that had happened. He was also able to answer some questions."

"Such as?"

Zane looked as though he was trying to decide what to say. "I asked him why he'd kept that postcard with your name on it. He kept it because he was sure Eddie was selling stolen goods and hoped he could use the card to prove it. He'd learned of the burglary down in Castle Rock and wanted to help with it, but then Rosa went missing and he had to put it aside."

Rachel lifted her brows. "Alex has good instincts. I hope he wants to return to work."

"He does, but the doctor ordered him to rest for the week first." Zane's jaw tightened. "Samuel Carrera is in a cell, right where he should be."

Thank You, Lord. Before she talked herself out of her next action, she grabbed him. "Zane, I've been telling you to trust God, when I was the one who should be doing just that. I really haven't trusted God for a long time, but I'm going to let Him guide my life now."

Zane looked down at her. He smiled. "Will you let Him guide both our lives? Together?"

"Toge—" She stalled her words as she gaped at Zane. "What are you saying?"

"I'm saying that on the way here, I realized that I have nothing to offer you, except my heart. I realized that is all God wants from us, so it has to be worth something. God will never leave us. That means that I need to trust Him when I return to Canaan to clear my name and make myself worthy of you."

"I don't want you to leave!"

"And I don't want to leave you. In fact, I'm not going to leave until Alex is on his feet. That gives you only a week to plan our wedding. I don't want to be apart from you for even one minute."

Then, getting down on one knee, he took her hands in his. His breath streamed out in the frosty evening air. She could tell his side was still aching. "I should be doing this properly. I love you. I want you to marry me and come with me. Without you, I wouldn't have found the strength to fight for my honor and my name. I don't know how that fight will end. I only know that I can't be a decent husband and provider with that disgrace hanging over my head. Back there near the mine, I wanted to tell you more, but I couldn't. Now, I can. However, the only way I will allow you to go to Canaan with me is if you marry me. You deserve nothing less."

"I love you, too, and yes, I'll marry you. We'll clear your name together." Love surged through her in a way she couldn't even describe. "You have taught me so much! Without you, I would never have learned to forgive Rosa. Your words back there as I stood beside her were so encouraging." She gripped his hands tightly and pulled him close. "You should stand up. We have a lot of things to do before our happily-ever-after starts!"

Epilogue

The warm summer sun hit Mrs. Rachel Robinson as soon as she allowed her husband to help her step from the train. She hadn't been back in Proud Bend since Victoria's wedding a few months back, and, even then, she'd returned the very next day to Canaan. To her husband, Zane.

He had given her good news that day when he'd met her train. The judge had finally heard the case and had agreed that there was sufficient evidence against Canaan's mayor and his son. They were charged with theft and conspiracy to hide evidence and falsifying official documents.

Zane was cleared of all wrongdoing. There hadn't been enough to charge the deputy with anything, but he was long gone from his position of authority.

Rachel and Zane were free, and having decided that Zane would open his own private investigator business, they were ready to return to Proud Bend.

Rachel smiled as her mother and Alex approached. Zane shot her a secretive look. "Are you sure she's going to like the news?"

"That your name is cleared?"

"No. Our other news."

Automatically, Rachel touched her still-flat stomach and smiled back. "Mother is terribly fickle, but if you could have seen her with Daniel that day Rosa took him and left, you'd know she's going to love our surprise."

Zane stole a kiss. "Let's go be a family, then. A free and happy family."

* * * * *

Don't miss Barbara Phinney's first story set
in Proud Bend, Colorado,

THE NANNY SOLUTION

Find more great reads at www.LoveInspired.com.

Dear Reader,

Thank you so much for reading *Undercover Sheriff*. I really enjoyed writing about Rachel. Ever since I first "met" her in *The Nanny Solution*, I have been intrigued by her and her ministry.

When we think of mission work, we probably think of far-flung places, but oftentimes, the best mission is close to home. The one discussed here may not be the most appealing, but we all know that it is a much-needed area in which to minister.

Zane refused to trust anyone, especially Rachel. He thought she was too much like those who'd betrayed him. Rachel may have enjoyed teasing Zane, but she was fully aware he could never be a part of her life if she was to reach the soiled doves in Proud Bend for Christ.

But our Lord always knows best, and He carefully used Rachel to teach Zane to trust again, while using Zane to teach Rachel to forgive herself. In a way, they ministered to each other.

Thank you again,

Barbara Phinney

Get 2 Free Books,

Love Inspired ® HISTORICAL

Plus 2 Free Gifts—

just for trying the *Reader Service!*

SPECIAL EXCERPT FROM

Love Inspired HISTORICAL

*After her disastrous wedding that wasn't, Caroline Murray
certainly isn't looking for love—but who could help falling
for an adorable set of triplet orphan baby boys in need of
a nanny? And how can she resist the handsome single dad
who has taken the babies in?*

Read on for a sneak preview of
THE NANNY'S TEMPORARY TRIPLETS,
the heartwarming continuation of the series
LONE STAR COWBOY LEAGUE:
MULTIPLE BLESSINGS.

"Why can't Miss Caroline be our nanny?"

All the grown-ups froze. David's eyebrows lifted. Had his
darling daughter just said "our nanny," as in she'd consider
herself one of Caroline's charges?

Caroline recovered from her surprise. "I'm sorry,
sweetheart. I couldn't."

Maggie's eyes clouded. "Why not?"

"Well, I'm not going to be here very long for one thing.
For another, I've never been a nanny before."

"Maybe not," Ida interjected. "But you certainly seemed
to have a way with the triplets. I can tell from the quiet in
this house that you finally got them to nap. Besides, we
wouldn't need you for long. Only until this nanny David's
trying to hire can get here."

"Ma, Miss Murray is here to visit her family, not work for
ours. It wouldn't be right for us to impose on that."

"Of course we wouldn't want to impose, Caroline, but your
family would be welcome to visit here as often as they want."

"Oh, I don't know." Caroline touched a hand to her throat

as she glanced around the kitchen. Her gaze landed on his, soft as a butterfly, filled with questions.

Did he want her to help them? The answer was an irrevocable no. Did he need her help? His mother's meaningful glare said yes. When he remained silent, Ida prompted, "We sure could use your help, Caroline. Couldn't we, David?"

He swallowed hard. "There's no denying that."

Caroline bit her lip. "Well, I'm sure my brother and sister-in-law could spare me now and then."

"We'd need you more than now and then." David offered up the potential difficulties with a little too much enthusiasm. "You'd have to stay here at the ranch. The triplets need to be fed during the night."

Caroline bit her lip. "What about the piano?"

David frowned. "What about it?"

"Would y'all mind ever so much if I played it now and then?"

Ida grinned. "Honey, you can play it as often as you want."

"In that case…" A smile slowly tilted Caroline's mouth. "Yes! I'd be happy to help out."

Maggie let out a whoop and reached for Caroline's hands. Somehow Caroline seemed to know that was her cue to dance the girl around the kitchen in a tight little circle. Ida sank into the nearest chair with pure relief. David opened his mouth to remind everyone that he was the man of the house with the final say on all of this, and he hadn't agreed to anything. Since doing so would likely accomplish nothing, he closed his mouth.

Don't miss
THE NANNY'S TEMPORARY TRIPLETS
by Noelle Marchand, available May 2017 wherever
Love Inspired® Historical books and ebooks are sold.

www.LoveInspired.com

LIHEXP0417

SPECIAL EXCERPT FROM

Love Inspired®

As a minister, blacksmith and guardian to two sets of twins, widower Isaiah Stoltzfus needs help! Hiring Clara Ebersol as a nanny is his answer—and the matchmakers' solution to his single-dad life. It'll take four adorable children to show them that together they'd make the perfect family.

Read on for a sneak preview of
A READY-MADE AMISH FAMILY
by *Jo Ann Brown,*
available May 2017 from Love Inspired!

"What's bothering you, Isaiah?" Clara asked when he remained silent.

"I assumed you'd talk to me before you made any decisions for the *kinder*." As soon as the words left his lips, he realized how petty they sounded.

"I will, if that's what you want. But you hired me to take care of them. I can't do that if I have to wait to talk to you about everything."

He nodded. "I know. Forget I said that."

"We're trying to help the twins, and there are bound to be times when we rub each other the wrong way."

"I appreciate it." He did. She could have quit; then what would he have done? Finding someone else and disrupting the *kinder* who were already close to her would be difficult. "Why don't you tell me about these letters you and the twins were writing?"

"They are a sort of circle letter with their family. From what they told me earlier, they don't know any of them well, and I doubt their *aenti* and grandparents know much about

LIEXP0417

them. This way, they can get acquainted, so when the *kinder* go to live with whomever will be taking them, they won't feel as if they're living with strangers."

He was astonished at her foresight. He'd been busy trying to get through each day, dealing with his sorrow and trying not to upset the grieving *kinder*. He hadn't given the future much thought. Or maybe he didn't want to admit that one day soon the youngsters would leave Paradise Springs. His last connection to his best friend would be severed. The thought pierced his heart.

Clara said, "If you'd rather I didn't send out the letters—"

"Send them," he interrupted and saw shock widening her eyes. "I'm sorry. I didn't mean to sound upset."

"But you are."

He nodded. "Upset and guilty. I can't help believing that I'm shunting my responsibilities off on someone else. I want to make sure Melvin's faith in me as a substitute *daed* wasn't misplaced. The twins deserve a *gut daed*, but all they have is me."

"You're doing fine under the circumstances."

"You mean when the funeral was such a short time ago?"

"No, I mean when every single woman in the district is determined to be your next wife, and your deacon is egging them on."

In spite of himself, Isaiah chuckled quietly. Clara's teasing was exactly what he needed. Her comments put the silliness into perspective. If he could remember that the next time Marlin or someone else brought up the topic of him marrying, maybe he could stop making a mess of everything. He hoped so.

Don't miss
A READY-MADE FAMILY by Jo Ann Brown,
available May 2017 wherever
Love Inspired® books and ebooks are sold.

"Exactly when did the stove catch on fire?"

The panicked blonde pushed back a lock of hair. "About five minutes after I turned it on. I was just trying to make tea."

Why did he have to find out the cottage he'd intended to buy had been sold this way? He forced kindness into his tone. "Don't ever hesitate to call on us, Charlotte. But why the sudden need for tea?"

She flushed. "I just signed the papers on the place today. I told Melba I just wanted to have a cup of tea on my new deck."

"You're Melba's friend?"

Chief Bradens had mentioned his wife's friend was buying a weekend cottage in town. Now, annoyed as he was, he'd have to be nice. A friend of the fire chief's wife deserved special care. Jesse pulled a business card from his pants pocket. "I'm a licensed contractor. If you like, I'll help you figure out what really needs work." If he couldn't have the house, maybe he could at least get the work.

She narrowed her eyes. "Why would you do that?"

"Because you're a friend of the chief's. Because I'm a nice guy." *Because I'm trying not to be a sore loser.*

Books by Allie Pleiter

Love Inspired

My So-Called Love Life
The Perfect Blend
*Bluegrass Hero
*Bluegrass Courtship
*Bluegrass Blessings
*Bluegrass Christmas
Easter Promises
  *"Bluegrass Easter"
†*Falling for the Fireman*
†*The Fireman's Homecoming*
†*The Firefighter's Match*
†*A Heart to Heal*
†*Saved by the Fireman*

Love Inspired Historical

Masked by Moonlight
Mission of Hope
Yukon Wedding
Homefront Hero
Family Lessons
The Lawman's Oklahoma Sweetheart

Love Inspired Single Title

Bad Heiress Day
Queen Esther &
  the Second Graders of Doom

*Kentucky Corners
†Gordon Falls

ALLIE PLEITER

Enthusiastic but slightly untidy mother of two, RITA®
Award finalist Allie Pleiter writes both fiction and
nonfiction. An avid knitter and unreformed choco-
holic, she spends her days writing books, drinking
coffee and finding new ways to avoid housework.
Allie grew up in Connecticut, holds a B.S. in speech
from Northwestern University and spent fifteen
years in the field of professional fund-raising. She
lives with her husband, children and a Havanese dog
named Bella in the suburbs of Chicago, Illinois.

Saved by the Fireman

Allie Pleiter

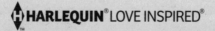

HARLEQUIN® LOVE INSPIRED®

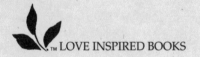

™ LOVE INSPIRED BOOKS

ISBN-13: 978-0-373-81801-3

Saved by the Fireman

Copyright © 2014 by Alyse Stanko Pleiter

www.Harlequin.com

Printed in U.S.A.

Unless the Lord builds the house, the builders labor in vain. Unless the Lord watches over the city, the guards stand watch in vain.
—*Psalms* 127:1

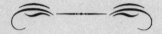

To Abbie
In faith that she'll discover many wonderful directions

Chapter One

Charlotte Taylor sat in her boss's office Friday morning and wondered where all the oxygen in Chicago had just gone.

"I'm sorry to let you go, Charlotte, I really am." Alice Warren, Charlotte's superior at Monarch Textiles, looked genuinely upset at having to deliver such news. "I know you just lost your grandmother, so I tried to put this off as long as I could."

A layoff? Her? Charlotte felt the shock give way to a sickening recognition. She'd seen the financial statements; she'd written several of the sales reports. Sure, she was no analyst wiz, but she was smart enough to know Monarch wasn't in great financial shape and a downsize was likely. She was also emotionally tied enough to Monarch and torn enough over losing Mima that she'd successfully denied the company's fiscal health for months. As she watched her grandmother's decline, Charlotte told herself she was finally settled into a good life. She'd boasted to a failing Mima—not entirely truthfully, she knew even then on some level—about feeling "established."

She'd patted Mima's weakening hands, those hands that had first taught her to knit and launched the textile career she had enjoyed until five minutes ago, and she'd assured her grandmother that there was no reason to worry about her. She was at a place in life where she could do things, buy things, experience things and get all the joy out of life just as Mima taught her. How hollow all that crowing she had done about becoming "successful" and "indispensable" at Monarch now rang. Who was she fooling? In this economy, did anyone really have the luxury of being indispensable?

Except maybe Mima. Mima could never be replaced. Charlotte and her mother were just barely figuring out how to carry on without the vivacious, adventurous old woman who'd now left such a gaping hole in their lives. It had been hard enough when Grandpa had lost his battle to Alzheimer's—the end of that long, hard decline could almost be counted as a blessing. Mima's all-too-quick exit had left Charlotte reeling, fabricating stability and extravagance that were never really there. Hadn't today just proved that?

Charlotte grappled for a response to her boss's pained eyes. "It's not your fault, I suppose." She was Monarch's problem solver, the go-to girl who never got rattled. She should say something mature and wise, something unsinkably optimistic, something Mima would say. Nothing came but a silent, slack jaw that broadcast to Alice how the news had knocked the wind out of her.

Alice sighed. "You know it's not your performance. It's just budgetary. I'm so sorry."

"The online sales haven't been growing as fast as we projected. I'd guessed the layoffs were coming eventually. I just didn't think it'd be—" she forced back the lump in her throat "—me, you know?"

Alice pulled two tissues from the box on her desk, handing one to Charlotte. "It's not just you." She sniffed. "You're the first of four." She pushed an envelope across the desk to Charlotte. "I fought for a severance package, but it's not much."

A severance package. Charlotte didn't even want to open it. Whatever it included, the look on Alice's face told Charlotte it wasn't going to make much of a difference. *Mima, did you see this coming?* Of course that couldn't be possible, but Charlotte felt her grandmother's eyes on her anyway, watching her from the all-knowing viewpoint of eternity. It wasn't that much of a stretch, if one believed in premonitions. Or the Holy Spirit, which Mima claimed to listen to carefully.

In true Mima style, Charlotte's grandmother had left both her and her mother a sizable sum of money and with instructions to "do something really worth doing." A world traveler after Grandpa died, Mima squeezed every joy out of life and was always encouraging others to do the same. Mima bought herself beautiful jewelry but never cried when a piece got lost. Mima owned a ten-year-old car but had visited five continents. She bought art—real art—but had creaky old furniture. Her apartment was small but stuffed with fabulous souvenirs and wonderful crafts. Mima truly knew what money was for and what really mattered in life.

That was how Charlotte knew the funds she'd inherited weren't intended for living—rent and groceries and such—they were for dreams and art and *life*. Having to use Mima's money to survive a layoff would feel like an insult to her grandmother's memory.

Alice sniffled, bringing Charlotte back to the horrible conversation at hand. Alice was so distressed she seemed to fold in on herself. "I wasn't allowed to tip anyone off. I'm so sorry."

She was sorry—even Charlotte could see that—but it changed nothing. Charlotte was leaving Monarch. She'd been laid off from the job she'd expected to solidify her career. It felt as if she'd spent her four years at Monarch knitting up some complicated, beautiful pattern and someone had come and ripped all the stitches out and told her to start over.

Over? How does a person start over when they suddenly doubt they ever really started at all?

Charlotte picked up the envelope but set it in her lap unopened.

"You've got two weeks of salaried work still to go." Alice was trying—unsuccessfully— to brighten her voice. "But you've also got six days of vacation accrued so…you don't have to stay the whole two weeks if you don't want to." The woman actually winced. Was this Alice's kinder, gentler version of "clean out your desk"?

The compulsion to flee roared up from some dark corner of her stomach Charlotte didn't even know she had. She didn't want to stay another minute. The fierce response surprised her— Monarch had been so much of a daily home to her she often didn't think of it as work. "And what about sick days?"

It bothered Charlotte that Alice had evidently anticipated that question; she didn't even have to look it up. "Two."

She was better than this. She couldn't control that she was leaving, but she could control when she left. And that was going to be now. "I don't think I'm feeling so well all of a sudden." Sure, it was a tad unreasonable, but so was having your job yanked out from underneath you. She had eight covered days out of her two-week notice. What was the point of staying two more days? Two more hours? Her files were meticulous, her sales contact software completely up to date, and next season's catalogue was ahead of schedule. There wasn't a single thing keeping her here except the time it would take to sweep all the personal decorations from her desk.

Alice nodded. "I'll write you a glowing recommendation."

It felt like such a weak compensation. Charlotte stood up, needing to get out of this office where she'd been told so many times—and believed—she was a gifted marketing coordinator and a key employee. "Thanks." She couldn't even look Alice in the eye, waving goodbye with the offending manila envelope as she walked out the door.

Monarch only had two dozen or so employees, and every eye in the small office now stared at her as she packed up her desk. Charlotte was grateful each item she stuffed into one of the popular Monarch tote bags—and oh, the irony of that—transformed the damp surge of impending tears into a churning burst of anger. Suddenly the sweet fresh-out-of-college intern she'd been training looked like the enemy. Inexperience meant lower salaries, so it wouldn't surprise Charlotte at all if adorable little Mackenzie got to keep her job. She probably still lived at home with her parents and didn't even need money for rent, Charlotte thought bitterly.

She reached into her file drawer for personal papers, her hand stilling on the thick file labeled "Cottage." The file was years old, a collection of photos and swatches and magazine articles for a dream house. Apartment living had its charms, but with Charlotte's craft-filled background, she longed to have a real house, with a yard and a front porch and windows with real panes. One that she could decorate exactly the way she wanted.

Just last week, Charlotte had nearly settled on using Mima's funds to buy a cottage in nearby Gordon Falls. It would be too far for a daily commute, but she could use it on weekends and holidays. She knew so many people there. Her best friend, Melba, had moved there. Her cousins JJ and Max had moved there. Melba's new baby, Maria, was now Charlotte's goddaughter. She'd come to love the tiny little resort town three hours away on the Gordon River, and there was a run-down cottage she'd driven past dozens of times that Charlotte could never quite get out of her mind. Mima would approve of her using the money to fund an absolutely perfect renovation in a town where everyone seemed to find happiness.

Well, not now, Charlotte thought as she stuffed the file into the bag. In light of the past five minutes, a weekend place had gone from exciting to exorbitant. *Get out of here before you can't hold it in,* she told herself as she stuffed three framed photos—one of Mom, one of Mima and one of baby Maria—in beside the thick file. She zipped the tote bag shut with a vengeance, yanked the employee identification/security badge from around her neck and set it squarely in the middle of the desk. Just last week she'd bought a beautifully beaded lariat to hold the badge, but now the necklace felt as if it was choking her. She left it along with the badge, never wanting to see it again.

With one declarative "I may be down but I'm not out" glare around the office, Charlotte left, not even bothering to shut the door behind her.

* * *

Jesse Sykes flipped the steak and listened to the sizzle that filled one end of his parents' patio. He'd built this outdoor kitchen two years ago, and this grill was a masterpiece—the perfect place to spend a Saturday afternoon. He planned to use a photo of the fire pit on his business brochures once they got printed. That, and the portico his mother loved. Filled with grapevines that turned a riot of gorgeous colors in the fall, it made for a stunning graphic. Only two more months, and he'd have enough funds to quit his job at Mondale Construction, buy that little cottage on the corner of Post and Tyler, fix it up and flip it to some city weekender for a tidy profit. With that money, he'd start his own business at last.

Move-in properties were plucked up quickly in Gordon Falls, so finding the perfect fixer-upper was crucial. He'd already lost out on two other houses last fall because he didn't quite have the down payment stashed away, but the cottage he'd settled on now was perfect. It was June, and he'd planned to buy the place in March, but that was life. He'd needed a new truck and Dad sure wasn't going to offer any help in that department. A few months' delay shouldn't make a difference, though—the cottage had been on the market for ages. It needed too much renovation for most people to want to bother.

"I'm pretty sure I'll have Sykes Homes Incorporated up and running by the fall. I can still snag the fall colors season if I can buy that cottage."

Dad sat back in his lawn chair, eyes squinting in that annoying way Jesse knew heralded his father's judgment. "Fall? Spring is when they buy. Timing is everything, son. You've got to act fast or you lose out on the best opportunities, and those won't be around in September."

Jesse flipped the next steak. "I'm moving as fast as I can, Dad." As if he didn't know he'd missed the spring season. As if it hadn't already kept him up nights even more than the Gordon Falls Volunteer Fire Department alarms.

"It might not be fast enough."

Jesse straightened his stance before turning to his father. "True, but learning to adapt is a good lesson, too. This won't be the first time I've had to retool a plan because I've hit a hitch."

Dad stood up and clamped a hand on Jesse's shoulder. "Son, all you've hit is hitches so far." This time he didn't even bother to add the false smile of encouragement he sometimes tacked on to a slam like that. Jesse thrust his tines into the third steak and clamped his teeth together.

"Is it that older cottage on Post Avenue?" his

mother asked. "The one by the corner with the wrought-iron window boxes?"

The wrought-iron window boxes currently rusting out of their brackets and splitting the sills, yes. "That's it."

He caught the "leave him be" look Mom gave Dad as she came over and refilled Jesse's tall glass of iced tea. "Oh, I like that one. So much charm. I've been surprised no one's snatched it up since Lucinda Hyatt died. You'll do a lovely job with that."

"In two more months I'll be ready to make an offer."

"You could have had the money for it by now if it weren't for the firehouse taking up all your time. You have no salary to show for it and it keeps you away from paying work. You'd better watch out or this place will be sold out from underneath you like the last one, and you'll be working for Art Mondale for another five years." Dad's voice held just enough of a patronizing tone to be polite but still drive the point home.

"Mike, don't let's get into that again."

Dad just grunted. Jesse's place in the volunteer fire department had been a never-ending battle with his father. Jesse loved his work there, loved helping people. And by this point, he felt as if the firefighters were a second family who understood him better than his real one. Chief Bradens was a good friend and a great mentor, teaching Jesse a lot about leadership and life. Fire Inspector Chad Owens had begun to teach him the ins and outs of construction, zoning and permits, too. It was the furthest thing he could imagine from the waste of time and energy his father obviously thought it to be.

Mom touched Jesse's shoulder. "You're adaptable. You can plot your way around any obstacle. That's what makes you so good at the firehouse."

Jesse hoisted the steaks onto a platter his mother held out. "That, and my world-class cooking." Then, because it was better to get all the ugliness out before they started eating, Jesse made himself ask, "How come Randy isn't here?"

Dad's smirk was hard to ignore. "Your brother's at a financial conference in San Diego this week. He said it could lead to some very profitable opportunities." Jesse's younger brother, Randall, would be retiring in his forties if he kept up his current run of financial success. Randy seemed to be making money hand over fist, boasting a fancy condo in the Quad Cities, a travel schedule that read more like a tourist brochure, and a host of snazzy executive trappings. It didn't take a genius to see Jesse fell far short of his brother in Dad's eyes. A month ago, when Jesse had pulled up to the house in a brand-new truck, Jesse couldn't help but notice the way his father frowned at it, parked next to Randy's shiny silver roadster.

"He's up for another promotion," Mom boasted.

"Good for him, he deserves it." Jesse forced enthusiasm into his voice. Somehow, it was always okay when Randy missed family functions because of work. It was never okay when Jesse had to skip one because he was at the firehouse.

"Someday, that brother of yours is going to rule the world." Dad had said it a million times, but it never got easier to swallow. Every step Randy took up the ladder seemed to push Jesse farther down it from Dad's point of view. While Dad never came out and said it, it was clear Jesse's father felt that a man who worked with his hands only did so because his brain wasn't up to higher tasks.

"I don't doubt it, Dad," Jesse admitted wearily. "I'll just settle for being King of the Grill."

Mom looked eagerly at the petite fillet he'd marinated just the way she liked it. "That is just fine by me. Jesse, honey, this smells fantastic. You will make some lucky lady very happy one of these days." Her eyes held just a tint of sadness, reminding Jesse that the ink was barely dry on Randy's divorce papers. His brother's raging career successes had inflicted a few casualties of late, and Mom had been disappointed to watch her grandma prospects walk out the door behind Randy's neglected wife. This past winter had been hard on the Sykes family, that was for sure. Was Dad clueless to all those wounds? Or did he just choose to ignore what he couldn't solve?

They were in love…once…his mom and dad. Now they just sort of existed in the same life, side by side but not close. Randy had married because he was "supposed to." As if he needed to check off some box in his life plan. Jesse didn't want to just make some appropriate lady "very happy." When he fell, it would be deep and strong and he would sweep that love of his life clean off her feet.

It just wasn't looking as though that would be anytime soon.

Chapter Two

"Done." Charlotte Taylor finished signing her name at the bottom of the long sales document. She put her pen—the beautiful new fountain pen she'd bought especially for this occasion—down on the conference table as if she were planting a flag. She was, in a way. The knot in her stomach already knew this was a big deal. A good big deal. The way to get her life back on track and prove Monarch was only a bump in the road, not the end of the line. She looked up and gave her companions a victorious smile. "The cottage is officially mine."

"I still can't believe you're going through with this." Charlotte's best friend, Melba, sat with her baby on her lap, trying to look supportive but appearing more worried than pleased. "I mean, I'm happy for you and all, but you're sure?"

Charlotte had done nothing but mull the matter over in the week since the layoff, and while the timing might look wrong on the outside, she'd come to the conclusion that it was actually perfect. She needed this, needed a project to balance the stress of a job search. When she'd gone to see the cottage again and the seller had been willing to knock down the price for a cash offer, Charlotte felt as if Mima was showing her it was time to act. "I am. If I do it now, I'll have the time to do it right. And you know me—I'll have a new job before long. This is exactly the kind of thing Mima would have wanted me to do with my inheritance."

"It's nice to see someone your age so excited to put down roots." The broker—a plump, older woman named Helen Bearson, who looked more suited to baking pies than hawking vacation properties—smiled back as she handed Charlotte the keys. The large, old keys tumbled heavy and serious into Charlotte's hand. "I'm sure you'll be very happy after the renovations. Gordon Falls is a lovely place to get away to— but you already knew that."

Melba gently poked the baby Maria's sweet button nose and cooed, "Aunt Charlotte always did know exactly what she wanted, Maria. Now you'll get to see her much more often."

Charlotte couldn't really fault Melba's sing-song, oh-so-sweet voice; new moms were supposed to adore their babies like that. It was charming. She'd probably be even more sugary when her time as a new mom came—if it ever came—and Maria was adorable. She'd been baby-perfect, happy and quiet for the entire long real estate transaction, and Charlotte had been grateful for the company at such an important event, even if it did take over an hour. Charlotte herself felt as if her hand would never uncramp from signing her name so many times.

Funny how even happy milestones could be so exhausting. Squeezing the new keys tight— well, new to her at least, for they looked giant and cumbersome next to her slick apartment and car keys—she exhaled. This wasn't an indulgence; this was a lifeline. Just for fun, Charlotte rattled the keys playfully over the baby's head. Maria's little gray eyes lit up at the tinkling sound, her chubby hands reaching up in a way that had all three women saying "Aww."

Awe, actually. She'd done it. The keys she held belonged to a cottage Charlotte now owned. It was an exhilarating, thrilling kind of fear, this huge leap. The cottage had become a tangible promise to herself, a symbol that future success was still ahead of her and she could still be in command of the blessings God had given her. No matter what her new job would be, no matter where her rented city apartment might shift, this cottage would be the fixed point, the home ready to welcome her on weekends and vacations. She'd boasted of feeling established in her job at Monarch, but the truth was today was what really made her feel like an adult. She'd never owned anything more permanent than a car before this. Her chest pinched in a happy, frantic kind of excitement.

"Thanks, Mima." She liked to think Mima was as pleased as she was, sending down her blessing from heaven as surely as if a rainbow appeared in the bank conference room. Once she'd prayed and made the decision, it felt as if Mima had orchestrated the whole thing—in cahoots with God to line the details up so perfectly that the purchase had been swift and nearly effortless. Yes, she was in command of the blessings God had given her—and that was what she'd sought: a firm defense against the uncertainties of a woman "between jobs."

Sure, Melba had made the same noise about practicality that Mom had made. Charlotte knew it might have been more sensible to buy a Chicago apartment and stay in the area to job-hunt, but Mima hadn't left her the money to be sensible. Mima was all about leaps of the heart, and right now Charlotte didn't know where her next job would take her, but she knew her heart kept pulling her toward Gordon Falls as her spot to get away. She'd spent so many weekends here, the guest bed at Melba's house had a Charlotte-shaped dent in it. The hustle and sparkle of Chicago would always be wonderful, but Mima's bequest meant she could own this cottage and rent a nice place in Chicago near her next job for the weekdays. That felt like a smart plan, and everyone knew smart wasn't always practical. Who knew? The way telecommuting was taking off these days, she might work full-time out of Gordon Falls someday in the future.

"Congratulations," Melba said, trying again to be supportive.

Poor Melba. She'd always be too cautious to ever launch an adventure like this. Melba had too many people needing her—a husband, until recently her late father, and now Maria—to ever throw caution to the wind. Charlotte would have to show her how exhilarating it could be. "I own a cottage. I'm landed gentry."

Melba winced as she untangled a lock of her hair from Maria's exploring fingers. "That might be overstating things, but I am glad you'll be here. Gordon Falls could use a few more of us young whippersnappers."

"I couldn't agree more," Mrs. Bearson confirmed as she slid the files into the needle-point tote bag that served as her briefcase. "I'm delighted to see so many of you younger people coming into town and settling down."

Settling down. The words fit, but the sensation was just the opposite; more of a leaping forward. It was the most alive she'd felt since that harrowing exit from the Monarch offices. Renovating this cottage was going to be about doing life on purpose instead of having it done to you by accident. Today declared Charlotte her own person, with her own roots to plant.

The older woman extended a hand. "Welcome to Gordon Falls, Charlotte Taylor. You'll love it here."

Charlotte shook her hand. "I know I will. Thanks for everything."

"My pleasure. Tootle-loo!" With a waggle of her fingers, she bustled from the conference room to the bank's lobby, where she headed over to say hello to several people.

Melba caught Charlotte's eye. "Tootle-loo?"

Charlotte winced. "She's said that every time we've met. Odd, but cute." She stared at the keys in her hand, cool at first but now warm and friendly to her touch. "I own a cottage."

"You do."

She'd been there three times in the past two days, but the need to see it again, to turn the key in the lock with her own hand as the owner, pressed against her heart. "Let's go see my cottage. My cottage. I want to make myself a cup of tea in my cottage. I brought some tea leaves and a kettle with me and everything."

Baby Maria's response to the invitation was to scrunch up her face and erupt in a tiny little rage. She'd been darling up until now, but it was clear that her patience was coming to an end. "I think Miss Maria needs to nurse and to nap. Much as I'd like to be there, I think we had better head home." Melba put a hand on Charlotte's arm. "Will you be okay on your own?"

"Just fine." That was the whole point of the cottage, wasn't it? When she thought about it, it was fitting that the first hours Charlotte spent in the cottage as its owner were on her own. "I'll be back for dinner, okay?" The cottage wasn't in any shape to call home just yet, so she'd opted to stay a few days at Melba's while she got things set up right.

"See you later, Miss Taylor of the landed gentry," Melba called above Maria's escalating cries. "Enjoy your new castle."

Jesse wrenched open another of the cottage's stuck windows and waved the smoke away from his face. The air was as sour as his stomach. He could barely believe he was standing in his cottage—only it wasn't his anymore now—talking to the new owner. Talk about a kick to the gut. "Exactly when did the stove catch on fire?"

The panicked blonde next to him pushed a lock of hair back off her forehead. "About five minutes after I turned it on." She pointed to a charred kettle now hissing steam in the stained porcelain sink. "Tea. I was just trying to make tea." Her eyes wandered to the fire truck now idling in her driveway, dwarfing her tiny blue hatchback. "I'm sorry. I probably overreacted by calling you all in for such a little fire. I was too panicked to think straight. I just bought the place today and I didn't know what else to do."

She was so apologetic and rattled, it was hard to stay annoyed at her. People were always apologizing for calling the fire department. Jesse never got that. It's not like anyone ever apologized for seeing their doctor or calling a plumber. She had no reason to be upset for calling the fire department, even for a little fire. Kitchen fires could be dangerous. One look at the dilapidated 1960s electric range told him any number of problems could have escalated from an open flame there. Sure it was a quaint-looking appliance, but he of all people knew suppliers who made stoves with just as much of that trendy vintage charm but with modern safety features. "Even a small fire isn't anything to mess with. Small fires can get very big very fast."

Of course, if *he* had been the new owner, he'd have had the sense to make sure the stove was safe before turning it on and starting the fire in the first place. The sting of his current situation surged up again. Why did he have to be on duty when this particular call came in? Why did he have to find out the cottage he'd intended to buy had been sold this way? He picked up his helmet from the chipped Formica counter, forcing kindness into his tone. "Look, don't be worried. You did the right thing, Ms...."

"Taylor. Charlotte Taylor." So that was the name of his pretty little adversary.

"Don't ever hesitate to call on us, Charlotte. Especially if you're on your own. It's why we're here, okay?"

Her eyes scanned the smoke still hovering close to the kitchen's tin ceiling. Jesse had always thought the ceiling was this kitchen's best feature. Stuff like that was hard to find these days. Would she appreciate that or tear it down and put in a boring ceiling with sterile track lighting? "Okay." She mostly mumbled the word, her face pale and drawn tight.

She didn't look anything close to okay. Her nerves were so obviously jangled they practically echoed around the empty kitchen. "If you don't mind me asking...why the sudden need for tea? You're not even moved in, from the looks of it." Her reply might let him know what her plans were for the place. If she was plotting a teardown and wasn't planning to move in at all, he could skip the preliminaries and get right down to hating her this minute.

She flushed. "It was a celebration thing. I just signed the papers on the place today. I told Melba I just wanted to have a cup of tea on my new deck."

How had he missed this? The facts wove together in his brain, making everything worse. "You're Melba's friend?"

Chief Bradens had mentioned his wife's friend was buying a weekend cottage in town. Never in a million years did Jesse consider it might be *this* cottage. Now, annoyed as he was, he'd have to be nice. A friend of the fire chief's wife demanded special care. "No harm done that I can see." He put his helmet back down on the counter as he swallowed his sore pride. "I should check the rest of the place. Just to be safe," he said over his shoulder as he began banging open the two remaining kitchen windows when they refused to budge.

She shrugged. "Probably a good idea."

He knew the rooms of this house. A visual inspection wasn't really necessary, but it might give him a last look at the place before she stripped it of all its charm. Charlotte followed him around the empty rooms while he peered at light switches, tested the knobs on heating registers and tried the fuses in the antiquated fuse box. Did she know what she was getting into here? This was no starter project for a hobby house flipper. "You can still keep lots of the place's charm, but you're gonna need some serious updating." He raised his eyebrows at her resulting frown. "You knew that going in, didn't you?"

"I did."

She did not. Now that was just dirty pool, letting someone like her beat him to a place like this.

Some jilted part of him wanted to tell her the house was chock-full of danger, but it wasn't true. Nothing looked dangerous to his contractor's eye, just old and likely finicky. The greatest danger she faced was blowing a fuse if she plugged her hair dryer in while the dishwasher was running. Charlotte had nice hair. Platinum blond in a city-sleek rather than elegant cut. She looked relatively smart, but what did he know? Do smart people set their teakettles on fire?

He avoided looking at her by inspecting the stove knobs. "Nothing about wiring came up in the home inspection?" He almost hated to add,

"You did *have* a home inspection, didn't you?" It was killing him—she looked as if she didn't even own a hammer, much less the belt sander it would take to bring those hardwood floors in the dining room up to snuff. Still, she had a certain spunk about her. It hadn't been there when he and the other guys first barged in the door, but he could see it now returning to her eyes. If she made the right choices, she might do okay. Not that he wanted her to succeed.

"Of course I did. Only now I'm thinking maybe it wasn't so thorough." She crossed her arms over her chest and her eyebrows furrowed together. "Honestly, the guy looked like he did inspections for laughs in between fishing trips. Mrs. Bearson said he was reliable, but…"

Helen Bearson. He could have guessed she'd made the sale. Helen was a sweet lady, but the kind Jesse referred to as a "hobby broker." Dollars to donuts the inspector was her brother. "Larry Barker?" Even someone he resented as much as Charlotte Taylor deserved better than that guy—Jesse wouldn't pay him to inspect a shoe box.

Charlotte raised an eyebrow. "A mistake, huh?"

He couldn't just sit there and let her make choices from what was likely bad information. Well, he *could,* but he wasn't the kind of guy who would—even under these circumstances. Jesse shucked off his heavy firefighter's coat and squatted down in front of the appliance, opening the oven door and peering inside. "Let's just say he wouldn't be my first choice," he said, giving Barker more benefit of the doubt than he deserved. "I haven't seen anything that should have stopped your sale." In fact, he knew there were no massive problems because he'd given the house a thorough once-over himself, far beyond his ten-minute walkthrough just now. Still, the word *sale* stuck in his throat. "This could really be just an old stove, not faulty wiring or anything." He stared at a layer of grime so thick he could sign his name in it with a fingernail. "I don't think this has been used in a couple of years. You'll want to replace it."

She groaned. "But I love the way this one looks. Does it cost a fortune to rehab a stove?"

Dark brown eyes and blond hair—the effect was striking, even with a frown on her face. "You can't really rehab a stove. Still there are ones that look old-fashioned but function like new. They're pricey, but you had to have known you were going to put some money into the place."

"Well of course I did, but I was hoping to wait longer than two hours before the first repair."

Despite his irritation, Jesse liked her sense

of humor. He glanced out the window to where the three other firemen were putting gear back into the truck. Normally he didn't fish for contractor work while on firefighting duty—especially given this particular circumstance—but she was pretty and clearly on her own and, well, seemed at a loss. Sure he'd regret it but unable to stop himself, Jesse swallowed the last of his pride and pulled a business card from his pants pocket. "I'm a licensed contractor over at Mondale Construction. If you like, give me a call tomorrow and I'll walk through the house with you over the weekend. I can go over what Larry said and either confirm it or tell you differently. I'll help you figure out what really needs work right away and what can wait until you've gotten over the sticker shock." If he couldn't have the house, maybe he could at least get the work, much as it would dent his ego.

She narrowed her eyes. "Why would you do that?"

He hated when people gave him "the contractor out to take you to the cleaners" look. "Because you're a friend of the chief's. Because I'm a nice guy." *Because I'm an idiot and am trying not to be a sore loser.* "And because I can make sure Mondale gives you a good price for work I could do and recommend a couple of guys for the other stuff—guys who will do it right and not empty your checkbook for the sport of it."

She took the card but still eyed him. Good. She shouldn't be trusting everyone who walked in here offering to help her, even him. She looked smarter than that, and he could bring himself to be glad she was acting like it. "So maybe you really are a nice guy," she said, still sounding a bit doubtful.

"Don't take my word for it. Look, you ought to know I don't normally pitch work on duty. Only I think Chief and Melba might ride me if I didn't offer my help, given the—" he waved at the smoke now almost completely gone from the kitchen "—circumstances. It's the least I can do."

She looked unconvinced, and a part of him was ready to be rid of the obligation. He'd tried, wasn't that enough? He gave it one last shot of total honesty. "Frankly, this place is a contractor's dream—good bones but needing loads of work. And I could use the work." After a second, he looked out the window and added, "Why don't you think about it? I've got to get back to the truck anyway—the guys are waiting for me."

She planted her hands on her hips. "No, I don't need to think about it. Can you come by after church Sunday?"

She went to church. Of course she went to church; she was a friend of Chief Bradens and his wife. Not wanting to look like the stranger to services that he was, he hazarded a guess based on when he usually saw his friends out and about on Sundays. "Eleven-thirty?"

"Perfect." She smiled—an "I'm rattled but I'll make it" lopsided grin that told him she'd do okay even if this wasn't the last disaster of her new home. Her new home. Life was cruel some days.

Jesse nodded at the kitchen's vintage molding and bay widows. "This will make a nice weekend place. You'll do just fine."

She made a face. "That's just what I was telling myself when the stove caught on fire."

"Everything looks okay, but I'd hold off on teatime until we check out all the appliances if I were you." His radio beeped, letting him know the rest of the crew outside was getting impatient. "Once you get the rest of your utilities up and running, turn on the fridge so we can check how cold it gets."

She perked up. "Did that already. Turned it on, I mean." To prove her point, she opened the ancient-looking refrigerator and made a show of peering inside. "Chilling down, nothing scary inside." Her head popped back out and she shut the door. "The dishwasher, I'm not so sure. It looks older than I am."

For an intriguing second, Jesse wondered just how old that was. She looked about his age, but he'd never been good at guessing those things. "Yeah, I'd hold off." He gestured to the single mug sitting beside a box of fancy-looking tea on the otherwise bare 1950s-era Formica countertop. "Not like you've got a load of dishes to do anyhow."

That lit a spark in her eyes. "Oh, I own tons of dishes. I collect vintage china. I've got enough to fill all the shelves in this house and my apartment back in Chicago twice over. Not that I'd put any of them in this old dinosaur, anyway." She shrugged. "Well, thanks, Officer—" she squinted down at the card "—Sykes." She held out her hand.

He shook it. "I'm not an officer, I'm just part of the volunteer brigade. So Jesse will do. I'll see you Sunday at eleven-thirty. And as for your new house celebration, go on down to Karl's Koffee and tell him what happened. If I know Karl, he'll give you a free cup of tea and maybe some pie to smooth things over. You deserve a better welcome to Gordon Falls than one from us." Jesse decided he'd call from the truck and ask Karl to do just that. Only, knowing Karl, he'd have done it with no nudging at all.

He felt a tiny bit better for pulling that sweet smile from her. "Maybe I'll do just that. Thanks."

Jesse tried to ignore the teasing looks that greeted him as he climbed into the truck. "Isn't she the prettiest run of the day." Yorky, an older member of the department who could never be counted on for subtlety, bumped Jesse on the shoulder.

"Of the week," Wally Forman corrected, waggling an eyebrow for emphasis. "Only it's not so fun for you given the circumstances, is it, Jesse?"

"Could have fooled me," Yorky snickered.

Jesse merely grunted and settled farther down in his seat. Maybe Wally would let it go.

Wally stared at him. "It is, isn't it? That's the one?"

Narrowing his eyes in the strongest "not now" glare he could manage, Jesse didn't answer.

Wally leaned back in his seat and pointed at Jesse. "It is. I knew it. Oh, man, tough break."

Yorky looked at Jesse, then at Wally, then back at Jesse again. "What? What am I missing?"

Jesse cocked his head to one side in an "I'm warning you" scowl aimed straight at Wally.

Not that it did any good. "That's the house. The one Jesse talked about buying. Sweetie-Pie up there just bought it right out from underneath him. How many more months before you would have saved up enough for the down payment, Sykes? It had to be soon."

Was Wally going out of his way to drive the sore point home? "Two." Up until this moment Jesse had managed to let Little Miss China Cabinet's sweet smile tamp down his irritation at being beat to the purchase table.

Yorky hissed. "Ouch!"

"Yeah," Jesse repeated, craning his neck back to look at the tidy little cottage. "Ouch."

Chapter Three

"Melba, I'm not the first person in the world to lose my job," Charlotte told her dear friend as they sat at her table after dinner that night. Charlotte had managed to avoid the topic of conversation with Melba for days, but tonight Clark was down at the firehouse for the evening and her friend had cornered her in the kitchen. "I wasn't even the last at Monarch—there were three other envelopes on Alice's desk."

Melba had Maria settled in the crook of her arm. "I'm just worried about you. Are you okay? You seem to be taking it well, but…"

Charlotte kept telling herself that she was handling it as well as could be expected, but she also spent too many moments stuffing down a deep panic. "Do I have a choice?"

"Not you. You'd never go to pieces, even at something like this." She caught Charlotte's eye.

"But you could. I mean, don't feel like you have to put on any kind of front with me. I've gone to pieces enough times in front of you."

While Charlotte was sure Melba meant what she said, the idea of giving in to the fear—even for a moment and even with a dear friend—felt like opening the big green floodgates at the end of town. Best to keep that door firmly shut. "I'm okay. I think I'm okay. I mean, I'm scared—you're supposed to be in my situation—but I can push through this. I'm choosing to feel more like I'm waiting for whatever God's got around the corner than I've been broadsided by a job change."

Melba leaned in. "The best part is you get to wait here. I'll be so happy to have you around."

"Well, part of the time. I expect I'll need to take lots of trips back to Chicago for job-search stuff and interviews eventually. Only it'll be great to have the cottage as a distraction. All the books say to take on inspiring new projects so it doesn't become all about the job search. This is a great time to get a serious creative groove on. I need a place outside of my résumé to channel all this energy."

All that was true, but there was still a small corner of her chest that felt as if she had planted her flag at the top of a very high mountain with no idea how to climb back down. She nodded to the thick file of plans, the one she'd taken from her desk on her last day at Monarch. "I wonder if Mima had any idea the incredible gift this is going to be. To get to fix this place up exactly the way I want it? To have enough to do that after I bought it? Debt free? It's a huge blessing."

Melba gave her a cautious smile. "I know you got it at a great price, but it needs so much work." She thumbed through the file of clippings and swatches with her free hand while Maria gave a tiny sigh of baby contentment in her other arm. "Don't you think it's a big risk to take at a time like this?"

Charlotte shrugged. "Yes, it is a big risk. But it's a worthwhile risk. Just the thought of being able to do this up right gives me so much energy. I don't care if I have to buy shelving instead of shoes. Or stop eating until October."

"You're not going to fix up the whole place and decorate it all at once, are you?" Melba turned to a magazine page showing chintz kitchen curtains. "Won't that cost more than you have?"

"I *have* to do some of the fixing up as soon as possible. The stove, the heating, the upstairs bathroom—they need renovation before they'll be usable, and all that stuff has to be done if I'm going to be able to live there. Do I need the designer concrete sink right away? Well, I don't know yet. It's probably smarter to get exactly what I want now—once you start ripping stuff out, you might as well do it right the first time rather than rip stuff up again a year later."

"Charlotte…"

"I know, I know. Stop worrying—I'm not going to take my aggressions out at the home decorating store. I should probably have the home improvement channels blocked off my cable service for now. But since I don't have a job, I can't even afford cable television, so that solves that anyway, doesn't it?" She leaned back in her chair, as if the sheer weight of Melba's doubts had pushed her there. "This is going to be fine. Really. I won't let this get out of hand."

Melba pushed the file back across the table to Charlotte. "Easy to say now, but these things have a way of snowballing. Even the remodeling costs for the house I inherited from Dad sent Clark and me reeling."

When Melba's father had died last year after a long battle with Alzheimer's, it left Clark and Melba to remake her childhood home into the one that now housed her new family. The transition had been complicated and expensive—going beyond what it would have cost in both time and money to start fresh with a new house—but it just proved Charlotte's point: the house gave off a palpable sense of history. She'd felt something like it from the cottage that first visit. The once-charming cottage seemed to beckon to her, begging to be restored. She knew it was a risky prospect, but she couldn't make herself feel as if she'd made the wrong choice. She'd chosen a challenging path, yes, but not a wrong one. "I'm going to be fine, Melba. Now let's drop the subject and let me hold that baby."

Melba stood up and handed Maria to Charlotte. As Maria snuggled in against her shoulder, Charlotte breathed in the darling scent of baby-girl curls. "You've got the best of both worlds, Maria. Your mama's curls and your daddy's red hair. You may hate it when you're five, but guys are gonna follow you like ducklings when you're seventeen."

Melba laughed as she warmed Charlotte's tea and set down a plate of cookies. "Clark's already informed me Maria will be banned from dating until she's thirty. And no firefighters."

Charlotte applied an expression of false shock. "Well, I'll back him up on the 'no fire-fighters' policy, but that's kind of a tough sell. He's the fire chief, isn't he?"

Sitting back down, Melba laughed again. "I think it's *because* he's chief. He's seen a little too much of the department's social life or heard a little too much in the locker room."

"They don't seem that rough around the edges to me. As a matter of fact, Jesse Sykes seems like a stand-up guy." Charlotte could feel Maria softening against her shoulder. Melba was right—the world was always a better place with a baby drooling on your shoulder.

"He's an original, that's for sure." Melba selected a cookie and dunked it in her tea. "I don't know about stand-up, but he sure stands out. You can trust him, though. He did some of the work here on the house. Good work, if you don't mind the singing."

"The what?"

"Jesse has a habit of breaking out in Motown hits. If you haven't heard him yet, you will. Don't you remember he sang at Alex and JJ's wedding?"

"*That* was Jesse Sykes?" Charlotte recalled a rather impressive version of "My Girl" at her cousin's wedding. She tried to imagine Jesse's soulful voice echoing in the cottage living room, but she couldn't conjure up the image. "Mostly he just made wisecracks when I talked to him this time. Funny guy."

"Oh, he's a cutup, that's for sure. And a good firefighter. Clark wouldn't put up with his antics otherwise." Melba got a conniving look on her face. "You should hire him. I think he'd be good for you. An upbeat guy to have around in a tight spot."

Charlotte narrowed her eyes. "Oh, no, you don't."

"Don't what?" Melba's innocent blink hid nothing.

Charlotte whispered into Maria's ear, "Your mama's getting ideas."

"I am not."

"Oh, yes, you are. I know you too well. Look, I know we were discussing behavior, not profession, but he's a fireman, Melba. I won't get into a relationship with a first responder no matter how well behaved. We've been through this how many times? Nothing's changed. I've got way too many memories of sitting up nights with Mom at the kitchen table."

"Your dad was a policeman, I know, but—"

"But nothing. Same stress, different uniform. Melba, I've got nothing against you and Clark, and goodness knows JJ's done terrific at the firehouse, but I know what I can handle and what I can't. I've never dated someone who does that kind of work and I don't plan to start now."

A tiny war was going on in Jesse's chest— and in his pride—as he walked up the overgrown sidewalk to Charlotte's cottage Sunday morning. This was supposed to be his cottage.

The place needed loads of work, and he knew he was the best man to complete it. He'd planned the rehab of this place a dozen times, imagining living in the home as he upgraded fixtures, appliances and wiring until he could turn around and sell it for a tidy profit. Or even stay there and use it as the showcase for what he could do with other properties. But that opportunity was lost now.

The only opportunity left in this situation was to be the guy hired for the renovation job. If a woman could afford a vacation cottage at Charlotte's age, she probably wouldn't haggle over the cost the place would require to be done up right. His business sense knew that made her an excellent customer even if she was a thorn in his side. The house needed loads of work, and loads of work could mean a big check for Mondale and for him. As he lay in bed last night, Jesse told himself a job this size could leave him with even more funds than he'd anticipated making over the summer. Funds to buy another house— bigger and better to soothe his wounded pride and show his father just how savvy a businessman he could be.

All this should have had him dreaming up the perfect sales pitch as he approached the door—and yet for some reason, he wasn't. He prided himself on knowing how to optimize a customer with deep pockets, only Charlotte Taylor didn't have that entitled look about her. In fact, she looked a little…lost. The way he'd looked when he'd first put on the bulky, cumbersome firefighter's gear—right at the launch of a dream, forcing an outer confidence that didn't quite cover the dazzled and doubtful person on the inside.

As he pushed the rusty doorbell button, Jesse still wasn't sure how he was going to play it for this meeting. *Just wing it,* he told himself. *You wing it all the time.* He pushed the button again, listening for the chimes inside the house once he noticed the living room window was open to his left.

No sound. Sometimes it was useful to start a customer off with a small project, but he'd planned on something larger than a broken doorbell. He knocked on the door loudly and leaned over the wrought-iron railing to yell into the window. "Charlotte!"

A second knock and another yell produced no reply. He pivoted to see her little blue car wasn't in the cottage drive. Maybe church ran long today. He could just start without her while he waited. After checking his watch, Jesse pulled out his notes.

He'd already made his own list of what the house needed, but he'd go through the process of re-creating a list to suit her taste. He just hoped it wouldn't clash with the character of the house he saw so clearly. Catering to a client's whims was one thing—ignoring his own clear ideas on this particular place was going to be quite another. Still, he'd do it to rack up enough funds to move forward. He was bone-tired of delays and detours, not to mention his father's ever-increasing digs.

Pacing the cottage's front stoop, he toed boards and pushed harder on the railing only to have it creak and pull out from its mountings. He added the doorbell and railing to his handwritten list and began scanning the front of the house for anything he'd missed.

He'd added four more items by the time Charlotte's small blue hatchback pulled into the drive behind his large brown pickup.

"Sorry!" she called, breathless and airy in a blue print dress with a lacy sweater that rippled behind her as she came up the steps. "Church went on forever. I mean, a good forever, but enough to make me late. I hope you weren't waiting long."

Jesse waited for her to say something like "I noticed you weren't in church." Or "Have you ever gone?" or the half dozen other thinly disguised recommendations he got from Melba, Clark and various other friends around town.

"No, I'm fine. Hey, JJ told me you're her cousin. You were at the wedding, too, weren't you? On the boat?"

"Wedding of the year, wasn't it?"

As the only female firefighter in Gordon Falls, JJ Cushman stuck out already before her legendary wedding to Alex Cushman on a steamboat on the Gordon River. "A big shindig, that's for sure."

"And then there's my other cousin, JJ's brother, Max." She fished for her keys and wrestled the old door lock open. "And Melba's baby is my new goddaughter. I know lots of people in Gordon Falls."

They walked through the front hallway to the kitchen, where she plunked an enormous tapestry handbag—a vintage artsy-looking thing, he was glad to notice—down on the kitchen counter. "And now I know Karl. You were right. He did give me a slice of pie for my troubles." She sighed, a happy, shoulder-heaving, contented sigh. "This is a nice town."

It was, most of the time. "It has its moments."

Charlotte began digging through the massive bag. "I made a list last night of the things I think the house needs—as a jumping-off point." She pulled out a notebook with Victorian ladies dancing on the cover. "I'm no expert, though."

Jesse put a hand to his chest. "That's okay,

because I am. Only there's an awkward question I really should ask first."

"Where do I want to hide the bodies?" She didn't need the pink lipstick to show off that dynamic smile; her eyes lit up with humor.

The joke made the next question easier to ask. "No, what's your budget?"

"Oh, that." He couldn't quite gauge her response.

"I mean, you don't have to tell me," he backpedaled, suddenly feeling his poor-loser wounds had run off with his diplomacy, "but it's better if I know. I can make smarter recommendations if I have a total-figure picture on the whole project."

Charlotte hoisted herself up to sit on the vacant countertop. "That's the best part—I don't have a budget. My grandma left me enough money to do this—at least I'm pretty certain she did. This place was a leap of faith." She didn't come out and say "unlimited funds," but her eyes sure looked as though she was ready to spend. *Must be nice to have that kind of cash.* Jesse ignored the sharp curl of envy wrapped around his gut.

Instead, he focused on how she fit in the house. Houses—even half-built or long since run-down houses—always had personalities to him. He'd sensed this cottage's personality way back, and looking at her perched on the counter, he knew her personality absolutely suited the vibe of this place. Had he just finished the remodeling, he'd probably have been delighted to sell it to her. He just couldn't get there quite yet—for all her charm, Charlotte Taylor was still the agent of the delay in his achieving his dreams.

She looked around the room with wistful eyes. "Mima was amazing." The grief was still fresh, glistening in her eyes and present in the catch of her words. Whoever this grandmother was, Charlotte missed her very much.

"Did Mima leave you her china?" Jesse wasn't quite sure what made him ask.

Her eyes went wide; big velvet-brown pools of curiosity. "How did you know?"

"You said you collect." Jesse began working his way around the kitchen, pulling drawers open, checking cabinet hinges, forcing himself to see the house through her eyes than through his own loss. "It seemed a natural guess that she'd leave you hers if you were that close."

"We were." Charlotte's voice was thick with memory. "Mima was the most astounding woman. She didn't have an easy life, but she got so much out of every moment, you know?" For a second Jesse worried Charlotte was going to break into tears right there on the countertop, but she just took a deep breath and tucked her hands under her knees. "She'd love this place."

Needing to lighten the moment, Jesse raised the charred teakettle from its place in the sink. "Even the smoke-signal tea service?"

Charlotte laughed. She had a great laugh— lively and full and light. "She might have liked the drama, but Mima was a coffee drinker. 'Strong as love and black as night,' she used to say. Drank four cups a day right up until the end, even when her doctors yelled at her."

It would be so much easier to begrudge Charlotte the sale if she weren't so…sweet. Sweet? That wasn't usually the kind of word he'd use to describe a woman, but it was the one that kept coming to mind with her. Only, she was more than sweet. She had an edge about her. An energy. She was probably more like her Mima than she knew. Spunky, maybe? No, that sounded ridiculous. Vivacious—that was it.

Jesse dragged his mind back to the task at hand. "Let's walk through the house and identify what needs doing."

It didn't take long. Half the needed improvements had already been in his head, and the other half came cascading down upon him as he assumed his contractor's mind-set and considered the house with her needs in mind. Every time the bitter thought of what he would have wanted threatened to overtake him, he wrote down a dollar figure next to a project to show himself what Charlotte's business could mean for his future. By the time he left, Jesse was looking at a proposal that might get him down payments on two different investment properties, and she didn't seem too fazed by it. Things were looking up.

Chapter Four

Jesse watched Charlotte reading through his written proposal on her back porch the next afternoon. Despite how easy it was to chat with her—and how unfairly easy she was to like—the entire situation still hung off-kilter and uncomfortable inside him like a bad joke. He admired her enthusiasm, but it felt like a punch to his ribs at the same time. Had he shown that kind of energy, the singular focus she now displayed toward this house, he'd already own the cottage by now.

Even though she'd been in town only a few days, he'd heard from several people—Chief Bradens, Melba, his fellow firefighter JJ, even JJ's brother, Max—about how Charlotte had gushed over her affection for the cottage. For crying out loud, it seemed even Karl at the coffee shop had gotten a speech about what she planned to do with the place. She'd spout off her plans to anyone who would listen.

Had he shown her initiative, acting more aggressively, more single-mindedly on his plans—the way Randy always acted when it came to business deals—Helen Bearson might have tipped him off that someone else had shown interest in the property. He could have found a way to inch past those final two months and purchase the property now. But no, his claim never went further than a comment to his folks or a vague remark to the other guys on the truck when they went past the vacant house. He'd never done anything more than occasional blue-sky thinking aloud. The plans had been there: real and detailed, meticulously compiled. But he'd kept them to himself, not wanting to be made the butt of more jokes or criticism if things didn't work out. Now the spreadsheet calculating his accrued savings toward the goal felt like a misfire. No, worse: a dud.

Of course, Jesse knew better. His nobler side told him he had no right to his resentment. He had no practical claim to the cottage. This was just another example of his biggest flaw: always hatching plans and spending too long perfecting them to get around to acting on them. Dad would probably be gratified that his trademark inaction had once again come back to bite him. He'd lost the cottage, fair and square. *You snooze, you lose. You've always known that. Maybe now you know it for real.*

The only consolation—and it was slim consolation at that—was how Jesse's gut still told him she belonged in that house. She had on these old-fashioned-looking shoes that would have looked ridiculous on anyone else, but with her flowing pastel dress and the fluttery scarf she wore, she looked as though she belonged right there on the cottage steps. "Vintage chic," his mom would probably call it. All soft and frilly around the edges but definitely not stodgy, and with an artsy edge that let him know she'd have great taste. She wouldn't gut the place and modernize it, stripping away all the history and charm—she'd do it right.

She flipped over the final page of the document he'd given her. "Wow, it's a lot, isn't it?" Despite her bright optimism, he could still read hints of sadness and confusion in her eyes. Trouble was, that determination just made him like her more. This job was starting to feel as though it could become a tangled mess all too easily—and even a mess-up like him knew it was never smart to mix business with pleasure. Even when the pleasure could land him a fat paycheck.

"It's a big job, yes. The results will be fantastic, though. You'd double your money if you ever sold."

"I won't sell." No buyer's remorse from this buyer, that was certain. He got the feeling that once Charlotte Taylor set her course, she was unstoppable.

"Okay, so you want to stay. Well, we know there are some basic repairs you'll need no matter what—like the stove and the upstairs bathroom—even if you do change your mind and decide to sell...."

"Which I won't."

"Which you won't," he echoed. "We can start with those and schedule out the cosmetic fixes and upgrades later. That way you start basic, but keep your options wide open."

She leaned back against the porch stair railing. At least this railing held, not like the wobbly one at her front door. Jesse grimaced as he remembered the photo of the gorgeous wrought-iron railing sitting in his file back home. "Maybe, but first on the list has to be my new claw-footed bathtub."

She'd gushed over the style of the old tub in the upstairs bathroom, saying she'd picked out some newfangled Jacuzzi version that still looked antique. "New is great, but you could also repair the one you already have. Old fixtures

like that are hard to find and worth keeping—
especially if you want to go the sensible route."

Her eyes flashed at the mention of *sensible,*
and she straightened her back with an air of defiance. "Or maybe I don't compromise. Maybe
I use all this free time to do the renovation *exactly* the way I want while I can."

"Free time?" Jesse couldn't help asking.

"I'm between jobs at the moment." There was
a flash of hurt in her eyes as she said the words,
but it faded quickly. "It's just a temporary situation. It's not like I won't find a new job. I'm
very good at what I do. Lots of companies are
ramping up their online commerce. Textile arts
are big business these days, you know."

She didn't strike Jesse as the sensible type.
More the artistic, impulsive type. Those customers were always the most fun—provided they
had pockets as deep as their imaginations—
which maybe still applied to Charlotte Taylor.
He didn't really know many details about what
her financial situation was, nor was it his place
to ask. Still, he'd seen this before, watching a
customer compensate for some loss in their life
by going overboard on a build. A guy's divorce-
driven five-car garage had bought Jesse his new
truck. After all, a smart businessman gives the
customer what they want, not necessarily what
they need. "You could do that."

"I could do that." Her face took on the most amazing energy when she got an idea. She was going to be a fun client to work with, and certainly easy on the eyes.

Jesse suddenly found himself wondering if he could walk the line on this. Could he encourage her, suggest the smartest choices for what she wanted? Could he balance the indulgence of her whims while warning her against something that would prove to be a foolish purchase? Viewed practically, her windfall of free time might allow him to get more work done in less time.

He nodded to the proposal. "I'm not saying you have to compromise. A job this big would be hard to do while you were working full-time. If you set your mind to it, we could be done by September. If you've got the cash now, the timing might be perfect."

She pointed at him, jangling the slew of silver bangles on her wrist. "Exactly how I see it. God's never late and He's never early."

"Huh?"

"Something Mima always said. About God's timing always being perfect, just like you mentioned. And I've always taken Mima's advice."

"You don't have to decide right this minute. You want some time to think about it?" He had to give her at least that much of an out.

She squinted up at the sky, making Jesse wonder if she was consulting her grandmother or God or both. After a long minute, she held out her hand for the pen he was holding. "Nope. I don't need any more time. This is what I want. I want it to be perfect." She signed the proposal in a swirly, artistic hand.

This was going to be fun. In the end, they'd both end up with a showpiece—his to boast about to clients, hers to call home. Win-win, right? "Then the pursuit of perfect begins tomorrow afternoon."

Charlotte 1, Cottage 0.

Charlotte congratulated herself on the tiny victory her cup of tea represented.

A few days ago, the scorecard might have looked a lot more like Kitchen 1, Charlotte 0, but a visit from the electrician Jesse had recommended and two hours of vigilant scouring this morning had put the kitchen in working order. Stopping in at the local housewares store, Charlotte had purchased an electric kettle to hold her over until a wonderfully vintage-looking but thoroughly modern stove came in on special order. At another downtown boutique, she'd found a charming bistro table with two chairs. It felt so satisfying to buy things for the house, to launch the project that was coming to mean so much to her. It made her long-overdue Owner of Cottage tea on her back deck just about perfect. Add one of Mima's teacups and her favorite teapot, and life was wonderful.

See? I'm still here, she thought, smirking at the bright green leaves of the overhead tree. *I will not be beaten by this bump in the road.* "You know what Eleanor Roosevelt says," Charlotte addressed a gray squirrel that was perched on the deck railing with a quivering tail and greedy black eyes, peering at the bag of cookies she'd just opened. "Women are like tea bags—you never know how strong they are until you get them in hot water."

"Quoting first ladies to the wildlife, are we?" Jesse came around the corner of the house lugging a clanking canvas bag and an armful of cut lumber. "Look at you, having a proper tea on your back deck and all."

Charlotte laughed. "This is not a proper tea. It's barely even an improper tea."

Jesse settled his equipment on the bottom step, leaning against the railing to look up at her. "A Mulligan, then."

"A what?"

He grinned, looking so handsome that Charlotte was suddenly aware she was probably covered in kitchen grime. "You don't golf, do you?"

"Not even mini."

"A Mulligan is a do-over. The chance to re-take a shot that went wrong."

Well, that certainly fit. "Yes, I suppose this is a Mulligan tea. I'd rather think of it as a victory lap. I'm declaring myself the winner in the epic battle of Charlotte versus the Filthy Kitchen." At least that was *one* thing she felt as though she'd won in this whole mess her life had become. "With a little backup from Mike the electrician, that is."

Jesse started rummaging through the canvas bag he had set down. "Mike made sure all your other appliances are going to work safely?"

"Everything's safe. He told me to tell you he's going to come back and do the upstairs bathroom wiring once you let him know the plaster is down."

Jesse's eyes lit up. "Demolition. My favorite part."

She cringed. "Somehow I'm not fond of the idea of you going at my bathroom with a sledge-hammer." *My bathroom.* Funny how little things like that made her heart go *zing* today in a way that almost made up for her lack of incoming paychecks.

"Oh, I'm not going at it today." He held Charlotte's eyes for a dizzying moment. "You are."

Charlotte nearly toppled her teacup. "Me?"

"It's a thing of mine. First swing of demo

always goes to the customer. If they're around, which you most definitely are."

"I'm sending a sledgehammer through my bathroom wall?" She'd seen such rituals on the home improvement networks, but she didn't think stuff like that actually took place on real jobs.

"Actually, it'll be more like a crowbar to the feet of your bathtub. Since you agreed to re-enamel it, I'm pulling it out today. Are you ready to start talking about color?"

Charlotte felt as if she'd been waiting a decade to pick the color of *something,* even though that was far from true. Colors—and how they went together—were a wondrous obsession for her, and part of the lure of the textile industry. Still, this choice felt new and exciting, in a way she couldn't quite define. She snatched the top issue from a pile of home decor magazines that were sitting next to the teapot. "I already have one picked out."

"Why am I not surprised?" Jesse walked up the last of the stairs. "Let's see."

She thumbed through the magazine to the dog-eared page, then held it up to Jesse to see. "That sink? The buttercream color with the brass fixtures? That's it, right there."

Jesse took the magazine. "Good choice. For a minute there I thought you were going to show me something purple or zebra striped. The guy who does the re-enameling work is good, but he's not a magician."

For a moment, Charlotte tried to imagine a zebra-striped claw-footed bathtub. Such a thing should never exist. "I have much better taste than animal prints for bathroom fixtures. He can do the sink to match, can't he?"

Jesse peered closer at the photograph. "It won't matter. You'll need a new sink no matter what—the newer fixtures won't fit on a sink like you've got. I'll bring you some catalogues with sinks that come in a color close to that tomorrow. When you pick the style and finish, Jack will make sure the bathtub matches perfectly." He looked up at her. "You're going to want one of those old-fashioned circle shower curtains, aren't you?"

"Absolutely. And in the brass finish. Not that cheap nickel finish."

"That brass finish is exactly that—not cheap. Are you sure?"

Parts of her were completely sure. Other parts—the edges of her chest that turned dark and trembling when she allowed herself to think of how her perfect life plan had been upended—balked at the extra price. Still, how many times in life did a girl get to pick out bathroom fixtures? Ones that would last for decades? A woman's bathroom was her sanctuary, her private escape from life's tensions. Hers *had* to be just right—especially when nothing else in life was. She nodded. Did he find that charming or annoying? His expression was unreadable, and she was growing a little nervous knot in her stomach. "I've even got the shower curtain and window treatment fabric picked out."

"You're going to be fun to work with, you know that?"

"I hope so." She really did. There was something so immensely satisfying about bringing the cottage back to life. As if the house had been waiting for her, holding its structural breath for her to come and pour her ideas inside. Charlotte had engineered some major achievements at Monarch, but those hadn't given her any security, had they? This cottage offered security, right down to the soul-nurturing buttercream color of her soon-to-be-reborn bathtub.

Jesse returned to his bag, making all kinds of rattling noises until he straightened back up with a crowbar, a pair of safety glasses and the daintiest pair of work gloves Charlotte had ever seen. Her astonishment must have shown all over her face, because Jesse waved the gloves and admitted, "These are from my mother. Don't ask."

She wanted to. The gloves were adorable,

white canvas with a vintage-looking print of bright pink roses. They looked like garden gloves from a 1950s issue of *Better Homes and Gardens*. "I love them." Then, because she couldn't hold the curiosity in any longer, "Your mother sent these?"

He ran his hands down his face, but it didn't hide the flush she saw creep across his cheeks. "I said don't ask."

Charlotte pulled her knees up onto the chair and hugged them to her chest, utterly amused. "Do all your customers get adorable work gloves on their first day?" Jesse's mix of amusement and embarrassment was just too much fun to watch.

"Was there something about 'don't ask' that wasn't clear here? Or do you want me to take away your crowbar and just have at the bathtub on my own?"

"No!" she cried, leaping off her chair. The thought of starting, of finally getting this project underway, whizzed through her like electricity. She lunged for the gloves and the crowbar, but Jesse dodged her easily.

"Wait a minute, Ms. Taylor. If we're going to demo together, there are some rules. I can't have customers getting hurt on the job or letting their enthusiasm run away with their good sense."

Charlotte planted her hands on her hips and

squared off against Jesse, even though he had a good six inches on her five-six frame. She raised her chin in defiance. "I never let my enthusiasm run away with my good sense."

The irony of that played out in Jesse's eyes the same moment her brain caught on to the idiocy of that statement made by an unemployed woman about to launch a major renovation project. He just raised one eyebrow, the corner of his mouth turning up in an unspoken, "Really?"

Charlotte used the distraction to pluck the crowbar from Jesse's hand. "Until now," she said, turning toward the door that led into what would be the dining room.

"Took the words right out of my mouth."

Chapter Five

Jesse watched Charlotte wiggle her fingers into the work gloves Mom had sent along. If they weren't so perfect for Charlotte, he'd have never agreed to something so unprofessional as a gift of fussy work gloves. Only these fit Charlotte's personality to a tee. Mom had won them in some social club raffle, and they were far too small for her arthritic hands, anyway. With a pang, Jesse wondered if Mom had been saving them for Randy's wife. Randy's ex-wife.

He'd wanted Constance and Randy to succeed, but even he could see she wasn't the sort of spouse who would continue to endure the kind of hours Randy kept. Jesse wanted his work to be a passion, surely, but not an obsession. That was part of why he loved the firehouse—it served as a constant reminder that there was more to life than a paycheck. There was a certain poetic justice in spending his work hours constructing when so much of the fire-fighting battled destruction.

Charlotte's wide-spread and wiggling floral fingers pulled his thoughts back to the present. He should have remembered pulling the bathtub would be a tight squeeze in this narrow bath-room—he was so close to her he could smell the flowers in whatever lotion she wore. Something sweet but with just a bit of zing, like her person-ality. Jesse held out the clunky safety glasses. "Time to accessorize."

He hadn't counted on her looking so ador-able, standing there like an enthusiastic fish with those big brown eyes filling the gogglelike lenses. Her smile was beyond distracting, and she looked so utterly happy. He'd been grumpy for days after he "lost" the cottage—for that matter he got grumpy when he lost a basket-ball game at the firehouse—but she managed to keep her bounce even when losing her job, not to mention her beloved grandmother. What about her made that kind of resilience possible?

He straddled the antiquated pipes that ran up one side of the bathtub, pulling a wrench from his tool belt to detach them from the floor. Best to get to work right away before the urge to stare at her made him do something stupid. Well, stupider than presenting her with fussy gloves and a baby crowbar. "Pry up that flange while I pull from here."

"Flange?"

Yep, stupider. More every minute. "The circle thing around the bottom of the pipe. Wedge the crowbar into the waxy stuff holding it to the tile and yank it free."

She was a parade of different emotions as she got down on her knees and thrust the crowbar under the seal. Anxiety, determination, excitement, worry—they seemed to flash across her face in split-second succession. He liked that she was so emotionally invested in the place, but it bugged him how transparent her feelings seemed to him. "Go on," he encouraged, charmed by the way she bit her lip and the "ready or not" look in her wide eyes. "You can do this."

Charlotte gave the fixtures a determined glare, then got down on her knees and thrust the crowbar under the seal. The yelp of victory she gave when the suction gave way and the ring sprang up off the tile to clatter against the pipe was—and he was going to have to find a way to stop using this word—adorable. She brandished the crowbar as she sat back on her haunches and watched him go through the process of unhooking the bathtub from its plumbing. He could have done this alone more quickly—maybe even more easily—but this was too much fun. Getting this porcelain behemoth down the stairs to his truck would be the exact opposite of fun, but he'd called in a few guys from the firehouse to help with that, even though they wouldn't add to the scenery the way Charlotte's grin currently did.

She ran a hand along the lip of the deep tub. "Mima would have loved this tub. You were smart to talk me into saving it."

The expensive Jacuzzi model she'd had her eye on seemed like a ridiculous indulgence he would have talked anyone out of buying. Especially when this one could be so easily repaired. "Tell me about her." The question seemed to jump from his mouth, surprising her as much as it did him.

Her eyes lit up with affection. "Mima? She was 'a piece of work,' Grandpa always used to say. Her real name was Naomi Charlotte Dunning, but when I was little I couldn't quite say Naomi, so I just said 'Mi' at first. Then it became 'Mima' and that stuck. I'm named after her. She was a great woman. Grandpa had Alzheimer's like Melba's dad, and Mima was a hero in how she took care of him. When he died, I know she grieved and was scared to go on without him, but she found her courage. So much so that she decided to scatter some of his ashes all over the world. And I mean all over the world. She'd been on almost every continent, and left a little bit of Grandpa everywhere she went." She shrugged. "It's hopelessly romantic, isn't it?"

"I guess." He was pretty sure his parents had already purchased grave plots at the local cemetery and probably had a file somewhere with precise instructions as to what was going to go on their markers. Dad was a firm believer in advance planning, which was why he was so quick to categorize Jesse's career as "unfocused."

Charlotte sighed. "I want to be just like that when I'm her age. I'd want to be just like that now, if I could."

Jesse couldn't think of a single family member—not even Mom—he would praise like that. Family just didn't spur that kind of adoration in his world. "Did you spend a lot of time with her?"

"Tons. She took me on a few of her earlier, smaller trips. Now I get...well—" she swallowed hard "—I *used* to get postcards from her adventures."

He hardly even needed to ask. "And you kept them, didn't you?"

"I'm going to buy beautiful silver frames for all of them and fill the dining room wall."

She had plans—ambitious plans—for every

room in the house. Jesse knew a thing or two about dreaming up plans. It made him wonder where he'd be right now if he had half the determination Charlotte had to put hers in play the way she did. "That will be nice."

Charlotte leaned in, pushing the safety goggles up on top of her head. "I loved her travels, but even when Mima wasn't going anywhere, she was great. You know those teenage years, when you think your parents are the world's worst? I would hang out at Mima's house and declare my life a disaster, and she would just sit there in her rocking chair with her knitting and let me rant. That's where I learned to knit— from Mima. She'd take me to the yarn store and buy me whatever I wanted—even crazy colors or wild novelty yarns—and then we'd go home and make something amazing with it together."

Jesse yanked the first of the two water pipes free and started on the second. "My grandmother taught me her beef stew recipe, but it wasn't quite the warm, fuzzy experience you described."

She cocked her head, sending the glasses askew so that she had to catch them with her hand. "What do you mean?"

"It was less of an 'I'm passing down the family recipe' thing and more of a 'Don't you mess this up and besmirch the Sykes family name' thing. She had no granddaughters, so I think I was just a stand-in. My brother's marriage didn't last long enough to permit any recipe sharing with his wife, anyway." He pointed to the claw foot of the tub nearest his foot. "Ready to pry that up?"

"I won't break it, will I?"

"This is a two-hundred-pound hunk of coated metal. I doubt you could even chip it."

"But it's cracked already." She really had become attached to the thing. It was a bathroom fixture, for crying out loud, not a family heirloom.

"You'll be fine." Because she looked so worried he added, "Just go slow and stop when I tell you."

That foot and the next came free easily, and Jesse was able to angle the tub out of the alcove where it sat and pry up the last two feet with no trouble at all. Once he'd turned the tub away from the wall, the offending crack could be seen. Charlotte ran her finger down the rusted crack, giving a little groan as if she was dressing a wound. "This can be fixed, can't it?"

Jesse made the mistake of hunching down beside her on the narrow floor. It put them too close. "I'm almost positive. The rust isn't that bad and my guy is an artist."

She ran her hands along the top again. "You

know, now I'm glad we're saving her. It'd be a shame to ditch such a beautiful old thing just for a few hotshot Jacuzzi jets, don't you think?"

He shot her a look. "You realize you're talking about a bathtub, right? You're not gonna give it a name or anything. Are you?" Boats, pets and people got names—not bathtubs—but the way Charlotte was looking, he couldn't be sure.

The corner of her mouth turned up. "I'm not the crazy lady who names her plants and has a dozen cats. Not yet, at least. I do plan to own a cat in the near future, though, so you never know."

Jesse chose not to hide his grimace. "A cat?" Maybe he could talk her into holding off until the renovation was complete. Surely he could scour the internet for home construction cat dangers and tell a few horror stories to warn her off.

Charlotte sat back against the wall and crossed her arms over her chest. "Well, if I didn't already guess you to be a dog person, I now have conclusive proof."

"I always heard cats and yarn were a bad combination." He began dismantling the hot and cold faucets from the end of the tub. "You know, jigsaw puzzle photos of kittens tangled up in yarn balls and all."

"I'll take my chances. I'm too enamored of my shoe collection to risk the damage a puppy could do." As if it had suddenly occurred to her, she asked, "How on earth are you going to get this thing down the stairs?"

Jesse checked his watch. "A few of the guys from the firehouse will be here in twenty minutes. I should have all these fixtures removed in ten minutes, and then we can start on the sink. That we can just whack apart with a sledge-hammer."

Her eyes popped. "You're not really—"

"No." She really was too much fun to mess with. "Unless you want to?"

It was the most amusing thing to watch. She was frightened of taking a hammer to her bathroom walls, but there was this corner of her eyes that lit up with the idea. The way that woman could run away with his practicality was going to be very dangerous, indeed. *Keep your distance, Sykes—the last thing you need to do is mess this up.*

"And then he took the sink out onto the driveway. I took that great big hammer, hoisted it over my head and split that sink into two pieces right there." Charlotte felt the ear-to-ear grin return, just as it had every time she remembered the sensation of cracking that sink right down the middle. "I didn't know I had it in me."

"I didn't know you had it in you, either." Melba laughed. "Honestly, I can't picture it. Sounds rather unsafe."

"No, Jesse brought me safety glasses and gloves and everything." She leaned closer to the circle of wide-eyed women at the Gordon Falls Community Church knitting group. "But I think even he was a little shocked that I broke it in half on my first try. The firehouse guys, when they came to help drag the tub down the stairs and into Jesse's truck? They were impressed. Guess all that upper-body work at the gym paid off. I'm telling you, it's satisfying. Demolition therapy is seriously underutilized."

The women all looked shocked—all except for Violet Sharpton, an elderly woman with a sweet expression and a quirky personality. She looked almost envious. "What fun!"

"It made me feel a little bit powerful." In fact, it had made her feel like a momentary superhero, a great memory to pull out when the surges of panic came. "For a woman in a job search, a little confidence boost goes a long way."

"Speaking of a confidence boost," said Melba, "show them your shawl, Charlotte. I want the ladies to see how really talented you are."

Charlotte reached into her knitting bag and produced a sky-blue shawl of mohair-silk lace. Stitched from a knitting pattern and yarn Mima had brought back from Ireland, Charlotte considered this shawl a personal masterpiece.

"Wow. You weren't kidding, Melba. That's beautiful!" Tina, one of the older ladies of the group, ran her fingers across the intricate stitch work.

"I told you, she's talented," Melba boasted. "Look at that lace work."

Charlotte held up the shawl. "It looks hard, but it's really not that complicated."

Violet somehow managed a friendly frown. "Didn't your mother ever teach you to hush up and accept a compliment? It may be easy for you, but some of us would never make it through the first inch." The older woman looked around the room to her fellow knitters. "Can you imagine how blessed someone's going to be when they get even a basic shawl knit with that kind of talent?" The purpose of the group was to make prayer shawls, hand-knitted wraps that were prayed over and given to people in need of healing or comfort. Charlotte had sent supplies from Monarch when Melba first started the group. "Thanks to Charlotte," Violet continued, "I think we've just taken things up a notch around here."

Melba looked pleased the group had taken so quickly to Charlotte. "You all remember it was Charlotte who set us up when I began to teach you all how to knit." Charlotte was pleased, too, feeling right at home in a matter of minutes. She'd always been that way with knitters—she could walk into a yarn shop anywhere in the world and feel as though she was among friends.

Her new friends all narrowed their eyes, evidently feeling the injustice of Charlotte's job loss as much as she did. "They shouldn't have let you go," Violet said. "It's a crying shame, that's what I say, even if Chicago's loss is our gain. Still, you seem a smart cookie to me. You'll land on your feet in no time."

Charlotte wondered whether she ought to admit she said something similar to herself in the bathroom mirror every morning, pep-talking herself into facing another day of unanswered queries and diminishing funds. Instead, she just quoted something Mima always said, "From your mouth to God's ears."

"That's right," another woman, Abby Reed, chimed in. "You've got yourself one powerful posse of prayer warriors on your side now. These ladies know how to storm the gates of heaven, I tell you."

"Good thing," Charlotte admitted as she began stitching. *Stitch,* she told herself. *Don't complain or whine, just stitch. Look confident and you'll be confident.*

"I admire you." Tina turned her knitting to start a new row. "Not too many folks your age would see the value in buying a home and setting down roots while you're still single. Shows confidence, independence, common sense—all those good 'ence' words."

"You should talk to my Ben." Abby groaned. "Since he graduated he hasn't shown any of those words except *nonsense*. You'd think a job was going to land gift-wrapped in his lap the way he lollygags around the house. Frank has threatened to force him onto the fire department in another two weeks if the boy doesn't step things up."

Violet held up the navy blue shawl she was working on, a textured piece with white stripes down the side. Melba had told her Violet was one of the newer knitters, but Charlotte would have never known it by the woman's work—she was a natural. "Think we could pray some sense into this and give it to him?"

Abby laughed. "You'd be better off praying some patience into one and wrapping it over my mouth. We keep fighting over this. I was so excited to have him back home from college, but I'll tell you the novelty has worn off."

"You were saying you needed more staff at

the shop," Marge Bowers suggested. "Can't he work there?" Abby ran the town gift shop, which also stocked a small selection of locally produced yarn. Charlotte had been in there numerous times—she wasn't a parent, but it didn't take a genius to know it wasn't a place most young men would ever want to work.

Jeannie Owens balked. "Can you see Ben making sales in Abby's shop? The only thing worse would be having him selling my candy— he'd eat all my profits."

"I thought about sending him over to bag at Halverson's Grocery just to get the employee discount—that boy eats enough for five people!"

Violet pointed her free needle at Abby. "You should do that. The bag boys at Halverson's don't show a lick of sense these days. Might do them good to have a college graduate in their midst."

"I just hope they motivate Ben to find a job that actually uses that expensive accounting degree." Abby looked up from her knitting. "Hey, this is sounding like a better idea every minute."

Charlotte let her gaze wander from face to friendly face. How often had she told Melba that this was what she loved about Gordon Falls? The people shared things, getting through life side by side, warts and all. These were the women who had held Melba up during the long, painful decline of her father's Alzheimer's. They'd held her friend close when he'd finally passed away, so much so that Charlotte never worried for Melba's support when she couldn't make it out to Gordon Falls. Why, then, did she resist telling them—and Melba—how frightening being jobless was to her? *End this wait, Lord,* Charlotte finished her row of stitching as she sent a silent prayer for God's favor over the dozen electronic résumés she'd sent out earlier this morning. *Send me a job.*

"Charlotte, if you could have any job in the world, what would it be?" Jeannie, who filled a room with sunny-eyed optimism wherever she went despite a host of personal challenges, posed the question as she poured herself a second cup of coffee.

"Oh, naturally, I've always thought about opening a yarn shop. I might do it someday, but I know enough to realize how much work it is."

Jeannie and Abby, both small business owners, nodded in agreement.

"I'm still looking to work for someone, to let all the managerial headaches be on someone else's plate for a while longer," Charlotte added.

She thought about Jesse. After they wrestled the bathtub free, she'd managed to get him to open up about his plans to launch his own business. He seemed pretty autonomous as it was, despite working for Mondale Construction, but was bursting with the urge to work for himself and call his own shots. She admired his ambition, but she could also see the dark edge of it. Jesse wanted success to show the world that he could do it, to prove himself worthy. From a few side comments he'd made, she suspected his father had a lot to do with that drive—and not in a good way. She was so fortunate to have Mom and Dad, who believed in her no matter what she did. When she owned her own business, it would be for all the right reasons. For now, it was enough that she owned her own cottage.

Chapter Six

"You've made quite an impression," Charlotte's cousin JJ announced when they ran into each other a few days later at Halverson's Grocery. This was another small-town phenomenon that still startled Charlotte—a trip to the grocery store turned into a social event every time. She'd yet to fill her basket without running into six or seven people she knew—not to mention being introduced to half a dozen new "neighbors." That certainly never happened at the city convenience mart.

"Jesse's account of your powerhouse sink demolition was the talk of the firehouse," JJ went on, as the two of them wandered down the frozen-food aisle. "As if your first-day kitchen fire hadn't endeared you to the guys already."

"I think I was hoping for less fanfare tied to my entrance into Gordon Falls," Charlotte admitted. "The past few months have been a bit more dramatic than I'd like."

"Well, if you're not into drama, you've hired the wrong guy. Jesse Sykes is as Hollywood as they come. You remember him singing at our wedding, don't you?"

Just the other afternoon she was upstairs measuring windows when Jesse either forgot she was home or didn't care that she heard him. His voice echoed stunningly throughout the empty house, and she'd stopped to lean against the wall and just listen. Smooth as silk and soulful to boot. Mima would have declared Jesse to have "a set of pipes" and Charlotte had to agree. "He's amusing, and he's got a great voice, that's for sure."

JJ's voice softened. "He's a great guy. A bit of a loose cannon sometimes, but a heart of gold." She grinned. "Mostly." When Charlotte narrowed one eye at her she added, "You could do worse."

She really didn't want to get into this with JJ again. Her cousin knew her concerns about getting involved with a first responder without them arguing it out for the umpteenth time. Anyway, it felt wrong to tell one firefighter that you didn't think you could do life alongside another firefighter. "Sure, he's got personality. He's not for me, though."

Was there anyone out there for her? She liked

to think so, though she was getting frustrated waiting for him to show up. In any case, now wasn't the time for a new relationship. Now should be about being her own person, stepping confidently—if not smoothly—into the future God had for her. Dating would just muck up her thinking and add to her anxiety. And really, the last thing she needed right now was the prospect of any more rejection.

"I thought you just said he was amusing." JJ selected a bag of frozen peas and placed them in her cart.

"Amusement is not the same thing as attraction." That felt dishonest, because she did feel an attraction to Jesse. She just knew better than to act on it. "I'll admit, we're having a bit of fun with this renovation project, and I could sure use a bit of fun right now, but that's all. Besides, from the little I heard, he's got all kinds of family baggage and I don't need anyone like that."

"Who's got family baggage?" Melba and Maria came up the aisle, waving hello. *Here we go again, a party in the frozen-food aisle.* It had its fun side, but Charlotte fretted her days of throwing on sweats and a baseball hat to duck into the grocery store were over.

"Sykes," JJ replied.

Melba sighed. "Everyone's got family baggage of some kind."

"Maybe, but your family baggage is adorable." JJ wiggled one of Maria's irresistible tiny pink toes, making the baby girl giggle.

"What would Mima have thought of Jesse?" JJ asked, surrendering the toe as, with the astounding flexibility of babies, Maria pulled it up to stuff it in her mouth. All three women laughed. Even though JJ and Max were Charlotte's cousins on her father's side, Mima left a big enough impression that both sides of Charlotte's relatives knew and loved the woman. Max and JJ had come to Mima's funeral, and not just because they wanted to support Charlotte and her parents.

Mima's opinion of Jesse—or what it would have been—was an interesting point to consider. Charlotte had to think for a moment, biding her time as she filled her own handbasket with a box of frozen breakfast sandwiches. "Hard to say. She'd like his sense of humor, but I doubt she'd have found him artistic enough."

"Your grandmother always was a pushover for the poetic types, judging from the way your grandfather won her over," Melba offered, gently removing the toe from Maria's drool-soaked mouth. "It's got to be too early for teething, doesn't it?"

JJ and Charlotte shrugged. Charlotte noticed a new weariness in Melba's voice and eyes.

"I still think you should publish all those love letters as a book," Melba went on. "Your grandfather was a heart slayer on the page in his day." The new mother sighed. "Nobody does that sort of romantic stuff anymore."

Charlotte leaned over and tickled Maria. "Is my darling goddaughter cutting into Mommy's love life?"

Melba's sigh turned into a yawn. "Right behind the firehouse. Between Clark's days and Maria's nights, I'm stretched to the limit. This parenting stuff is hard."

"The chief has been wound pretty tight these days, too," JJ added.

Charlotte eyed her friend. "When's the last time you and Clark had an evening to yourselves?"

Melba's only response was a sad smile. "It's worth it."

JJ put a hand on Melba's sagging shoulder. "You two deserve to be off duty. No offense, but you look exhausted. And honestly I could use a less grumpy boss."

"That's it, I'm babysitting." Charlotte pulled out her smartphone to check her calendar. There was nothing like helping others to get her mind off her own problems. And she adored Maria. *This should be a fun task.* "When is the next night Clark has free?"

Melba rolled her eyes. "Who knows?"

"Clark does," said JJ. "Text him right now and ask him."

"Right now?" Melba seemed more interested in the choice of green beans, and that was bad news in the romance department.

Charlotte shut the freezer cabinet door in front of Melba's face. "This instant. You're outnumbered three to one."

"Three?"

"Maria agrees with me."

Two minutes and a package of ground turkey later, Melba peered at her phone and declared, "Thursday night."

"Mission accomplished. Okay, ladies, I have to get going." JJ's face took on a glow. "Alex is heading out of town again, and I promised him one home-cooked meal before he gets on another plane."

Melba gazed after the lovestruck firefighter and then pushed out a breath as she deposited a box of biscuit mix into her cart. "I'm pretty sure Clark and I looked that smitten once."

"Exactly my point," Charlotte replied. "I'm babysitting next Thursday night so you and Chief Bradens can have some time to rekindle your flame."

"I'm likely to fall asleep at the restaurant table," Melba admitted. "I can't remember the last time I sat down for a whole meal. They don't call 5:00 p.m. 'the fussing hour' for nothing. By the time Clark pulls in the driveway I'm ready to take a hot bath and tell the world goodnight. At least until Maria wakes up again."

The strain in her friend's eyes tugged at Charlotte's heart. Melba had been through so much since moving to Gordon Falls—the long, hard struggle to care for her father, his eventual death—she'd thanked God for sending Clark to Melba a million times over the past year. And now baby Maria added more joy to their lives, but they were both clearly tired. While Melba never complained, Charlotte knew being married to the fire chief wasn't the easiest job in the world. Dad had been only a police captain, and it had taken a lot out of Mom. She touched Melba's elbow. "You need this. Let me do this for you. It's one night. Even if Maria screams the entire time, I can handle it."

Jesse set down the nozzles he was cleaning a few days later and stared at Chief Bradens. "Really?"

Chief nodded. "With your background, you never thought about taking the inspector's training?"

"Well, no." Fire inspectors were career guys. The Gordon Falls department had only two paid employees, Chief Bradens himself and the fire inspector, Chad Owens. While some volunteer guys looked to shift to a paid professional post, Jesse never counted himself among them. As his father never missed a chance to point out, this job asked enough of him on a volunteer basis. He wasn't eager to expand that. "Chad's not retiring or anything, is he?"

"Not that he's told me. It's just that I see the potential in you."

"I don't know. Sounds like a whole lot of paper pushing to me." Chad spent more time at a desk than on a truck, and Jesse knew enough of the Gordon Falls building codes to know they could tax a guy's patience. "I'm allergic to administrative tasks."

The chief leaned up against the truck that sat parked behind where Jesse was working. "I thought you wanted to own your own business someday."

"I do."

"You'll have to get over your allergic reaction to paperwork."

Jesse gave a grunt. "Mondale doesn't do paperwork."

"That's because his wife does his billing and filing. You planning to marry into an administrative family anytime soon?"

then there was the subject of Sunday mornings. "I don't think I spend enough time in church to be her type anyhow."

The chief's expression made Jesse regret his choice of reply. "You can change that if you want. The congregation talent show is soon, and we're still looking for an emcee."

That made Jesse laugh. "Me? Master of ceremonies at the GFCC talent night? Don't you think that's a bit ridiculous?"

"Have you ever seen our talent show?" Bradens smirked. "Ridiculous is nearly a requirement. It's the talent that seems to be optional."

"Why don't *you* do it?"

"I'll have to if I don't find someone else. This year providing the emcee is the firehouse's contribution. We could really use someone who has some actual theatrical tendencies."

Sure, he was a born show-off, but Jesse still shook his head. "I think I'll pass."

"Will you at least think about it? That, and the inspector's training?"

Some days Bradens just didn't know the meaning of the word *no*. "Yeah, fine, I'll give it some thought. I doubt I'll change my mind, though, so keep looking for someone else."

"You're my first choice. On both fronts. Just know that, okay?"

Both of those fronts, but not first choice for Charlotte, huh? That stung just a little, but suited him fine, anyway. "Sure, okay."

Chapter Seven

Charlotte was regretting her final "I can handle it" words to Melba. It was eight-thirty, and Maria hadn't stopped crying since Melba went out the door at six. Charlotte had fed her, changed her, rocked her and done just about every other baby-soothing thing she could think of, but still Maria wailed.

"All right, Maria, it's a nice night, so you and I are going to go for a walk. Any more of your cries bouncing off the walls in this house and I'm going to go a little bonkers. If the river doesn't soothe you, nothing will."

Charlotte found the stroller (complete with an adorable hand-knit baby blanket) on the back porch, penned a quick note and stuck it to the fridge—all one-handed because the red-faced Maria occupied the other arm—and headed out into the warm June night.

Gordon Falls was at its best on summer evenings. The town spread itself out along the Gordon River, filling the hillsides with quaint homes and dotting the town's main thoroughfare of Tyler Street with a collection of charming shops and restaurants. It was a picture-postcard small town. Charlotte had joked about the overwhelming quaintness of the place on her first visit, but she'd come to really love the community. It was as far away from the hustle and concrete of Chicago as she could get, and she could always feel her stress peeling off her soul as her car pulled through the big green floodgates that stood at the edge of Tyler Street. Even Maria simmered down to a steady whimper punctuated by a few bursts of crying.

Charlotte headed toward Tyler Street and the far end of Riverwalk, sure to be filled with people enjoying the evening but far enough from the restaurant where Clark and Melba were dining so that she wouldn't risk running into them. She already had a host of memories connected to places in town: the housewares store where she'd purchased the new kettle. The hardware store where she'd gotten her first spare set of keys made. The grocery store where she seemed to meet everyone she knew on every visit. The boutique that was sure to be her favorite place for clothes—once she spent time and energy on clothes instead of curtains. Abby Reed's craft and gift store, which held just enough yarn to make Charlotte feel as though she hadn't abandoned all artistic civilization. She hadn't been back to her Chicago apartment in almost three weeks, and she hadn't even missed it. That place was boxy, ordinary and noisy. The cottage was on its way to becoming quiet, filled with charm and a thing of beauty to help the rest of life's stress disappear.

What are You up to, Lord? Why am I so drawn to this place? Charlotte wondered to God as she pushed a fussing Maria through the town. *I've never felt a place could make me so happy before this. It's always been people that made me happy. Only now I've lost my colleagues and Mima. The things here—the things in my house, even—are what make me happiest now. Is that wrong? Or just different?* Charlotte looked down at Maria's frustrated mad-at-the-world pout and thought, *Kiddo, I know how you feel.*

Her Tyler Street journeys led her down by the firehouse and Karl's Koffee. It wouldn't hurt to meet a friendlier face than Maria's frustrated red cheeks and tiny balled fists.

Maria's wailing ensured that most people heard her coming before they saw her. Two grandmother-types outside of Karl's had offered some tactics, but neither of them had worked, and Charlotte admitted to growing a little anxious that maybe her goddaughter was suffering from something more than simple fussiness. It wasn't much of a surprise that Maria's cries caught the ears of the firefighters on duty as Charlotte walked by.

"Hey, is that the Charlotte?" A stocky man from the firehouse called as he rose from his lawn chair on the driveway.

Charlotte stopped, startled that he'd called her by name. "Um, hi."

A younger fireman—in actual red suspenders, Charlotte noted with amusement—came out from behind one of the bright red trucks that stood ready in their enormous garage spaces. "Yorky, you gotta stop calling Chief Bradens's kid 'the chieflette.'" He wiped his hands on a towel that he subsequently stuffed into a back pocket. "Chieflette's not a name. It's not even a real word. It's just weird."

He hadn't been saying "Charlotte"—he'd been saying "chieflette." Charlotte felt a twinge of satisfaction that the baby's firehouse nickname sounded so close to her own. After a second she remembered Yorky from her ill-fated first day as cottage owner.

He was currently balking at the younger guy. "Everybody in here has a nickname, why not the baby?" His eyes popped in recognition. "Hey, you're the cottage lady."

"I am." She held out her hand. "Charlotte. And I think 'chieflette' is kind of cute. It's certainly original." Which kindled a fierce curiosity as to what name Jesse had been given. Smiling at Yorky, she made a mental note to discover a sneaky way to find out. Maria gave a wail of disapproval as if to counteract her godmother's endorsement.

"She's certainly cranky." Yorky peered into the stroller. "Gas?"

Charlotte sighed and picked Maria up out of the stroller to settle her against her shoulder. "I've burped her. Twice. Some lady even tried some special colic hold outside of Karl's, but nothing seems to help."

"Is she running a fever?" The younger man went to reach for Maria's head, but Yorky swatted his hand away.

"Wash your hands before you touch a baby, son—everybody knows that." When the man pulled the towel back out from his pocket, Yorky frowned. "And no, that's not enough." For a big, burly guy, Yorky was evidently a softie for babies. "Shame JJ's not on tonight—women always have a knack for that stuff."

If women always have a knack for this, why am I pushing a screaming baby down Tyler

Street? Charlotte thought, suddenly fighting a wave of insecurity. She tried to give an educated touch to Maria's forehead. "No fever that I can tell."

"Go see if Pipes is still here," Yorky said to his companion, cocking his head back toward the firehouse kitchen window.

"He left an hour ago. Him and Wally are grilling out down by the river with some of the probies."

Pipes? Probies? Some days firemen seemed to speak a different language. "Is Pipes a parent?"

That brought a guffaw from Yorky. "Jesse? Now wouldn't that be a hoot. Nah, Jesse's just got silver pipes. The guy sings to kids when they're scared from the fires. Honestly, it'd be hard to keep him around if he weren't so good at it."

So Jesse's nickname was "Pipes." The singing she'd heard echoing through her house certainly validated the name. Jesse's silky voice struck her as a Frank Sinatra–Harry Connick Jr.–Michael Bublé sort of croon, but with a decidedly soulful edge. Based on the wails she'd been enduring for the past pair of hours, getting Jesse to sing Maria to sleep seemed like the best idea in the world. "I'll go find him, if you don't mind. Where on the riverwalk is he?"

"Just south of the footbridge. Go a block far- ther than Karl's Koffee and you should be able to smell the meat burning."

Maria gave a yowl as if she was working up to another good fit again, spurring Charlotte to settle the fussy baby back into the stroller and turn them both toward the river. She'd pledged to herself to do anything necessary to present Melba and Clark with a happy baby when they got home from dinner—those two deserved some peace and quiet. They deserved to not feel one pang of guilt for taking an evening to themselves. "Thanks, I'm sure I'll find him."

"He'll probably hear you coming," Yorky of- fered with an understanding smile. "But I can page him if you like."

"No, I think we can make it to the footbridge in one piece. Thanks, Yorky." She took an im- mediate liking to the stocky, middle-aged fire- fighter. He was a big bear of a man with a heart of butter—who wouldn't like a man with that smile? "And extra thanks—you know—for playing hero the other day at my cottage."

"Nothin' doing, Charlotte. That's why we're here. You just take care of the little chieflette there and we'll call it even."

Charlotte started walking toward the river. "Chieflette, huh? You could do worse, Maria. You've got two dozen uncles looking out after you, little lady. That's good, because with those red curls and that smile—the one you haven't shown me in hours, I might add—you're gonna need 'em."

"Aw," Wally groaned as he bit into his hamburger. "Aw, Sykes, this is carnivore perfection." He wiped a smear of Sykes's Special Sauce from his chin, a look of gastronomic pleasure on his face. "What's in here?"

Jesse smiled as he passed off a burger to another firefighter in training, or "probie," as they were known around the firehouse. "Wouldn't you like to know."

To be known for an awesome burger was a small satisfaction, but Jesse liked the appreciation. The firehouse boasted only three decent cooks, so meals were a gamble most nights. If they ever went to a professional model where the firefighters lived on-site in regular shifts, it'd become a serious issue. As it was with rotating shifts of volunteers on call, meals were more of a perk than a requirement. Jesse liked to make sure he was around on Thursday nights when the butcher always sent over burgers. It was a crime to see good meat destroyed by bad cooks.

A sharp cry caught his ear as he slid his spatula under the final burger and handed it off to another grateful probie. There was a baby nearby, and an unhappy one at that.

Jesse put the cover back on the grill and wiped the spatula clean on a towel. He dipped a finger in the plastic bowl of Sykes's Special Sauce, licking a tangy taste before snapping the lid into place. Man, that stuff was delicious. Maybe someday he'd consider bottling it and selling it wholesale to bars and burger joints. His thoughts were interrupted as the high-pitched wail grew louder, and he turned to see the source of the drama.

It was Charlotte Taylor. Chief Bradens had mentioned she was babysitting his daughter tonight. The strained look on Charlotte's face told him it wasn't going well.

He left the bowl on the table and walked toward the noisy pair. "Somebody having a rough night?"

"She's been like this for almost two hours. I've tried everything I know and a few things complete strangers have suggested." Charlotte pushed her hair back from her face in exasperation. "In another hour I'll be ready to cry myself."

Jesse reached back to the table to pull an antiseptic wipe from a container and used it to clean the last of barbecue and Sykes's Sauce off his hands. "I'll bet."

"Smells great." Charlotte nodded toward the grill with a weak attempt at a smile. Poor thing, she really did look at the end of her rope.

"Just gave out the last one, sorry."

"No, I've eaten. I just didn't realize your skill set included cooking."

"Oh, it sure does," one young man said with a mouth full of burger. "Sure does."

"It's nice to have an appreciative audience," Jesse admitted, peering into the stroller to see a puffy red face surrounded by a halo of Bradens-red curls. "Seems Chieflette's got a temper to match her locks."

Charlotte laughed. "I heard Yorky call her that." She gave Jesse a slightly panicked look. "I also heard they don't call you Pipes for nothing and that you're great at calming down kids. Care to work some of that vocal medicine on Little Miss Fussbudget here?" She looked just short of desperate.

It was the chief's baby. It was Charlotte asking. What kind of fool would say no? "No guarantees, but I'll do my best." A surprising knot settled in Jesse's stomach. Normally he was never given to nerves—especially about singing—but for some reason the stakes felt higher at the moment. Distracting five-year-olds at the preschool fire drill was one thing. Soothing a fussy baby in front of a pack of probies and

Charlotte Taylor? Well, that was quite another. "Okay," he said, infusing his voice with confidence he didn't fully feel, "hand Little Miss Crankypants over and let's see if we can calm her down."

At first, Maria didn't care at all to be handed over to a strange set of arms. As he settled her against his shoulder, she wailed, and out of the corner of his eye Jesse saw Charlotte wringing her hands. Starting down in as low a register as he could manage, Jesse launched into a slow, soft version of Ben E. King's "Stand by Me." He remembered reading somewhere that the rumble of a deep voice in a chest was soothing to babies. When that didn't have much of an effect, he modulated up a key and began to sway around the grass with her, holding her tight and patting her back the way he'd seen his grandmother do. Halfway into the second chorus, Maria gave a little hiccup and softened her wails.

A natural tenor, Jesse was more comfortable in higher keys, and the tiny bit of progress he'd made bolstered his confidence. He was "Pipes," and while he mostly used his voice for laughs, he also knew this was his gift, the particular talent he brought to firefighting. He could serenade somebody calm in the back of an ambulance, as they made their way down the ladder or as they waited for their loved ones to emerge from a smoking building. And, okay, he was a bit of a born show-off. Showing off for a good cause like helping Charlotte help Chief Bradens? Well, that ought to be a cakewalk. When Maria calmed further, Jesse took it up another key and began dancing with Maria. He caught Charlotte's eye, winked and spun Maria in a tiny turn that actually produced a sigh from the baby.

"Will you look at that?" one of the probies said with astonished eyes. "It's like he's the baby whisperer or something."

By the third chorus, Jesse had produced an actual laugh from Maria. Well, at least it sounded like a laugh. He ignored the growing wet spot on his shoulder, focusing instead on the steady small breaths coming under his hand on Maria's back. By the end of the second song, Maria was out cold, Charlotte was astonished and Jesse felt downright victorious. He'd sung victims to calm—or something at least close to reasonable—before, but he'd never actually sung a baby to sleep. There was a startling satisfaction in the accomplishment, which fueled a warm glow under his ribs. Very, very carefully, he lowered a contented Maria back into the stroller and then looked up to catch Charlotte's wide smile.

"Better keep walking so she stays asleep," one of the probies said behind him.

Jesse turned, head cocked in annoyance. "If you know so much about babies, Carson, why wait until now to speak up?"

"Hey," Carson replied, "I'm the oldest of eight. But no way was I going to step in and miss a chance to see the Great Sykes at work. Just keep walking for another ten minutes or so and you'll be golden."

Jesse wasn't really in the mood to see Charlotte take off down the Riverwalk. Tossing the package of hamburger buns to the trainee, Jesse said, "Okay, then, we'll walk. You clowns finish up eating and take everything back to the firehouse. Don't forget to study those handouts before the next session." Turning to Charlotte, he said, "I'll go along as a precautionary measure. In case my outstanding talents only have a temporary effect. It is the chief's baby, after all."

Charlotte shrugged as if to say, "Better safe than sorry," and began rolling the stroller down the path. Jesse caught up with her, enjoying the victory of the moment. They walked along in cautious silence for a few minutes, ensuring that Maria was safely off in dreamland.

"That was amazing," Charlotte whispered after a bit.

"Actually, that was Ben E. King. 'Amazing'

is a different tune." The soft laugh his joke pulled from Charlotte was even more satisfying than Maria's dozing. See? He could do the casual friendship thing here. Bradens's warnings weren't necessary. He was just helping a client help a friend, that was all. Besides, he always liked to make people laugh—why not Charlotte, as well?

"The guys at the firehouse said you've done that on calls. Sing to kids, I mean. How do you manage it?"

It was like having someone ask how he breathed. "It wasn't something I really thought about. The first time was my second or third call on the rig—my first real fire. I was scared. You never really lose the fear. You just sort of make peace with it. Anyway, back in the upper bedroom there was a little boy. We're scary looking with all our gear on, so it's always a challenge to get kids to come to us." The memory of that little boy's dread-filled eyes had never left Jesse. At that moment, he would have done anything it took to gain that boy's confidence and pull him to safety. "I saw a poster from a television show on his wall and I just started singing the theme song."

"And he came to you?"

"Well, it was more like he didn't run away. I just kept singing and walking toward him. I didn't think about whether anyone could hear me on the radio, I was so focused on doing anything to keep that kid from ducking back under that bed. When I got close enough, I grabbed him and just kept singing the whole way down the stairs and out the door so he'd stay still and not struggle."

Charlotte smiled. "Jesse, the singing fireman."

Jesse shot her a look. "Please. I've heard every version of that you can think of, and I don't like a single one of them. It works. It keeps kids—and even some adults—calm when calm is the hardest thing to manage. Bradens does it with his eyes. I do it with my voice."

"Clark's eyes?"

"Every firefighter has a particular gift, a talent. Chief Bradens has a way of looking right into your eyes so that you believe whatever he says. You don't question stuff like that when lives are at stake." He caught Charlotte's gaze and held it. "I take my work at GFVFD very seriously. We all do. We put our lives on the line for it."

"I'm sorry." Her voice was soft, and he regretted calling her out for her teasing. "Really."

"It's okay. Just no cracks about it, all right?" He reached out and touched her hand as it rested on the stroller handle. Something not at all casual and not at all like friendship zinged through his fingers when he did. "I think I've knocked her out cold, poor thing."

Charlotte looked up at him for far longer than was necessary. "You're my hero."

If you choose to go after her, I'd want to know you really mean it…. I don't want the department's most confirmed bachelor to stomp on the heart of my wife's best friend. The chief's warning echoed sensibly in Jesse's brain. Trouble was, the rest of him was busy losing the battle to Charlotte's big brown eyes.

Chapter Eight

Jesse stood in the doorway of Chief Bradens's office Monday morning. "You wanted to see me, Chief?"

"I did. Come on in."

Jesse crossed the room to take the guest chair in front of the chief's desk. "What's up?"

"First off, it seems I owe you some thanks for serenading my daughter the other night." Clark shook his head. "Man, that sounds odd to say."

Jesse made a serious face. "I'm not taking your daughter to the prom, sir."

Clark laughed. "Not on your life, even if she was eighteen years older."

"At least twenty-two years older, boss. And not even then." That was true. If Chief were older—and Bradens was one of the youngest fire chiefs in the state—and his daughter was anything close to Jesse's age, Jesse still wouldn't touch that with a ten-foot pole.

"Okay, well, thanks are in order anyway. It was a pretty nice thing to come home to a sleeping baby. Melba was sure Maria would give Charlotte a load of trouble, and it seems you kept that from happening. The probies were calling you 'the baby whisperer.' It's pretty funny, actually. I think they wonder if you have superpowers or something."

"Feed those boys a decent burger and they'll believe anything," Jesse joked.

"Anyway, I wanted to know if you've given any more thought to the talent-show thing or the inspector's training."

Bradens was not usually one to push on stuff like this—Jesse was beginning to feel the pinch of his predicament. Didn't singing the man's daughter to sleep gain him a "cease-fire" on the church invitations? At least he wasn't riding Jesse for spending an hour walking around the Riverwalk with Charlotte. That hadn't been such a smart idea—that woman had begun to really get under his skin. He'd spent the next hour in the firehouse weight room burning off energy and listing all the reasons to keep clear of the pretty client.

"Yeah, look, I don't know."

The chief leaned in. "I'd take it as a personal favor if you'd emcee the show for us."

Chief's attempts to drag Jesse over the GFCC threshold were getting less subtle every time. It was bad enough when Melba had joined the choir a few months ago, and Bradens went on about fun and fellowship—which Jesse found ironic, because everyone knew the chief couldn't hold a tune if it had a handle tied to it. To Jesse, choir sounded like a bunch of people who barely knew how to have fun standing up singing old songs in silly, shiny robes. Not that he could confirm his theory; the only time he'd darkened the doors of Gordon Falls Community Church had been for Melba's father's funeral a while back, and there had been only community singing in that service.

When Jesse didn't respond, Bradens played his trump card. "Charlotte was the one who came up with the idea, actually. I'm surprised she didn't mention it to you given the success of your little command performance in the park." That settled it. Charlotte could be relentless. Jesse was sure if he said no to Bradens, Charlotte would just take up the campaign and double it.

"Tell you what. I'll do the talent show if you lay off about the choir."

"Thanks. Think about what I said regarding the inspector, though. Actually, I think you could go further than that. You're a good fire-fighter, but your real talent is connecting with people. Catching their focus in a crisis. Those are skills I can't really teach. You may think I'm nuts for saying this, but I think if we could rein in that crazy side of yours, you have the makings of a good chief."

Jesse sure wasn't expecting that. "Me? A fire chief?"

"Well, we've got to find some way for you to harness all that charisma for good."

He'd heard some version of that speech—one slightly less complimentary of his personality—regularly from his father. Grow up, settle down, fly straight, take action; it came in a dozen sour flavors. Jesse had really hoped the launching of Sykes Homes would put a damper on that sort of talk. He knew Chief Bradens was demonstrating faith in his abilities; it was just that the topic was a raw nerve. He liked his own plans—even if they had been detoured by the loss of the cottage—and suddenly Bradens was piling new expectations on him. "Thanks for the vote of confidence," was the best answer he could give at the moment, "but like I said, I'm allergic to administration."

"I'm trying to talk the town council into finding the funds to pay for a deputy chief."

Jesse shrugged. Bradens could sweeten the deal all he wanted, but it still didn't really fit in with Jesse's plans for where life was supposed to go from here. He switched to what he hoped was a safer topic. "Speaking of administration, Charlotte will get her occupancy permit this afternoon—we're turning the water back on later today. You'll get your house back." That little benchmark still stung, but the chief had no way of knowing that—only a few of the guys on the crew knew about Jesse's thwarted plans to buy the place. "The place is still rough around the edges but livable. It'll be a beauty, though, when she's done. That woman knows how to make full-blown decorating plans, that's for sure."

"I feel better knowing she's working with you and Mondale rather than some contractor from out of town. She's in a bit of a weird place right now when it comes to that cottage."

At that moment, Jesse saw in Chief Bradens's eyes a glimmer of the niggling suspicion that had bothered him for days. The growing sense that Charlotte might not be thinking with her head right now so much as her heart. "How so?"

"Well, don't you think she's going at this with a little too much—" he searched for the word "—drive?"

Charlotte was indeed going full out on the renovation. It was keeping him busy and swelling his paycheck, but it was also making him a bit worried. "She wouldn't be the first person to take her stress out on the Home Shopping Network, if that's what you're saying." The desire to honor her grandmother and take her mind off her job problems could easily get twisted up in a craving to do things that might not make the most financial sense. "She's taking advantage of the free time in between jobs to give the place the attention it deserves. I can spot the difference."

Could he? He'd accepted her order for premium kitchen fixtures yesterday that were three times as expensive as the ones he'd recommended. While he felt oddly protective of Charlotte, he was also becoming aware that with the right smile, she could make him agree to just about anything. Not that it was his role to rein her in, but hadn't he promised himself to do just that? Let her splurge but splurge wisely? What she'd ordered yesterday couldn't be called a wise splurge by anyone, and yet he hadn't challenged it at all. Charlotte wasn't the only one in a bit of a weird place right now.

"Melba's worried about her." The chief gave a weary sigh. "At the same time, I'd kind of like my house to contain only two females again, if you catch my drift."

"Relax, Chief. Like I said, I should have your

guy-to-girl ratio back down to one-to-two by tomorrow." As for what the additional woman would do once she was living in her project and could focus on it full-time…he'd worry about that later.

Charlotte held up Violet Sharpton's latest prayer shawl Wednesday morning with genuine admiration. Karl of Karl's Koffee had fallen and hurt his hip again, and Violet had made him a brown shawl with coffee cups dotting either end, their plumes of steam rising to meet in a swirly pattern down the middle. "Honestly, Violet, if I were still at Monarch, I might ask to put this one—and your flame shawl and the flamingo one—on the cover of a catalogue." Violet had made a fabulous one-of-a-kind prayer shawl, with a flame motif to match his thrill-seeking style, for Max Jones after he'd been hurt in a paralyzing fall. She had exceeded that effort a few months later with one for Max's fiancée, Heather, bearing her favorite birds. A Sharpton Shawl was on its way to becoming a hot Gordon Falls commodity.

"How is the job search going?" Violet asked tenderly. "Seems like there's no loyalty to hardworking people anywhere these days." She handed Charlotte a cup of tea. "I'm just glad the Good Lord sent us another tea drinker." She took back the "Shawlatte," as she'd christened it a minute ago. "It's getting hard to hold my own against the Gordon Falls caffeine junkies." The petite woman's eyes fairly sparkled at her own joke.

"It's still early," Charlotte replied, pasting a smile on her face. "But there have been lots of nibbles, so I'm sure an offer will be here soon." She knew most of the life stories of these women, and none of them had easy lives. Seeing their zest for life despite some whopping challenges gave Charlotte courage. Compared to some of the things these woman had endured—loss of spouses, fires, debilitating diseases, children gone wrong—one layoff seemed barely worthy of complaint.

She did her best to ignore Melba's disbelieving look. The truth was, things weren't going well at all. She'd expected to be choosing between offers by now, not staring into a gaping void of tepid responses to submitted résumés. So much of this loomed out of her control, and it was driving her crazy. She needed action, momentum, anything that felt like results—but the only place she could come close to any of those things was on the cottage renovations. To do that, and do it with excellence, proved such a saving grace. It made her feel successful when success seemed to be edging out of her grasp.

Marge Bowers tugged on Maria's hand as she held the baby. "I saw the sweater your godmother made you, Maria. Your aunt Charlotte knows her stuff." It felt lovely to have her knitting skills receive compliments, especially from these ladies. Maria's biological grandmothers might be gone, but she had a dozen honorary ones here. This morning Charlotte couldn't be certain a fight wasn't going to break out over who got to hold Maria first. "Between Charlotte and your mama, I doubt you'll ever be short of hats or mittens."

"Or scarves," Charlotte added. "Scarves are my favorite."

"I like dishcloths myself," Tina Matthews piped up. "Quick, practical and there are hundreds of designs to choose from."

"Tina gives six as a housewarming gift," Melba related. "I still use my set every day."

"And now I can make you a set, too," Tina said. "Do you know your kitchen color scheme yet?"

Melba started to laugh. "Are you kidding? There are four file boxes, a set of computer files and two scrapbooks on the subject. And that's only the ones I know about."

Charlotte hoped she hadn't been too fast to pull out her smartphone and display an image of the "china-blue and white with yellow accents" color scheme she'd chosen for the kitchen. The resulting *ooh*s and *ahh*s were highly gratifying. The hand-painted porcelain cabinet knobs and handles had arrived the other day, and they were worth every premium penny.

"You've got an eye, Charlotte. Now I know just what color yarn to buy."

The idea that her kitchen sink would someday be graced with both designer weathered copper fixtures *and* a set of handmade color-coordinated dishcloths settled a warm hum in Charlotte's chest. She wasn't quite sure when it had happened, but Gordon Falls was starting to feel like home. Whole days would go by where she didn't even think of Monarch or her city apartment. That made it easier to stomach how she wasn't shuttling back and forth between multiple interviews right now.

"However long you stay, we are glad to have you," Abby Reed replied. "Gordon Falls was starting to feel a little gray-haired before Melba came along."

"And JJ, Alex and Max," Melba added.

"My two cousins have done all right for themselves here," Charlotte admitted, turning her knitting to start a new row. She hadn't really meant "married off" as her version of "done all right," but the knowing looks some of the ladies passed between them meant they'd clearly made the connection.

"Clever you, meeting the town's most charming bachelor fireman your first day in the cottage," Marge teased.

Charlotte rolled her eyes. "Oh, you wouldn't think it was so clever if you saw my kitchen filled with smoke."

"It brought Jesse Sykes to your doorstep." Vi chuckled. "Handsome and handy, that one." For a widow in her seventies, Violet had more energy than anyone else in the room. And more nerve.

"Violet, you really are a piece of work," Jeannie Owens chastised, then broke into a smile. "I hope I grow up to be just like you."

The group erupted in laughter. "Why go for home repair when you could shoot for a man who knows his way around the kitchen?" Marge said in a loud whisper. "I've seen the way Karl looks at you. He already gives you free pie. Wait until he gets that shawl—you'll be eating free for a year!"

Violet snorted her disagreement. "Nonsense. Karl comps anybody who has to move for Hot Wheels, you know that."

Charlotte's cousin Max, who had received his knitted "FlameThrow" when a climbing accident confined him to a wheelchair, could fit at only one table in Karl's Koffee. It was common knowledge that when someone had to shift seats to make way for Max "Hot Wheels" Jones, Karl gave them free coffee. "I know we all get coffee," Marge countered, wagging her finger, "but you're the only one I know who gets pie. You're special."

Violet, usually never at a loss for a good comeback, didn't reply. She scowled at Marge, but Charlotte was pretty sure the pink in her cheeks wasn't from anger. Anyone who thought Gordon Falls was a quiet, quaint little tourist town on the river where nothing ever happened would get a surprise if they met with this group. The ladies had always been pleasant acquaintances, but they were becoming fast friends. This group had scooped up Melba when she'd come to Gordon Falls in the throes of her father's progressing disease, and now it felt as if they had scooped up Charlotte, as well.

Abby, who had offered to talk retail yarn over lunch after today's knitting session, spoke up. "You know, you could do lots of your job from just about anywhere, couldn't you? You could work for a company in France right from your home."

"If I spoke French," Charlotte admitted. "I have done international work for Monarch, and for my job before that. I used to travel quite a bit, actually. Now that's not so necessary with all the digital communication."

"There was a woman in the shop the other day buying yarn for her grandchildren. She had their video up on her phone and was holding up yarn so they could pick colors right there in front of her. And they were in New Jersey!" Abby picked up Maria, who had started to fuss a bit in her carrier. "I don't really know how all that stuff works, but it was fun to watch."

"I text my grandchildren all the time," Violet said. "I know stuff that would curl their mother's hair, but I'm keeping my mouth shut. I want them to think they can come to me if they're afraid to talk to Donald and his wife."

"You really are the coolest grandmother ever," Melba said. "I hope you'll be texting Maria when she's in middle school and hates me."

Melba's mother had been gone for years, but Charlotte recognized the still-constant loss that pressed on her own heart. How many times had she picked up her phone to send a photo or text to Mima, only to realize she was gone? It felt as if the huge hole in her life still had ragged, painful edges. Until she had a family of her own, Charlotte vowed to be the kind of support to Maria that Violet was to her grandkids. *I want to trust you'll find me a job, Lord. I want the*

*panic to go away. Until it does, thank You for
this amazing circle of women.*

She felt fresh tears sting her eyes until Tina
thrust a ball of yarn into her view. "Charlotte,
what on earth did I do wrong here? It looks like
tumbleweeds."

Charlotte held out her hands. "Let me look at
it. I'll have it straightened out in no time." Here,
at least, was one thing she knew she could fix,
one problem she knew she could solve.

Chapter Nine

Jesse put down his wrench and turned the knob on Charlotte's gorgeous new kitchen faucet. "Drumroll, please."

Charlotte laughed and drummed her hands on the counter. "Ready."

The pipes under the faucet made a host of disturbing noises from behind their cabinet doors. Then, after a few tentative spurts and a gurgle or two, water cascaded from the graceful copper fixture. "Hot and cold running water for Miss Charlotte Taylor, thank you very much," Jesse boasted. "You can move in."

Charlotte was thrilled. This last renovation made the house officially livable. She'd spend her first night in the cottage tonight, even though it meant sleeping on the mattress on the floor, since she hadn't taken delivery yet on the majestic four-poster bed she'd found at the local antiques store. While waiting on some of the final utilities—and a disturbingly empty e-mail inbox—Charlotte had poured over catalogues, invaded furniture stores and even scoured local flea markets in search of perfect finds. Even Jesse had remarked that the place managed to boast a surprising amount of furniture already. It was much better to focus on the decorating progress she *could* control than to ruminate on the employment process she could not. A dozen curtains came in, but the two dozen résumés she'd most recently sent out hadn't produced any response.

She poked her head into a cabinet to produce a brand-new stovetop kettle and two mugs. "Shall we celebrate? Without the smoke signals this time?"

Jesse pulled a rag from his toolbox and wiped the worst of the grime from his hands. He had a royal-blue T-shirt on today that did distracting things to his eyes. "Tea?"

"Yogurt doesn't feel very festive, and that's all I've got in the fridge right now. I was heading out for groceries this afternoon."

"Well, if it's either tea or yogurt, I'll opt for tea. As long as it's really strong." He clearly had no interest in the brew and was consenting for her benefit. Charlotte hadn't seen that level of consideration in a guy for a long time. How nice that he sensed what an important moment this was for her, how it was much more than two mugs of tea on a flea-market table—it was a declaration of resilience. Jesse held up one finger. "Go ahead and put the kettle on…I'll be right back."

Turning the brand-new faucet lever warmed her all the way out to her fingertips. The perfection of it felt like the best antidote to the sagging job search—satisfying and empowering. This house had been waiting for her. Okay, the first welcome hadn't gone well, but despite that kitchen fire she knew the house loved her.

That was silly of course; a house was incapable of loving her. Still, how many times had she felt her knitting comfort her—or mock her when things went horribly wrong? Charlotte drew strongly from her surroundings; her tactile world had always affected her deeply. The scent of her favorite tea filling this kitchen would feel like an anointing; a blessing of her life here. A promise that it would all work out in the end. Not that she could or would explain such a thing to the likes of Jesse Sykes.

The porch door slammed as she was placing the tea cozy—one she'd knitted herself—around the steeping pot, and Jesse entered the room with a small handful of flowers and a package of cookies. "What's a tea party without cookies?" He waved the package and the flowers at her. "Although they've been in the backseat of my truck for a week—we may be looking at more crumbs than cookies."

Charlotte didn't think her smile could get any wider. He'd understood her need to celebrate. And yet his gesture wasn't forced or overwhelming; it was just an honest gift of what he could scramble together. "Are those from Mrs. Hawthorne's yard?" She didn't know her new next-door neighbor well enough to judge how much of a trespass Jesse had just committed.

Jesse made a "who me?" face. "Could be. Could be I just happened to have black-eyed susans in my glove box. Or a flat of flowers in the back of my truck. You'd have no way of knowing. You're completely innocent."

The closest thing Charlotte had to a vase was a tall blue glass canning jar, which she filled with water and set in the center of the table. She grabbed a small tin tray from a box in the hallway, laid a paper towel across it and arranged the rather sad assortment of broken cookies on the towel. The tea, flowers, mugs and cookies made a comical vignette, and he couldn't help but laugh as she placed a few restaurant packets of sugar by the teapot. "One lump or two?"

"With only a brother in the house growing up, I'm not exactly up on my tea party etiquette."

He pulled the chair out for Charlotte with a dramatic gesture, then made a show of easing himself into the opposite chair. He winced a little when it creaked a bit under his weight, looking like the proverbial bull in the china shop of her furnishings. "What am I supposed to do?"

Charlotte laughed. "Drink tea and eat cookies—or what's left of the cookies. This isn't a test." She poured his cup, then her own. "This is a chai tea—it's strong like coffee, so you might actually like it."

Jesse smelled the aroma wafting up from the mug, his face scrunching in suspicion. "Doubtful. Might be good for dunking, though." He caught her eye. "I am allowed to dunk, aren't I?"

"I heartily encourage the dunking of cookies. I'm a dunker myself, you know." After a second, she felt compelled to add, "Thanks."

"For putting in your sink?" His eyes told her he knew exactly why she had thanked him, and that it had nothing to do with the sink.

"No." The word slid soft and warm between them. The aroma of chai tea in her new kitchen settled around her like a consecration, with all the comfort of a fluffy shawl on a cold evening.

Jesse added two sugars before even tasting the tea, then lifted the mug to his lips. "Um—" he paused, clearly looking for the right description "—delicious?"

"You hate it." Charlotte found she wasn't offended at all. In fact, she was more enchanted by his efforts to hide it. "No, really, it's okay."

"I'm a coffee guy," he explained, spreading his hands in admission.

"I like coffee, too," she said, then wondered why she was trying to build connections with him. "I just don't have any in the cottage right now. I'll get some this afternoon." Why had she said that? Why was she extending social invitations to a guy she'd already decided wasn't a good match, even if she was looking for someone? "So you can have coffee while you work and all."

Plausible as the excuse was, they both knew that wasn't what she'd meant. Things were tumbling in a direction Charlotte didn't really understand or endorse. Only she knew she didn't want Jesse to leave—now or even soon. She told herself it was that she wasn't ready to be in the house all alone, but that rang as false as Jesse's compliment of her chai tea.

"So your Mima wasn't a tea drinker? Even with all the china cups and all?"

Why was it that every time Charlotte talked herself into dismissing the tug she felt toward Jesse, he'd say something that pulled her to him again? She needed to talk about Mima. A lot. Charlotte didn't like how it felt as if Mima were slipping from her memory, as if she had to speak aloud to secure all those wonderful memories in her life now that Mima was gone. It was silly— she'd never even spoken that often to Mima. Their communication in the last few years was mostly fun texts or postcards or jots of short correspondence. Why the burning need to keep talking about her? Grief did funny things to a person.

Charlotte wrapped her hands around the warmth of her mug—despite the June afternoon heat—and wished for the dozens of china plates, cups and saucers to be surrounding her here in the cottage kitchen instead of still back in Chicago. "Mima drank tea, coffee, cocoa, anything. She was always bringing exotic blends of coffee and tea home to me. And that spicy Mexican hot chocolate. She loved that, too. When I was little, she would make me tea or coffee in my own special cup that she kept at her house just for me. A real china cup, not a plastic kiddie thing. Of course, the drink was more milk than coffee or tea, and it was loaded with sugar, but I felt so grown up when I drank it." Tears clamped her throat again. "Important, you know? She was great at making me feel like I meant the world to her."

"That's nice. A rare thing." There was a shadow in Jesse's eyes as he looked at her. A dark place behind all the sympathy. After a second or two, Charlotte realized it was envy. Hunger, even. It made her wonder if Jesse had ever had anyone in his life to make him feel important. Was that where the showmanship personality and the hero-rescuer drive came from? She'd had so much affirmation in her life, it stung to see the lack of it played out so clearly in his features.

Even though she knew it might not be a safe question, she asked anyway. "Anyone like that in your life?"

Is there anyone like that in my life?

Jesse swallowed hard. Charlotte had asked the million-dollar question, and he found himself unable to dredge up one of his smart-aleck evasive answers. Not here, not when he was faced with the collection of sweet memories playing across her face. To be so loved—it must be amazing. And then again gut-wrenching to have that love taken away. She had on a peach-colored tunic, and he watched her finger the simple gold cross that sat in the V neckline of the top. He knew, without having to ask, that it had been her grandmother's. He realized he'd never seen her without it, and that she touched it whenever she talked about Mima. He could guess that she'd put it on the day the beloved old woman had died and she hadn't taken it off since.

To love someone so hard and know they loved you just as much—that hadn't ever really been the case in his family. Sure, he'd mourn his parents when they were gone, but it wouldn't be like the loss he could see in Charlotte's eyes when she talked about this amazing grandmother of hers.

"Not like that." It seemed the safest way to answer her question. His memories of his grandparents were mostly about instructions and expectations. He and Randy got along, but they'd never been particularly close. His mom loved him—in a safe, mom kind of way—but not with the fierce, lasting affection Charlotte seemed to have known. And Dad? Well, he supposed Dad thought the pushy way he treated Jesse was what parental love was supposed to look like.

"I'm sorry." Charlotte looked at him—really looked at him, as though she could see all the regrettable things going through his head. No judgment, just awareness. A sad sort of understanding that wandered a little too close to pity.

Guilt twisted Jesse's gut. "Don't get me wrong, my parents love me and all, but they don't really—" he couldn't find a word that didn't sound ungrateful and even petulant "—root for me." He pushed out a sigh and took another swig of the tolerable tea just to buy time to think. "I have a younger brother, and he does all the expected stuff. All the right, successful things moms and dads think their kids ought to do when they grow up. Great job, big house, all the trimmings. They say they don't compare, but..." He found he didn't want to finish that sentence.

"You save people." She said it with something close to awe. The wideness of her eyes pulled at him. He was wrong; it wasn't pity he saw in her features—it was "you deserve so much more." It wasn't fair what that did to him. He wasn't prepared for how she got to him without even realizing what she was doing.

"Yeah, I think that confuses them most of all. The whole volunteer firefighter thing makes no sense to them. Why risk myself for nothing? At least that's how they see it. Mom never comes out and says it like that, but Dad never minces words on the subject."

Charlotte picked up a broken cookie. "Your dad doesn't like you in the volunteer fire department?"

"He thinks of it as a waste of time. Or close to that—I don't think he's been quite that harsh. More like an unnecessary distraction that seems to be keeping me from reaching my professional potential." Jesse picked up a piece of cookie and dunked it in the mug. "He'd be happier if I were more successful."

"More like your brother?"

"If you mean my brother whose marriage just fell apart and who is working on his second ulcer, then you can see why maybe I don't share the old man's opinion." Jesse hadn't meant the words to come out with quite that much edge, but Charlotte had hit a nerve. "I have my own idea of success. I have big plans for a remodeling business." He stopped himself there, afraid that if he launched into those plans he might reveal how he'd wanted this cottage as his first project. Right now he didn't want Charlotte to know that. It would make everything weird, and it was weird enough already.

"You're different than him."

The simple words struck a completely separate nerve. The hungry nerve, the unfed craving. She managed to meet some need in him he wasn't even aware of until she'd waltzed into Gordon Falls and stymied his plans. How had she managed to articulate the one thing, the one thought, that he could never seem to get his parents to understand? "Completely." He didn't trust himself to go any further than that.

"I don't think I'd like this brother of yours very much." She'd said it casually, before either of them realized the natural progression of that thought. It unwound itself in Jesse's brain like a mathematical equation: *if C dislikes R and J is the opposite of R, therefore C must like J.* She knew it, too, for suddenly she stared too hard at her cookie instead of looking at him.

He had to find some way out of this too-close moment. "You'd hate his cooking."

"Most guys can't cook their way out of a paper bag." Charlotte was trying, as he'd done, to lighten the moment, but it wasn't working for either of them. "Well, evidently, except for chefs, and you and your burgers."

Ah, now she'd done it. Had she knowingly thrown that door open, or just by accident? He puffed up his chest. "I am an outstanding cook. I could probably cook circles around half the restaurants in Gordon Falls, and not just on firehouse fare. I'll have you know my skills extend far beyond chili and burgers."

Her eyes narrowed at his boasting. "Do they? So not only can you install ovens, but you can use one, too?"

There was just enough tease in her words to seal her fate. "I'm on duty tomorrow night, but Friday you are going to find out just how well this man can cook his way out of a paper bag. As a matter of fact, I could probably cook a paper bag and you'd think it was delicious." Before Charlotte could put in one word of protest,

Jesse stood up and began opening the mostly empty cupboards and fridge, taking stock of what was here and what he'd need to bring. "You said you were going to the grocery store and back to Chicago for a load of stuff tomorrow, right?"

"Yes?" She looked as if she had just opened Pandora's box and wasn't sure if she should start regretting it.

"You're coming back Friday? You've got a saucepan?" He circled his hands to mimic a deep round pan just in case she didn't know her way around a kitchen.

"I'll be back Friday. And of course I have a saucepan." Her hands crossed over her chest.

"Frying pan?"

"Yes. Two, in fact."

He scratched his chin, the meal planning itself in his head already. "Bring both." Grabbing a receipt from off the counter, he started writing. Within five minutes he'd given her a list of items and suggested tableware. This was going to be fun. If there was anything Jesse Sykes knew how to do as well as build things, it was cook things. Delicious, incredible things. Friends cooked for friends all the time, right? It wasn't a date. Not even close.

Charlotte sat there, running her hand down

the list with her mouth open. "Um, I've got everything on here but a cheese grater."

"I'll bring mine. And my spices. I don't trust the grocery store stuff most people get—no offense, but it makes all the difference. Can you be back in Gordon Falls by five-thirty?"

She shrugged. "Works for me."

Charlotte's smile held the tiny hint of "you gotta be kidding me" that touched the edges of her eyes. It kindled an insane need to put that doubt to rest and flat-out amaze her. Jesse knew—down to his boots knew—that he could. He just wasn't going to take the time to analyze why.

Chapter Ten

Charlotte pulled open her back door Friday night to the sight of Jesse holding a pair of stuffed grocery bags. A bouquet of flowers tottered on the top of one bag while a loaf of delicious-smelling bread poked out of the other. He grinned. "Hungry?"

She grabbed one of the bags and held the door open. A whiff of "clean guy"—that extraordinary mix of soap and man and a hint of whatever it was he put on his hair—wafted by as he passed, and Charlotte felt her stomach flip. Maybe she should have stayed in Chicago and said no to this little feast. That probably would have been the smart thing to do, but this didn't really feel like a date, and besides, Jesse didn't strike her as the kind of guy who took no for an answer.

Still, there was no denying the guy was seriously attractive. And toting incredible food. God must have known what He was doing when He ensured she wouldn't be hosting Jesse alone.

Just as he put the bag down on the counter, Jesse caught site of Charlotte's new housemate. His entire face changed.

"You have a cat."

Jesse said the words slowly, biting off the end of the last word with a sharp *t*. This was clearly not a welcome revelation.

"I do." She forced ignorant cheer into her voice. For the fifth time today, Charlotte wondered if Melba had known *exactly* what she was doing when she'd presented her with the furry little wonder when Charlotte got back from Chicago this afternoon. She walked over to the kitchen seat where her new companion sat staring suspiciously at her guest cook. "Jesse, meet Mo."

Mo curled up the end of his tail in something Charlotte hoped did not translate to "I was here first."

"Hello, Mo." Charlotte could practically watch Jesse's back straighten. Dinner was in danger of becoming a territorial battle, and the man had been here all of thirty seconds.

"You brought a cat into a house under renovation." Charlotte could practically hear Jesse's brain trying to link the two ideas. While he never said it, and was trying hard not to look it, the man's every pore seemed to seep "Are you out of your mind?" She watched him mentally sift through potential verbal responses before he settled on "That will make things interesting." Then he set down the bag of groceries they'd both forgotten he was holding.

Charlotte, who'd already set down the bag with the bread, walked over and stroked Mo. He arched his back up to meet her hand, keeping one yellow eye on Jesse as if to say "See? She likes me." "Melba gave him to me as an early birthday present. She has a cat she loves very much."

"I remember." They weren't happy memories, that much was clear. He chose his next words carefully. "I'm surprised Melba failed to remember that working on the house with Pinocchio didn't go especially well."

Mo apparently took offense to that, leaping in a brown, black and white streak toward what would be the dining room. Evidently he wasn't going to stand around and listen to Jesse defame his character. She imagined he'd head up to the bedroom soon, as the mattress on the floor had become his favorite spot since this afternoon. "She mentioned it might be a bit of a bumpy ride at first. But I love Pinocchio, and he was great company curled up next to me in the guest room at Melba's. Mo's been fine and settling in all day. It'll be nice to have company. You told me you were a dog person, but I didn't realize that meant you were an anti-cat person."

Jesse began taking items out of the bag. "I'm not an anti-cat guy. I just recognize that construction can stress animals out. You may be in for a bumpier ride than Melba let on." She watched him choose to get past it, pushing out a breath and turning to her with the bouquet of flowers from the grocery bag. "These are for you. Paid for, fair and square."

She didn't want to let Mo ruin the evening, either. She'd considered Mo a convenient excuse, a way to cut the evening short if things felt as if they were getting too close. Now, looking at him all spiffed up and offering a bouquet of flowers, Charlotte realized she liked Jesse. She *really* liked him. And that could still be okay; one dinner with him didn't constitute a lifetime of sirens and anxious nights. It was just a friendly dinner. She didn't have to stress over it the way she might have over a *real* date.

She took the flowers, delighted that he'd chosen a mixture of wildflowers and sunny pastels rather than something serious like roses or ordinary like carnations. The arrangement fit the room, fit the sturdy little table that would host their meal. "Thank you. They're lovely. I brought a vase from my Chicago apartment, too. I was going to put some greenery from the backyard in it, but this is much nicer." She reached into a box on another counter, found a doily Mima had crocheted and set it on the table with the vase right in the center.

They worked together on the meal as easily as they had worked on the bathtub. Jesse was masterful in the kitchen, doling out small jobs like chopping shallots while hovering over four different pans of delectable-smelling food. It made the cottage feel like a true home. A meal with friends.

Only it didn't seem to want to stay just "a meal with friends." Jesse would catch her eye every now and then, smiling confidently as he explained why this had to boil for just a minute more, or why that ingredient had to be added just a little at a time, and her pulse would catch just a bit. He sang snippets of Sam Cooke's "You Send Me" while he worked, and his voice swirled around her as it filled the kitchen. Then he lifted the lid on one saucepan and spooned up a creamy white sauce that smelled delicious. Jesse tasted it, eyes closed in assessment, added a little more of something, then tasted again. His resulting smile beamed of victory. "Here, try this." He held out a spoon, and Charlotte couldn't have refused for all the world.

Had someone told him Alfredo sauce was her favorite? Had he run into Melba or Clark at the grocery store? Or was this just another way Jesse Sykes knew how to keep his customer happy? "Oh," she said, going beyond just a taste to lick the spoon completely clean. "Oh, my. Wow."

"My family may be Anglo, but Italian is my specialty. Douse that handmade fresh spinach fettuccine with this, add the Brussels sprouts I've got going over there, and you'll think you've died and gone to heaven."

Charlotte winced. "I'm…um…not really a fan of Brussels sprouts." Actually, she didn't know anyone who was a fan of Brussels sprouts.

"You haven't tasted mine." He said it as if resistance to his particular brand of vegetable would be impossible. The tone of his voice made her believe him. Or at least want to believe him. "Close your eyes."

She gave him a look. "A bit dramatic, don't you think?"

He gave her a look right back. "You'll eat those words right after you eat my Brussels sprouts."

Parking a hand on one hip, Charlotte countered, "You know that sounds ridiculous, don't you?"

Jesse wagged his fingers in front of her face

until she rolled her eyes before squinting them shut. She heard him fiddle with the top of a saucepan, then the sound of his voice very close and soft. "Open." He sang the word more than said it, his tone smooth and coaxing. She felt him close with her eyes closed, smelled the soap on his skin now mixed with the marvelous scents of his cooking. Maybe Brussels sprouts had been given a bad rap. She felt the fork against her tongue and bit down on what he offered.

Oh.

Brussels sprouts were the epitome of gross vegetables, the thing universally turning up child and adult noses everywhere. These could not have been Brussels sprouts. They were crunchy and a bit crispy, with something savory hiding between the tiny green leaves. Half a dozen different tastes and textures mixed on her tongue. This was the chocolate cake of vegetables. It couldn't be those nasty green orbs everyone avoided in the produce aisle. He was tricking her; he had to be.

Charlotte opened her eyes wide, unprepared for the closeness of Jesse's triumphant face. There was a second piece on the fork, which she immediately ate. "Wow," she said with her mouth full. He was so close, so dauntingly handsome, and he had just fed her his cooking. At this very moment, Jesse Sykes was the most attractive man on earth. Denying it was just plain impossible. "That's a vegetable?" she whispered, just for something to say because his nearness was fogging her thinking.

"You should see what I do with butternut squash," he boasted, "but this is a personal specialty." He reached out and brushed a bit of sauce or butter or whatever that splendid concoction was off her chin. She shivered at his touch, fighting off the dizzying sensation his brown eyes kindled in the pit of her stomach.

Talk. Talk before you do something else, something you don't want to do right now. "Every Brussels sprout on earth should stand up and thank you." She hated how flustered she sounded, hated how he knew exactly how he'd wowed her and was currently reveling in it. "I hope you made a lot of those." She ducked out of the dazzle of his eyes to peer into the covered pan.

"Pace yourself. You'll want to save room for dessert."

The man had made dessert. That was just plain fighting dirty. If this man produced a cheesecake then all hopes of sensibility were lost. Charlotte puttered around the kitchen, fighting the sinking feeling that was like drowning but a whole lot sweeter.

Jesse stood still, watching her, as in control of the moment as she was out of it. "You want to slice up some lemon for the water?" The words were mundane enough, but his eyes seemed to say "So I don't kiss you right now up against the refrigerator?"

There was a journal page upstairs in Charlotte's bedroom listing all the reasons why dating a firefighter was a bad idea. Right now Charlotte couldn't remember a single one of them.

Jesse had eaten in some pretty spectacular restaurants, had even done the firehouse's entire Thanksgiving dinner last year, but no meal had ever filled him with the satisfaction of Charlotte's little table currently spread with his cooking. Even Mo—the predatory little beast—had come in from the living room to view the spectacle, perhaps hoping to leverage his cuteness into a little creamy Alfredo sauce.

Jesse gave him a "my turn" glare as he walked over to pull out Charlotte's chair for her. The urge to run a hand through the cascade of her blond hair caught him up short, and he nearly tripped on his way around to his side of the table. His plan to keep the evening light and friendly was falling prey to the look of utter delight on her face. It sank deep into his chest and settled there like a craving. She took such a rich pleasure in the world, in small things, in things he often took for granted. What gave her such a rare capacity for joy like that? Even in the face of all the obstacles life had thrown at her recently?

He settled himself in his chair and reached for the serving spoon. "Dig in."

She cocked her head at him. "No grace?"

It took him a minute to realize what she'd said.

"Grace," she repeated. "Over the food."

"Um, sure," he said, fumbling. "Why not."

Charlotte extended her hand for his. Jesse was sure a man ought not to feel the sparks her hand left in his palm while saying prayers. He told himself not to luxuriate in the softness of her hands while he closed his eyes. He'd never been the hand-holding kind of guy, but right now holding her hands felt to him like whatever he saw shoot through her eyes when she tasted his cooking.

"Thank You, Father, for this wonderful meal Jesse has set before us."

Jesse wasn't prepared for her words. He was expecting some rote little poem, some Sunday school verse said in memorized monotone. Charlotte was praying. Real, actual, as-if-she-talked-to-God-every-day conversation. Over his food. "I'm grateful for this house, for all You've made possible, for all the work that went into this delicious food. I am, quite surprisingly, thankful for Brussels sprouts, too. Who'd have thought?"

Jesse opened one eye to see her smiling, eyes closed as she carried on the easy dialogue. He'd not seen grace—or even prayer—ever look like this. It startled him, shaking something loose that felt as if it didn't belong rattling around under his ribs.

"Bless the hands that prepared this food," Charlotte tightened her grip on Jesse's hand, making his pulse gallop for a moment, "and may it nourish our bodies. In Your Son's name, Amen."

"Amen," Jesse gulped out, hoping that was the right thing to say. He was still trying to work out what had just happened. Chief Bradens had been known to say a formal grace over meals at the firehouse, but they never sounded like that, and they never made him feel as though someone had just hit him with a thousand-watt floodlight, dazzled and blinking for focus.

"This looks incredible. I want to stuff myself silly—I've tasted all of it and I think you're about to meet my piggish side."

"Knock yourself out." He wanted to see her piggish side. He wanted to see her unrestrained enjoyment, to hear her groan with delight and lick the sauce off her fingers and ask for seconds if not thirds. He'd enjoyed lots of compliments on his food before, but those mostly fed his ego. Her pleasure in his cooking only made him want to make her happier. That wasn't the kind of selfless gratification Jesse was used to, and he didn't know how to deal with the feeling. He only knew he liked it, and he wanted more of it.

He ate with enthusiasm. He watched her eat with relish, going on about this project and that fixture between raves over the food and sighs of what could only be termed gastronomic infatuation. The combination of Charlotte gushing over his food and espousing big renovation dreams was like catnip to Jesse—to put it in Mo's terms. His insides were buzzing like live wires, sparking with every small touch, every adorable look. More than once he yearned to kiss the Alfredo sauce off her cheek, off her lips, no matter how stridently Chief Bradens and his own sense of caution had warned him off. He had found women disarmingly attractive before, but this was a whole new scale of allure.

"I think I should go ahead and get the custom ironwork for the front steps. I just don't see anything I like as much in the catalogues. I love the idea about Mima's quilt motif worked into the front railings." He could see it as clearly as she could. The price tag started not to matter. There was something about being near her, as if she gave off some kind of magnetism he was helpless to resist. "Irresistible" suddenly wasn't a clichéd description—he found Charlotte wholly, genuinely irresistible. This was becoming dangerous on any number of fronts.

By the time he made coffee and doled out French vanilla ice cream to start melting all over the berry cobbler he'd pulled out of the oven for dessert, Jesse felt his personal and professional warning system completely short-circuit. She was talking about imported glass tile backsplashes and granite countertops while she tore off a piece of bread and mopped up the last bit of sauce off her plate. He knew just the color stone that would set off her eyes, and it no longer mattered that it was the most expensive. She was Charlotte. The world would line up to do her bidding because at that moment, he would have said yes to anything she asked. Even the dumb cat. She had him hooked. What made him most nervous of all was that he could already feel the ache that would start when he walked out this door tonight and never let up until he was near her again.

It scared him to death. He knew he was on the verge of a terrifying loss of control he wouldn't have predicted and couldn't contain. Jesse knew guys who got this way about fire—it drew them, fascinated them, nearly possessed them in a way that made them fearless. *It's also what gets them hurt or killed,* he reminded himself. When emotion overpowered thought, damage happened. The very thing he'd hoped to give Charlotte in this project—an objective eye, a grounded opinion as to what was a worthwhile splurge and what was reckless spending—was about to go out the window. This was not good.

Jesse turned back from returning the ice cream to the freezer and found her already digging into the cobbler right there at the counter— she hadn't even waited for him to set them down at the table. She had a spot of purple right at the corner of her mouth, and she let out this intoxicating little hum as she found it with the tip of her tongue.

That was it. Without a thought to the consequences, without even wondering if she'd welcome the advance, because every cell in his body already told him she would, Jesse kissed her.

The taste of his cooking on her lips was enthralling. When her initial surprise melted into surrender, he lost the ability to think straight. But when Charlotte began to return his kiss? That put him over the edge. Who cared what

Bradens thought? It was one night, one dinner, one kiss. One really amazing kiss.

"Jesse…" She gasped his name, falling back against the counter as if the house had shifted off its foundations. He felt the same way, as if the world was whirling around him, spiraling out from the place where her hand still lay on his chest.

He put his hand atop hers, wondering if she could feel the pounding. "I…um…" He knew he should say something smooth, something casual and clever, but he came up empty. She'd undone him with one kiss, frightening as it was. He craved another kiss so much that he feared being able to control himself if he took one.

Not good, Sykes, not good at all.

Chapter Eleven

Crash. The moment came to a loud halt when a dish clattered to the floor. Mo had, at some point, leaped up onto the countertop in an effort to get at the melted ice cream and had succeeded in knocking over the cobbler dish. The cat screeched and bolted back into the dark of the living room. They both looked down to see white cream and purple cobbler splattered all over the floor and Charlotte's light-colored pants.

Charlotte didn't know whether to thank Mo or to kick the furry, meddling feline to the curb. The moment—whatever it was—was gone, replaced with a sticky mess and the casualty of one of her favorite pairs of pants.

Jesse had already grabbed a towel from the counter and was picking the pieces of the plate off the floor, muttering unkind things about cats. She stared at him, wanting to blink and shake her head, needing to know what had just happened and whether or not she should regret it.

It had been a spectacular kiss. The kind that made her sensibilities go white like an ·old-fashioned flashbulb, the kind that ought to be the first kiss between soul mates. Only now that the bubble had popped, she could name half a dozen reasons why Jesse Sykes was not the mate of her soul. And as for Jesse himself, if the kiss had affected him the way it had her, it no longer showed.

"See, not too hard to clean up." Jesse slid the broken china into the wastebasket and tossed the purple-blotched towel into the sink. "I don't think you can say the same for those pants." He turned to her, an "oh well" smile in his eyes, as if it had been a simple kitchen mishap. "There's enough dessert to start over."

"I don't think we ought to." She knew she didn't sound at all convinced. She wasn't—confused was closer to accurate.

His disappointment was so appealing. "Really? My cobbler's even better than my Brussels sprouts."

Charlotte leaned against the cabinets. "Jesse…"

He leaned up against the same cabinets, inches

from her. "Hey, it's okay." He shrugged. "But it was a really nice kiss."

She shut her eyes for a moment, slipping her hand up to press it to her own lips while she launched a prayer up to heaven for the right words. "I know there's something...here." She opened her eyes again, wanting to make him understand. "The meal, the kiss—you know how to sweep a woman off her feet. It's just that..." How could she make him understand when she wasn't even sure what she wanted at the moment herself?

He put a hand to his chest as if wounded. "I feed you fettuccine Alfredo and you shoot me down? Ouch." His words were harsh but his eyes held that teasing glint she found most irresistible about him.

"I need to take it a whole lot slower than this." That much was true. She still hadn't figured out if, in the space of one meal, Jesse Sykes had truly disintegrated her conviction not to get involved with men in his line of work. Had she truly overcome that fear? Or was it just pushed aside by Jesse's....*Jesseness,* just to return later when her guard was down? "I like being with you," she admitted, "but we have a lot of ground to cover and a bunch of things we have to...I have to work out. Or through. Or something."

She let her head fall back against the cabinets. "'It's complicated' sounds so stupid, but it is."

"It doesn't have to be. I don't think this has to be a big, complicated deal. I do know I don't want tonight to end here, like this."

"Maybe it's better that it does. At least for the sake of my pants." *If not my convictions.*

Jesse ran one hand through his hair. "I'll tell you what. Why don't you go upstairs and get those into water or soap—or whatever you do to get blueberry out of something—and I'll clean up here? Then we'll figure out what comes next. No sweeping off of any feet."

It seemed as good a plan as any. She needed fifteen minutes out of the pull of his eyes, away from the way he seemed to fill the room and cloud her thinking. "Okay."

Charlotte dashed upstairs, slipped into a pair of jeans and filled the bathroom sink— the beautiful bathroom sink Jesse had installed three days ago—with cold water and soap. She dunked the stained pants into the sink and scrubbed a few seconds before stopping to stare at herself in the mirror.

What do you want, Charlotte? What do you want to do about that man downstairs in your kitchen?

She knew Jesse. Knew his character and personality as if they'd spent years together instead

of weeks. He probably thought she hadn't noticed his reaction to her prayer over the food,
but she'd seen it. It was so strong she'd nearly
felt it. Still, all that awareness wasn't the same
as a man of faith, a man whose soul could match
with hers. In all the time they'd spent together
they'd only skittered around the topic of church
and God. She knew his dreams, but not his val-
ues. And quite frankly, it wasn't hard to guess
at his reputation where women were concerned.

And then there was the question of firefighting. It wasn't his whole life, as the police
force had been for Dad, but it was a big part.
Would it always be there, or would his volunteer
duties eventually fade as his business grew to
take more and more of his time? And was dating your general contractor ever a good idea?
The questions seemed to rise up and swallow
her clarity the same way the rising bubbles rose
up to cover her hands.

Mo wandered into the bathroom, drawn out
of his hiding spot in her bedroom by the lights
and sounds of her spontaneous load of laundry.
Charlotte pulled her hands from the suds and
pointed a finger at the cat. "The jury's still out
on you, mister."

Mo simply sat down on the tile and wrapped
his tail around his legs, a picture of all the calm
and patience she currently lacked. If he had any

advice or warning, she couldn't decipher it from his eyes. Charlotte would have to work this one out on her own.

She touched the framed photo of Mima as she passed it on the hallway table at the top of the stairs. *What do I do, Mima? Why is this man in my life now when you aren't here to tell me what to do with him?*

Charlotte had enough married friends to know that to come downstairs to a man responsible for a spotless kitchen was a wonder indeed. He had his stuff packed up in the grocery bags but his face told her he wasn't the least bit ready to leave. "Talk to me," he said as he sat down at the table she now noticed was set with two cups of coffee. "Tell me what's whirling around in that pretty head of yours."

She sat down. Talking about this was a good idea, and she was glad for the table between them. She knew he wasn't clouding her thinking on purpose, but that didn't mean he wasn't very good at it. "I'm worried this won't turn out to be such a good idea."

"Because I'm working on your house."

She owed him the further explanation. "That's just part of it." She ran her hands across the thighs of her jeans, wiping the last of the water from the upstairs washing project. "My dad was a policeman."

His face changed, understanding darkening his features. "I didn't know that."

There was a lot he didn't know. That was the whole point. "I've spent a lot of nights watching my mom get eaten alive from the stress of waiting for bad news. I made a promise to myself that I'd never let myself in for that kind of life."

Jesse leaned back in his chair. "You've known I was a firefighter literally from the moment you met me."

"I didn't say I couldn't be *friends* with you." That felt like a weak defense.

"Friends don't kiss like that. But this doesn't have to become superserious overnight, Charlotte. It's not an all-or-nothing proposition."

Charlotte's chest was filled with a mixed-up host of reactions. He'd felt it. Of course he'd felt it—how could he not feel what she felt humming between them? Only Jesse looked so much more in control of the situation than she felt. "Look, I'm kind of an impulsive person." Was she explaining her choice in backsplash tiles or how she'd kissed him back?

"Really? I hadn't noticed." Did he have to smile like that? All velvety and cavalier?

She struggled forward, telling the flutter in her stomach to behave itself. "It makes it hard to hang on to certain…challenging convictions."

Jesse gave her a look that said he rather enjoyed challenging people's convictions. Right—there was one of the problems with this whole situation. "Okay."

"My faith is really important to me. Maybe more now than it's been at any point in my life. It'd be a bad idea to get serious with someone who couldn't share that with me. I know you don't get that, but—"

"I do get that."

She hadn't expected that response. "You do?"

"I liked your grace. Never heard it done quite that way before. I'm okay with it."

"I'm glad to hear that, but it goes a bit deeper for me than table grace. There are—"

He cut her off. "Do you know I said yes to emceeing the talent show at your church tomorrow night? I figured maybe it was time I stopped ditching that stuff."

Oh, he'd managed to say the one thing that made resistance harder. "Clark didn't tell me you'd said yes."

"I told him I wanted to tell you myself. Surprise you at the end of tonight. I've seen you, and Chief, and Melba, and even JJ when you talk about going to church. I want to know what it is you all have over there. I just don't know how to try it or if it will stick. But you came up with the perfect introduction, didn't you? Doesn't that count for something to you?"

Lord, couldn't he be a jerk or something? You know me, I'm going to go all optimistic and hopeful now and I'm having enough trouble thinking practically already. "If we're going to be..." She didn't know how to finish that sentence without revealing how very attractive she found him, and Jesse surely needed no encouragement in that department.

"Hey," he said, taking her hand. She knew she ought to pull away, but she couldn't muster up the resistance. "Who actually knows what we're going to be? I'm not so sure why you have to plot this out right now. Can't we just wait and see?"

He meant well, but Charlotte knew herself, and she had a bad habit of throwing herself headlong into relationships that ought never to have been pursued. It didn't take a rocket scientist to know there was some serious chemistry between them, and that could make it hard to pull back before it was too late. "Well, the term *playing with fire* does come to mind."

"I'm a fireman. I think we'll be safe. How about I finish my coffee and leave like the gentleman I am? I'll see you at the talent show tomorrow night, and maybe we can try a dinner Sunday. Someplace easy and friendly, like Dellio's."

Those events—she refused to call them dates, even in her head—felt safe.

"I won't even be sitting near you at the talent show. There'll be something like sixty people between us. Then at dinner we can talk some more," he continued. "I can hear you say grace again."

If he was willing to come to church and be part of the talent show, if he was willing to let her say grace over burgers in public, there had to be an openness to faith about him. He was putting in an effort; she ought to at least meet him halfway on this. "Okay."

Jesse finished his coffee in one gulp—something she'd seen Melba's fireman husband do, so it must be a professional requirement—then stood up to leave. She stood up, as well.

He held his hand out, an oversize request for a formal handshake. "Friendly, see?"

When she offered her hand, he pulled it to his lips and left a soft kiss there. "Well, mostly." Without any further explanation than that, Jesse gathered up his things and headed out the door.

Jesse stood in his kitchen, staring at the still unemptied grocery bags, sorting through the puzzle of his feelings. Exactly what had happened tonight? He knew how to wow a lady, always had. It was an extension—however egotistical—of his urge to please people. He liked making customers happy, helping fire victims, making women feel special.

Whatever it was he felt for Charlotte, it was a whole new thing. He found himself disturbingly desperate for her—but not at all in a physical sense; it was so much more than that. This was much more consuming than a merely physical attraction. There was some gaping, empty hole he couldn't seem to hide from her. Worse, not only could she see it, she effortlessly filled it. As he paced his kitchen, Jesse had the uncomfortable sensation that his life had just cracked open to make room for her and nothing else would ever fill the space that made.

He tried to tell himself that urge to make her happy, to watch the delight spark up in her eyes, was ordinary, an ego boost, the way it was with everyone else. Only with Charlotte, it wasn't. It was the closest thing to a purely selfless urge he'd ever had, and he had no idea what to do with that. Oh, sure, lots of people thought of his work at the firehouse as selfless, but it really wasn't. It was a hero thing. He liked playing the hero—the stakes at the firehouse were just a bit higher than when he built someone the garage of their dreams.

The old Jesse would have kissed her again even when he knew better. He'd never, ever have pressed his advantage with a woman, but he would have been far bolder than he was tonight. It was as if someone had changed the rules on him without notice.

Without his consent. Chief Bradens really was right: Charlotte hadn't learned how to go in small steps—not in relationships or renovations or maybe even in life. Could he be the man to show her how to slow things down? Lighten up and have a little more fun? Learn that a few dates and kisses could be just that—a few dates and kisses? It was worth a dinner at Dellio's to find out.

And beyond that…he'd figure it out when he got there.

Chapter Twelve

Well, who would have guessed it?

Jesse stood on the stage of Gordon Falls Community Church's meeting hall, hand on the microphone, about to open the church's talent show as its guest emcee and baffled by the open welcome in all the faces he could see. He'd thought of himself as an intruder—an impostor up here on the stage, where someone well-known in the church should have been. No one else seemed to see it that way. Everyone had been nothing but warm and friendly.

"Good evening and welcome to tonight's Taste of Talent. If you haven't filled your plate from the dessert table at the back of the room, you don't know what you're missing. And hey, if any of you find yourselves overcome with the urge to bring me some of that raspberry cheesecake, by all means don't hold back." He couldn't help himself from directing that last remark right at Charlotte.

Instead of feeling awkward, the past half hour of setup had been surprisingly fun. What he'd told Charlotte was true; he'd never had anything against going to the church. So many of his friends already did. It was just that he dreaded the hurdle of that first visit. By happenstance—or design—this gig handed him the perfect opening. "We're going to start things out tonight with a touch of class, and a lot of brass. Let's listen to the Senior High bell quartet."

He looked out over the sea of friendly faces from his stool at stage left, seeing proud, smiling parents among them. Honestly, even here he felt like a bit of a celebrity—and he was a man given to enjoying attention. "Aren't they talented?" he asked the audience, as the quartet cleared their many bells from the stage. "There's more where that came from. This is one talented congregation, I'm telling you. Here's what's up next…"

And so the evening progressed, act by surprising act. Jesse's initial comments about the flood of talent were just to be nice at first, playing to the audience. Eventually, they gave way to genuine astonishment, soundly trouncing Jesse's preconceptions of hokey church festivities. Max Jones, Charlotte's cousin and no stranger to the firehouse through his sister, JJ, did a hysterical lip-synch of an Elvis tune with the high school boy he'd been mentoring for almost a year, Simon Williams. "Talk about true rocking and rolling," Jesse cracked as the pair—who both used wheelchairs—popped a dual pair of wheelies and spins as they moved offstage. Jesse felt a warm glow as he watched Simon's dad, Brian, also a firefighter, give his son a standing ovation. The kid had come a long way, and he knew that Brian credited the support of this church as much as the partnership Simon had with Max. Jesse and Max—and a few of the other younger firefighters—had made a few mistakes in their efforts to help Simon, but everyone had learned their lesson, and even Simon's mom had given Jesse a warm welcome.

And where had Fire Marshal Chad Owens hidden his surprising juggling talents? He was normally a laid-back guy, but the audience hung their mouths open when he proved a pretty talented trickster. Those open mouths served them well, for Chad's finale was to juggle a dozen of his wife, Jeannie's, beloved chocolate caramels, tossing them into the audience as his final trick. Jesse would have eaten a handful if the sticky confections wouldn't have rendered him speechless for five minutes at least. He stuck with one, making a big show of chewing with the appropriate *mmm*s. "Well now," he managed, still sounding as if he had a mouthful, "guess they really meant it when they called this Taste of Talent."

There were other acts—some silly, some heartwarming. Even the regrettable ones—someone needed to tell Nick Owens an eleven-minute drum solo was hard on the ears—brought a smile and a hearty round of applause from the audience. The trio of curly-blond-haired girls who couldn't have been more than five didn't do much more than sway and spin in their frilly pink tutus, but no one cared. Instead, everyone cheered and snapped photos like paparazzi when the ballerinas took their bows, bursting into louder applause, mixed with laughter, when one little girl rushed over and hugged Jesse's leg, leading him to take her hand and twirl her like a ballroom dancer as she left the stage.

Every time Jesse thought the evening couldn't get more enjoyable, some new moment would capture his heart. He was having such a terrific time, Jesse decided he'd have to eat his words and thank Charlotte for pulling him in to the event. Charlotte must have been thinking the same thing, for every time he caught her eyes, her smile broadcast "See, I told you this would be fun."

What really brought the house down, however, was one of the final acts. Jesse knew JJ's husband, Alex, played the ukulele and was known for his campy musical sense. As such, it wasn't a big stunner when he took the stage and began strumming "By the Light of the Silvery Moon." What no one saw coming was when Violet Sharpton and Karl Kennedy—of Karl's Koffee fame—sashayed onstage and broke into a snappy duet. No one knew either of them could sing, but they were fabulous. When they added an adorable half-limped, cane-assisted little soft-shoe dance on the final verse, Karl yelping, "Slow down, son, I can't hoof it that fast with my bad hip," to a guffawing Alex, the crowd spared no effort to urge them on. They got a standing ovation, and deserved one. Jesse himself was smiling and laughing so hard he could barely take the microphone as the curtain behind him closed.

"I don't know how we're going to follow that act, folks," Jesse proclaimed, wiping his eyes. He hid his satisfaction at the frantic scrambling behind him from the other side of the curtain. "Oh, no, wait," he said in mock surprise. "As a matter of fact, I do." Drums behind him hit the *ba-dump-ching* that was the standard musical punctuation for bad jokes, and Jesse knew his own surprise was nearly ready. He'd successfully managed to keep his contribution a secret.

If a church was going to ask him to emcee a talent show, they'd better be prepared for what they got.

A hidden set of drums began a steady beat behind him. "Ladies and gentlemen, presenting for the first time ever on this or any stage, for your listening enjoyment..." A base guitar joined in with a bluesy swagger. "I give you... Jesse Sykes and the Red Suspenders!"

The curtain parted to reveal a band composed entirely of hidden talents from the Gordon Falls Volunteer Fire Department, decked out in black shirts and those cheesy red plastic fire helmets Wally's sister had found at the local party store. And, of course, red suspenders. The applause and laughter from the audience was enough to fuel Jesse's gloat for a month.

It had started out as a joke, a wisecrack from Yorky when they found out Jesse had been cornered into serving as the evening's master of ceremonies. A "wouldn't it be funny if..." that took on more and more momentum until the idea seemed too good to pass up. When Wally shared that he played the drums and Tom Matthews offered to fish his bass guitar out of the attic, the Red Suspenders were born. Jesse reached behind him, knowing Tom held out his next props. As the lead guitar riff began, the hoots of encouragement and surprise doubled.

When Jesse donned the red hat and a pair of sunglasses, the crowd went wild. Chief Bradens was laughing so hard he was alternating between wiping his eyes and hiding them.

Going to great lengths to rehearse in secret, the guys had worked out a squeaky-clean, church-worthy four-song list that dipped into gospel, soul and just enough rock to enthrall the youth group. By the second song, the audience was clapping along. By the third song, they were on their feet. When the bass guitar and drums kicked into the familiar introduction to "Stand by Me," Jesse was pretty sure he saw Charlotte go pink. This was going to be fun.

Charlotte watched Jesse up there on that stage and felt her heart run off against her wishes. She didn't want to be falling for this boisterous, all-too-charming fireman, but there didn't seem to be much she could do to stop it. Melba sat next to her and would catch her eye after this remark or that heart-slaying grin, and she tried to feel neutral about the guy. Clearly Melba could see she was failing. Of course, Melba had no qualms about pairing off with a man from the fire department, even if she was kind about Charlotte's resistance.

Charlotte had gone so far as to talk to Clark about it. Clark had grown up in a firefighting family—the son of the former chief—and he had freely shared that things had been hard on his mom. He told her he understood her hesitation and respected it. "I remember how much my mom had to endure," he said. "I understand why you'd choose to avoid it. I'll say this, though. If the right guy comes around and happens to wear a uniform, I think you'll find a way to handle it."

Charlotte was terrified the right guy was standing right in front of her. She shut her eyes for a moment, even as she felt Jesse's presence from the distance across the room. Jesse was dead wrong about a crowded room making being with him any safer. *Lord, You know the effect that man has on me. If this isn't where I should be heading, I'm going to need an escape. I'm losing perspective.*

Melba leaned over and whispered in Charlotte's ear, "He keeps looking right at you, doesn't he? I mean, it sure looks like it."

That was not helpful. Charlotte had spent the past twenty minutes trying to tell herself the sensation of Jesse singling her out in the crowd was just an emotional illusion. The trick of a good entertainer—an *amazing* entertainer, really, Charlotte admitted to herself as she watched him sing on the stage, backed up by the rest of the Red Suspenders. The combination of silly plastic fire hat and bad-boy black sunglasses was downright irresistible.

As the band began the introduction from what Charlotte knew had to be "Stand by Me," Jesse took off his sunglasses and made a show of peering into the crowd. Charlotte told herself to slump down in her chair, useless as that tactic might be. Her breath—which had momentarily stopped—let out when Jesse called, "Maria? Maria Bradens? Where are you, darlin'? I know you like this one."

Oh, please let him just play this to Maria. Don't let him realize what his voice singing this does to me.

"Home with the sitter!" Clark called back, laughing.

That was right. Maria wasn't even in the building. With a pulse that ricocheted between fear and thrill, Charlotte watched as Jesse unhitched the cordless microphone from its stand. He stared straight at Charlotte, those high-voltage eyes at full force. "Well now, I'll need someone else. Another fine young lady who might be partial to this song." His voice was silken, all confidence and charisma as he stepped down off the stage and began walking right toward her. "Any takers?"

Charlotte felt as if her cheeks were as red as his hat. She tried to hide her face behind her hands but Melba pulled them down. As the fireman behind the keyboard launched into the song, Jesse passed his hat to Clark, pulled Charlotte to her feet and began to sing the lyrics, about not being afraid even when the night was dark. It was as if he sang directly to every fear and every worry. His voice seemed to find every bit of resistance she was trying to hang on to, every memory of her mother alone and staring at the unused place setting on their kitchen table. He was pulling all the stops out, pulling her under in the process.

When he turned back toward the stage, Charlotte practically fell into the chair. She'd forgotten how to think. She'd forgotten how to breathe. When he pitched his voice up into a soulful wail for the second verse, showing a level of talent she'd never expected—nor had anyone else, from the level of applause that was roaring up from the audience—she'd have followed him anywhere.

And that, right there, was the problem. *He is irresistible.*

What he did next hit Charlotte as clearly as if someone had tossed a glass of water in her face. Two rows down, Jesse found the high school French teacher and began singing to her. The woman looked exactly as Charlotte had felt when she'd been in that position: dazzled. Jesse asked her how to say "Stand by Me" in French and began singing the chorus in French, even getting her to sing with him.

Was his attention—the attention that, a moment ago she thought was just for her—an act? She watched the woman lay her hand on her chest and sigh, realizing she'd done the exact same thing herself. When he picked a third woman out of the audience and charmed her just as effectively, a foolish, hollow feeling crept up Charlotte's chest. She had no idea if Jesse was genuine in his attention to her, genuine in his attention to each woman he'd singled out of the audience, or simply applying his talents at showmanship.

Either way, it drove home a point she'd managed to miss—or chose to miss. Hadn't Jesse made it clear after that kiss back at the cottage that he felt no pressure for them to be serious? She'd been too dazed then to recognize what he was really saying—just as she was barely clear-headed enough now to realize the truth.

He wasn't ready to *offer* her anything serious.

Jesse, who displayed so much of his charm but hid so much of his nature, who gave away his talents but locked up his dreams, who was as impressed by her drive as he was bewildered by it, didn't know how to truly, deeply commit.

Not to God, not to a woman, not to his business plans that never seemed to get off the ground—not even to just one woman when it came to dedicating a special song.

Worse yet, part of her didn't even care. Even in the face of all her reservations, he enthralled her as he caught her eyes one last time before he stepped back up onto the stage. Despite everything she just saw, her breath caught as it felt as though he was singing just to her.

Charlotte was defenseless. The past few minutes had startled her into the awareness that she would fall for him far too easily—and get her heart broken when he stopped short of returning that love. On her good days, her resistance might stand up for a while. On a bad day, she'd give in instantly. Hadn't his kiss in her kitchen proved that? Her attraction to Jesse overrode her good sense even when she tried to stop it. With a gulp she realized that if he had tried to kiss her right in the middle of that song, with his eyes pulling her in like that, she very well might have let him, and returned it with the same intensity if not more. In front of everyone. Despite all the reasons she knew she didn't want to get involved with him. Because she *wanted* to get involved with him. She hadn't stopped thinking about him. She'd always imagined herself falling that hard for the perfect guy—and Jesse Sykes was not the perfect guy. He was a great guy, an amazing guy, but he was not the right guy for her.

Sure, it was impulsive. It was probably even cowardly and childish, but none of that stopped Charlotte from making the quickest exit possible while the crowd moved toward the stage to congratulate the Red Suspenders for stealing the show.

She was glad she'd walked to the church tonight, grateful for the space and dark and calm to help sort out her thoughts. Jesse was magnetic—in every sense the word implied. As she worked the brand-new lock on her front door, she recalled the unsettling realization she'd come to the other night: her extravagant renovation plans were partially to keep Jesse around.

Lord, I'm a mess. I'm getting all tangled up here. Help!

As she dropped her handbag in the hallway, her cell phone rang. She didn't even have to look at the screen to know it was Jesse. "Hey, where'd you go?" He sounded so exuberant.

"I'm home."

"Home? You went home?"

"I'm sorry," she replied, leaning against the

wall without even switching on the light. "Look, that was just a bit much for me."

She heard him push out a breath. "What? The song? I know you like that one. I was just having fun."

Could he have picked worse words? "Just having fun."

"Wait, what's wrong here? Did I embarrass you? I'm sorry if I did that, okay? I thought you'd like it. I like singing to you. You looked like you were having fun."

She couldn't help her reply. "Oh, they were all having fun, I'm sure. You're quite the showman."

Someone tried to grab his attention, and she heard Jesse shoo them away. "Are you upset that I sang to you in front of everyone like that?"

She wasn't, and that was part of the problem. "No. It's just... I don't know. I just wanted to get out of there, okay?"

"No, it's not okay. I'm not quite sure what I did wrong here, but I don't want to leave it like this. Talk to me. Better yet, give me ten minutes and I'll be over there."

"No, don't." She squeezed her eyes shut, knowing what a stab that might be but then wondering—with the way he was always careful to hide what he was feeling—if that would be any kind of a dent to him at all.

"I'm at a loss here, Charlotte. C'mon, talk to me."

"It's… I'm okay. Stunned, maybe. Give me time."

"I sang to lots of people. But I especially sang to you. We've got a history with that song, don't we? Wait…are you upset that I didn't sing it only to you? Is that what this is about?"

It sounded so petty, so hopelessly infatuated when he said it, that Charlotte cringed and sank against the wall. There was more to it than that, but she couldn't put it into words. She couldn't even answer him.

"Whoa. It's not like that. It was an impulse, an entertainer thing." After a moment he said, "I'm a jerk. A show-off. Let's talk about this. Dinner tomorrow, right?"

It wouldn't help. She'd just see his eyes and the whole tumbling would start all over again.

"Charlotte…don't make this into something it wasn't. If you won't let me come over there now, at least let's do dinner like we planned."

"I just need to…I don't know, sort this out somehow. Good night, Jesse, you were amazing. Really, really amazing."

She heard him fending off someone else, then come back to the phone. "Dinner. I'm not hanging up until you agree to dinner."

She didn't have the nerve to fight him off right now. "Okay. Dinner." She ended the call.

Would anything change in twenty-four hours? Was she being fair if she didn't allow Jesse a chance to explain himself? Charlotte had no idea. Half an hour of sitting still and trying to listen for God brought no clarity. Fifteen minutes of petting Mo and staring into his wise yellow eyes didn't help, either. Knitting—her usual solace of preference—lasted less than ten minutes. Finally, in desperation, Charlotte turned on her laptop to look over her e-mail.

There, at the top of her inbox, was an e-mail from Borroughs Yarn and Fabric Supply in Stowe, Vermont. Every knitter knew Borroughs was a great company, a maker of high-quality yarns. Now they were developing an admirable reputation for inventive patterns and clever supplies for all kinds of textile arts. They'd already taken many of the steps she'd been trying to get Monarch to consider in utilizing digital media. Their blog was gaining serious traction—they were getting it right and seeing results. And they were asking her to come out for an interview after the upcoming Fourth of July holiday to discuss the possibility of heading up their new online commerce department.

I need this. Even if I don't get the job, it will put a bit of space between Jesse and I so

I can think. Thank You, Lord. I knew You'd make a way.

Charlotte replied that she'd let them know as soon as her flights were booked. Now she'd have something to put some space between her and that charismatic, problematic fireman.

Chapter Thirteen

"Vermont?" Melba looked as shocked as Charlotte had expected her to be.

"Well, just part of the time. Or all of the time if I want it, and the company and I can come to an agreement." They were having a spontaneous post-church picnic on a blanket in Melba's backyard, watching Maria kick and wiggle.

"Vermont?" Melba said again. "And you're actually considering it?"

"I was laid off a month ago today. I've been putting out feelers every day since then, and all I've got to show for it is a few phone interviews that made me feel inept and a stack of carefully worded deflections." Maybe it wasn't such a smart idea to have kept how badly the job search was going from Melba all this time. "There aren't as many jobs out there as I thought there were. Monarch's not the only company feeling the pinch."

"But you're here. You want to be here." Melba scooped up Maria as if to shield her from the news. "Don't you?"

Charlotte sighed. "Of course I do. But I need a job, and there don't seem to be any jobs for me here." It was the first time she'd spoken that truth out loud, and it let loose the growing tendril of fear in the pit of her stomach she'd been trying so hard to ignore. She'd been so sure of her path up until now. So convinced God had led her straight to Gordon Falls.

So sure she never wanted to be attached to someone like Jesse Sykes.

Melba settled Maria into her lap and furrowed her brows. "Did your mom finally get to you?"

Charlotte's mom, usually supportive, had lately begun to express concerns about Charlotte buying the cottage and sinking so much of her inheritance into the renovations. She hadn't said anything during the sale and the first days, but telling comments had started sneaking their way into conversations. A doubt here, a question there, a disapproving silence after renovation updates on the phone. The unspoken current of "and you still don't have a new job" ran constantly under every conversation. "Let's just say she hasn't been enthusiastic in her support."

Normally she didn't let her mother get to her that way, but the undeniable truth was that Charlotte was starting to worry about it herself. The gorgeous high-end kitchen faucet that cost twice as much as the standard—was that really what she needed? The armoire from the antiques store—was that really "the most darling thing she'd ever seen" or had it seemed that way because she'd gotten two rejections that day? The credit card bill had come last night, and it hadn't been pretty. Sure, she had the funds for now, but she couldn't—shouldn't—keep up the spending like this. Things were starting to come unraveled around the edges; she knew it on some level, just didn't know what to do about it.

"Don't let her get to you, Charlotte. You love that house. You belong in that house."

That was still true. Charlotte leaned back on her elbows, admiring the emerald-green of the leaves as they fluttered in the breeze overhead. It was so wonderfully green here. Everything seemed to be thriving—well, everything except her. "I didn't say I was going to sell the house. I just may not get to live here for a while."

"What are you going to do?"

"I'll still finish the renovations, but I might have to rent it out for a while."

Melba twirled a leaf over Maria's head,

watching how her eyes followed the shapes and colors. "I can't imagine anyone in that house but you. You can't rent it to just anyone."

"Actually," Charlotte said carefully, keeping her voice as neutral as possible, "I was thinking of asking Jesse if he wanted to rent it. I know he just lives in an apartment now and it might make it easier to finish the renovations."

"Yes." Melba raised her eyebrows. "Let's talk about Jesse. About what's going on between you two. You could have lit half the valley on the sparks flying between you two at the talent show last night."

"He's a showman."

"Yes, he is. But while he sang to some other people, it was a whole different thing when he sang to you. And you still haven't told me about Friday's dinner in your kitchen. I want to hear it all—everything from dinner to why you disappeared after the talent show."

Bit by bit, Charlotte unfolded the entire story of dinner at the cottage. It felt useful to put the thing into words, to try and describe—if she couldn't hope to explain—what had sprung up between her and Jesse. Melba's response was an unlikely mix of surprise and "I told you so." She, of all people, could understand the pile of conflict mounting in Charlotte's heart.

"Wow," she said when Charlotte finished her

tale and fell flat on her back on the blanket. "I mean, really, wow. This is a side of Jesse I don't think anyone's ever seen. He's mostly just a goofball around the firehouse, but it seems the man is an insufferable romantic."

Charlotte put her hands over her eyes, the vision of Jesse's magnetic gaze heating her cheeks all over again. "So what if he is? That doesn't mean he's capable of—or even looking for—commitment. Come on, your own husband called him 'an insufferable bachelor.' I don't want to be just another member of the Jesse Sykes fan club."

"I'm sure you can tell the difference."

"No, I can't. Not yet," Charlotte admitted, rolling onto her stomach to bury her face in the blanket. "I was defenseless when he sang to me in my kitchen, too. 'You Send Me' while he made the Alfredo sauce."

"The Sam Cooke song? I think I'd melt right into the Alfredo."

"I'm pretty sure I did. And the kiss…" She rolled back over and draped her hand over her face dramatically. "Glory, but that man can kiss. I was a goner. If it hadn't been for Mo, I'd have been in serious trouble. I *am* in serious trouble." She sat up. "That's what makes it so hard—I can't tell what's genuine. If he was just a guy on the make, I don't think he would have backed off when I asked him to in my kitchen. There's really something there. But you saw what he did to those other women in the audience. I don't know what's real. I'm not even sure he knows."

"I don't, either, but I'm pretty sure moving to Vermont isn't the answer."

"But it could be. I've lost my job and Mima. I'm not in a good place to think smart right now."

"Have you talked to him about any of this?"

"We were going to talk at dinner tonight, but he called me earlier and said he got pulled onto duty and we have to postpone. What if some time and distance is exactly what I need? The cottage will still be here in a year, and I'll be stronger."

"And Jesse? What if he's not here?"

That would be okay, wouldn't it? That would mean God had helped her shut a door she wasn't strong enough to shut on her own. That was what she'd prayed for, what she'd come to understand as the opportunity this Vermont job offer presented. Only if that were true, where was that sense of assurance, that ability to leap forward that had always been her strength? "Then I'll know it wasn't supposed to work out."

Melba gave her a doubtful stare. "You need to talk to him, Charlotte. You need to tell him in person that you're thinking about the Vermont offer. You need to ask him outright what's going on between the two of you."

"I know. I know. We'll have dinner tomorrow and I'll do it then."

Chapter Fourteen

There was a reason most firefighters hated the Fourth of July.

It was as if the world was ganging up on him to make sure he didn't have enough time to think through what was going on with Charlotte. Three false alarms, two parades, multiple firecracker-related incidents and four guys sick on the squad. As Jesse was fond of joking, "Some weeks it just didn't pay to be a volunteer firefighter." And that wasn't even counting the two construction jobs that were stymied by the holiday and back-ordered supplies.

He'd used the time away from Charlotte to go over that night at the talent show a dozen times in his head. It wasn't as if he'd planned what he was going to do when he went into the audience, but the way Charlotte looked at him had practically pulled him offstage. He loved what his voice did to her eyes, the way his touch could raise color in her cheeks. They had such a strong connection that he felt just a bit out of control when he sang to her.

That wasn't how it was supposed to happen. The leap in his gut made him pull back, made him resort to old tricks and play up to other women in the audience. He'd known exactly what he was doing when he'd shifted his attention to the high school teacher, had even guessed how Charlotte would react. It didn't surprise him that the other women were as entertained as Charlotte was. It did stun him that he didn't enjoy their blushing smiles. He'd walked back to the stage that night not wanting to sing the final chorus to anyone but Charlotte. That was not who Jesse Sykes was. He wasn't ready to be so serious with Charlotte, or with any one woman right now.

Still, he couldn't stay away. The tone of her voice—the hurt and confusion when they'd spoken on the phone—echoed in his head no matter how hard he tried to shake it off. He told himself it was okay, maybe even a good thing, that things felt off-kilter when they'd talked. It was for the best that things had cooled off considerably when he was forced to postpone their date for Dellio's until after the Fourth. This unpredictability was part of his life, part of why he couldn't get serious with a woman. It was better that they'd have to take separate cars, because he was still wearing a beeper tonight, on call in case one of the other firefighters called in sick with whatever nasty bug was still making its way around the firehouse.

If he got called in out of their dinner, the interruption would be a sore spot for Charlotte. Still, the firehouse and its demands were part of who he was. If anything were ever to work out between them, they'd have to figure this part out. He just didn't know if that was possible. He still wanted to take this in small steps, and he just didn't know if Charlotte was capable of small steps in anything.

Even though it had been his idea, Jesse found Dellio's an annoying opposite of their first dinner. It was a local favorite; a noisy, greasy, delicious diner—one of the few places Jesse felt produced burgers nearly as good as his own. And the French fries? They were legendary—everybody loved them.

She was waiting in his favorite booth. That had to be a good sign. Despite all the complications, he still wanted tonight to go well, still wanted to move things forward and halt the backward slide they'd taken. Other women had never wandered continually into his thoughts like this—even on the job, where he used to be known for his single-minded focus.

"Glad you finally made it." She was trying to make a joke of it, to keep things light, but it was clear the long postponement had hit a nerve.

"Yeah." He surprised himself by hiding the beeper in his pocket and switching it to Vibrate so that she wouldn't see he was on call. *Cut her some slack, okay, God?* He was equally surprised to feel the tiny prayer rise up out of him, hoping the God she spoke to so easily had enough kindness not to rub salt in the wound tonight. *No calls—I'd consider it a favor.* He switched subjects. "How's Mo settling in?"

"Generous of you to ask, considering. He's doing okay. He hasn't broken or shredded anything, if that's what you mean, but there isn't a lot to shred just yet. I can't really hang curtains downstairs until the new windows get installed."

Of course she had to mention the back-ordered windows. "They'll be here in ten days, they tell me. The two new doors are supposed to come in tomorrow, along with the closet fixtures, so I can get started on those as soon as things calm down." She'd ordered top-of-the-line interior doors for the upstairs bedrooms, but the master bedroom closet was the thing that really stunned him. She'd moved one wall and taken a corner of the upstairs hallway to build out what she termed "a decent-sized closet." Jesse would have considered something half that size "decent." This was edging closer to decadent. And expensive. She'd gotten defensive when he made even the tiniest remark about the cost.

"The sink's working great, and everything in the bathroom is just perfect." She was picking at the edge of her menu with one fingernail.

"Glad to hear it. That tub looks just as good as a new one, don't you think?" *Come on, you're supposed to be patching things up with the lady and the only conversation you can manage is plumbing fixtures?*

"It was a good idea. I've got a few more ideas I want to try out on you, but let's order first."

Things eased up once the food came, but while he waited for her to bring up the subject of the talent-show night, she failed to raise the topic. Should he bring it up first? That didn't feel right—it was mostly her issue; he should follow her lead.

Instead, Charlotte said a quiet grace over the food—not as long as the prayer she'd said over their previous dinner, but it had the same effect on him. To be continually thankful like that—over something as mundane as burgers and fries—it got to him. When she added a plea for safety for Jesse and all the Gordon Falls Volunteer Fire Department, his heart did a startling twist in his chest as if the prayer had physically embedded itself there. Her voice took on a different quality, soft and lush, lively and yet peaceful at the same time. Jesse found himself easily and even gladly saying "Amen" to her blessing over the food.

The effortlessness he was so drawn to in her cottage came back to their conversation bit by bit. Maybe things had settled on their own—and that was okay, wasn't it? He didn't want to make this more complicated than it already was. That smile—the one that managed to tumble his insides in a matter of seconds—came back. Still, it was easy to see she had a lot on her mind, and at some point they were going to talk about whatever went haywire between them the other night.

"So." He decided to press the issue when they were halfway through the heart-attack-on-a-plate hamburgers and they still hadn't talked about whatever she needed to say. "What's up?"

"You mentioned your apartment lease was nearly up the other day." He'd expected a deluge of emotional questions and concerns, not that. She fiddled nervously with a French fry, drawing artistic circles in the puddle of ketchup on her plate. What was going on?

"I did," he replied slowly, cautiously.

"I don't know if you'd find this at all appealing, but if I ended up taking a job offer out of town, would you consider renting the cottage for a year?"

Where had that come from? And what did a question like that mean given everything that had gone on between them? "You're leaving?"

"No. I mean, I don't know. What if I have to? It hasn't…well, it hasn't been as easy to find a new job as I'd hoped."

If this was about how he'd behaved at the talent show, the cottage was no place to take it out on him. Rent? Why? "Well, sure it's a tough market out there, but…" It surprised him how much the thought of her leaving stung him.

"I don't want to spend my days marketing widgets just because it's the only marketing job I can do from home. I want to work in the fiber industry. Textiles at the very least. There are only so many companies big enough to hire. I've gone a whole month with no serious prospects. Now there is one in Vermont that's starting to sound promising and…well…I may need to go where the work is."

This seemed a hundred miles from the impulsive, passionate Charlotte of just a few days ago. He reminded himself that she'd wanted to slow things down. She'd put the brakes on their relationship, and he was happy about that. Wasn't he? That didn't explain the irrational annoyance climbing up his spine. He hadn't wanted to get serious with anyone, least of all her, so he knew he shouldn't be ticked that she was considering an out-of-town offer. It made no sense. "I suppose that makes sense," he said, just because he couldn't come up with anything else to say.

"What do you think?"

Was she asking him if he'd take the lease? Or was she looking for him to ask her to stay? How was he supposed to know the right answer to a question like that—especially after the other night? He sat back in the booth. "Are you leaving?" The words made her flinch just a bit—they'd come out sharper than he would have liked.

"I just said I don't know yet. I don't want to go—" she gave the words an emphasis that made Jesse's insides tumble in eight different directions "—but what if I don't have a choice?"

"You always have a choice, Charlotte. If you really want to stay here, then you can find a way to make it happen." He looked at her. "Vermont? You don't really strike me as the rural New England type." He knew it wouldn't sit well, but he had to ask anyway. "So now you're sorry you bought the cottage?" If she were to walk away from it now, it would feel like rubbing salt on the wound she'd dealt him by buying it out from under him in the first place.

"No. I'm not sorry. I'm not saying Vermont's perfect, but it may have to do for a little while. And I don't want to sell the cottage. I'll want to come back to it. I love it and I want to keep going on the work on it. But I can't stomach the idea of just anyone living there."

So I'm a convenient stand-in? "I'm not so sure that would work." It was time she knew the full story. It was clear she needed to know. "Look, Charlotte, you should know that this hasn't exactly been a cakewalk for me seeing you in that house. I'd been plotting to buy the cottage for months before you showed up."

Surprise widened her eyes. Maybe now she'd understand why this might be an especially touchy subject.

"The reason why I have all those good ideas on what needs to be done is that I've been thinking about it all year. I just needed two more months to save up enough for the down payment. Not all of us get windfalls from loving grandmothers, you know."

Windfalls from loving grandmothers? The edge in Jesse's words cut off Charlotte's breath. Did he realize how hurtful that sounded?

"The home you **were** going to buy to launch your business **was** my cottage?" Suddenly everything that **had transpired** between them became suspicious, **as** if he'd been working some hidden **agenda she** wasn't clever enough to notice. Was **it so hard** to believe he'd played to her just as **he played** to other women in the audience—that she **was** just a customer like any other—after hearing that fact?

"Was. So you can see that renting it from you might be a bit of a touchy business for me?"

"Why didn't you say anything about this before?" It made no sense that he'd keep it from her unless there was some reason behind his silence.

He pinched the bridge of his nose. "Leave me just a little bit of pride in this, won't you? I didn't have any legal claim to the cottage—I just hadn't moved fast enough when you struck like lightning. The gracious loser thing doesn't come easily to me. I figured it'd just make things uncomfortable between us if I brought it up."

"So if you couldn't be the owner, you'd get the owner as your biggest customer, is that it?" She began to think through every decision he'd encouraged or discouraged, wondering if his charming helpfulness was ever fully genuine.

"No, that's not it." He planted his hands on

the table, his eyes darkening at the accusation. "My offer to help was mostly on the level."

Well, that was a telling choice of words. "Mostly?"

"Of course I saw it as a good business opportunity. Your house represented a big job for me, and I needed a big job. I won't say I wasn't ticked at first. I was. But you clearly needed help, and I knew that I was the best guy for the job. And it wasn't long before it became more than business. You know that." He tossed his napkin on the table, and for a moment she wondered if he'd simply stand up and walk out. He didn't.

Instead, he leaned in. "I'd procrastinated on my plans too long and it came back to bite me—that's not a new lesson for me. This one just hurt a bit more than the others, and maybe that's good." His eyes took on that intense quality that always pulled her in, always made her heart skip. "Charlotte, you belong in that house. Every time I said that I meant it. You belong there. Why on earth are you leaving it? Leaving here?"

At that moment, it struck her that she was waiting to hear "Why are you leaving *me?*" Only that was not what he said, and that omission said everything. "I don't know that I'm leaving. I don't want to leave. But if I can't find a job here, I may not have a choice. I'm just trying to find a good solution for the property if I have to go." She paused, struck again by the enormity of his omission. How could he spend so much time with her in that place and keep his original intentions from her? It felt so manipulative. All the intensity of his persuasion at dinner, his attentions at the talent show, they all felt fabricated now.

"So that's what I am? A useful solution?"

She was not using him. She'd made the suggestion to be helpful. Yes, to both of them, but she hadn't used him the way he'd used her. "That's not fair. I didn't know you wanted the cottage. And the reason I didn't know was because you hid it from me."

"What, exactly, would have been the point of telling you? The only thing it would have done was made things awkward. As it was, things were pretty great." He ran one hand down his face. "Well, to tell the truth, I don't know what things are right now." His phone vibrated loudly in his pocket. "I thought we had something going on at dinner the other night, and I thought we had fun at the talent show, but how it got all serious and complicated all of a sudden is beyond me." His phone continued to go off and he grumbled while he fished it out.

This whole thing was a mess. "Jesse…"

Jesse practically threw the device on the table as the firehouse sirens began to wail through the night air. Charlotte realized it wasn't his phone at all, but the firehouse beeper. "You're on duty?"

"I'm on call," he growled. "And now I have to go in." He muttered a few unkind words under his breath as he slid out of the booth and tossed a pair of twenty-dollar bills on the table. "We're going to have to finish this—whatever this is— another time."

Charlotte stared at her food, the delectable burger having lost all its appeal. Jesse couldn't have picked a worse moment to be called into the firehouse. She tried to summon a prayer of sympathy for whoever's home or business was facing the threat of fire, but self-pity overpowered her better nature. Right now, she selfishly despised the siren.

Here, in a single moment, was every reason why she and Jesse wouldn't work. They didn't consider the same things important. He should have told her the minute they'd sat down that he was on call. He should have told her he'd been eyeing the cottage before she bought it.

He should have told her he wanted her to stay in Gordon Falls.

I got it all wrong, Mima. This isn't what you would have wanted. You were looking to give me adventure and I turned it into foolishness. If I had only waited, thought some more about what I was doing, I wouldn't be in this mess.

She fought the urge to do something, to move or talk or do anything to stem the discomfort now crawling under her skin as if her emotional state had taken on physical symptoms. *Sit and think, don't react,* she told herself, but it didn't help. She was a whole ball of reaction.

Charlotte ate two more bites of her burger before giving up. She flagged the server and asked to have both meals boxed up, grateful most of the Dellio's staff was familiar with the firehouse and used to people dashing out mid-meal. She added a few more bills to cover the tip and left the restaurant, knowing she'd hold the sight of that half-empty booth with two meals in her head for a long, long time. One person with two plates of food—how she knew and detested that view.

She made sure her route home didn't take her past the firehouse. When she pulled into her driveway, the glow through the curtainless front windows looked forlorn instead of expectant. The house that had always spoken of possibilities struck her tonight as a giant pile of things undone. The feeling she'd fought off since she'd signed the sale papers rose up huge and undeniable. It was clear now that she'd bitten off far more than she could chew.

I need to think this through.

She knew, as strongly as she recognized the truth, that she needed time and space away from Jesse and Gordon Falls in order to do that.

Charlotte stood in the hallway, half paralyzed with indecision, half desperate to do something. She tried to pray but she had no idea what to pray for. *I need something to do, Lord. I can't just stand here.*

With no visible path, Charlotte simply kept doing the next thing that came to mind. First, she turned the oven on low and tucked the food in to keep it warm until her hunger returned. Then she put the kettle on to make a cup of tea. While she drank the tea, she opened up her laptop and booked the flight to Vermont. Then, in what felt like the first clear thought of the night, she packed her bag to head back to the Chicago apartment. It'd be easier to catch a cab to the airport from there, and she needed to be gone when Jesse got off duty.

She picked up the cat carrier Melba had brought for Mo and opened the door. "If we leave now, we'll be in Chicago a little before ten. We'll figure out tomorrow when tomorrow comes." Astonishingly, the cat walked right in as if he thought that was a smart idea. What more encouragement did she need? She was packed and turning onto the highway before an hour had passed.

Chapter Fifteen

Jesse winced as the emergency room doctor wrapped the plastic splint around his swollen ankle. "Is it a bad break?" He'd seen the X-ray and could guess, but he wanted confirmation.

"I've seen worse. If you stay off it—and I mean really off it, no weight on that ankle for three days until the swelling goes down enough to put a hard cast on it—you'll be back in action in six weeks."

"Six weeks?" Jesse moaned and let his head fall back against the examining bed, listening to its paper cover crinkle in sanitary sympathy.

The doctor peered over the top of his glasses. "You could be off crutches and into a walking cast in three or four weeks if it heals well. But if you push it and try to go faster, you could end up needing surgery. You may need surgery anyway." He peered again at the bandage on

Jesse's leg. It covered a nasty gash just above the break. "Come back tomorrow to get the dressing changed. We'll see how the swelling has gone down by then. Ice every twenty minutes, ibuprofen for the pain, keep it elevated, you know the drill."

Chief Bradens pulled aside the curtain, looking weary. "Another down. What the flu started, that porch railing finished. I'm going to have to call another department to send a few guys to hold us over until some of the others are back on their feet."

"Sorry." Jesse knew injuries were part of the job, and no one could have foreseen that the porch railing wouldn't hold when he tripped and fell into it. Some small part of him—the part that keenly remembered Charlotte's prayer for his safety not hours before—knew he was fortunate not to have been more badly hurt. Still, a larger and angrier part of him was ticked off at all the trouble this break would cause.

"Come on, Sykes, it's not your fault. I'm just glad you'll be okay to come back eventually."

"Sure, in mid-August."

"More like September, actually," the doctor cut in. "You'll need another two weeks of physical therapy after getting the cast off to get back into enough shape to go out on call."

"And let's not even talk about my time off

the job," Jesse moaned. Mondale wouldn't take kindly to having to call someone else in to finish his jobs. Someone else working on Charlotte's cottage? And the loss of income? Even with insurance, it would set his plan for the launch of Sykes Homes back a month if not more. Tonight was turning out to be a lousy evening on every front.

"Let's worry about that tomorrow and get you home." Chief Bradens began the paperwork while Jesse hoisted himself up with the pair of crutches that would be his constant companions for the next few weeks. "Have you got someone who can help you out tonight?"

His mom would be here in minutes if he called. Even Randy, busy as he was, might find a way to stay overnight if asked. Only Jesse didn't want any of those people. He wanted Charlotte. Despite everything that was getting tangled further between them, the urge to do his recuperating in that overstuffed old plaid chair in the corner of Charlotte's living room came over him like a craving. He'd even put up with Mo to spend his days sitting on that chair watching her putter around the house with that elated, decor-planning look on her face. Go figure.

That option, however, was off the table for now if not forever.

"I'm set," he hedged, knowing the chief himself would find someone to stay with him if he wasn't convinced Jesse had it covered. Right now he really wanted to be alone with his frustration. "Just get me home and I'll deal with the rest." His car was still at the firehouse, and he didn't think he could drive it, anyway. One of the guys could bring it over later.

He and Bradens hobbled out to the chief's red truck, the radio still chattering in the dash with all the usual post-incident communication. It had been a small fire, a holiday fish fry spilling over onto a back deck, more smoke and mess than any real damage. Only the deck was old and rickety, as Jesse and his left tibia had soon learned. Those mishaps—the ones that were so infuriatingly avoidable—made Jesse angry even if he didn't end up hurt. If people would just bother to repair things like stairs when they broke, or—better yet—call in someone who knew what they were doing instead of trusting structures to a lethal combination of lumber store supplies and an internet tutorial. As every paramedic in the department knew too well, sometimes "do-it-yourself" turned into "hurt yourself" or "hurt someone else," as tonight well showed.

"It's late." Chief Bradens sighed, looking at the digits on the dashboard clock.

"It's so late it's early," Jesse managed to joke, pointing to the "12:25 a.m." with a strangled smile.

"I hope we get a quiet night from here on in," Chief Bradens said, breaking his own rule. It was a standing joke at the firehouse that hoping aloud for "a quiet night" nearly always guaranteed the opposite. The holiday incidents and short-staffing had really wiped the chief out.

"I hope we get a quiet weekend," Jesse added. "We need a break." He caught his own unintentional joke and laughed, glad to see a weary smile come to the chief's face, as well. "Well, a different kind of break, that is."

They drove to Jesse's apartment in tired silence, listening to the back and forth of the radio chatter slowly die down as the department settled in. The guys on duty would be up for another hour cleaning and restocking before they got to go home to their families. Nights like this were hard under the best of circumstances, much less when they were short of staff, as the GFVFD currently was.

They pulled into the driveway of Jesse's duplex. "I guess it's a good thing you have the first floor." Chief Bradens nodded to the pile of Jesse's turnout gear in the truck's backseat. "I'll take your stuff back to the firehouse for you."

Jesse opened the door and put his good foot—

now sporting a paper hospital bootie, since he'd gone in wearing fire boots—on the sidewalk. He angled the crutches out of the truck and stood up. Everything hurt.

Chief came around the car. "You're sure you'll be okay?"

"Fine." He'd keep his cell phone nearby and call Mom if he needed anything other than the ten hours of sleep he currently craved.

He was fishing in his pocket for his house keys when the beeper went off and they both noticed the radio in the truck spouting a crackle of commands. "Not again," Bradens groaned.

If the chief didn't look so drained and his own body didn't hurt so much, Jesse would have made some crack about Bradens jinxing the night with his hope for quiet. Mostly he just shook his head as the chief hoisted himself onto the passenger seat to grab the radio handset.

"Gotta go. Smoke at 85 Post Avenue."

"Go," Jesse said, turning toward his house. "I'll be fine once I…" He halted, frozen by the facts his tired brain had just this moment absorbed. Then Jesse spun around as fast as his crutches would let him, only to see Bradens's truck speed away, lights blaring as the firehouse siren sent up its second wail of the night.

85 Post Avenue was Charlotte's cottage.

Chapter Sixteen

It no longer felt like home.

That was the single, constant impression Charlotte's Chicago apartment left her with as she rattled around the dull white box of a dwelling. A month ago she'd found the urban apartment dripping with character, but now it felt sadly ordinary. Impersonal, even, despite the fact that it still contained many of her personal belongings. Even the addition of Mo didn't seem to liven up the place. How could a stuffed full apartment feel more vacant than a half-empty cottage?

When she'd pulled out of the driveway in Gordon Falls, she'd doubted the wisdom of that purchase. Now, back in Chicago, she recognized it for what it had become: her home. Sitting in her favorite chair in her Chicago apartment, she still felt uncomfortable and out of place. She wanted to be in Gordon Falls. She wanted to *live* in Gordon Falls for more than just weekends and vacations.

It didn't seem possible—at least not any way that she could see right now. *I want to be there, but there isn't a job for me there. Is there one that I've missed? Lord, why are you opening a door so far away when You've knit my heart to Gordon Falls? Is it because I need to be away from Jesse? We're not good for each other, even I can see that, but my heart...*

Charlotte curled up under a lush afghan, welcomed Mo onto her lap and began to make two lists. One list held ideas for jobs she could do in Gordon Falls or one of the neighboring towns— "make do" jobs like marketing for the local hospital or some other company, office work or finding online work she could do from home. None of these felt at all exciting or motivating. The second list held all the arrangements—like finding a moving company or renting a storage facility—that would be necessary if she went to Vermont. Both lists left a sour taste in her mouth, and she abandoned the task in favor of knitting with Mo purring beside her until she dozed off.

The loud ring of the apartment's landline phone woke her, clanging from the single receiver in the kitchen. She bumbled her way to the phone, the alarm of a middle-of-the-night call fighting with the fatigue of her difficult day. Mo tangled around her feet and she almost tripped twice. Her answering machine was kicking in by the time she lifted the receiver. "Hello?"

"Charlotte, what on earth are you doing in Chicago?"

"Melba?" How had her friend even known to call her here? She hadn't told anyone she was leaving. She'd planned to call Melba in the morning, but she knew if she talked to Melba before she left, her friend would have talked her into staying over. She needed to be farther away from the cottage than the Bradenses' house. "I decided to come to my apartment. What's wrong?"

Charlotte heard Maria crying in the background. "I only tried this number because you didn't answer your cell phone. Charlotte, it's the cottage. One of your neighbors smelled the smoke and called the fire department."

Charlotte fumbled for her handbag, knocking a tote bag to the ground and sending Mo scurrying back out of the kitchen. "The cottage is on fire?" Panic strangled her breath and sent her thoughts scattering. "The cottage?" she repeated, as if that would help the news sink in.

"I don't know any details yet. No one knew where you were."

She found her cell phone and saw three missed calls—two from Jesse and one from Melba, not to mention multiple texts from both of them. All within the past ten minutes. She'd set the phone to Vibrate during dinner with Jesse and hadn't turned the ringtone back on. "I drove here earlier tonight." Charlotte sat down on one of the tall stools that fronted her kitchen counter. "My house is on fire?" Tears tightened her throat. She couldn't stand to lose something else. She just couldn't.

"Not fully, and the guys have it under control. Clark said it was mostly just smoke but he called me when they didn't find you in the house." Her voice jostled as if she were bouncing Maria to try and soothe the crying child. Charlotte squinted at the cell phone screen to see that it was nearly 1:00 a.m. "I'm so glad you're okay. I've been praying like crazy since I couldn't reach you on your cell phone."

"My house is on fire." She couldn't think of another thing to say. "My house. My cottage." She began stuffing everything back into the tote bag she'd knocked off the counter. "It'll take me hours to get there. Oh, God…" It was a moan of a prayer, a plea for clarity where none existed.

"What if you took the train? Maybe you shouldn't drive."

She couldn't wait for a train. And she surely wouldn't sleep anymore tonight. No, the only thing for it was to head back to Gordon Falls and pray along the way for safe travel. "No, I don't think there's one for hours anyway. I'll call if I need help to stay calm, and I promise I'll pull over if I need to rest." *My house is on fire.* Her brain kept shouting it at her, making it hard to think. She was supposed to be the calm head in a crisis, the problem solver, but none of that felt possible now. "I'll be on my way in ten minutes." She reached into the fridge and stuffed the last three cans of diet cola—a faster caffeine source than waiting for the coffeemaker to brew—into the tote bag. Mo, in a move she knew no other cat owner would probably ever believe, calmly walked into his carrier as if he knew they were getting back into the car. "Call my cell if you learn anything more, okay?"

"I will. Stay safe, Charlotte. The cottage is important, but you're more important than all of that. Don't speed, and call me if you need me. I'll talk to you the whole way in if you need me."

The cell phone buzzed on the counter. Jesse's information lit up the screen.

"Where are you?" his voice shouted over a lot of background noise, including sirens.

"I'm in Chicago. I just talked to Melba."

"Chicago? What are you doing there? I went nuts when they couldn't find you in the house."

There was so much noise behind him. The thought of Jesse standing outside the cottage watching flames eat her house made it harder to fight off the tears. She sat down on the stool. "How bad is it?"

"Not as bad as it could have been. If you had been inside…" Someone barked questions to him and she heard him pull the phone away from his ear and answer, "No, no, I've got her on the phone right now. She's in Chicago. Yeah, I know."

"I'm coming." She was desperate to see the cottage, to know how badly it had been damaged. The 160 or so miles between Chicago and Gordon Falls felt like a thousand right now.

"I would." His voice was unreadable over all that noise. Did he say that because he would have made the same choice? Or was it so bad that she needed to be out there as soon as possible?

"Whoa, Sykes! Ouch! How'd that happen?" She recognized the voice as one of the firemen but couldn't begin to say which one.

"Hey, not now, okay?" came Jesse's quick

reply. His voice came close to the phone again. "You be careful driving. Things are under control here, just try and remember that."

What did he say just now? "Jesse, are you okay?"

"I'm fine. Just rattled, that's all. The cottage and everything. Call me when you get to the highway exit." He paused before adding, "I'm glad you're okay. Really glad."

She heard emotion tighten his words and felt her own chest cinch with the awareness. "I should be there sometime before four." She took a minute to breathe before she asked, "Jesse, what aren't you telling me? Is the cottage gone? Just tell me now—I need to know."

"The cottage isn't gone. Looks like mostly smoke and water damage. I didn't get close enough to know anything more than that."

Not close enough? Jesse had been brought in on duty tonight. Why wasn't he in the crew that went to her house? "But I'd have thought you—"

He cut her off. "Just get here. The longer we talk now, the longer it takes for you to get on the road. I promise, I'll be here when you pull in and I'll answer all your questions then."

"But what—"

"Look, I've got to go. Please promise me you'll drive safely, and you'll pull off if you get sleepy."

She had a gallon of adrenaline running in her veins. "No chance of that. I've got a bunch of Diet Cokes besides." She had to ask. "It's going to be okay, isn't it?"

"Yes."

She wanted him to turn on the charm, to launch into that irresistible persuasion that was his gift, to sweep her up in that bold confidence he had, but really, how could he? A phone conversation in the middle of what might be a disaster couldn't do that. The only thing she knew that could do such a thing was prayer.

"Jesse?"

"Yeah?"

"Pray for me? I know it's not really your thing, but God will hear you anyway, and I'll feel better knowing you're asking Him to keep me safe until I get there." It was a drastic thing to ask, but if this wasn't a time for drastic measures, what was?

"I'll give it a shot."

That was all the foothold she needed. "Okay. Mo and I are on the way."

"Wait...you have the cat with you?" He sounded surprised.

"Evidently he likes car rides."

He pushed out a breath. "I had the guys scouring the neighborhood for the beast. I thought he was a goner, or at the very least ran away." He actually sounded relieved. "Glad to hear he'll live to torment me another day."

Even on the phone, even faced with disaster, he'd managed to pull a smile from her—one just large enough to get her on her way. "See you soon."

Every single bone in his body ached. His leg injury was down to a dull fire thanks to the pain medicine, but Jesse felt the sorry combination of wide awake and exhausted pound through his muscles and thud in his brain.

He should go home. It was feat enough that he'd hobbled all the way here on his crutches—it wasn't that long a walk but still, that had to have been damaging. He should take himself back to his apartment and at least make an effort to get some sleep.

Only he couldn't. He sat on the curb, his splinted leg sticking out in the deserted street atop his crutches in a makeshift attempt at "keeping it elevated," staring at the cottage. He was trying to make the place feel like his cottage, striving to muster up the sense of ownership he'd privately claimed before Charlotte came along. It wouldn't come. This was Charlotte's place, and two things were currently driving him crazy.

One, that he needed to make it Charlotte's perfect place—wonderfully, uniquely hers.

Two, that no matter what he told himself, no matter how "unserious" he claimed to be about that woman, he couldn't stand the thought of her gone.

What had swept through his body when he realized Chief Bradens's radio was crackling out orders for Charlotte's cottage was sharper than fear. It was the bone-deep shock of loss. A loss that wasn't about bricks and shingles, but the woman who'd come to invade his life. He'd told himself it was better to keep things cool, to play their mutual attraction the way the old Jesse would have done. Only he couldn't. She'd done something to him. He'd told himself that his balking over her rental suggestion was just the legendary Sykes ego, a refusal to live in the house over some sore-loser impulse. That would have been a good guess for his personality a month ago. That wasn't it, though—he'd bristled because he hated the idea of the house without Charlotte inside, even temporarily. Somehow he knew—had known since the beginning in a way he couldn't comfortably explain—that she belonged there. Living there instead of her seemed just plain wrong.

Sitting there, feeling something way beyond

sidelined, Jesse added two more items to the list of things that were bugging him:

Three, that he couldn't help with the cottage. Normally, Jesse wasn't the kind to rush in toward a fire. There were guys like that, firemen who were nearly obsessively drawn to a crisis, driven by an inner urge to save the day that made ordinary men heroes. He'd never felt that pull—until tonight. It buzzed through him like a ferocious itch that he could only watch from the sidelines. It gave him nothing to do.

Which brought up number four: Charlotte's request that he pray. He could no more help her get here from Chicago than he could march into that cottage, and the sense of helplessness crippled him worse than his leg. The prayer she'd requested was the only thing he could do for her... but he wasn't sure how. He was not a praying man. He wasn't opposed to the idea—he took some comfort in the prayers Chief Bradens or Chad Owens or any of the other firefighters had been known to offer, and he found himself drawn to Charlotte's prayers of grace over their dinners. Still, none of those people had ever directly asked for prayer from him. It was like being told to use a complicated new tool without being given the owner's manual.

Only, was it complicated? Charlotte never made it look like anything more difficult than breathing. Prayer seemed to come to her like singing came to him—something that just flowed out of a person.

Singing.

Jesse searched his memory for a gospel song. He owned nearly every recording Sam Cooke, Aretha Franklin and Bobby Darin ever made, not to mention Ray Charles and Smokey Robinson. One of them had to have a gospel song in there somewhere.

He couldn't remember the title of the song, but his mind recalled Sam Cooke's mournful voice singing, some song about Jesus and consolation. That's what Charlotte needed. And so, after a guilty look around to see if there was anyone who could hear, Jesse began singing the couplets he remembered. Charlotte needed consolation to return to the assurance she'd first proclaimed to him: *God is never late and He's never early; He's always right on time.*

He kept on singing, letting the words soak into his own tangled spirit as he remembered more and more of the lyrics, letting the song undo the knots in his shoulders and the grip in his chest that wouldn't let him breathe. Letting him know that it might not be a bad thing that he felt so bonded to her, and her alone. Slowly, he felt his own words form—not out loud, but like a sigh inside his head, a breath waiting to be exhaled.

"She knows You're there, God. Give her consolation." With something close to a grin, he switched the lyrics so that they were about Charlotte, about her knowing there was consolation. She ought to be halfway by now, closer to Gordon Falls than Chicago. Exhausted as he was, he felt his heart rate pick up at the thought of seeing her soon.

Why was he so frightened of being serious with Charlotte—why be scared of something that had already happened? Getting serious with Charlotte was no longer a proposition; it was a fact. A done deal, whether he was ready for it or not. *I'll sing you home, Charlotte. I'll sing you prayers to bring you home.*

He began improvising a little bit on the melody, stretching it out into long phrases he imagined could cross the miles between himself and Charlotte, bonding them further, reaching into that little blue car as it made its way through the dark. "Charlotte knows You're there. She knows there's consolation."

Do I?

The question from somewhere in the back of his brain startled him so much he bolted upright. *Do I know God is there?*

It was the "know" part that brought him up

short. He didn't not believe in God, in the grace of Jesus forgiving sins. He liked to think God was around, working in the world. He'd certainly seen what it did for the lives of people he knew. But did he know, really know in the rock-solid way Charlotte seemed to? The way Charlotte would need him to? The way that offered the consolation he felt himself lacking?

It was then that the title of the song surfaced out of his memory. "Jesus Wash Away My Troubles." It could not be coincidence that of all the gospel songs recorded by all the Motown artists in history, that was the song that came to him on this forlorn street corner in the middle of the night. *You are. You're there.* Jesse felt the astounding sensation of his soul lifting up and settling into place.

He looked around, feeling…feeling what, exactly? *Transformed* was such a dramatic way to put it, but no other word came to mind. He felt lighter. Looser. In possession of a tiny bit of that peace of Charlotte's that pulled him in like a magnet.

This was what made her the way she was. What made her able to ride through life with that indescribable trust that everything would work out in the end, and the courage to leap into situations without hesitation. It was the exact opposite of that drive he had, the one that made him plot and plan and scramble to bend life to his advantage. He'd never trusted that things would work out, because he'd never had anything to trust *in*. But he did now.

Consolation.

He felt consoled. Nothing in tonight's circumstances had changed—the cottage was still a wreck, his leg was still broken, the next six weeks up in the air and all of it beyond his control.

Yesterday's Jesse would be gnawing on his crutches by now. Tonight, he felt absurdly okay with it all.

All of it except the fact that Charlotte was not here. The sting of her absence, the bolt of ice down his back when he thought she might be harmed, the unsettling power of his need for her—those things weren't consolation. They were powerful, a bit wonderful and a great big hunk of terrifying.

Okay, God, this is me, doing the prayer thing. No songs, not someone else's lyrics, just me. And I'm asking You—begging You—to bring her home safe. Keep her head clear enough to drive or smart enough to pull over if she's too tired. I'll wait if I have to. But I figure You already know that I don't want to. Just keep her safe, because I can't. Not from here. That's

*going to have to be Your department. You get
her here and I'll take it from there.*

He sat there on the curb in the fading darkness of near dawn, listening to the steady drip
of water off the cottage. They hadn't soaked the
house, but even a small fire like the one tonight
called for a fair amount of water, and firemen
never had the luxury of being careful with their
hose. He sang all the verses he could remember
from "Amazing Grace"—Aretha Franklin had
a dynamite ten-minute version on one recording he owned—humming in the parts where
he couldn't remember the words. He was seg-
ueing into Ray Charles's "O Happy Day," feeling the beginnings of a second wind, when his
cell phone rang.

He grabbed it like a lifeline, a gush of "Thank
You" surging from his heart when he saw Charlotte's number on the screen. "Charlotte?"

"I just got off the highway. I pulled over on
the shoulder on Route 20 to call."

Jesse was glad she was only ten minutes
away. She sounded weary. "You're almost here.
I'll be up by the floodgates, waiting for you."
He wanted to hold her, to give her every ounce
of support he could before she saw the cottage.

She guessed his strategy. "That bad, huh?"

"No, not really. It's all fixable from what I
can see. But you have to be so tired."

"I am. You must be, too. This was your second fire of the night and you weren't even supposed to be on duty."

Jesse saw no point in giving her the details yet. She'd see the crutches soon enough. "No worries, Miss Taylor. This is what I do. Get back on the road and I'll see you soon."

"Okay." If she hadn't already been crying, she was close to tears. Who wouldn't be in her situation?

Jesse pocketed the phone, picked up his crutches and hobbled toward the floodgates humming "O Happy Day."

Chapter Seventeen

Charlotte worked it out, somewhere west of Rockford. The force of her own idiocy had struck her so hard she'd nearly had to pull over and catch her breath.

She had set her own house on fire.

She'd left the oven on with the paper bag and tin containers of food inside to keep them warm. The greasy nature of Dellio's fries made them downright addictive, but probably also made them something close to kindling if left unsupervised. *Father God, I burned my own house down. How could I have been so foolish?* She wanted to ask Jesse—had tried to, in a roundabout way with her repeated question of "How bad is it?"—but she knew he'd never say. Not while she was driving. He'd save the lecture for when they were face-to-face. *Why did I have to leave right then? Why couldn't I have been sensible and waited until morning or at least until I was calmer?*

Part of her knew the answer: what she felt for Jesse was frightening her. She wasn't ready to love a firefighter. She wasn't ready to accept the life that she saw beat Mom down over the years. Needing someone who could be yanked away from you on a moment's notice? She didn't think she could handle that. Hadn't she already proved how poorly she handled that? The facts that Jesse didn't have a relationship with God— and seemed to have trouble with relationships in general—were just the icing on the cake.

She wouldn't worry about that right now. Right now she would just get to Gordon Falls, fall exhausted into his arms, thank him for saving her house and praying her safely here, and let him save her for now. The rest of it would have to wait until she could think straight. Charlotte pulled off Route 20 and sighed out loud when she caught sight of the familiar green floodgates that marked the official entrance into Gordon Falls.

The sigh turned into a panicked yelp when her headlights shone on Jesse. He was standing on a pair of crutches with a bandage over one eyebrow, and a splint on one leg.

He'd been hurt. And he hadn't told her. Had he been injured fighting the fire at her cottage?

A dozen thoughts slammed together in her head as she threw open the car door and raced up to him.

"You're okay!" He reached out to her as much as the crutches would allow.

"You're not!" As much as she wanted to melt into his arms and cry buckets of tired tears, the shock of seeing him injured wedged between them. "You're hurt. What happened? Why didn't you tell me?" It was as if the omission of that detail let loose a deluge of her own panic, and everything she'd been holding in check the entire drive came gushing out of her in a choking wave of sobs.

"Hey." He tried to grab her but she darted out of his grasp. "Hey, I'm okay. I didn't think you needed the extra stress of the news on the drive."

She noticed the bloody bandage on his leg above the splint and felt a bit dizzy. In her mind she heard her mother yelling at her father. The one night he'd been seriously injured—a stab wound in his shoulder—he'd simply waltzed in the door with his arm in a sling and Mom had gone through the roof. Now she knew how that felt. "You were hurt and you didn't tell me? You were hurt fighting the fire *at my cottage* and you didn't think I could handle knowing? So it's bad enough that I started the fire, why add to my guilt? Is that what you think of me?" Some part of her knew she was being unreasonable but she couldn't stop the spiral of panic and guilt that wrapped itself around her.

Jesse managed to grab her arm, the force of his grasp startling her out of the tailspin. "Look at me. Charlotte, *look at me.*" His eyes were fierce, but in a protective way. He pulled her toward him. "I am fine." He spoke the words slowly, clear and close. Charlotte latched on to them like an anchor line. "I'm hurt, yes, but I'm going to be okay. We're both going to be okay."

She didn't see how any of this was going to be anything close to okay. She started to shake her head, but Jesse tugged her closer, crutches still under both arms, and held her close.

"You're here. You're safe. That's what matters." He let the crutches fall against the side of her car, holding her face in his hands. "I went nuts when I realized it was your house. I would have run there in my bare feet if it weren't for this." He wobbled a bit, standing on one leg, and she helped him hop over and sit on the hood. "When they couldn't find you…"

His words struck her. "You were hurt at the first fire?" It was still awful, but the weight on her chest eased up a bit. She looked at his leg. "What happened?"

"I tripped and fell into a porch railing. The

railing was in bad shape, so it gave way and I went down. Kind of hard."

Only Jesse would make light of something like that. "And…"

"Broken tibia and sixteen stitches."

She put her hands to her mouth. "Oh, wow. That's bad."

"Well, it's not the 'put some dirt on it and walk it off' kind of thing, but I'll be all right." His hands came up to her hair. "I was worried about you. I was close to banging down your cousin JJ's door and getting one of those corporate helicopters her husband uses rather than forcing you to make that drive."

She knew Jesse would have, too. She hadn't imagined what had sprung up between them; it was real. "Alex doesn't run a huge corporation anymore, you know that."

"I just kept thinking about you all alone on that dark highway, tired and scared. For a guy's first prayer you sure picked a doozy. I'd say 'baptism by fire,' but I think that would be in poor taste."

Charlotte touched the bandage over his eye. His eyes. He could never fake what was in his eyes right now. It was no trick of entertainment; it was deep, true care. "So you did pray?"

"Of course. You asked me to. I couldn't work out how at first, so I just started singing what-

ever gospel song I could remember. It got easier after that. I just tried to believe as much as I
know you do, hoping it would rub off."

"Did it?"

The warmth in his eyes ignited further, and
she felt his hands tighten around her waist as
she stood next to him beside the car. "Yeah, it
did. I couldn't help you from where I was, but
I began to feel like God could. Like He would."
He looked down and shook his head. "I don't
know how to explain it, really."

She lifted his chin to meet her eyes. That
wasn't just warmth or care, it was peace. "No
explanation needed. I get it. And I'm glad." The
peace that had momentarily abandoned her—
or had she abandoned it?—returned bit by bit.
She allowed the strength of his embrace to seep
into her, felt his head tilt to touch the top of hers
and leave a handful of tender kisses there. Real.
True. Trustworthy.

"You may not be so glad in a few minutes.
The cottage is a mess. It's still there, it didn't
burn, but there's a lot of damage."

She cringed. Her beautiful cottage—undone
by a burger and fries with a side of stupidity.
"I started it. Oh, Jesse, the fire is my fault. The
oven…"

He tightened his grip on her. "I know. Clark
told me they found the Dellio's tin in the oven.

Or what's left of the oven." He put his face close to hers. "We'll get through it. Just…"

"Just what?"

His entire face changed, the fierceness leaving to reveal a heart-stopping tenderness. "Just don't leave. Don't go to Vermont, Charlotte. I don't want you to go. You belong here. You belong with me. You know you do, don't you?"

She knew how much it cost him to admit that, to make the request, and the last piece of her heart broke open for this incredible man. "I want to, but how?"

"I don't know yet. But if God is never late and He's never early, then maybe He's never wrong. I'm pretty new at this, but you told me yourself you felt like God led you here. It's got to still be true. We'll just have to figure out how to trust that."

Jesse's work with the GFVFD put him in the position of dealing with friends and neighbors after a fire, so he should have been used to this. None of that explained how his heart drummed against his ribs as he rode in Charlotte's little blue car, crutches banging against his shoulders, frustrated that he was forced to let her drive.

The damage on the outside wasn't especially visible in the predawn light, though there were *some* signs. The loose front railing had given way when knocked by one of the firefighters, and it lay propped up against the side of the cottage. The bushes Charlotte had just trimmed after months of neglect were trampled, and there were divots and gashes in the front lawn, scraggly as it was.

He caught her gaze as she turned off the ignition in the driveway. "See, it's still here. Not even a window broken. You should realize how fortunate you are." He wanted to reassure her, bolster her up before she saw the inside. He'd not been in there yet, but he knew what to expect. He dreaded watching her eyes take in the overwhelming sooty blackness he knew would cover her home.

"Yeah, I know." She said the words for his benefit, her tone hollow with disbelief.

He grabbed her hand, needing to make her understand. "Your neighbor called when she heard your smoke detectors go off and she didn't see any lights come on in the house. If it had become fully involved in open flames, I don't think you'd have much of a cottage left." He tried to put it into the terms that would mean the most to her. "You're blessed, Charlotte. It could have been so much worse."

Her grip on his hand tightened. "You put those smoke detectors in for me."

"And boy, am I glad." There was no way he

was going to let her sleep in that house without the best smoke detectors he could get. It was the one extravagance he endorsed without a hint of guilt. He couldn't help drawing the connection between that urge and her current safety. He knew Charlotte wouldn't call that coincidence, and it was starting to sink in that it wasn't. He'd been placed in Charlotte's life right at this time. *God is never late, and He's never early; He's always right on time.* "Come on, let's get the first look over with. It gets better after that."

She hesitated, one hand still white-knuckled on the steering wheel. "What's in there?"

"I don't know. I haven't been in yet."

"Yes, but you know what to expect. Tell me what I'm going to find."

Jesse took a deep breath. Perhaps this was the least he could do—lessen the sensory shock so that it didn't hit her like a brick wall. He pulled her hand into his lap and stroked it softly while he kept his tone low and calm. "It will smell bad—at least for now. It's good that you don't have a lot of furniture in there yet." He thought of the little plaid chair where he'd imagined resting his leg. "Most of the textiles might need to go or be professionally cleaned."

"All my yarn and fabrics are still in Chicago. And my china, too—well, most of it." Her grappling for positives unwound his heart.

"Yep, that's good. Most of the kitchen will be covered in black soot and probably some whitish powder from the extinguishing agent. Probably some of the dining room and hallway, too. None of the windows are broken, so that's good, too."

"My new sink and faucet are goners, aren't they?"

"Maybe, maybe not." He gave her hand a final squeeze before he let go and opened the car door. "There's only one way to find out." When she winced, he added, "I'll be right beside you, Charlotte. Now and all the way through this."

Before he could get himself out of the car, Charlotte grabbed his shoulder and gave him a tender kiss. If there had been any resistance left in him, the need he felt in that kiss dissolved the last trace. The small, insistent longing to make her happy swelled into a consuming urge. He returned her kiss as if he were sealing a promise. *I will see you through this. I will stand by you.*

"Thank you," she said, their foreheads still touching.

He started to say, "You're welcome," but the words weren't near adequate. Instead, he kissed her again, hoping his touch spoke more. "Okay." He forced a grin and a wink. "Enough necking in the driveway. Let's get the hard part over with."

Her hands were shaking as she pulled aside

the yellow tape that held the door shut. They'd had to break down the door. "Oh well, I was thinking about a new front door anyway."

"That's the spirit. Ready?"

"No." She managed the smallest slip of a smile, a weak and wobbly thing that still looked breathtaking on her.

"Want me to go first?"

She pushed back her shoulders and raised her chin. "No. I can do this."

You can. I know you can. In that moment, Jesse knew she'd come through this even stronger. Chief Bradens said he could always tell which people would beat the fire, and which people would let the fire beat them. In this case, Jesse could see it, too. Charlotte wouldn't let this keep her down for long. Jesse felt his heart slip from his grasp as she stepped across the threshold.

The acrid scent of smoke hit them with a force that was almost physical as he followed her into the house. Her hands went up to her face. "Oh, Lord, help me." It wasn't a casual expression—it was a heartfelt plea to heaven. Jesse, to his own surprise, felt a similar plea launch up from his own heart—*Help me help her.*

The front hallway and living room weren't as bad as they could have been. Thin black film covered everything, but he'd seen far worse. In the gray-pink light of dawn, it was as if the room had been poorly erased; everything blended together in a smudge of colorless dust. He made his way over to the windows and began opening them up. He'd go through the house with Charlotte and open every working window until the worst of the smell had eased up a bit. It would feel like progress to her, and he knew all she really needed was a first foothold.

He heard a whimper and turned to find her staring at the plaid chair, now damp and smudged with soot. He could tell her something optimistic, but he owed her the respect of honesty. "You'll have to trash it. I'm sorry."

She hugged her elbows and shrugged. "It was so perfect." It was true. She'd grown ridiculously attached to that chair ever since the day she'd brought it home, half hanging out of the hatch of the tiny blue car. It had made him wonder how it hadn't fallen out on the way home and why she hadn't asked him to pick it up in his truck, which would have held four such chairs easily.

"You'll find another perfect one. Maybe a pair this time." He wanted to swallow the words back—a pair?—what kind of dorky misplaced romantic comment was that?

Opening two more windows, Jesse made his way to the kitchen, taking care not to slip on anything with his crutches. He was due back at the hospital in three hours, where he would have to explain why he had not, in fact, done anything close to "take it easy and keep it elevated." The last dose of painkillers had worn off and his leg was throbbing.

"Oh." Charlotte's word was more of a gasp. "It's ruined. It's all ruined."

Jesse went over to one of the blackened cabinets, which looked like someone had set a dozen cans of black spray paint on the stove and triggered them in every direction. The new stove was a total loss, as were the cabinets directly above and around them. He had kissed her up against one of those cabinets. Every scorched corner of the room held a memory for him.

Even more so for her. Charlotte was pacing around the room, hands outstretched as if she needed to touch everything but couldn't bring herself to do so. "Everything is covered in black."

He opened one of the cabinets, wanting to show her one thing that hadn't been blackened. The interior wasn't scorched, but the plastic containers inside were slumped into melted, distorted forms. Her teapot lay in pieces on the far corner of the kitchen floor. The mason jar that had held his flowers the first time he'd brought them for her lay cracked with a big chip out of the top. One chair lay sideways on the floor, a leg bent in on itself and smeared in black. Footprints and smudge marks covered the once cheery lemon-colored linoleum floor she'd wanted so badly to keep.

"I did this." She stood in the center of the room, losing her battle to the returning tears she'd been trying so hard to fight off since the floodgates. "I'm so stupid to have done this."

She wouldn't hear any argument he might make right now. So Jesse did the only thing there was to do. He leaned against the counter for support, and pulled her to him. He let her cry it out, holding her tight and singing "Jesus Wash Away My Troubles," with his eyes closed and his heart wide open.

Chapter Eighteen

"Charlotte! Charlotte, where are you in here?" Melba's shocked voice called from the hallway.

"Kitchen," Charlotte called out, then sniffed and wiped her eyes with the corner of the zip-up sweatshirt she'd been wearing. Already it had black streaks on it, the fabric beginning to give off the tang of soot and smoke. Her eyes stung from more than the onslaught of tears.

"Look at this place. Thank heavens you're safe." Melba's hug somehow brought everything into full reality, making Charlotte instantly exhausted. She needed to sit down but didn't have a single clean spot to do so. "Clark told me it wasn't as bad as it could have been, but it looks awful enough to me."

Jesse seemed to sense her weariness. "Let's go out onto the back porch. There's still a lot of smoke and soot in here, and I could use a dose of fresh air."

"And Mo. He's yowling in the car, you know."

"I forgot about Mo!" Charlotte rushed to the car to find a disgruntled Mo protesting his neglect from the backseat. In the emotion of the past hour, she'd not even remembered he was there. She pulled him from the carrier, keeping one hand on his collar. "Oh, big guy, this isn't a place for you to be inside right now. We'll get you set up in a little while, but I need you to stay put." Guilt over Mo piled on top of her grief and stress over the house. "This isn't much of a new home, is it? It'll get better, I promise." She found some strong yarn in one of the bags in her trunk and tied it to Mo's collar. "The back porch is the best I can do for you right now. Be nice to Jesse, okay? He's done a lot for us and he even went looking for you."

She walked around the side of the house, wincing at the dark streaks around the kitchen window and wondering if they would wash off or if she'd have to repaint.

She walked up the back porch steps, Mo still in her arms, to find Melba had pushed open the back door and propped it wide with a sooty box of books. Jesse had maneuvered himself into one of the porch's bistro chairs. He looked exhausted and uncomfortable.

"Clark told me you were hurt in the first fire," Melba was saying to Jesse, as Charlotte practically fell into the other chair and settled Mo on her lap. "It's broken, huh?"

Jesse nodded, one eye on Mo. His regard toward the animal had softened a bit. Charlotte was so touched that he'd gone in search of "the little beast" before he knew Mo was with her in Chicago.

Melba settled herself on the porch steps. "I was worried sick, Charlotte. I wished you'd called me when you got into town."

Charlotte leaned back in the chair, fatigue growing stronger with every minute. "You were asleep. You had Maria to tend to. I knew Jesse was waiting." Charlotte yawned. She'd been up for almost twenty-four hours now, and it was taking its toll.

Within seconds, Melba had her "mother face" on. "Have either of you slept at all?"

"Not exactly." Jesse yawned the words, although they had more of a wince quality to them. He hadn't said anything about the pain he was in, but it was obvious he hurt. Badly. The bandage on his leg was starting to grow pink at the center.

Melba stared at Jesse's bandage and splint as well, coming to the same conclusion. "Clark's dropping Maria off with JJ and Alex. He'll be

here in ten minutes. Charlotte, you're coming
home to shower and sleep at our house while
Clark takes you to your apartment to do the
same, Jesse. Clark's dad is skipping church to
come pick you up for your hospital appointment
at ten-thirty and deliver you back home. I should
tell you, Chief George has orders from Clark
to tie you to your couch if that's what it takes."
Melba's father-in-law was fire chief before
his son took over the job, and Charlotte knew
George now served as an unofficial guardian of
sorts to the firehouse. Jesse could use that kind
of support right now.

"I don't think I have the strength to argue
with that," Jesse said, shifting his weight tenderly. "Charlotte needs to sleep."

"So do you," Charlotte added, a surge of gratitude for all Jesse had done in the past hours
welling up and threatening a new bout of tears.
"You've probably done a million bad things to
that leg in the last eight hours."

"I haven't exactly kept it rested and elevated,
if that's what you mean." He held Charlotte's
eyes for a long moment. "I had other priorities."

"These firemen," Melba chided. "They think
they're invincible." She walked over and stood
over Jesse. "Where are your pain meds? Your
antibiotics?" She was on full mother alert now.
Charlotte had seen it when Melba was caring

for her ailing father. It was not wise to mess with Melba when she was in caregiving mode.

"Back at the apartment." He had the good sense to look sheepish, like a kid caught skipping his chores.

"A fat lot of good they're doing you back there."

"Yes, I hurt. Everything hurts. I need my medications. I'll go home with Chief and I'll keep my doctor's appointment—after some sleep. Okay, Mom?" His half-exaggerated pout told Charlotte he was nearing the end of his good humor, and so was she.

"It isn't like we can do anything right now except air the house out anyway." Melba planted her hands on her hips. "I'm going to go see how many windows I can get open."

"You'll need my help on some of those." Jesse made to rise but Melba pushed him back down.

"I'll do just fine. And what I can't get open, Clark will. You sit tight, both of you." She fished around in her handbag until she produced a pair of granola bars. "Eat something." Then she disappeared back into the house, a few expressions of her dismay echoing from the mudroom and kitchen.

Jesse sighed and tore open the wrapper. "She's a total mom now. Like someone threw a switch inside her, you know?"

"She's always been the caregiving type. It's why she came here to take care of her dad." Charlotte tied the other end of Mo's yarn leash to the porch railing and went over to kneel at Jesse's feet. "How are you, really?"

Mo, after giving Charlotte a "you gotta be kidding me" glare and swatting once at his makeshift leash, sauntered over to brush against Jesse's good leg. With a small "harumph," Jesse reached down and ran one hand over the cat's fat back. They were making friends after all. "I wasn't kidding. I hurt. Everywhere, it seems."

Charlotte noticed a bruise on his forearm and some scrapes on his knuckles. The risks of what he did clashed with the care she felt for him. It was an awful tug-of-war inside her, and she was too tired to endure it. She couldn't think of anything to say other than "I'm sorry."

He ducked his head down to meet her eyes. "It's not your fault."

It was the wrong thing to say. Tears welled up in her eyes and she nodded back toward the house. "Oh, this most definitely is my fault."

"The usefulness of that debate right now aside, my leg is not your fault. Firemen get hurt. It comes with the territory. Always has."

And that was the problem, wasn't it? "Have you been hurt before?"

She watched Jesse start to give her some

wisecrack answer, then stop himself in favor of the honest truth. She was glad he didn't try to brush this matter off—it was important. "Not this badly. Mostly cuts and bruises. I chipped a tooth once. Usually I'm a pretty careful guy."

"What happened, then?"

A hint of a smile reached the corners of his eyes. "I had an argument with someone I care about. Something about Vermont, but it's all kind of fuzzy right now." He leaned down toward her. "I meant what I said, Charlotte. I don't want you to go. I know it's not my decision and I can't tell you what to do, but I don't want you to go to Vermont. Even for a year. Even for a month."

Charlotte touched the bandage, the splint. "I don't know if I can do this. I told myself I'd never do this."

"I told myself I'd never do church, but I prayed so hard tonight I thought God Himself would drop His jaw in surprise. Maybe it's not as hard as we think."

Charlotte let her head fall on Jesse's lap, feeling Mo curl up beside her. "Maybe it's harder. Maybe we're kidding ourselves."

She felt Jesse stroke her hair. "I'm not saying God allowed your house to burn, but what if He knew it would take something this drastic to get us together?"

She angled her head up to look at him. "Are we together?"

"That depends on whether or not you need to go to Vermont." There was a cautious pleading in his eyes that broke Charlotte's heart wide open.

"I don't know," she admitted. "I want to stay here, but I don't know if I can."

"We can find a way. I believe that."

She let his confidence bolster her own. "I believe you."

Clark's voice came from the mudroom doorway. "Okay, kids, it's time for bed."

Jesse frowned. "And *he's* become a total dad."

Jesse held up his hand as he sat on the exam table. "Don't start on me, please. Chief George has been laying into me for the last twenty minutes." Chief George hadn't been fire chief for over a year now since his son Clark took over, but no one had ever stopped calling him by that name.

Dr. Craig crossed his arms over his chest. "Let's just say I don't agree with your definition of 'keeping off it.' You didn't help yourself last night."

"Well, no." George, after his brisk lecture, had been amazingly supportive once Jesse opened up about what happened to him in the heart sense, and yes, in the soul sense—although it felt weird to talk about his own soul—during that long wait on the curb outside of Charlotte's cottage. Truth be told, Jesse was still grasping for ways to understand what had happened last night and this morning, much less explain it. He just knew his life had made an important turn.

He was glad Chief George seemed to understand. The former chief had unofficially adopted every single guy in the firehouse—and many of the married ones. The GFVFD was his family, even though he was only Clark's actual father. More than once in the conversation, Jesse had been stung by the thought of what his life might have been like if he'd had a father as supportive as George Bradens. He was pretty sure his own dad loved him; it was just that Dad's love came with so many requirements before it was paired with approval. Jesse always felt as if he had to earn his father's affections, whereas George seemed to be so generous in giving his—even if it came with a lecture or two.

"He didn't help himself at all, medically," George asserted, placing a fatherly hand on Jesse's shoulder. "But let's simply say the evening evened out." George offered a wink. It made Jesse wonder if Clark had sent his dad for this task by convenience or by design. He'd tried to give Clark a sense of what the night had been for him, but he was far too tired to make much sense. Explanations and talent-show serenades aside, Jesse was pretty sure Clark could have been fast asleep and still have sensed the bond now strung between himself and Charlotte.

And what exactly was that bond? That song at the talent show had shown him Charlotte was different from any other woman. Even as he'd taken steps not to single her out, his gut was telling him he wanted to single her out. *Exclusive.* That wasn't a term Jesse had ever cared to apply to women before Charlotte. Did that mean he was in love with her? Maybe. Whatever it was, Jesse knew it was powerful and worth whatever last night had cost him. That didn't change the worry in the pit of his stomach at the doctor's scowl. His leg looked awful and felt terrible.

"It's gonna be okay, right, Doc? I mean, I didn't do any real harm." He knew he was fishing for reassurance.

Dr. Craig seemed in no hurry to give it. "I can't say for sure. You broke it on an angle. Any weight you put on it last night could have shifted the bones and made things worse. How's your pain today?"

He didn't want to admit how badly it hurt. "Well…"

"Son," George cut in, "there are three people

you should never hedge your answers to, ever. One's your lawyer and the other's your doctor."

"And the third?" Jesse felt the punch line of a bad joke coming on.

"Yourself."

Okay, that wasn't so funny. "All right, it hurts a lot. The medicine takes it down to a dull roar, but I'm dying before I get to the next dose. And…I sort of skipped a dose overnight. I was out at the fire site and I left all the prescriptions back at my apartment."

Was the pop-eyed shock from the doctor really necessary? "You went to a fire scene last night?" His face went from surprise to annoyance to dismissal in a matter of seconds. "You hero types make my job a lot harder than it needs to be."

"I'd classify last night as extenuating circumstances, if that helps," George cut in. "Jesse did what he had to do. We can't change that, so can we just move on from what we've got here?"

It seemed as though Dr. Craig dropped any pretense of gentleness as he bent to examine Jesse's throbbing shin more closely. His leg had turned a startling shade of purple, among other pessimistic medical appearances, and Jesse fought the nagging sense that the night had cost him far more than he realized. Personally and professionally, he could take an enormous hit here.

"We'll need another set of X-rays to see if the bone has shifted, but given how it looks—" the doctor doubled his scowl "—and from what you've told me, I'd say we're looking at surgery. Maybe even pins or a plate."

Jesse slumped back against the examining table, all his bleary-eyed wonder at last night giving way to a rising dread. "It's just a break. People break their legs all the time."

"It's a bad break that you put weight on— all night long, evidently. I've half a mind to schedule you for surgery just so I can admit you right now." Straightening up, the doctor put his glasses back in his lab coat pocket. "Mr. Sykes, would your cooperation be too much to ask for here?"

"I'll be a good patient from here on in, Doc. I promise." He folded his hands on his lap, trying to look penitent. "Where do we go from here?"

Dr. Craig picked up a chart and began writing. "I can't cast you—the swelling hasn't gone down sufficiently. I'm sending you for X-rays. We'll change the dressing on that wound and then see what the X-rays tell us. You might get lucky, but I think you should be prepared for the possibility of surgery tomorrow morning." He put the brace back on, which made Jesse wince. "When was your last dose of painkillers?"

Jesse had yearned to swallow a double dose the moment he woke up from his nap earlier. The twenty minutes it took for the stuff to kick in felt almost longer than the wait for Charlotte to pull into Gordon Falls last night. This morning. Had it all really just happened? He felt as if he'd lived a year in the space of those hours. "Six this morning. I'm due. Believe me, I'm due."

George padded the pocket of his windbreaker. "I've got 'em right here."

"I'll have the nursing assistant bring you some water when she comes in to change the bandage. You'll want them—the boys in radiology aren't known for their tender touch." He closed the chart. "I'll see you back here afterward and we'll talk about next steps."

"Okay, Doc." Jesse tried to look cooperative and hopeful, but it was hard with his leg screaming at him. In five minutes he'd down those capsules without water if that nurse hadn't shown up yet. The pain—and his doubts—were beginning to make it hard to keep his trademark humor.

As the examining room door closed, George pulled his cell phone from his pocket and began tapping with youthful speed. "Time to call the cavalry." The former chief had taken to texting with enthusiasm; he sent more "Gexts"—as the firehouse had come to call the numerous electronic check-ins the man was prone to send—than most of the teenagers Jesse knew.

"Huh?"

"Church."

He'd heard stories about the ladies of GFCC swooping in to care for people, but he wasn't sure casseroles were what he needed right now. "You don't need to do that."

George kept typing. "Oh, yes, I do. We need to pray that leg into cooperation. We want those X-rays to show you haven't hurt yourself further by what you did last night. That's going to take prayer."

This was foreign territory. People praying for him? Him praying for himself? For Charlotte? The world had tilted in new directions overnight, and Jesse still wasn't quite sure how to take it all in. "Um…okay…I guess." It probably was going to take divine intervention to keep him off the operating table. "I'll be okay, though, if I have to go under." He rubbed his eyes, reaching for a way to explain his foggy thoughts. He looked at George. "I mean, it was worth it."

One end of George's mouth turned up in a knowing grin. "I agree. But I'm still lighting up the prayer chain for that leg of yours. After all, you're part of the church now."

He was part of a church. Jesse waited for that to feel odd, or forced, but it just sort of sank into his chest like a deep breath. "I guess I am. Not such a bad thing, is it?"

George's grin turned into a wide smile that took over the old man's entire features. "Best thing there is."

Chapter Nineteen

Charlotte found her way to the kitchen, hoping for a cup of steaming tea to face what was left of the day.

"Hey there." Melba looked up from feeding Maria. "They prayed for both you and Jesse at service this morning. Feeling better?"

Charlotte walked over to the sink and began filling the kettle. Did she even have a teakettle at the cottage anymore? What kind of person has a life that destroys two teakettles in so short a time? "Not really. Less exhausted, but now I feel like I have twice as many thoughts slamming through my head." She sat down at the table opposite Melba and Maria. They looked so peaceful and happy.

"You'll be okay, Charlotte. You know that, don't you?"

She ran her hands through her hair. Even with

a long hot shower, Charlotte felt as though she still smelled of smoke. "It's a little hard to see today."

"Maybe today's not a good judge of everything. Clark says it takes two days for the shock to wear off, longer for some people." She looked at Charlotte with such warmth in her eyes. "You can stay here for as long as you need to. Really."

Charlotte knew she meant it, but Melba and Clark had played host to her long enough. She didn't want to stay any longer than absolutely necessary. They deserved to be a family on their own again. "Thanks. I know I need a few days to get my feet underneath me, but I've still got my place in Chicago."

That wiped the warmth from Melba's eyes. "I hate the thought of you being back there. I hate the idea of you going to Vermont even more. I know it's selfish of me, but I really feel like you belong here. Even with everything that's happened."

Charlotte didn't have an answer. Her brain felt far too clouded to think. She was grateful the kettle's whistle gave her something to fill the silence.

Melba settled Maria on her shoulder and began patting the baby's back to burp her. "You want to tell me what happened with Jesse last night? And don't say nothing, because it's all over both of your faces, not to mention what Clark told me last night."

Turning to her friend, Charlotte asked, "What did Clark tell you?"

"That Jesse went crazy with worry when the call came and they realized it was your cottage. That he ignored the doctor's orders and walked to the scene because Clark had already left. That he was frantic to know you were okay, and it was all the guys could do to keep him from trying to help."

Mo, who had thankfully made fast friends with Melba's cat, Pinocchio, darted into the room to weave his way around Charlotte's legs as she set the tea to steeping.

"And that he hobbled around the neighborhood calling for Mo when no one was found in the house." Melba stood up and walked over to Charlotte. "That man has it bad for you. And you have it bad for him."

"It's just that after the display at the talent show, and all he said about not wanting to get serious with any one woman—well, he didn't come right out and say that, but it wasn't hard to guess—I didn't know if I could trust his charm. I don't want to be dazzled."

"But he's gotten to you, and he cares about you—a lot, obviously. I know it's not perfect, but do you really want to walk away from that?"

"*And* he's a firefighter. I know that's okay for you, but—"

"And then there's the whole faith thing, and that's big, too—especially now that he's made the first steps, from what I've heard."

"That's just it. Those things are sort of working themselves out. And for the first part…what he told me, the way he treated me last night at the fire, you can't fake that. His heart is true, I know that now. Only, is that really enough?" She told Melba the entire story of Jesse's night, how he'd come to terms with the God she knew had been pursuing him since the night of the talent show. "It wasn't really God Jesse was resisting, it was his preconceptions of church and judgment. His father's been putting him down for years. That made it hard for him to grasp a Father who loves unconditionally, you know?" She remembered him holding her in the destroyed kitchen, singing a gospel song she'd never heard before but now felt engraved on her heart. What could be a deeper truth than that? "He has such a huge heart, Melba. It's been aching for grace for so long."

Melba started to get mugs down from the cabinet, only to stop and look straight at Charlotte. "Do you think you're in love with him?"

Charlotte leaned against the counter, squinting her eyes shut for a moment. "Shouldn't I *know* if I'm in love with him?"

"I think it slams some people clearly like that, but I think more often it is something that slowly takes shape. Like knitting with a striped yarn—sometimes you don't see what it really looks like until you get further along."

"The attraction is certainly there." Charlotte thought of the head-spinning serenade that had made it hard to breathe back at the talent show. "The man knows how to sweep me off my feet, Melba, but just because he can doesn't make him the right man for me." She poured the tea into the pair of mugs Melba set on the counter. "You know how impulsive I am. Vermont was going to give me the space to think about this. Maybe it still should."

"Are you running to or running from?"

"What?"

"It's something Clark always says. About jogging or even guys at a fire. People rarely get hurt running to something, but they often injure themselves running *from* something. If you go to Vermont, are you running to what could be a good job or running away from what could be a good man?"

Melba had managed to boil the whole storm of Charlotte's thoughts down to one piercing question. Was she really enthused about Borroughs's offer, or was it just an escape from facing the scary prospect of loving a man who risked his life for others? "I don't know. I don't even know how to figure it out."

"Maybe that's why you ought to talk to Abby Reed this afternoon. She's coming by in an hour if you're feeling up to it."

"Abby?" Abby had a reputation as a notorious matchmaker. If she'd taken Jesse on as her newest project, Charlotte didn't see how she'd lend any clarity to the situation. "What's she got to do with any of this?"

Melba's smile was sweet but a little secretive. "I think you'd better hear that from Abby herself. I'm going to go put Maria down for her nap. Why don't you go sit on the deck and just relax for a while. It's a beautiful day, and you need all the doses of fresh air you can get."

The next thing Charlotte knew, someone was gently tapping her on the shoulder as she lay slouched in one of Melba's back deck lounge chairs. She forced her eyes open. "I must have dozed off."

"I'll bet you needed a nap." Abby Reed sat down on the chair opposite Charlotte, a kind smile on her face and a bag of chocolate-covered caramels in her hands. "I know chocolate doesn't make everything better, but it makes most things better."

Charlotte sat up and accepted the bag, reaching in for one of the sweets. "I guess it pays to be good friends with the candy lady."

"Jeannie wants to help in any way she can. She's been through a fire, too, you know. She lost everything a while back, and she knows how it can pull the rug out from underneath you."

"I keep trying to remember I haven't lost everything, but it still feels like I have. There's soot over everything." She smoothed her hair out, thinking she probably looked like a mess today. "The fire was my fault, you know— food that I left in the oven and forgot about. I've made such a mess of things with my own stupidity. I used to think of myself as such a clever person."

"You're still a clever person. You're just a clever person in a tight spot. We've all been there. Gordon Falls is full of people who are great helps in tight spots."

Charlotte knew that. She could feel the pull of Gordon Falls's tight-knit community calling to her even before her house filled with smoke. "I'm not going to end up with a refrigerator full of church-lady casseroles, am I?" She winced. "I don't think I even have a working fridge anymore, much less a stove to heat them in."

Abby laughed. "You might. GFCC is good

at crisis management with food. It's a universal church thing, I think. Jeannie will tell you one of the blessings of a crisis is all the help that comes to your side. I know it may not feel like it this morning, but I'm sure you'll come out of this fine."

"I'm not so sure."

"Then I'd have another caramel if I were you."

No one had to twist Charlotte's arm. When the delicious, sticky confection allowed her to talk again, she prompted, "Melba said you had something you wanted to talk to me about?"

Abby settled her hands on her lap. "I've had an idea for a while now, and before last night I was going to wait until the fall. Now I think I shouldn't wait. Charlotte, I'd like to ask you to consider running a new shop for me. I want to expand the store to open a full yarn and fabric shop in the space next to mine. I'm looking to knock the wall out between the stores and create two connected spaces—one dedicated to gifts and art, the other for crafting. Only I can't run the both of them—really, I don't want to. When Ben finally moves out, I don't want to spend my newly earned free time behind a cash register or in a stock room."

Charlotte's brain struggled to comprehend what she was hearing. "You want me to work for you? Open up a yarn shop next to your store?"

"I'd thought of it more as a partnership, but that was further down the road. I figure that's a bit much to take on right now. I'd mentioned it to Melba a while ago—just as an inkling I'd had when you first said something about job hunting at the knitting group—but when she told at church this morning that you were considering going to New Hampshire or wherever it was, I had a long talk with God about whether I might need to speed up my time frame."

"Vermont," Charlotte clarified, and then thought that was a stupid thing to say. She blinked and ran her hands down her face, reaching for a focus that she couldn't quite attain. "Not that it matters." She straightened up, planting her feet on the ground as if that would help. "You're serious? You're offering me a job? Here?"

"There are probably lots of details to iron out, but yes. I want you to know you have an option to stay here if you want to. I'm not at all sure I can match whatever you were making at Monarch, but—"

"I want to stay here," Charlotte cut in. She blinked again. "I don't think I even realized how much until just this moment. I don't want to go to Vermont." She held Abby's gaze, feeling a bit dizzy. "Thank you. I'm sure we can figure something out."

Abby's smile told Charlotte this was no pity offer, this was God at work, moving things to His perfect timing. "I'm sure, too. After all, we both know you are a very clever person."

Charlotte was sitting on his front steps by the time George pulled into Jesse's driveway. Jesse was glad to see a little more of the old Charlotte back in her eyes. That smile did more for him than all those painkillers.

"Well now, look who's waiting to take over nurse duties," George teased as he pulled the crutches out of his backseat while Jesse opened the passenger door. "Toss me your keys, son, and I'll get your front door open while you say hello to the lady."

Charlotte ran a hand down Jesse's cheek, and he felt his whole body settle at her touch. "Hello, you."

He leaned up and gave her a small but soft kiss to her cheek. She smelled just-showered; clean and flowery. It was like fresh air compared to the disinfectant-soaked doctors' rooms. "Hello to you, too." He stood up and tilted his head close to hers, closing his eyes and stealing another breath. "You smell amazing, do you know that?"

He felt her smile against his cheek. "Flattery just might get you better nursing care." She pulled away to eye him. "How'd it go?"

He'd have to tell her sometime, might as well get it over with on the front sidewalk. "Not well."

Alarm darkened her features. "What do you mean?"

He started making his way carefully to the front door. "I messed my leg up pretty badly. I'm going to need surgery. I have to be at the hospital tomorrow morning at some cruel hour." He tried to keep the anger out of his voice, but her eyes told him he hadn't been successful. George's "prayer warriors," as he called them, hadn't won this particular battle.

"Surgery? Oh, Jesse."

Somehow the worry in her voice just made it worse. Weren't church people supposed to get happy endings from God? His twenty-four-hour venture into faith wasn't going very well, even though George had spouted some platitudes about God still being in control. "I'm more of a Motown guy than a heavy-metal one, but it seems I'm going to get chrome-plated tomorrow. I get fifteen whole hours at home before I have to report for surgery." The further he got into his explanation, the less it seemed worth the effort to keep the annoyance out of his voice.

"I'm sorry. I know that's not what you

wanted." She hugged her arms. "You should never have stayed out there waiting for me."

He stopped, nearly losing one crutch in his effort to grab her elbow. "I don't regret it. Don't you think that for a second, Charlotte. I'm just mad I didn't get a clean getaway, that's all."

"You're going to be okay," she offered, even though she had no way of knowing that was true.

He simply nodded, not having a good comeback for that one.

Once they got him settled on his couch, George ticked off a list of instructions to Charlotte and bid goodbye with a promise to visit Jesse tomorrow at the hospital. "Make sure he calls his folks," George ordered on his way out the door.

Charlotte pulled an ottoman up to the couch. "Want me to get your cell phone?"

"No." He took her hand, pulling her in for another gentle kiss. "Not yet. How are you? Did you go back over there?"

She smiled and brushed the hair off his forehead. Her fingers were gentle and soothing. He wanted those hands nearby when he woke up from surgery tomorrow. He wanted those hands nearby every waking moment. With a sort of slow-motion burst of light, he realized he loved her. Exclusively her, absolutely her.

"No. I slept most of the morning, and then Abby Reed came over to talk to me." Something bright danced in the corners of her eyes.

"That's nice." That struck him as a dumb response. "What'd she say?"

Charlotte took his hand in hers. It was much easier to push the pain out of his thoughts when she was near. "She offered me a job, Jesse. Evidently she's been thinking about expanding her business into a full-fledged yarn shop next door, but hadn't planned on doing it until the fall. When Melba told her this morning I was looking at a job in Vermont, Abby decided maybe it was time to speed up her time frame."

Jesse wished the pain medicine didn't sludge up his thinking so much. "A job? Here?"

The brightness in her eyes now lit up her whole face. "A job. Right here. We're still working out all the details but I think it's going to be perfect. I've always wanted to run a yarn shop— it's almost what I did with Mima's money. Now I can learn, only as part of another business and with a partner."

"Me?"

She laughed and slid off the ottoman to bring her face close to his. "No, silly, Abby. You'd be terrible as a yarn salesman."

He kissed her again, needing her close. "Nah,

I'd be great." He reached up to touch her cheek. "You're staying."

She nodded. "I think so."

Maybe George's prayer army had pulled off getting him what he truly needed after all. "What about…us?" He didn't think he could stand the thought of her being in Gordon Falls and not being with him. As he looked into her eyes, Jesse realized, with a crystal-clear shock of certainty, that he'd do whatever it took to be with her. Whatever it took. "I need us to be… us." He knew he wasn't being eloquent by a long shot, but the look in her eyes told him she understood. "Tell me what you need for that to happen." He'd never in his life placed someone else ahead of his own interests, never laid his own plans at the feet of someone else's needs. A fire rescue was one thing, but his whole life? How did that work? He was pretty sure faith was what made such a thing possible. Clark had said it before—even Charlotte had talked about it—but he'd never really believed it before now.

Jesse wanted to see certainty in her eyes, but saw honesty instead. She settled in against him, sitting on the floor and laying her head on his chest. "I don't know. At least not yet. I've got a lot of…baggage…in that department and I'm not sure how easy it will be to lay that all down."

"I'd leave it. The firehouse, I mean." He didn't

even know that until it leaped from his mouth. He waited for the regret to come, but it didn't arrive. "It'd be hard, but I would."

A tender pain filled her face. "I don't want it to come to that. It's so much of who you are. I don't know what the answer is, but I have to think there is one out there."

For the first time, waiting didn't feel like procrastination. "We've got some time here. I'll be off duty for a while after the surgery." He grinned. "Look at me, all silver lining and stuff. Maybe God really is always right on time. This is going to take some getting used to. I've got authority issues."

Charlotte laughed, and Jesse felt the hum of it against his chest settle somewhere deep inside. "I've noticed." After a long spell of staring into his eyes, she ran one finger across his stubbled chin and whispered, "I love you. I don't know when it happened, but I'm glad it did."

The glow in his chest had nothing to do with any prescription. "I know when for me. I mean, I didn't at the time, but looking back, I know exactly the moment."

"You do?"

He nodded. "Berry cobbler." Just remembering the moment doubled the glow under his ribs.

"Then?"

"The face you made when you dug into it? A

man can only take so much. I lost it right then and there. I didn't know it yet, but that was the end of it."

Her face flushed. "So that's why that kiss pulled the rug out from underneath me."

It had yanked him way off balance, too. "I didn't work it out, though, until the fire. I figured it was just a great kiss...until I thought maybe you were in that cottage. When that call came and I didn't know if you were safe... And then later when I thought about you driving back all that way all alone..."

She lay her hand across his chest, and he felt the warmth of her palm against his heartbeat. "Maybe that's what it took for both of us. All the stuff we thought we needed—lots of it is gone right now. Maybe that leaves more room for the stuff that really matters."

It was so clear, right then, what really mattered. He slid his arm around her shoulders and pulled her closer. "I love you. We'll work it out. Right here."

"On this couch?" Her laugh was soft and velvety against his cheek.

"It's a good place to start."

If he'd thought the kiss over the cobbler sealed his fate, he was dead wrong. The kiss she gave him now beat that one by a mile.

Epilogue

Ouch.

Jesse's head felt as if it had been stuffed with cement and he couldn't feel the tips of his fingers. His mouth was dry and something was beeping with annoying regularity off to his left. He forced his eyes open to a bright room.

"Hey there, hero."

It took him a minute to recognize the voice as Charlotte's. He rolled his head away from the beeping and saw her eyes in the glare.

"Welcome back."

He winced and grunted, no words coming beyond the dusty dryness of his mouth.

"Thirsty?"

He felt Charlotte's fingers feather across his forehead as he nodded.

She held a cup and straw up to let him drink, and he felt the cool water pull him back to life.

"You came through beautifully, Jesse. There's a plate in your leg now but it'll be okay."

Jesse recognized his mother's voice and turned his head toward the foot of his bed, where his mother and father stood looking like twin parental pillars of worry.

"I always wanted to be in hardware," he choked out, the voice sounding as if it came down from the ceiling rather than from his own body.

"At the moment, you're in plastic. You get a fiberglass cast later." His father's voice filled the room, but without the edge it usually had. "You'll be back to your usual antics in a few weeks."

Not really. Jesse still hadn't figured out a way to tell his parents how drastically things had changed for him in just a matter of days. As he watched his mom's eyes dart back and forth between himself and Charlotte, it was clear she had caught on. Dad still looked a bit confused. "Maybe. Right now it hurts."

"I imagine it does."

"You always had a flair for the dramatic." Jesse turned to find Randy sitting on the guest chair. Randy was here. "Or should I say heroic?" He rose and offered Jesse his hand.

"That's me, your friendly neighborhood hero."

"That *is* you," Randy said, squeezing Jes-

se's hand. "You're pretty amazing. I may have
to take back all my wisecracks about the firehouse." It was as close to a declaration of support as Jesse had ever gotten from Randy. "Let
me know how I can help. I'll find the time."
Jesse blinked hard, almost unsure he'd heard
Randy correctly. The world really had been
turning inside out lately.

"You will be off your feet for a while," Charlotte said. "George already has a schedule up
at the firehouse for when your parents, Randy
and I can't be there. And your church fan club
will keep you in food clear through Thanksgiving if you need it."

"Why didn't you call us earlier?" His father's
voice was tight with worry.

Jesse's first response was a knee-jerk "Why
are you so concerned all of a sudden?" as the
usual wound of his father's inattention roared
to life. Only something made Jesse stop and
look at his father's eyes rather than just react
to his voice. He was genuinely concerned. It
wasn't just the "Why do you do that firefighting thing?" Jesse always read into his father's
inquiries. Today it looked more like "You were
in danger." He wasn't quite sure what brought
on the distinction. Had his father changed? Had
even Randy changed? Or was it his ability to
see his family that had altered?

An honest answer—instead of his usual wise-crack—came to him surprisingly easily. "I didn't really have time. And I knew I'd be okay."

"Oh, you knew, did you?" Mom did not look as though she shared that opinion. "Surgery is not my version of okay, son."

"I called you for the surgery part, Mom. And look at me, I'm fine." He wasn't fine—not yet, really—but he wanted that worried look to leave his mother's eyes. "Mom, Dad, Randy, this is Charlotte."

Charlotte laughed softly and his father smiled. "We had a chance to meet while you were getting your new hinges put in."

"So this is who bought the cottage," Dad said. His words hinted at more than a real estate transaction, and Jesse found himself wondering just how well his parents now knew his favorite customer. "I'm glad you weren't hurt in all that the other night."

"We have lots of work to do—" Jesse felt Charlotte's hand tighten on his "—but I think it will all work out in the end." She caught Jesse's eyes. The fact that she'd used the word *we* planted a grin on his face that had nothing to do with the postoperative painkillers.

Only he couldn't really help with the renovation work for now, could he? "Who are we going to get to help you finish the cottage?" He didn't really like the idea of anyone else working on that place—he liked to think of the project as his and Charlotte's alone.

"I think we can worry about that tomorrow. Chad Owens helped me call in a cleaning company that specializes in these things, and that will take a few days anyhow. And then there's all the insurance to be settled." She ran her thumb over the back of his palm and Jesse felt his eyes fall closed at the sensation. "We have time."

God is never late, and He's never early, Jesse thought as the fog began to fill his head again.

"What did you just say?" His father sounded baffled.

"It's something my grandmother taught me," he heard Charlotte's voice explain. "About how everything works out. 'God is never late, and He's never early. He's always right on time— His time.'"

"That's a lovely thought." His mother sounded pleased.

She's a lovely woman. I'm in love with her, Jesse thought to himself as he began to slip back asleep.

"You don't say?" Randy actually sounded amused. When had Randy learned to read minds?

"And I'm in love with you," he heard Charlotte whisper in his ear. "But we've got time for that, too."

"I think we'd better leave these two alone for a bit," came his mother's voice. "We'll meet you back here later to bring him home."

Jesse fought the fog to push his eyelids open. Charlotte had the sweetest look on her face. "I'm loopy," he admitted, realizing what had just happened. "But I still mean it." He brought his hand up to touch the delightful softness of her cheek. "I'm head over heels for you. Well, maybe just one heel at the moment."

She laughed. "One heel is enough. Though, I thought you were sweeping me off my feet, not the other way around." She parked one elbow on the bed beside him. "Your family is sweet. Your dad tries to hide it, but he's really worried about you. He cares, Jesse. He just isn't very good about knowing how to show it."

"I think they like you."

Her smile made his head spin. "I hope they do. I think they were onto us before your little pronouncement a moment ago."

"They'll have to get used to it sometime, why not now?" Jesse yawned and blinked. He needed her to know before he slipped away again. "I'm absolutely, one hundred and ten percent in love with you." The words were taking more effort to get out as the fog settled back in. "So you have to stay. You have to." He couldn't keep his eyes open any longer. "I need you. Stay, please?"

The last thing he remembered was the cool softness of her kiss on his forehead. "I know where home is now. I'm not going anywhere."

* * * * *

Dear Reader,

There is an old saying that "God laughs at our plans." I don't know that I believe that as much as I believe He smiles at *our* version of our plans, then gently remakes our striving into His better purpose. Sometimes not so gently, as many of us need a hefty shove to be headed in the right direction, yes? Jesse and Charlotte have dramatic turns in their lives, turns that pull them together but are by no means smooth transitions! I hope you draw faith for your own challenges from their story. If you'd like information on how to start a prayer shawl ministry at your church or just want to say hello, feel free to contact me at www.alliepleiter.com, "Like" me on Facebook or drop a line to P.O. Box 7026, Villa Park, IL 60181—I'd love to hear from you!

Questions for Discussion

1. Would you have bought the cottage if you were in Charlotte's position? Why or why not?

2. Why is it that cautious people like Melba become friends with daring people like Charlotte? Has it been true in your life?

3. When have you had your plans yanked out from underneath you like Jesse has? What did you learn from it?

4. Do you have a "Mima" in your life? Are you a "Mima" to someone? Could you be?

5. Abby tells Charlotte she's got a "powerful posse of prayer warriors." Do you have people who pray for you regularly? If not, how could you create your own posse?

6. Are you a cat person or a dog person (or something else)?

7. Have you ever been drawn to a town the way Charlotte is drawn to Gordon Falls?

8. Is it a good thing to go full throttle at a project as Charlotte does on the cottage? Is there a wrong time to have that kind of enthusiasm? A right time?

9. What foods bring out your "piggish side"?

10. Was Charlotte wise to offer Jesse the chance to rent the cottage if she left?

11. Jesse uses his music to open himself up to faith. What first opened you up to faith?

12. When in your life have you needed consolation? How did it come to you?

13. Jesse says, "I couldn't help you from where I was, but I began to feel like God could." Have you ever found yourself in a situation like that?

14. Chief Bradens said he could always tell which people would beat the fire, and which people would let the fire beat them. Which do you think you are? How do you know?

15. Charlotte and the church ladies use their knitting to bless others. What gifts can you use to do the same?

LARGER-PRINT BOOKS!

GET 2 FREE
LARGER-PRINT NOVELS
PLUS 2 FREE
MYSTERY GIFTS

Love Inspired®
SUSPENSE
RIVETING INSPIRATIONAL ROMANCE

Larger-print novels are now available...